Praise for *The Marmalade File.*

'Seasoned political journalists Steve Lewis and Chris Uhlmann
have come up with a satirical political thriller designed to tell
a ripping yarn at the same time as it confronts issues to do with
power and leadership, our relations with China and the United
States, and the changing face of the media and political reporting'
Canberra Times

'The book opens on a freezing morning after the 2011 press
gallery midwinter ball, with world-weary journalist Harry
Dunkley chasing a lead for a cracking yarn. It goes haywire
from there to Beijing, Washington and back to Canberra, with
no sacred cow left unmilked, no media outlet untainted and no
character unbesmirched'
Australian Financial Review

'Both authors are heavy hitters in the political scene yet
scrupulously insist that their book is all harmless fiction. You've
got to hope so. Imagine if these clowns and schemers really were
running our country?'
Australian Women's Weekly

'The Monument Men went to war on cultural barbarians whereas
the Marmalade Men target political barbarians. Much more fun'
Phillip Adams

'It's definitely fun. It's got sex, it's got politics, it's got spooks, it's got a transvestite disco. I table *The Marmalade Files* and commend it to the honourable members of *The Australian*'s readership'

The Australian

'The book's blurb says it's a romp through "the dark underbelly of politics" and for once the blurb doesn't lie ... the result is *The Marmalade Files*, a banquet of bastardry'

Daily Telegraph

'The novel is regularly hilarious, inserting much fiction into a perfectly factual Canberra setting ... and teases unmercifully the readers' perceptions of Australian politics and the secret world'

National Times

'It is indeed a romp – often hilarious and always great fun'

Weekend Gold Coast Bulletin

Steve Lewis arrived in Canberra in late 1992 and spent more than two decades tormenting the nation's political elite. He worked for the *Australian Financial Review*, *The Australian* and News Corp's big-selling metropolitan dailies. He currently works as a senior consultant with Newgate Communications. He is co-author, with Chris Uhlmann, of the best-selling *The Marmalade Files* and also works as a freelance journalist.

Chris Uhlmann is a Walkley Award winning journalist and one of Australia's best known and most respected political broadcasters. His career in reporting began at the *Canberra Times* in 1989, after failed stints as a student priest, storeman and packer and security guard. He was editor of the *Canberra Weekly* before joining the ABC in 1998. As political editor for ABC TV, and now host of ABC radio's flagship current affairs program *AM*, he has earned a reputation for his fearless pursuit of the nation's politicians.

THE MANDARIN CODE

POLITICS PEELED BARE

a novel

STEVE LEWIS
CHRIS UHLMANN

FOURTH ESTATE

Like all works of fiction, this story was inspired by events in the real world, but it is a work of fiction and none of the main characters in this book really exists and, more importantly, none of the acts attributed to these fictional characters ever took place. So please do not interpret anything that happens in this book as a real event that actually happened or that involved any person in the real world (whether living or now deceased).

Fourth Estate
An imprint of HarperCollins*Publishers*
First published in Australia in 2014
by HarperCollins*Publishers* Australia Pty Limited
ABN 36 009 913 517
harpercollins.com.au

HarperCollins*Publishers*
Level 13, 201 Elizabeth Street, Sydney, NSW 2000, Australia
Unit D, 63 Apollo Drive, Rosedale, Auckland 0632, New Zealand
A 53, Sector 57, Noida, UP, India
1 London Bridge Street, London SE1 9GF, United Kingdom
2 Bloor Street East, 20th floor, Toronto, Ontario M4W 1A8, Canada
195 Broadway, New York, NY 10007, USA

Lewis, Steve.
The mandarin code / Steve Lewis and Chris Uhlmann.
978 0 7322 9475 5 (pbk.)
978 0 7304 9966 4 (ebook)
Journalists – Fiction.
Satire, Australian – 21st century.
Australia – Politics and government – Fiction.
Other Authors/Contributors:
Uhlmann, Chris.
A823.4

Cover design by Darren Holt, HarperCollins Design Studio
Author photograph by Gary Ramage, News Ltd
Typeset in Baskerville Regular by Kirby Jones

For Flint, Charlie, Rosie and Harry.
And Rosemary, who's playing with the good angels, somewhere.

For Mary Rose and Gai Marie,
1 Corinthians 13:13.

There is a devil there is no doubt,
but is he trying to get in us or trying to get out?

THE MANDARIN CODE

CHAPTER ONE

Canberra

When he woke in a knot of panic, the sheets were stained with sweat. He'd not meant to sleep, for fear of the dark angels that had begun to haunt his dreams. His eyes flashed open to a void beyond black, and the still breath of midnight amplified his every heartbeat.

Canberra usually cooled with the sunset, but an unnatural heat lingered in this blast-furnace summer. A faint scent of smoke hinted at fire licking at the city's edges. The hour was nearly upon him.

Cradling a USB drive in his sticky palm, the Chinese national wondered how future generations would judge him. As a delusional zealot, or as a good man who'd tried to warn them?

Somewhere outside, a generator chugged its diesel drone. In the cramped cabin, the heavy, even breathing of his two roommates signalled they were asleep. It was time to move. But fear pressed down, a malign and unyielding weight.

Six months earlier, he'd been sent to this strange, empty land to help build an ultra-secret frontline. Listed as Asset 53, he was one of China's revered cyber-warriors. But he was a rebel who longed for intellectual freedom, who yearned to break the shackles of the stultifying regime that choked its people as the old dynasties had once bound the feet of its women. He'd lost faith when they'd forced an abortion on his mother for the crime of conceiving a second child. The botched procedure had taken the one person whom he had loved unconditionally. So he'd made a vow – to work within the system just as long as it took to gather the weapons that he needed to destroy it.

And now he had them, his own personal arsenal, carried on a tiny memory stick that he placed, carefully, in his left trouser pocket.

He mentally rehearsed his escape route. Nine hundred and eighty-seven steps to freedom. He'd measured the distance in cyberspace: from the compound that was his home, feverishly being transformed into a new Chinese embassy, to the fortified front gates of the embassy of the United States.

Briefly, he'd contemplated defecting to the Australians, but the risk was too great. Having witnessed their kow-towing at the altar of China's wealth, he feared they would hand him back if pressure was applied. No, the Americans were his best hope, and he would buy his freedom with the evidence in his pocket and the trove of priceless information in his head.

Now, lying as if paralysed on his bed, he willed himself back twenty years to focus on a ten-year-old child's last memory of his mother. He recalled the grimace of her death; the two lives butchered by a heartless, soulless state. The exercise worked its tonic: he was resolved. He would embrace the terrifying future and be ruthless with the past.

It was nudging 12.30am. There was no moon, but powerful arc lights lit the building site. Months of meticulous planning had collapsed to this moment. He had placed cloth under his mattress to dampen the squeak of his bed-springs, practised easing back the sheets without the faintest telltale rustle.

He had hoped for a breeze to muffle his footfall. The distant throb of the diesel engine offered some cover, but to him every step was a shouted betrayal of his escape.

He visualised what stood between him and freedom. He'd memorised the shortest path. One hundred swift paces to the fence, two rows of razor wire, then a dash to the US embassy.

With furtive steps, not glancing back, he stole out of the cabin to the expanse of the compound, hurrying to the shadows that would hide him from cameras on either side of the three-metre fence.

His heart beat a staccato pulse as he pushed a makeshift ladder into place and climbed to a narrow opening in the perimeter wire.

He leapt into the dark and landed with a crunch, his weight flattening the tinder-dry grass. The impact shuddered through his legs, and he rolled to cushion the fall, then took a breath to check his route.

Eucalypt bark, curled and brittle-dry, littered the ground. His every step would echo until he reached the concrete path. Slowly he navigated a glade of trees. A sticky web grabbed at his face and he stifled a gasp, clawing frantically at the gossamer threads wrapped across his cheeks. He froze. A creature slowly traced a path from his hairline to his temple. Its legs on his exposed skin. With a panicked flick he sent it to the bushes.

Exhaling, he continued towards the path that ran along the side of the compound. Soft-glow streetlights ahead marked a long avenue towards a city he had never seen. On his right, the dirt-block site that had been his home − his prison − for the past six months. Through a final stand of long grass, he reached the path, turned right and forced his limbs into a steady jog. He knew he was not safe. The path ran beside the compound for two-hundred metres. He could not relax until the fortress of the building site was behind him.

The quiet was shattered by a harsh voice, familiar, ordering him to halt. 'Ting! Ting!'

Two shadows emerged from the gloom, stepping out from a gate to the compound sixty or seventy metres ahead, blocking the path. He turned, and raced into the unknown.

He charged across a roadway, a route that he'd never intended to take. A hotel loomed on the right. Should he go there? No. His course was set. There was a bridge ahead, a well-lit route across the lake. This was his best chance. The city was there, on the other side. Freedom was there, on the other side. Could he lose his pursuers in this foreign place? He scanned his surroundings for signs of life, of help, but the street leading to the bridge was empty.

The footsteps were getting louder.

Harder. Faster.

He was still young, and had once been athletic. But in the panic to avoid capture, he had sprinted the first few hundred metres. Within a minute his muscles were burning more oxygen than his lungs could deliver and his body began to rebel.

Keep going.

The well-trained security men were closing on him, and were now, maybe, only fifty metres away. His chest was lead-heavy as he pushed up the incline to the bridge.

The lights of the city teased him, called to him. He could feel the pursuers on his heels now. They would catch him in seconds.

There was no time to think, little time to act. With one final effort, he surged towards the bridge railing on his left; pushing his hands down hard, he vaulted over the edge.

Four seconds of panic and a crack as his head met the water. His mother's face appeared, beckoning him to a better place.

Then everything went black.

CHAPTER TWO

Washington

Earle W Jackson III reclined in the sturdy leather chair, soaking up the majesty of the room, and considered the staggering improbability that he belonged in it. The three months since his election had passed in a blur of meetings and briefings that gave him few moments to reflect on the miracle of his becoming the forty-fifth President of the United States of America. In November's ballot, he'd shocked the fancied Democratic incumbent, winning with a populist blend of good ol' boy southern charm and homespun protectionism. Not since Truman's upset victory over Thomas E Dewey in '48 had the White House welcomed such an unexpected occupant.

Now here he was in the Oval Office, the epicentre of world power, an unrivalled, near-mythical place. The heart of the American empire. The new Rome.

Jackson turned to the three bay windows behind the desk carved from the timbers of the British ship, the *Resolute*. He looked through bulletproof glass to the South Lawn, dusted with snow, imagining the Republican lions who'd stood here before him. Ted Roosevelt, Ike, Nixon – the weight of the world on their shoulders. A cancelled phone call had given him exactly five minutes to himself. He interlocked his fingers and lifted his hands above his head, pushing his palms towards the ceiling, stretching his shoulders and back. He rocked his head from side to side. It helped relieve the stress in his neck, which was already stiff and sore. If it got worse, his head would be thumping by day's end.

What would Reagan have done?

It was one of his regular mind games, imagining how his favourite president might have reacted to a difficult challenge. It was based on the question his strict Presbyterian mother had frequently asked him: 'What would Jesus have done?'

Despite serving eight years as Governor of Mississippi, he was ill-prepared for this role, Leader of the Free World, the most powerful man on the planet. Trained for a life of law, he had risen steadily, though unspectacularly, through the Republican ranks to chair the deeply conservative Rankin County, Mississippi district, and had been picked as an observer during the controversial 2000 Florida Presidential re-count. He'd risen to public prominence in a referendum battle over the State flag: the last in the union to have the battle cross of the Confederacy emblazoned on it.

A 2001 court ruling had opened the door for civil rights activists and local businessmen to move to expunge the Civil War

7

remnant from the standard. That outraged Jackson and he was a man made for the fight. A direct descendant of General Thomas Jonathan 'Stonewall' Jackson, he was not about to stand by as his heritage was airbrushed to appease liberal do-gooders.

Never an original thinker, Jackson lifted his rallying cry from the National Rifle Association: 'You can have my flag when you peel it from my cold dead hands.' It appealed to and amplified the many prejudices that fortified his natural constituency. It also helped that the proposed alternative was a circle of stars, suspiciously similar to the European Union banner: 'The Euro fag flag,' Jackson called it.

It was a fight he couldn't lose. The flag was retained with a two-thirds majority. Three years later, he was elected Governor. His charisma, crisp-good looks, folksy yet polished style of public speaking and impeccable Conservative credentials were a heady cocktail and he emerged from the pack to storm the 2012 Republican primaries.

Jackson went into the presidential poll a rank underdog but he surprised the pundits, tapping into American trauma over the financial crisis and growing anxiety about the nation's diminishing global authority. The people were hungry for a return to past glories so that's what Jackson promised them.

In a twist on the Reagan *Morning in America* campaign, Jackson's crusade anthem was the theme from *Star Wars* and his slogan the aspirational 'The Empire Strikes Back.' It was an aggressive mix of hope and xenophobia, which blamed outsiders and their liberal allies within the US for the nation's decline.

In a stroke of genius Jackson built a cartoon version of a rising China to replace the Axis of Evil as America's new enemy-in-chief. He toured the rust belt, pointing to manufacturing jobs that had been 'stolen' by the emerging communist power. 'Every "Made in China" tag you see is a pink slip handed to an American worker,' was his mantra on the stump. 'Every dollar you spend on foreign trinkets is money taken from American pockets and food taken from our children's mouths.' His campaign centrepiece was a solemn promise to declare China a 'currency manipulator', if he won office.

Against the advice of every sane Republican, that's what he did. And from day one in the Oval Office, his foreign policy battles began to rival his considerable domestic woes.

The President checked his watch. 'Lesley...' he bellowed.

His efficient PA pounced on the intercom. 'Yes, Mr President?'

'Send in my eleven o'clock.'

'Yes sir. Coffee?'

'No. I've had enough. Thanks.'

Jackson stiffened as a high-powered group strode through the door: the cream of his national security team, accompanied by the Secretary of Treasury. He already knew that the CIA and the State Department were in rare agreement: his decision to declare China a currency manipulator had knocked over a domino and others were falling.

China had responded belligerently. It declared currency to be a sovereign issue and called the US stance an act of aggression. It cancelled the annual meeting of the joint economic strategic dialogue and recalled its Ambassador to Beijing for 'briefings'.

9

Eight Chinese warships had then sailed through the twelve-nautical-mile zone, off the disputed Senkaku Islands, and the Japanese were threatening retaliation. China's riposte was to schedule missile tests for the Taiwan Strait, something it had not done for nearly two decades. There was no way of telling how far the sabre-rattling would go.

The President surveyed the room then motioned to the director of the Central Intelligence Agency.

'Mr President,' Travis Manning spoke as directed. 'As I explained in our last meeting, when I suggested we move slowly on the China front, the problem is that we don't yet have a clear idea of the temperament of the new leadership. At almost the same time you were elected, the Communist Party's 18th Congress appointed the people who will lead China for the next five years. As I said in January, we needed time to let them settle in and for us to get some feel for just who we are dealing with. There's a growing view that this new team is more deeply nationalist, and more dangerous, than the last.'

'And as I told you, I am not going to break a pledge I made to the American people on my first day in office.' Jackson spoke more loudly than necessary, meeting reason with volume. His tone dropped as he searched for an argument. 'And for God's sake, Clinton declared China a currency manipulator in '94 and things didn't go to hell in a handbasket then.'

The Treasury Secretary jumped on the opening. 'Mr President, China's Gross Domestic Product in '94 was $500 million. Ours was $7 trillion. Today, China's GDP is $9 trillion, closing on our $15 trillion. Based on these growth rates, their economy will surpass ours before the end of the decade. And in 1994 we did about $10 billion worth of trade with China. Now it's over half a trillion and rising.

'In 1994 China was an insignificant player in the government bond market. It now owns more than $1 trillion worth of our bonds. To put that another way, Mr President, only the Federal Reserve controls more US Government debt than China.'

'The point is: pissing them off is a bad idea,' interjected Manning. 'And there's more. George has come back from Beijing with some disturbing intel.'

George Blake, the CIA's Beijing station chief, was a hardened intelligence careerist, and he knew China, its nuances and instincts better than anyone.

'Sir, the new Chinese president, Meng Tao, was billed as continuing the market-oriented reform of Deng Xiaoping. But we have reason to believe his sympathies actually lie with the New Left, which is pushing back against growing inequality in China and wants the party to return to its Maoist roots.'

Blake reached into his folder for a one-page briefing note and handed it to the President.

'We intercepted a conversation between Meng and one of his allies, Jiang Xiu. It's clear that they know your currency declaration is a domestic political ploy and could easily be negotiated in financial forums. But they see an opportunity to play Chinese public opinion against the US by painting us as an aggressor that's trying to strangle Chinese growth before it becomes a threat.'

Blake paused for a moment to allow Jackson to absorb the brief before continuing. 'China is mobilising its considerable assets: military, financial and virtual, opening the way for serious retaliation. I believe they will rub up against their neighbours to test our will. They might even be looking for an opportunity to roll back economic and social reform under cover of a "national emergency". We could be playing right into their hands. They sense we are weakened by a decade of war and economic decline. Sir, they are looking for an excuse to demonstrate that they are the rising global power.'

The Secretary of State tagged in, determined to pressure Jackson into relenting.

'We urge you, Mr President.' Henry Wilenski leaned forward to press home his appeal. 'Make it plain, today, that you do not intend to proceed with the next steps of your currency declaration. Make a statement saying you won't be imposing tariffs and restrictions on Chinese goods. You can make a credible argument that your warning has been heeded and that talks should come before any more action.'

Jackson rose to his full 6 feet 3 inches and slammed both hands on the desk. 'Except that's not what I said. I said I would impose tariffs on Chinese goods within ninety days of the declaration if China did not lift the value of its currency and level the goddamn playing field.'

He turned his back on the group and looked out the window, the defiant gesture of an insecure man.

'Mr President, that would not be wise.' Wilenski was pushing hard. 'This will not help American workers and it threatens the peace at a time when we are in no shape to fight.'

Jackson raised his hand and turned to eyeball the group.

'I need to think about this,' he said. 'We'll talk again tomorrow. That's all for now. Thank you, gentlemen.'

Dismissed and disgruntled, the group shuffled out.

As the door closed, the President picked up his phone. 'Lesley, get Big Mac on the line.'

CHAPTER THREE

Canberra

They ran squealing down to the lake's turbid waters, a tangled knot of excited children, two-dozen playful pups and their handlers. The year six class from Birchgrove, a smallish public school in Sydney's inner west, was on its annual pilgrimage to Canberra.

Fuelled on fast food and pre-teen adrenalin, they'd spent the morning at Questacon, mixing fantasy with science. It was now time for a picnic lunch on the shores of Lake Burley Griffin before continuing to the National Museum.

'Slow down and be careful. Maddie, watch the muddy banks,' a teacher bellowed.

Several errant boys were creeping stealthily towards a bushy thicket by the water's edge, intent on slipping from their handlers' gaze, courting those moments of freedom every schoolboy yearns for. Corey, a tousle-haired blond with attitude beyond his years, spotted it first. Half-submerged, the body was maybe ten metres from shore. Corey called his mates over to make sure he wasn't imagining things. From the bank, they couldn't see a head or even a pair of feet, but there was no mistaking that this was a corpse. Playtime was over.

The senior teacher called the police as the others shepherded the children away, comforting several distraught girls. A small crowd was gathering, drawn by human fascination with the macabre, wanting to catch a glimpse of the body in the shallows.

Ten minutes later the police arrived, two constables who donned waterproof clothing and set about their work, all purpose and professionalism. Their first task was to ensure they were not the victims of a hoax, then, if necessary, to call for assistance.

Aidan Steele, with five years experience in the ACT Policing branch of the Australian Federal Police, took charge initially, working with his junior colleague, who answered questions from a *Canberra Times* reporter. Steele had never before seen a body in Burley Griffin, but he was familiar with the lake's unfortunate habit of giving up the dead: the headless body of '79; the female torso washed up near Scrivener Dam in '93; the Nigerian diplomat whose corpse was found in 2005, bloated and disfigured, a homicide that remained unsolved.

He cast his eyes over the still water. *What was it about this drowned landscape?*

Like the capital, the lake was placid on the surface, but beneath its coffee-coloured water lurked hidden danger. The remnants of the eucalypts that once crowded the Molonglo riverbanks before the dam was built lay in wait below the lake's smooth skin: a trap for the unwary and the foolish.

There was no pulse. Steele reckoned the body had been submerged for more than a few hours. He also knew police procedure; it was time to call in the top dogs.

Within the quarter-hour, six of the ACT's finest had arrived and had begun to take statements from witnesses.

Four hours later, the initial forensic examination had been completed, the body having been gently hauled from the lake by the ACT water police.

The body was an Asian male, likely aged in his thirties. Of slender build, he was clothed in plain trousers and a light-coloured shirt. A pair of joggers weighed down his spindly legs. And that was it. An initial search had turned up nothing else – no wallet, no ID, no jewellery or other personal items.

The task now fell to the morgue for a thorough examination of the body and to the water police for a sweep of the muddy inlet.

Steele gazed out over the lake, its quiet waters now empty. He shook his head before turning to his colleagues.

'Christ, it's a funny old place to be seeking asylum.'

CHAPTER FOUR

Beijing

Alone in his sanctuary, Jiang Xiu cradled a mug of green tea in one hand as he tapped an ink block with a favoured brush. A Chinese melody drifted in the background, a hymn of praise for the plum blossom of spring. Thick walls offered protection from the city and its suffocating barrage of sound, and he savoured the serenity of his early morning ritual, a rare respite from the burden of leadership.

In five days he would turn fifty-six, still young compared to the dinosaurs who stained the party's upper ranks. Curmudgeon communists, he called them.

For the past six months, Jiang had headed China's propaganda agency. His appointment as minister was part of a coup that had seen a number of his nationalist comrades elevated to the helm of the ruthless political machine that would rule this vast ambitious empire for the next five years. Dubbed the 'Magnificent

Seven', the Standing Committee of the Political Bureau of the Communist Party of China Central Committee had the destiny of 1.35 billion people in their grasp. They would not disappoint. And they would not relent.

Unlike many of his contemporaries, Jiang had started with nothing but the unbridled love of his mother. He was no princeling, no Maserati-driving poseur who'd leveraged the family name to earn his wealth. He despised nepotism, a cover for the weak and lazy. He had gained power through cunning and intellect, and through a fierce political drive first unleashed as an undergraduate at Jilin University, studying economics and international management. He'd garnered plaudits from party elders for his organisational skills, but he was also a keen student of China's compromised history, and was determined to forge a new era for the Middle Kingdom, to place it on its rightful path to global supremacy.

Now, in his small studio in House No 2, near the centre of Beijing, he dipped his brush into a pool of oily black liquid. Two blank sheets of paper were set several feet apart on a long timber bench. On each, stone blocks were placed to keep the paper from ruffling.

With the first touch, his brush skimmed a white sheet and left a perfect stain of black.

Like dancing, rippling ribbons ...

He loved calligraphy's effortless grace, each stroke a link to the past. And with each practised touch, Jiang recalled the words of his master: 'Deviation from the model is a failure.'

It was a dictum that applied to all of nature and politics. He had dabbled in Western philosophy and was struck by the parallel

18

he saw with Plato's theory of forms: that this world was merely a copy of a perfect one. Jiang believed a universal template existed and his role as a politician was to make China the best replica of the model. Any deviation was a step towards chaos.

The traditions of calligraphy spanned several thousand years. Each character had its appointed place, set within pre-ordained boundaries. It was much like his expectations for China.

The only Western figure he respected, other than Plato, was Napoleon, a rare military leader gifted with great insight. 'Let China sleep, for when she wakes she will shake the world,' the French general had said.

China would certainly shake the world, as it had done through the ages, if Jiang could shake it awake. In the sweep of history, the West walked in the shadow of China's majestic past. China had gunpowder when the peasants of the West were still hurling stones at castle walls. All of mankind's great achievements had been conceived here, in the Middle Kingdom.

For a millennium China was the greatest civilisation on earth. The envy of the world.

Then a familiar rage surged. Jiang's face tightened. He gripped his brush hard.

The fall. The great indignity.

The West's interruption of China's ascendancy was an outrage. And it awaited punishment for the century of humiliation that began in 1839 with the First Opium War. The West and its brutal lackey Japan had brought China to its knees – shackled, humbled and impoverished. It had been on the long march back since 1949.

Jiang flinched. Some memories were hard, painful, personal.

His mother had been celebrating her fifteenth birthday in her Nanking home in December 1937 when the Japanese invaded. They had stolen her childhood as they raped her. She witnessed the massacre of countless innocent Chinese, butchered by that evil force. She had spent every birthday since in mourning and her suffering and memories were seared on her son's soul.

She had forged Jiang as a warrior, and he had spent his life readying for war.

Two lines, refined and flowing, perfectly intersected …

He had disguised himself, playing the role of an acolyte of Deng Xiaoping, a market liberal. But he believed that the Chinese economy had to be managed like a bird in a cage, allowing the centrally-planned system to define its limits. Yes, the cage could be made larger and, occasionally, other birds might be let in, but the bars ensured order.

China's growth, and the yearning of its fast-growing middle class for greater freedoms, had to be tightly controlled. The delusions of those who believed China could take its place at the helm of the new world order while relaxing its iron grip enraged him. Who were they, these free-market liberals preaching discredited Western ideals? The emergence of the internet had allowed this Western infection to spread. With Jiang's guidance the Politburo would tame those who believed the future of China was more entwined with Coca-Cola and McDonald's than with Mao and the State.

Swift running script, an infinite power …

Leaders often need a crisis to precipitate decisive action and the 1997 Asian financial meltdown, which hit China hard, had offered Jiang – then a rising star within the Communist Party – the first opportunity to rein in those who sought to mimic the West. The shadow capitalism that China had pursued meant that many of its banks tottered as the meltdown struck. Jiang had been given responsibility – and unfettered power – to right the creaky financial system.

It was a challenge that he took up with relish. He was dubbed the 'Dragon Titan' for his zealous pursuit of regional officials who thought they could continue to operate with autonomy.

Smooth top-down vertical lines, mellow like pearl and jade ...

After three years, he'd been rewarded with appointment to the Party's finance committee, a high-level role that gave him access to the upper echelons of the Politburo. He was determined to impress.

Jiang had soon been charged with running one of China's biggest state-owned companies, and he became a familiar name to the bankers from Wall Street and London who'd initially expected the same riches they'd milked by flogging off lazy, capital-starved enterprises from the former Eastern Bloc. But while Russia and its Soviet allies were easy pickings for these vultures, Jiang was formidable.

He married a sharp economic brain with determination and dogma. He championed the workers, arguing that China had a responsibility to ensure that its most vulnerable had the same rights as those who, through accident of birth or other connections, had risen to the top.

21

A curved arc, flexible and vivid …

He was centre stage as China made giant strides to catch the West. He became associated with a group of conservatives, the 'New Left', who were convinced that the greatest threat was not from outside forces, but from those within the party who wanted China to become a pale imitation of America and Japan.

He was an ultra-nationalist who believed the adoption of Western ideas poisoned his country. Now he was able to make change. And exact revenge.

Not since its imperial glory had China possessed the wealth and the power to strike at a weakened foe. He would need resolve, but he was not alone. Other key figures on the committee shared his view. Oh, and that fool in the White House had opened the door. President Jackson's declaration that China was a currency manipulator represented an opportunity to push back. Hard.

The challenge was to take the Chinese people with him. To harness their sense of nationalism and direct their anger towards the West. Once that began he would pour oil on the fire. He would not stop until China emerged victorious.

And if the world had to be torn asunder and remade, then so be it.

Jiang stood back and admired his work. His brush dripped, glistening black, as he soaked up Mao's revolutionary edict.

When the enemy advances, withdraw; when he stops, harass; when he tires, strike; when he retreats, pursue.

CHAPTER FIVE

Canberra

The trembles. The slightest of trembles. George Papadakis studied his hands for the telltale sign that one of the most powerful men in the nation was as nervous as a sixteen-year-old at a school formal.

He switched on his iPad, flicked to that journal of torment. It was nudging 6am and today marked the first Newspoll of the year. An election year. The numbers would not be a surprise because Papadakis, the Prime Minister's chief of staff, was always given a preview the night before the results went public. It was how *The Australian* interpreted the raw data that really mattered. How the views and prejudices of 1200 voters were spun, twisted, beaten up and spat out would dictate the sort of day that Martin Toohey and his minority Labor Government would have.

Every radio and television station, every two-bit 'analyst' with a Twitter handle, would be waiting to wring Newspoll for every last drop. For just over two years, the broadsheet had used the fortnightly measure of the national pulse to persecute Labor. If the numbers fell, the *Oz* would boldly predict an imminent move against Toohey, despite there being no viable alternative. No change would be dubbed 'flat-lining', conjuring images of a government on life support. A miraculous rise was a 'dead-cat bounce' that briefly masked Labor's long-term, irreversible decline.

Since the last election *The Australian* had not written one positive word about the minority government that had survived despite the conservative cliques' ceaseless predictions of its imminent demise. The paper had glossed over the fact that the government's legislative agenda had scarcely missed a beat as Toohey deftly herded the hundred and fifty cats in the House of Representatives to relative order.

But as the online edition downloaded, Papadakis knew the latest numbers would tell their own devastating story without the paper applying the mix-master.

He plunged a half-cup of caffeine down his throat as he digested the horror.

TOOHEY HITS HISTORIC LOW

Support for the Toohey Government has crashed with Labor's primary vote slumping below 30 per cent for the first time in Newspoll history.

Toohey, Papadakis's political soul mate, would be dead but for the fact that his only possible challenger, Catriona Bailey, remained stricken in a Canberra hospital eighteen months after being felled by a stroke during an interview on the ABC's *Lateline*.

The bastards at the *Oz* blithely ignored this inconvenient truth and kept including Bailey in their 'preferred prime minister' poll.

> In further dire news for Martin Toohey, bed-ridden Foreign
> Minister Catriona Bailey remains an overwhelming favourite, out-
> ranking the Prime Minister as preferred leader by 44 per cent to
> just 17 per cent.

Mongrels.

The only sniff of good news was Emily Brooks's continuing struggle to gain traction. The Opposition leader was paying a price for denying Bailey a parliamentary pair after her stroke stopped her attending Parliament. Focus group testing showed Brooks rated as cold and heartless. Voters were turned off by her calculating approach and Tory grandees were murmuring that she'd have to soften her steely exterior.

The big winner in the poll was 'Other' which had climbed to 20 per cent as voters turned away from the major parties.

Papadakis glanced out at the courtyard.

Who can blame them? We are our own worst enemy.

The Toohey Government had been the gift that kept giving for the press gallery. Any success was always trumped by spectacular own goals. Among a raft of contenders, the most extraordinary was Bruce Paxton's fall from ministerial grace. He had failed to declare that his first election campaign – way back in 1996 – had been funded in part by China Inc. That bombshell had nearly undone them.

Paxton, a one-time ally of Toohey, had initially accepted his demise, taking his place among the wasters and plodders on a surly backbench. He was thrown a few parliamentary crumbs and, for the most part, played the loyal footsoldier. But his mood changed when Toohey made it clear he would not be reinstated.

He'd first sounded off to Lucy Gibbs, an ambitious press gallery newbie. Her story 'Paxton Marks Toohey a Fail' was the first of many. Now he routinely threatened to resign from the Labor Caucus to sit on the crossbenches as an independent.

Despite his many failings Paxton wasn't the government's biggest headache. That dubious honour went to Bailey who had an almost supernatural capacity to upstage the government. Her rock-star status had forced Toohey to retain her as Foreign Minister, despite her incapacity. And every time the PM was getting some traction, Bailey would steal the limelight.

It's like we're trapped in a B-grade horror movie being stalked by the Zombie Queen.

And the diplomatic poseurs at the United Nations had made it worse by awarding Bailey a special peace prize based solely on the Foreign Minister's non-stop string of heartfelt Tweets during the early months of the Syria crisis.

Bailey's online tirade had achieved nothing. Not a jot. But it triggered favourable press – which was just the kind of 'action' those UN pretenders adored.

If she dies, we're dead at the by-election. Catch 22. I wish I had stayed in Treasury.

Papadakis tried to calm the rage that pulsed within whenever he thought about Bailey. He turned back to his iPad. There was work to do. He had to think clearly to apply the finishing touches to a plan he and Toohey had been hatching for months.

They called it the Big Bang, their bid to break the cycle of dire news. To change the national conversation. To lay down a platform for an unlikely election win.

We can claw this back.

The truth was, Labor's own research matched the public polls. The party was heading for decimation. But the internal polling also showed there was a glimmer of hope amid the ruin. While it confirmed that barely 30 per cent of the population was prepared to vote Labor, a surprising 38 per cent still identified themselves as 'Labor voters'. If the Toohey Government could win back its base it could be competitive.

We need to capture their imaginations and their hearts. To show only we can deliver jobs and a fair go.

And that was what the Big Bang was designed to do. It was the ultimate circuit-breaker, a multi-pronged, multi-billion-dollar plan to boost jobs, skills, education and health.

Privately, Papadakis admitted its purpose was to dig the government out of a hole. But he also firmly believed it was visionary and 'Labor to the bootstraps'.

Its long-term cost was breathtaking, and only partly offset by cutting existing spending, particularly on Defence. The real genius of the plan was the revenue stream tapped to fund it. The bulk of the money would flow from a yet-to-be-signed deal with a Chinese state-owned energy company. It had been two years in the making, driven by the PM and a trusted few in Cabinet.

It was unique. The Australian Government would sign a 99-year lease ceding control over a massive gas-field just off Darwin to Sinopec, the world's fifth-largest company. It would give the Chinese what they coveted: real energy security through effective ownership of every step in the supply chain.

And it would give the Toohey Government what it desperately needed: cash. Money was a big problem: revenues were falling, government spending kept rising and the Treasurer, ridiculously, had staked Labor's economic reputation on a return to surplus this very year.

The beauty of the plan was that the gas-field was offshore and located in a territory, not a state. That meant all the bountiful tax revenues would flow directly to the Commonwealth, and as a bonus the Northern Territory would enjoy the benefits of massive investment. And the money would flow from the moment the deal was signed, with a $10 billion down-payment on the lease. Sinopec would then pay $1 billion a year, tied to inflation. At the end of the lease the site would revert to the Commonwealth, hopefully helping to combat the inevitable claims of 'selling off the farm'.

And we will deliver a massive social dividend. Whitlam-on-steroids.

The beating heart of the Big Bang was a plan for universal mental health coverage.

A Medicare-like set-up to cover a yawning gap in the health system. It would deliver to every family what the expensive advertising blitz would repeat ad nauseum: 'Peace of Mind'.

Even the economic hard-heads in the party agreed: the social benefits easily outweighed the cost. Secret focus group testing showed that the punters loved the idea.

Papadakis scribbled small patterns as he pondered Toohey's grand vision. This could work, could get the government back in the game.

Sure, it was a high-wire gamble, Labor's last desperate chance, and the Tories would ensure there was no safety net if Toohey stumbled.

CHAPTER SIX

Canberra

Amanda Wade cast her emerald eyes across the paperwork, straining to find a clue that would shed light on the mystery of this Asian corpse. Facts were proving elusive.

For nearly two years, Detective Sergeant Wade, the chief coronial liaison officer for the ACT Police, had worked in this gleaming warehouse for the dead. The state-of-the-art morgue had cost ACT taxpayers $5.5 million, replacing the dilapidated forty-year-old centre at Kingston. It had been designed to store up to one hundred bodies – ambitious, because most days in sleepy Canberra no more than a dozen were stored on the slabs of polished steel.

The body had arrived the previous evening, brought in by a funeral contractor, after its discovery by a group of schoolchildren visiting from Sydney.

Makes a change from PE and maths.

Vincent Duffield, a forensic pathologist with nearly thirty years experience in trying to tease secrets from the dead, had carried out the post-mortem examination five hours ago. Wade had played spectator.

The cause of death was drowning. Although the man suffered a blow to the head, consistent with falling from some height, the water in his lungs confirmed the head trauma had not been fatal. All the signs indicated that he had taken a tumble into the lake, most likely from Commonwealth Avenue Bridge. Or maybe Kings Avenue.

But why?

There were no traces of alcohol in the body, so the chances that he'd been part of a group skylarking around the lake were slim.

Suicide?

That too was unlikely. A fall from either bridge could kill if the person landed awkwardly, but the structures weren't terribly high and didn't usually attract those wishing to end their lives.

The policewoman gazed out at the light industrial landscape of this southern suburb. Late afternoon ho-hum. Nearby, a salesman was closing a deal on a Hyundai, while the local office supplies outlet looked as if it was shutting early.

And here she was, troubled and restless, trying to commune with the dead.

Wade was nearing retirement. Then what? Twilight days in the garden, the odd overseas trip supported by a generous super scheme, she supposed.

I'll miss it.

Wade had begun her career as a beat copper in Canberra nearly thirty-five years earlier, earning her stripes as she climbed the ladder at the Australian Federal Police. She was one of its first female recruits, gaining respect and promotion due to her unrelenting eye for detail.

She'd exploited the career opportunities that only the AFP offered. In the wake of 9/11 she had trained for the Specialist Response and Security Team as the then Commissioner turned the AFP into a paramilitary force. She'd served with the United Nations – first in Cyprus, then Timor-Leste in 2004 and South Sudan in 2006. And finally, in the dirt and blood of Afghanistan in 2008.

The AFP was family and, not for the first time, Wade wondered how she would cope with retirement.

'Amanda, are you there?' The voice of Heather Rose: the front office clerk, roused Wade from her reverie.

'Yeah, Heather, what's up?'

'Two people to see you, from the Chinese embassy.' Rose emphasised the name of the country as if she was swallowing a razor blade. 'They want to chat about a deceased Asian man.'

Chinese? Maybe that's one part of the puzzle solved.

Wade gathered up a few papers, folding them neatly, before walking the short distance from her office to the foyer.

'Amanda Wade,' she said, extending her hand to a man dressed in a dull grey suit. She then turned to an attractive woman clad in a smart-looking outfit.

The man spoke with a heavy accent, wrestling with his English.

'Hello. I am Zheng Dong, First Assistant Secretary, Embassy of China.' He looked uncomfortable and glanced at his companion.

'Weng Meihui. I am also from the embassy. Thank you for seeing us, Ms Wade. Is there somewhere we can talk in private?'

Weng spoke with the faintest of accents, all diplomatic charm. She offered a warm smile.

Wade's practised eye studied the pair. Weng had the poise and beauty of a model. Tall for an Asian woman. Her face was open and friendly, and she did not look Han Chinese. From one of the regions, Tibet perhaps. Her age was elusive, but there were hints about her eyes that she was older than she appeared. The man's cheap, ill-fitting suit could not disguise the hardness and athleticism of his body. Wade caught the calluses and scars on the knuckles of his hands, a sign of someone who had spent years training in hand-to-hand combat. But it was his eyes that sent a chill through her. So black that the pupil vanished into the iris. An assassin's eyes.

'Of course. Why don't we go to my office, it's a little way along here.' Wade led her visitors down the hall, turning into a room furnished in bland government chic.

Once seated, Zheng spoke politely, but Wade sensed a hint of menace beneath the diplomatic veneer.

'Ms Wade. The man who was found in the lake, dead. He is, we believe, an official from the embassy. He was deeply troubled and not happy with living far from his home. Unfortunately it would appear that he took his own life. My colleague and I would like to see the body. Now. Please.'

A few moments later Wade and the two diplomats were standing alongside a sheet-covered body. She drew back the cloth.

'Is this your man?'

Zheng nodded and turned to Wade.

'The People's Republic of China has legal responsibility for this man, who was in Australia on a diplomatic passport. We will take the body with us. Now.'

Wade was on her turf and not about to give ground to visiting bureaucrats. They knew their rights and she knew hers.

'That may be, Mr Zheng, but the body has not been cleared for release. I can tell you, though, that nothing was found on the body, or among the clothing. We found no identification, no money, nothing.'

Weng opened her black handbag and removed an envelope, offering another winning smile as she handed over an official letter from the embassy, attached to which was a passport photograph. 'We don't wish to cause any trouble. But we are the legal guardians of this man. His name is Lin An.'

Wade dug in. She wasn't to be taken for a fool.

'I'm not sure that I even have the authority to release the body, particularly given that we haven't concluded the formal investigation. I'll have to take advice on that. In any case, it's too late in the day for it to occur now.' She sized up Zheng, who was now clearly displeased. 'We just don't allow bodies to leave the morgue without all the proper paperwork and procedures being completed. I'm sure you understand that, Mr Zheng.'

The Chinese pair stole a quick glance at each other. Clearly there would be no cutting corners, or getting around this green-eyed *gweilo*. Finally, Weng spoke.

'Thank you Ms Wade. We appreciate your time and, ah,

assistance. We ask respectfully that you check with your superiors about making arrangements for us to retrieve the body … once all proper procedures have been completed.'

'Of course, Ms Weng. If everything goes to order, the body should be available for consular pick-up in the next few days. But I stress this will depend on the final results of the forensics.'

With that, she led the two diplomats out to the foyer, shaking their hands as she bade them farewell. The slightest of grins ghosted across Zheng's face … or were Wade's sharp eyes deceiving her?

She returned to her office, preparing to make detailed notes of the visit by the Chinese, the sort of rote police work she wouldn't miss. What she had not told them − and had not yet documented anywhere − was that the body had yielded one fascinating clue: a small USB had been secreted in the man's intestine. It had showed up on the MT scan and Vince Duffield had retrieved it with a deft cut.

Wade opened a locked desk drawer and held a small plastic bag up to the late afternoon light. The USB carried a single word, UNIS. It had 10GB of memory − and heaven knows what it contained on its digital circuit board.

Earlier, she'd plugged it into her PC. It was encrypted and that alone was fascinating. Now the visit by the two Chinese diplomats had deepened her suspicions that there was a far more intriguing story behind this death.

That meant Wade needed to push matters up a very different chain of command from the routine coronial hierarchy. She picked up her mobile and flicked through its address book, locating a man she'd first met in Afghanistan in 2008. He had been attached to a contingent sent in to track the faint footprints of Osama bin Laden. Ware had forged a bond with him in the ancient war-torn wasteland, often sharing a non-alcoholic beer as an antidote to the daily assassinations and bombings. She punched the dial button.

After four rings, a cultivated voice answered.

'Hello?'

'Charlie, it's Amanda. How are you?'

'Amanda, what a nice surprise. I haven't seen you for months.'

'Yes Charlie, it's been a while. I'm counting down to retirement but I'm not ringing to discuss how best to spend my super. I do have something for you, though. Something intriguing.'

CHAPTER SEVEN

Canberra

He paced the bare room, illuminated by a single fluorescent light that buzzed softly. His schoolboy error had left the knuckles on his right hand badly bruised and he counted himself lucky that no bones had broken. But he knew from long experience that his fingers would ache for days. He cursed.

Never, never lose your temper.

That it was imperative to stay in control had been drilled into him. His instructors had been determined to instil discipline in their promising disciple, to harness the unquenchable rage that coursed through him. That needed to be managed. Directed. But never extinguished.

If he was honest, he would admit that he enjoyed these rare moments of letting go a little too much. The tools of his trade, strewn across the floor, were useful. But he always liked to get 'hands on' once the groundwork had been laid. And rage, too, could be a useful tool.

The bunker where he was working had not yet been completed; it would one day be an embassy storeroom. It required none of the artistry that would grace the rest of the mansion. Below ground level, it was a windowless concrete box with minimal ventilation.

The air had grown fetid as he'd worked. Others would have found it oppressive, but he felt exhilarated. He took a deep breath. The smell. It was one of the things he loved. The mud-like tone of fresh concrete mixed with stale sweat and the acidic tinge of urine. And the top note: the sweet, familiar tang of blood.

And fear.

Others scoffed but he had always known that fear had a smell. He had been close to it all his life. His own fear, as a child, when his father's rages made the taste of his own blood routine.

Then the smell of his father's terror as he lay helpless before the blade as the rage that had been brewing exploded for the first time. That moment of sweet revenge had made him feel powerful, alive. Both his crude savagery and calm demeanour had shaken the police when they'd found him by the brutalised corpse.

It led the State to save him from execution. Instead they would train him, still a teenager, to be a special breed of footsoldier. Because the State knew that such men were valuable. That terror had its place.

The interrogator stopped rubbing his hand and returned his focus to the centre of the room where a shattered body was bound to an office chair. Builder's wire bit deeply into wrists with the subject's every agonised wrench. His white shirt was covered in blood and sick. His head flopped unconscious to the right, exposing the ragged flesh and cartilage that had once been his left ear.

A thread of spittle dribbled from split lips. The little fingers from both hands were missing: tossed on the floor near a kitchen cleaver, some pliers and several teeth. A hammer had crushed toes, smashed a kneecap and broken several ribs.

A welt just under the subject's left eye was beginning to swell. The interrogator knew his last, ferocious blow had broken a cheekbone. And the subject had passed out, again.

Yet he had learned nothing of the incident that had so enraged his masters. The subject had shared a room with the traitor and seen and heard nothing on the night of the escape. It had been the same with the other one.

Both, it seems, were innocents.

So what remained of his day's work was simply for pleasure.

'Wake up!' he barked, as he poured water over the battered head. Slowly a mind muddied by pain and terrorised by what a fellow human was capable of cleared enough to rouse from one nightmare to another.

His mouth tried to form a plea. A futile effort to evoke some pity.

'Please ...' His single word came out a guttural sob.

The interrogator felt the tingle of excitement that always came with the last desperate entreaty for life.

'I now understand you know nothing about the escape.' His voice was low, measured. 'But you need to know this. He betrayed his nation. And you. You are suffering because of him. Believe me, I will make it end. Soon.'

He dangled a blade before swollen eyes.

'Now, let's get rid of those pants.'

He emerged as early evening shadows were turning to night. It was warm, the air was clear, and birds chattered in the trees that surrounded the compound. In the nearby suburbs the mundane dinner-time rituals were well under way.

If anyone had been paying attention, they would have noticed that the lights that usually lit the building site had been extinguished.

The interrogator paused for a moment.

So quiet. Like the moment when death comes.

He was still astounded by the silence of this place, its proximity to nature, so different to the relentless noise of the city that he knew.

He motioned to the two men behind him who were labouring with the body. Another carried a plastic shopping bag, its contents heavy. They shuffled fifty metres to a trench that would form part of the foundations of the embassy's administrative wing.

The body was dumped next to another and the plastic bag thrown in alongside. The interrogator rubbed the aching knuckles of his right hand as he nodded to the men. Concrete flowed down the slipway of the mixer as a worker expertly guided the grey liquid over the small pile of human remains.

The half-dozen men looked at the interrogator only for instructions. Otherwise they steadfastly avoided his jet-black gaze and busied themselves with their appointed tasks.

He smiled as he lit a cigarette. Fear. He could not smell it mixed with this sweet night air or see it in the shadows that shrouded the faces of his peons.

But he knew it was there because they knew what he had done.

CHAPTER EIGHT

Canberra

Martin Toohey took a break from the mountain of paperwork piled on his desk, looked up and shook his head. Again.

Burnt orange.

Which genius in the Department of Prime Minister and Cabinet had chosen this catastrophe in 'contemporary furniture' to grace the most important office in the land? The four leather armchairs and one long lounge looked like they had been retrieved from the set of a tacky '70s sitcom.

The decor was another symbol of the hung parliament. If Labor had a clear majority, Toohey could have banished the monstrosities. But with his government under constant surveillance, the cost of a replacement suite would be splashed across the Murdoch tabloids. So he was snookered. Even the green leather chesterfield chosen by John and Janette Howard would have been preferable.

Maybe not.

It was close to midday and the first pangs of hunger prompted thoughts of lunch. But the poached salmon would have to wait. Toohey was expecting a VIP visitor.

A quiet knock signalled his arrival. His long-serving PA opened the door.

'The Ambassador to see you, Prime Minister.'

'Thanks, Barb. Please show Brent in.'

Brent Moreton had landed in Australia several years earlier and had quickly forged a reputation for telling it as it was. Or as the Americans wanted it to be. A charmer nonetheless, his Savile Row suits marked him as one of the sharpest dressers in Canberra's competitive diplomatic community. Moreton was highly regarded on the social circuit and his dinner invitations stretched out almost a year.

'PM, nice to see you. The President sends his regards.'

'Thanks, Brent. How's the family? You were taking the boys up to Sydney for a weekend the last time I saw you.'

'Yeah, and man, didn't we have some fun? Not sure that Luna Park is used to seeing a bunch of security guys talking into their wrists, though.'

The two men had forged a solid relationship despite their different world views. Both were professional advocates for their respective causes and when from time to time conflict between the Toohey Government and the US arose, they were mature and sensible enough to work through it.

But the challenges were growing. China and America were amping up the rhetoric to a level not seen since the end of the

Cold War. The Republicans had won the White House and President Jackson seemed to be taking his cue from the Tea Party loonies who believed in guns, God and slashing government. His foreign policy was an extension of his domestic tub-thumping – his decision to declare China a currency manipulator was just the most significant of several early blunders.

And China was increasingly combative, pushing out its elbows. Testing its growing power and the will of the United States to confront it. Some think tanks had begun to speculate that conflict between the two powers was inevitable, and might occur sooner rather than later.

Toohey was trying to chart a middle course: needing Chinese dollars *and* the security of the US alliance.

'The Switzerland of the Pacific,' one Canberra-based analyst had sneered.

Above all, the PM wanted to avoid being pushed into making an impossible choice between two rival powers. That made talks with the two nations' envoys a delicate dance between raindrops.

While Moreton had been appointed by Barack Obama, and expected to be replaced in time, he was first and foremost a loyal servant of the Stars and Stripes. He was a former marine and had effortlessly fallen into step with the new administration and its determination to adopt a tougher stance in relations with China.

Moreton had rung Toohey to lock in this meeting. The two men had blocked out forty minutes from their busy schedules. Moreton opened, smoothly shifting to a business-like tone.

'Prime Minister, thanks for making the time so quickly. I wanted to bring you up to speed on events. The President has been ringing several world leaders – David Cameron, Angela Merkel, Shinzo Abe – and he would like to speak with you this evening.'

The Ambassador paused as if searching for the right tone.

'We are concerned about the direction Beijing is heading. The new Chinese leadership seems determined to test its power. It's as if we have gone back to the bad old days before Deng got his hands on the political and economic levers.'

Toohey began his practised tightrope walk.

'I'm not sure I share your pessimism, Brent. We've had two ministers – senior ministers – visit China in the past month. Their feedback has been quite positive. The Trade Minister actually believes we are closer than ever to a free-trade deal, and that would be terrific not just for us but for this part of the world more generally.'

'It would be quite a coup, I grant you that, Prime Minister. And yet China shows little interest in being part of our bid to free up trade across the entire region through our Trans-Pacific Partnership.'

Toohey knew exactly what the Chinese thought of that, another exercise in the US writing the rules and expecting Beijing to follow them.

'Well, we support it and are optimistic that China will too, one day,' Toohey lied.

The main game was yet to unfold and he left space for Moreton to fill.

'We'll see,' Moreton said. 'I'm not sure I share your optimism. But one thing is clear: what China is spending its money on. Its military. It admits to lifting defence spending 11 per cent this year to $120 billion. We think it's much more than that.'

Moreton had his brief well-rehearsed.

'Their J-20 program is well advanced; the prototype stealth fighter they've been developing at Chengdu is not on par with ours, but it ain't far behind. China's air capability has moved ahead in leaps and big bounds.'

The Ambassador reached for a cup of tea, grimacing slightly at its heat, before continuing.

'Our intelligence isn't as definitive on China's submarine program but, Martin, they are putting together a very nice fleet. The Taiwan Strait is getting very crowded and they aren't pleasure craft out for a Sunday paddle.'

Toohey was trying to recall his latest briefing on the relative strengths of China's and America's military machines. Infuriatingly, he couldn't remember specifics but he did know Uncle Sam was well ahead. Toohey wanted to inject some common sense into the debate.

'Brent, you and I both know China is miles behind the US when it comes to military capability. You – the US – spends what? More than four times what China outlays on defence. Right now your country accounts for just under 40 per cent of the world's military spending. Even if they are hell bent on catching up, it would take decades. '

Moreton leaned forward, determined to make his friend understand.

'Martin, they don't need to spend what we do right now to be a threat. They just have to have the kit to push out into the neighbourhood and push us back across the Pacific. And this new leadership is something else; it is much more aggressive than we expected. And not just in the real world. You have no doubt read the latest Five-Eyes briefs on China's cyber-espionage activities?'

The Ambassador left the words hanging, knowing Australia's genuine concern about the threat posed by Beijing's cyber-thieves. The Prime Minister's own emails had been stolen by the Chinese, and Toohey had only learned of this when the US alerted Australia to the audacious intrusion.

'We are entering a new phase in our relationship with China.' Moreton said. 'President Jackson is very concerned by the latest briefings.'

Toohey was worried about activities on both sides of the Pacific.

'Frankly, Brent, I am more than a little concerned by the tone out of Washington. Declaring China a currency manipulator was a mistake. It would be better if your President let the calmer heads in his national security team prevail, rather than being dictated to by the Tea Party. It would be wise to take a step back on that. If China feels boxed in, it will retaliate. You are handing them a reason to do so. Stop yelling at China and start talking to it.'

Toohey almost immediately regretted the Tea Party line, realising that even if the Ambassador secretly agreed he would be forced to come to his President's defence.

'We needed to send a shot across China's economic bow.' Moreton swiftly manned the President's barricade. 'For too long, they've been able to get away with using their fixed currency to damage our economy. We will not meekly sit back and allow

Beijing to game the system. If they want to enjoy the benefits of the international economic road rules, they should abide by them.'

With a politician's instinct for seizing on just those words that served his argument, Toohey grasped the opening offered by Moreton.

'Australia wants everyone to obey the international rules that help ensure the peace, Brent. Because if we keep the peace we can all prosper. And if we accommodate China's rise we can guarantee the peace. If you attempt to ring-fence it, no good will come of it.'

Toohey reached for a glass of water, perching it on his knee before continuing.

'Brent, I – we – can appreciate the concerns you may have, but my government believes it is critical that China and the US attempt to forge a more constructive relationship. A true partnership. And that might mean that, occasionally, the US has to step back and give China space to mature. The twenty-first century rests on peace between your nations, and as a friend to both of you, that is our counsel.'

Toohey knew that the idea of the US taking a step back on anything wasn't one that had a lot of currency in Washington. But he believed that it was a powerful argument and one he intended to make as strongly as he possibly could.

The two men had been talking for close to twenty minutes when Moreton lifted the stakes.

'A free-trade deal is one thing. But Washington is very worried that you are about to get strategically entangled with China. Martin, we hear that a massive gas deal that involves effective

Chinese ownership of Australian resources will be at the heart of your Press Club address.'

Toohey was stunned. The China deal was top secret. Just a handful of people knew about the Northern Territory gas hub plan.

'As usual I am staggered by your intelligence.' Toohey was measuring each word and wrestling with his emotions. 'That plan is not yet finalised, and if and when it is I will act in the best interests of my nation.'

'Don't commit yourself to this, Prime Minister.' Moreton was treading carefully. 'If you do, it will put us in a very awkward position.'

'Brent, I will promise you just this. I will do what is right for my country. And the party I lead. Labor has always been the party of big ideas, just like your Democrats. We owe our political success to our ability to marry good economic policies with progressive social reforms. That is what I intend doing.'

Moreton looked unconvinced and Toohey suspected the cable back to DC would be quite something.

'Martin, our relationship – our friendship – has endured for many decades. Australia has always, *always*, been one of our closest allies, through good and bad. The President will be calling soon and I think our conversation has given you a good flavour of what is on his mind. He treasures this alliance and hopes he can count on you in what may well be difficult times ahead.'

'Always happy to talk.' But Toohey had run out of patience with the conversation and was keen to begin another with his chief of staff to try to track down the source of this latest damaging leak. 'And as a friend of America I will repeat the advice I have offered you.'

The Ambassador had delivered his message and glanced at his Seiko Velatura before continuing. 'Your government has some big decisions ahead of it, my friend. Now, I must away. Lunch with the Brits awaits.'

He stalled at the door, and looked back.

'And Prime Minister, don't forget who your mates are.'

CHAPTER NINE

Canberra

This was his daily god moment, an intersection of nature and music, played out in the private amphitheatre of his home.

Most mornings around 7am, Charles Dancer would sit Buddha-like, meditating, as the Canberra sun streamed in, a soft tune thrumming in the background. The spears of light created a natural kaleidoscope as they played across a row of jade statues, sourced from back-alley dens in Laos and Cambodia. His obsession with the art of Asia was evident in the paintings and portraits that covered the walls, while a custom-made set of shelves tastefully showcased fertility figures, dolls and masks. They were his nod to the romance of the East, a reminder that he – ostensibly a dry-as-dust bureaucrat – had led a life of intrigue.

Dancer was nudging sixty, an age when most public servants were contemplating retirement, or seeking out a quiet corner of some overlooked agency in which to eke out their time. But

Charles was no ordinary mandarin. Officially he was an analyst who worked for the Department of Foreign Affairs and Trade. Unofficially he considered himself an invisible diplomat, a senior member of the nation's spy force paid to find, and fix, the dangers ordinary people couldn't even imagine. He reported directly to the Secretary, and was one of the trusted few given unfettered access to the government's darkest secrets.

Dancer stretched and ended his yoga session. He walked to the kitchen and poured a shot of black coffee, adding two sugars. For the past fifteen years, he'd lived in a bungalow close to the bustling village of Manuka, a few kilometres from the R.G. Casey building that housed a thousand of Canberra's most cunning bureaucrats.

He loved the smell of secrecy and conceit that permeated DFAT. They really did consider themselves a special breed, he mused, artisans trained to make gunfire sound harmless.

Along with many of his colleagues, Dancer had a taste for the good life. He got a thrill whenever he came across a new treasure – an antique shadow puppet, a Chinese *ta* – while overseas and occasionally would leverage his status to ensure its smooth passage through Customs. His walk-in wardrobe – built by a fireman friend who dabbled in carpentry – reflected a refined taste in clothing. He seldom shopped at home, relying on regular international travel to maintain a steady supply of tailor-made suits and shirts. Recently, he'd experimented with internet shopping and was pleased with his first online purchases.

Not that money was an issue. A lifetime of living alone, a steady and well-paid job with generous allowances, and the hand-me-down benefits of his parent's estate (three houses and a mini-horse stud in the Hunter Valley) ensured financial security.

Dancer had followed a standard path into DFAT's ranks, graduating from the Australian National University with honours in International Relations, earning a special commendation for an insightful thesis on Australia's relationship with Indonesia. Hired through the graduate program – Class of '77 – Dancer was considered a stand-out among the many who, each year, jostle for one of the handful of positions on offer. He'd adapted easily to the culture of the time, had worked hard and been rewarded with a posting to Jakarta after just five years.

On the surface, he was a boilerplate public servant. Under the radar he had been recruited by the Australian Secret Intelligence Service, and he'd become one of their very best.

Dancer was fastidious and uber-fit, enjoying long rides on a custom-made Kona that could whip down the narrow mountain trails that flanked the national capital. For thirty years, he'd maintained a steady weight of 85 kilograms, underpinned by an obsession with healthy eating. While his wine cellar was graced with prized vintages, he drank in moderation and considered a hangover to be a sign of frailty.

On this crystal-cut morning in Canberra, however, the tastes and habits of Charles Dancer mattered little. He contemplated a plastic-and-metal USB that he'd been given by Amanda Wade.

His mate from the morgue had rung out of the blue. She'd explained, over a glass of wine, about the body in the lake and the visit from the Chinese embassy staff, their clumsy attempt to retrieve the corpse before the investigation had finished.

What they didn't know was that a memory stick had been retrieved from his stomach during the autopsy. Wade had used discretion to ensure there was no record of it on the official police file. She'd given Dancer brief details about the man – identified as Lin An – and a copy of the forensic notes.

According to the Chinese, Lin was a construction worker sent to Australia to help build the fortress-like embassy that was taking shape on the lake's edge, four hundred metres from the existing buildings. The story didn't fit though; his pallid body displayed none of the brawn or weathering you'd expect of a labourer exposed to Canberra's punishing climate.

Someone wasn't telling the truth.

Dancer fired up his MacBook Pro as the voice of Angelique Kidjo flowed from Bang and Olufsen speakers. Her blend of home-grown activism and sultry French vocals always relaxed him.

The file was encrypted. That reinforced the notion that Lin was not a labourer. Clicking through the unreadable documents, Dancer surmised it would take quite some time before they could be cracked.

And if Lin had locked it with keys that only he possessed?

That might take weeks.

Once opened, the file would have to be translated, although that would pose little trouble for Dancer who'd been stationed for several years in Beijing. Prior to his posting, he'd studied Mandarin at the RAAF School of Languages at Point Cook and graduated R4S4, the highest levels of reading and speaking.

Dancer had a particular passion for China and its rich and painful history. It was something he'd shared with Kimberley

Gordon, a former security analyst with the Defence Signals Directorate whose death eighteen months ago had left a searing wound.

Kimberley had been DSD's shining light, a gifted agent who had risen to the top of a naturally paranoid organisation, despite the fact that she, in her early forties, had transformed from a man to a woman. Ben Gordon had become Kimberley without missing a beat in his/her career.

Dancer had envied her courage in resolving her sexual confusion because it had been very different for him. As a teenager in a strict Baptist home, Charles had fought the attraction that he felt for men. Denied it and himself. He could never admit it to his parents and his father's words still haunted him.

All mankind is depraved, sinful and lost.

He had quit his family's stern religion as soon as he left home. But it clung like a cancer on his soul. Dancer loathed himself and his homosexuality. He had grasped at relationships with women, but they ranged from the awkward to the embarrassing.

Eventually he had given in to his desires but only when he was far from home. Even in his late forties, he had never had a long-term love.

Until he met Kimberley. Then he was besotted. She seemed to offer an answer. Outwardly female, bodily male. For a while, they revelled in each other, liberating each other's lustful yearnings. But, in time, Dancer's doubts and his loathing returned. Kimberley had fought to maintain their special bond, to try to get him to find peace with himself. But the relationship was doomed.

I pushed her away.

They avoided each other for more than a year before Kimberley had sought his help with a difficult job. He had been thrilled to hear from her. Tried to help her. To point her in the right direction.

And then she was killed.

More than once, Dancer had caught himself muttering 'For you, Kimberley ...' as he set about some onerous task, trying not to douse himself in self-pity and blame.

Now, on a summer's day promising to soar into the high thirties, Dancer began to run the first pass of a decryption program over the USB. A nervous twinge whisked down his left arm, the anticipation of stumbling onto something big.

An hour later Dancer had extracted a few shards of information from one of the hundreds of files on the memory stick. The lines of the decrypted code did not disappoint, confirming that Wade was right to be suspicious of the Chinese claim that the dead man, Lin An, was a labourer.

The first file was a dossier on Lin.

My my my ...

Dancer had seen enough secrets in his time that he could usually cover his excitement with a studied indifference. It was something he practised, even in the isolation of his own home.

But this file showed Lin was attached to one of China's most dangerous institutions: Unit 61398. The unit had been the subject of cables from Beijing and knowledge of it had even spilled on to the internet. It was an arm of China's People's Liberation Army, and its headquarters had been tracked to a twelve-storey building in the middle of Shanghai. Unit 61398 was the nerve centre of

China's hacking empire, home to hundreds of cyber-warriors who'd launched assaults against corporations and even countries.

Dancer had read top secret files blaming China for infiltrating key assets in Australia. Rumour had it that the Australian Security Intelligence Organisation's Director-General, Richard Dalton, believed China was responsible for stealing the building plans of the new spy HQ on the edge of Russell's Defence complex, a stone's throw from Lake Burley Griffin.

Dancer's mind was racing. The fact that a Chinese cyber-warrior was here in Canberra confirmed his worst suspicions about the real nature of the new embassy being built on the opposite side of the lake – and within cannon shot of Parliament House.

He weighed his options. Of course, he would present the information to his superiors. But that was no longer enough. He had watched with alarm as each warning issued by intelligence chiefs about the growing threat of China went unheeded by this appalling government.

He had always worked in the shadows and his natural instinct was to keep secrets. But as the Toohey Government forged ever closer ties with the Chinese, the danger to the nation grew. He knew his masters shared his concerns and believed the Australian people would too.

If only they knew.

The people needed to know how *serious* the threat was. If they did they would be horrified. And that would force the Toohey Government into making the right decisions. To act in the national interest.

The best way to influence public opinion was through the mainstream media. Despite the rise of online news, tweeting and blogging, Dancer wanted to leak this information to the outside world the old-fashioned way.

First he had work to do. Dancer saved the material from the USB onto a portable hard drive, then put it into a safe hidden behind an early Mapplethorpe. Next he uploaded a few lines from the document he had opened onto another memory stick, editing the raw data to ensure that it offered no more than a tantalising taste.

Dancer had a low regard for journalists, but there was one he trusted, the press gallery veteran Harry Dunkley. They'd met eighteen months ago, after Kimberley's death, drawn together by a deeply ironic intersection of work and their mutual affection for her. Just days after the funeral, Dancer had 'outed' himself to Dunkley as his Deep Throat on a story that had struck at the very heart of the Toohey Government and eventually forced the resignation of Defence Minister Bruce Paxton. Dunkley, displaying the cynicism of a seasoned reporter, had been cool, even hostile, at first.

His anger had eventually dissipated and he and Dancer had shared the odd bottle of wine as balm for their common grief. Not that Dancer considered himself the sentimental type.

He flicked on his mobile and scrolled through an impressive contact list. Six rings later, a gruff voice answered.

'Well, well. Look who the fucking cat's dragged in ...'

CHAPTER TEN

Fort Meade, Maryland

The steel door slid open with a sound like air rushing from a tyre valve and Matthew Sloan stood transfixed as it revealed a scene drawn from a childhood fantasy.

The chair of Australia's Parliamentary Committee on Intelligence and Security had stepped onto the bridge of a spaceship that was immediately, eerily, familiar. The skin on Sloan's scalp tightened and his arms tingled with goose bumps.

The circular room was built on two levels. He'd stepped onto the upper deck where the focal point was a single high-backed chair on a raised platform. It looked towards a massive plasma screen displaying a satellite image of the world, with the United States dead centre, that arced from floor to ceiling across both levels of the bridge. Also on the top deck, just below and in front of the captain's chair, was another command module where two senior crew sat monitoring a bank of computer screens. Three sets of stairs ran down to the lower deck where more crew clustered around duty stations of monitors and keyboards dotted around the outer circle.

The bridge was alive, pulsing with energy. An electronic wonderland.

So, it was true. The US National Security Agency's Intelligence and Security Command's 'Information Dominance Centre' at Fort Meade, Maryland, had been designed as an exact replica of the bridge of a Constitution Class starship. To be specific, the USS *Enterprise*.

In the late 1960s, like so many Australian kids, Sloan had tuned in avidly each week to watch Captain Kirk and his crew go boldly where no man had gone before. Now he was one of a very privileged few to venture here. The Labor MP swelled with pride. He had been assured he was the first Australian parliamentarian to be invited into the beating heart of the most sophisticated signals intelligence operation on Earth.

The main chair swivelled and an athletic-looking military man rose to greet him. Sloan had not previously met four-star general Dick Hargreaves, but was intimately acquainted with his formidable career. Hargreaves was the longest-serving leader of the NSA and the inaugural commander of US Cyber Command, which included the Navy's 10th Fleet, the 24th Air Force and the Second Army. From this bridge he listened to the world's secrets and battled shadowy adversaries.

'Mr Sloan, I presume.' Hargreaves spoke with a gentle southern drawl. 'I am delighted that you could join us.'

'General, the pleasure and honour are mine. Please call me

Matthew.' Sloan glanced about the impossible room. 'This is ... extraordinary.'

'Yes, Matthew, the great folks at Imagination in Hollywood helped us put it together. Our idea was we're going into a new area – information warfare and cyber – so how do we build *esprit de corps* and help the army think about this in a new light? We've got to get people energised about carrying out this mission set. We've got to have them be creatively inspired to bring disparate data together to help secure our nation.'

'Forgive me for asking ...' Sloan was still gawping, '... but is it true that the number on your car space here at Fort Meade is 007?'

Hargreaves laughed. 'That's correct. It shows you that the folks at NSA have a sense of humour. But I drive a Chevy pickup, not an Aston Martin. And I'd rather be remembered like an Arnold Schwarzenegger in *True Lies*. My daughters would be much more impressed!'

Both men chuckled and Sloan, knowing his time here would be strictly limited, moved to the main game.

'General, the reason I requested this meeting is so I might give my committee a proper feel for how you work. We're particularly interested in trying to replicate your cyber-war capabilities. We want America's assessment of the threats.'

'Sure, come join me on the bridge, I've pulled up a chair for you.'

As the two men sat, the general pressed a button on a console in the armrest of his chair. The giant screen flicked to a flow chart headed 'NSA Operations'.

'NSA has two main tasks. First, it collects, decodes, translates, analyses and disseminates foreign signals, or communications, for intelligence and counter-intelligence purposes and to support our military operations. Those signals are transmitted over many mediums including copper, fibre, radio, satellite and other wireless channels.

'NSA's second job is information assurance. That is, to prevent adversaries from gaining access to the nation's most sensitive secrets – our government's intellectual property, so to speak.'

The general punched the button again and the screen flicked to another diagram.

'Cyber Command's mission is three-fold: first, to defend the nation from cyber-attacks; second, to operate and defend the Defence Department's information networks; and, finally, to support our military combat commanders with the cyber-capabilities they need, including conducting full-spectrum military cyberspace operations, when directed, in order to enable our military actions across the air, land, sea, space and cyber domains. In short, Cyber Command's task is to ensure the military has freedom of action in cyberspace – and to deny the same to our adversaries.'

Sloan was already across a lot of the theory. What he wanted was an idea of how it worked in practice.

'So does all this help in a real-world war zone?'

Hargreaves shifted forward in his seat and Sloan could see this keeper of secrets was enjoying the chance to boast about his work.

'One of my proudest moments is how we responded in Iraq in '05 and '06. The casualties were mounting with a dozen allied soldiers being killed or wounded daily, driven by a surge in roadside bombings.

'We started collecting a much broader range of insurgent communications and then, crucially, compressing the time it took us to get actionable intelligence back into the hands of the end users. We successfully reduced that disconnect from about sixteen hours down to around one minute. We saved lives.'

Sloan wanted to talk about another kind of war. One waged in bits and bytes in the ether. One Australia was ill-equipped to fight.

'General, how serious is the threat of cyber-war?'

'Matthew, I believe the rise of globalisation has made the world a more dangerous place. What keeps me awake at night are terrorist and cyber-attacks, for both your country and America. Those are the two threats where adversaries can reach far into the homeland and really hurt populations. Those risks are growing, and we need to be out in front of them.'

'What are the risks?'

'What we're seeing is more folks testing boundaries with mounting numbers of state-on-state cyber-probes and sometimes cyber-attacks. So the main risk is miscalculation. Assume one country believes it can hit your nation with a cyber-attack, and that it won't lead to physical conflict.

'But in launching that cyber-attack, suppose they actually knock down your stock exchange or temporarily disable your banking system, which is a very real possibility. And if you extend those attack vectors to take out power grids, transport systems and other infrastructure, they can have devastating effects.

'Your government then feels it has to retaliate. Then we have an unpredictable chain reaction that could lead to outright war. In the virtual world no one knows where the red lines are.'

Sloan felt uneasy listening to a new doomsday scenario. Now he understood why the spooks he knew were paranoid, always glancing at the shadows in search of an enemy that may or may not exist.

'So how do we protect ourselves?' the MP asked.

The general's eyes wandered over his gleaming twenty-first-century war-room.

'When you think about success on the battlefield, you say your artillery has to be the best. Your armour has to be the best. Your infantry has to be the best. The same logic applies in the cyber-domain.'

Sloan had worked his way towards the one question that was keeping *him* awake at night.

'So who should Australia fear the most?'

The general caught Sloan's gaze and didn't miss a beat: 'China.'

'Why?'

'You matter to China. You're a reliable source of the resources it needs for it to rise as the next superpower. But it sees you as tied to us, the current superpower, through ANZUS. That presents a problem. No matter what you say in public, in China's mind you can't straddle that divide forever. One day you'll have to make a choice.

'So China needs to know your deepest thoughts. The relationships at the heart of your leadership, right down to who is literally fucking whom, if you'll pardon my French. That's why they opened up your parliamentary communications systems. When we found out about it we warned you. But we believe that they had access for a year.'

Sloan's heart sank. He was well aware of the damage. 'Yes, it was like a fucking open-cut mine.'

'Indeed, and right now there's a warehouse full of Chinese analysts poring over every line of what they took, looking for weaknesses.'

'I don't doubt it.' Sloan shook his head.

'And since our President decided to muscle up to China on its currency manipulation we've been recording attacks on our systems every day that are off the charts. You could be in the line of fire, too.'

'Why? What have we done? If anything our government is doing too much to appease China.'

The general frowned. 'Yes, we've noticed that. But in the end, you're our ally. You have access to all this.' Hargreaves swept his right arm across the bridge. 'So that makes you a target.'

Suddenly the general rose from his chair. The audience was over. The spymaster had real work to do, but he had one last message to send. He leaned in close to deliver it.

'Matthew, if there is one thing that you should tell your government, back in Canberra, it is this: the enemy is already through the gates.'

CHAPTER ELEVEN

Canberra

Harry Dunkley rolled out of his double bed, the remnant of a dream already fading. It was nearly 7am and the press gallery veteran rubbed an ache in his hip, a reminder of too much rugby in his reckless youth.

The soft early morning light cast a glow over the sleeping Celia Mathieson. She seemed to shine from within and looked younger than her thirty-two years. Her beauty and their fledgling relationship still astounded him.

They'd met in October when Mathieson, back in Canberra after eight years overseas, was hired by *The Australian* as a 'data journalist'. Dunkley had rolled his eyes when told of the new position, assuming it was something dreamed up by Gen Y back-office types.

Mathieson was the only daughter of one of Canberra's most senior mandarins, the fearsome Roger Mathieson – AO and all-round shit. Mathieson snr had bulldozed his way to the top of the public service, serving as deputy secretary in half a dozen agencies. Perhaps it was to escape from her father's long shadow that Celia had taken off overseas soon after graduating with honours in Advanced Computing from the Australian National University. She'd only returned when her mother was diagnosed with breast cancer.

A month after she'd started at the *Oz*, Dunkley had enlisted her help to trawl through the entitlement records of every MP and senator. She'd taken her time completing the task but Dunkley had been astounded by her computer skills. He'd shouted her a joint byline on the subsequent story and asked her out for a drink after she'd given him a tantalising 'thank you' kiss that lingered a tad too long.

Their relationship had blossomed from spreadsheets to bedsheets, and now, as Dunkley watched his sleeping angel, he felt the guilty lust of a man who couldn't quite believe his luck. He shook his head in wonder. *What does she see in me?*

He headed to the bathroom, splashing his face to wash the sleep from his eyes before examining last night's damage. He tried to convince himself he was still handsome despite the creased face that looked all its fifty-five years and offered a little too much history. Still, the first flourish of grey added a certain Clooney lustre, he thought.

Not too shabby, mate.

His hands pinched at a belly several kilos heavier than he would have liked. But the back was ramrod straight and his arms retained enough muscle tone to suggest this body was a fine athletic specimen. Once.

He was still entangled in his physical stocktaking when the bathroom's digital radio burst into life. The familiar trumpet of the ABC's NewsRadio heralded a lively discussion with Marius Benson about the morning's headlines. Dunkley turned down the sound so as not to disturb his sleeping beauty.

A cursory run through the Fairfax papers and Murdoch tabloids was the warm-up for a full-scale dissection of *The Australian*'s front page. Not all of it complimentary, either.

'Thank you Marius,' Dunkley muttered caustically.

He stifled a yawn as he opened the front door to his small apartment. He avoided reading the papers online whenever possible, and was pleased to see real-world print resting with reassuring tactility on the porch.

As he carried the five mastheads inside, he was dismayed by their meagre weight. The rise of the internet and changing reading habits were strip-mining advertising dollars from the old media, by the millions. And as the cash dried up and profits shrank, the farewells for journalist colleagues were becoming routine. Every paper in the country was fighting for its survival, slashing costs as it shed hardcopy readers. Jesus, even his local newsagent, Chris, was toying with scrapping the paper run.

'It's costing me money,' Chris had told Dunkley recently as he'd settled his monthly account. 'I only do it 'cause of customers like you. And you're getting fewer every year.'

It had hit Dunkley like a punch. Something that he'd assumed would be a permanent feature of his life was about to vanish.

That reassuring thud of paper-on-grass would soon, like the clink of the milk run, become a story that grandparents told to wide-eyed youngsters. He thought about that often. He had always revelled in unwrapping the papers and spreading them out on his kitchen table, as he did now.

A quick scan of the headlines to see if he'd been scooped by one of his colleagues in the blast furnace of the federal parliamentary press gallery, still the most competitive marketplace in journalism.

Patrick Lion from the *Tele* had a small-beer yarn about yet another Coalition MP forced to pay back money for a dodgy travel claim. The MP had retreated with a template excuse. The jaunt across the country to attend a colleague's birthday was a legitimate expense given the important matters of state that were inevitably discussed. But, just to clear the matter up and 'to ensure the right thing is done by the taxpayer and alleviate any ambiguity', the MP had agreed to repay $5000 clocked up in airfares and expenses.

You grub.

He knew Lion and his other rivals would be frothing over his own story – and, more importantly, so would their editors.

By habit, Dunkley saved the national broadsheet until last.

Despite nearly thirty years in the game, Dunkley still felt the same kid-in-a-toyshop thrill when he broke a yarn that would set the agenda. One that would be the envy of his mates and enemies on the Hill.

A tingle took hold as he gazed at today's headline: TOOHEY IS TERMINAL.

Farrrkkkk.

Dunkley shuddered and for once it was not the result of a late-night drinking bout but the sheer thrill of re-reading the lead on a yarn that hit like a prizefighter.

Labor risks electoral annihilation with just one in four voters now backing the embattled Toohey Government, secret internal ALP polling reveals.

The credibility of Prime Minister Martin Toohey has also crashed with voters abandoning a government that has been rocked by crisis.

The polling, details of which have been obtained by *The Australian*, shows voters in battleground seats in western Sydney and Brisbane have lost faith in the government's ability to manage the country.

Labor insiders fear the party is beyond salvation and the public has stopped listening to the Prime Minister.

'They are waiting with baseball bats and chainsaws,' one senior source said. 'When the election is held, the streets will run red with our blood. Toohey's a great guy but this can't go on.'

This government is in more strife than Speed Gordon.

But unlike the mythical superhero, there would be no salvation in the final frame. Half the front page of the national broadsheet was devoted to delighting in the latest piece of bad news for the Toohey Government, dissecting the troubles of a once great and proud Labor Party. Pointers promised more thrills inside, including a thundering editorial which would point out that, once again, the judgement of the *Oz* had been vindicated.

A historical analysis revealed that Toohey was the least popular prime minister since Billy McMahon. The paper's caustic 'Cut and Paste' column amused itself with a series of quotes from the ABC and Fairfax ripped from Toohey's days of early promise, all designed to show the multiple delusions of the 'Love Media'.

Just to make sure that not a single reader was left in any doubt as to where the newspaper stood, *The Australian*'s chieftains had published a photo of a glowing Opposition leader, Emily Brooks, as she left a function full of cheering Tory types, with the caption 'Headed for the Lodge'.

Dunkley flinched. He had no trouble going in hard with the facts and Labor had brought most of its woes on itself. But he did worry that the paper looked as if it was barracking for the Opposition when it ran puff pieces on Brooks, as rarely had he met a more objectionable individual. While the country seemed poised to throw the government out, the punters weren't hungering for the alternative. Would Brooks be better able to provide the three key things Dunkley believed Australians craved from their leaders – predictability, certainty and competence?

Dunkley blamed most of the government's grief on the now catatonic Foreign Minister, Catriona Bailey. The deposed prime minister had laid such rocky foundations in the first two years of her chaotic reign that she had been on track to be the first PM since Scullin in '32 to be tossed out after a single term.

Bailey had pissed record ratings up against the wall. She had started dozens of grand projects and never finished a single one. Her obnoxious and high-handed style coupled with a deluge of demented demands had alienated the bureaucracy inside six months.

She'd lost Cabinet in the first year. But the real problem was the scorn she'd heaped on Caucus, totally misunderstanding that in a parliamentary democracy a prime minister is selected by her party, not the people.

Caucus despised her.

So they pulled the trigger in a minute-to-midnight coup just months out from a general election. But the unexpected and largely unexplained shift to Martin Toohey shocked and confused the public. The election had seen the major parties' share of the vote split down the middle, leaving neither with the numbers to form government.

Toohey had cobbled together a minority government. But the compromises, and the messy aftermath of the Bailey era, had crippled him.

Bailey refused to go quietly, undermining him at every opportunity.

At another time, under different circumstances, Dunkley believed Toohey might have made a decent PM. But that was a fantasy. History had punched Toohey's card and before the end of the year his brief, unhappy term in office would be over.

The sun pouring through a small eastward-facing window lit up a dust-covered Walkley Award, among a pile of other ill-treated honours on a cluttered shelf. The chaos of the Bailey–Toohey years had been the most successful of Dunkley's long career covering politics. Labor had been good for journalism and he'd led the pack.

So what.

No award could mask the pain that followed the death of his only real friend, Kimberley Gordon. It was only after she was gone that he realised how alone he really was.

He'd met Kimberley at university when she was a he: Ben Gordon, a hard-running rugby forward. The two were both instinctively loners, destined to find one great friendship in each other. They clicked instantly and shared every high and low for over two decades. They'd grown even closer through the years of Ben's torment over his sexual identity. He'd finally decided to make his way as a woman. Dunkley wasn't good at life advice but he was the one thing his friend had needed: someone to talk to.

When Kimberley died Dunkley had no one to talk to. His marriage was over and his daughter distant. Kimberley had always been there, and her loss was a constant raw welt.

Only now, in his budding relationship with Celia, had some of the pain begun to fade. But Dunkley knew he would always be tormented until he unravelled the mystery of Kimberley's death. And avenged it.

The official line, that she had been the victim of a gay-hate crime while cruising in a public toilet, infuriated Dunkley. It was a lie, a lazy bureaucratic dismissal of a rich and beautiful life. The police had cast Kimberley as a freak who'd invited her own death.

But he was convinced her murder was linked to former Defence Minister Bruce Paxton and his murky ties to China.

I pushed the rock that started the landslide.

Dunkley had asked for Kimberley's help with a photo that eventually implicated Paxton in electoral fraud. But she had turned up a more astonishing story: that Paxton and former prime minister, Catriona Bailey, had been courted by Chinese spies.

The allegation was unprovable, the evidence circumstantial at best. And he was well aware that spooks were naturally paranoid and prone to conspiracy theories. But Dunkley could not reconcile one undeniable fact: within hours of Kimberley stumbling onto the links between Bailey and Chinese intelligence, she was dead. If she wasn't the victim of a senseless crime there was only one logical conclusion.

Someone knew what she knew and wanted it to die with her.

Every day he felt the weight of guilt. She had died helping him.

Dunkley had used his considerable investigative skills to try to track down the killer. All roads led to China, and he believed a third secretary, who had abruptly left the Chinese embassy in Canberra following Kimberley's death, was the key. Dunkley had taken long-service leave to follow the trail to Beijing, but turned up nothing.

So he'd come home and thrown himself back into his job with vigour. But the experience had hardened him against China. He'd written opinion pieces warning of the strategic risks that came with the opportunities of its rise, reminding Australia to remember who its real friends were. Since the Second World War, the United States had provided the security environment that had allowed China to flower peacefully. Dunkley doubted that China would be as benevolent when it was fully grown. Everything he saw confirmed his prejudice against a nation that seemed to be ever more aggressive in its dealings with neighbours.

Dunkley's opinions were at odds with the prevailing view and drew much criticism. But he'd found some in Cabinet, Defence and Canberra's diplomatic community who were deeply grateful. The Japanese Ambassador was particularly helpful.

Later this morning, he had an appointment with an old contact. He'd received the call a day earlier, out of the blue, from someone who kept more secrets than a Catholic priest.

He licked his lips at the prospect of entering the confessional, just as a piece of toast, burned beyond recognition, sprang from the toaster. It was his last piece of wholemeal, too.

CHAPTER TWELVE

Canberra

THE clean sheets felt pleasant against her skin, soothing and soft. The fresh linen acted as a balm for Catriona Bailey.

For eighteen months, the Foreign Minister had lain paralysed, her world reduced to a small private hospital room, the hum-and-whirr of life-support machines as familiar as her own voice had been.

This was her life, lungs, heartbeat. And her prison.

Medical science had kept her alive, but every day was a battle against despair.

The small things mattered, sustained her, like the daily change of linen.

A stroke had robbed her of agility, and she could no longer speak. Her rare condition – locked-in syndrome – meant she was reduced to communicating through the one bodily function she could still control: her eyes.

Bailey would have descended into madness but for the wonders of the information age that liberated her mind and unshackled her from these life-giving machines. Sanity had come from the computer that turned her eye-movements into words, and the internet that allowed her brilliant mind to wander the world.

This had allowed her to retain her ministry. She'd become a *cause célèbre*, the disability lobby using her fame to press a weak government to keep her on the frontbench. And the Opposition, led by preening fools, had helped when it announced plans to deny her a parliamentary pair. It had been forced to retreat under a barrage of outrage, but Bailey feared the Coalition would try again.

I must be ready.

There was one other thing that sustained Bailey.

Revenge.

In the few quiet hours when she wasn't blinking commands, or keeping up a steady stream of online banter, she was plotting the demise of the man responsible for her descent to in-patient: Martin Toohey.

It began with his smash-and-grab plot to steal her prime ministerial crown. Although she'd been tagged the Tungsten Lady, her downfall, swift and unexpected, had been devastating.

She was convinced her paralysis was directly linked to Toohey's treachery.

So the thought of revenge, of making him pay for his duplicity, sustained her. Hope, she'd learned, was a powerful elixir. With hope, miracles could happen.

I must believe I can walk again. Talk again.

Now, in the small hours of the Canberra morning, after finishing a discussion on Syria with her online disciples in the United States, she turned her mind to finding a cure for her condition. She scoured the internet for the latest information on anyone who had recovered from locked-in syndrome.

The news was largely bad. The syndrome was rare, usually the result of a stroke which damaged the ventral pons at the base of the brain. It left sufferers paralysed and needing life support. Even medical journal articles admitted it was the stuff of nightmares.

Bailey read one from the Texas Medical Association that neatly described how she felt.

Imagine waking from a deep sleep to find yourself fully conscious but unable to move any voluntary muscles save for the muscles that control your vertical eye movements. You can see, hear, smell, taste … However, you are unable to speak or make any vocalizations at all. You are, in essence, locked in your own body. This scenario is not a fantasy that Rod Sterling would have written for a *Twilight Zone* episode but a recognized, though rare, neuropsychological syndrome.

Enough of that.

Bailey knew the problem all too well. What she was searching for were solutions.

The gold standard was Kate Allatt, a forty-year-old who had almost completely recovered after two years. But Allatt was so rare as to be unique. Bailey feared she would never regain her old abilities.

But there has been progress.

Hours of painful therapy had seen some movement return to her hands. And as she tested the long disused muscles in her neck and back she felt that she would, before long, be able to sit upright.

Even better, the doctors believed she would soon be able to breathe unassisted. That meant she would be able to test whether the tracheotomy in her neck had done permanent damage to her voice box.

And if she could sit up, be taken off life support and speak she would be able to leave this room behind. She'd find liberation in a wheelchair, for her body and mind.

If it is humanly possible, I will triumph.

But time was pressing. An election was due later this year. She would take short-cuts if necessary, even if these were risky and untested.

Bailey needed to rise again, more quickly than was humanly possible. And when she achieved that, she would turn off Martin Toohey's life support.

CHAPTER THIRTEEN

Beijing

The seven men filed on stage, all purpose and swagger, dressed in identical dark suits with bold red ties, a neat symmetrical march of the recently elected, all-powerful Standing Committee of the Political Bureau of the Party's Central Committee. The ones chosen to steer the nation through the next phase of its inexorable rise, to the peak of global power. This was a pantomime staged for the three hundred and seventy-six Communist Party central committee members drawn from every corner of the republic, stacked with the people who really ran China. Regional governors sat beside generals who nodded sagely at those who ran state-owned enterprises. A gathering of the communist elite. They had come together in the cavernous Great Hall of the People for the third plenum of the 18th Central Committee. Their task: to debate a five-year economic and strategic plan.

Jiang Xiu stole a quick glance at the painting that spanned the stage, nearly thirty metres wide and eighteen high, 'This Land So Rich in Beauty'. He loved its majesty, its aura of rugged charm. He stood near the far left of the elite line-up, his number six stamped on the floor, and obediently followed his comrades as they answered the audience applause with soft handclaps of their own.

A surge of elation and responsibility pulsed through him. His poor debilitated mother would have been so proud.

But Jiang knew this public forum was purely for show. Here in Beijing, the future direction of this autocratic State had already been thrashed out behind heavy wooden doors, fortified to resist armies.

Jiang, his lush jet-black hair slicked back and glistening, gazed into the audience, seeking out familiar faces. An urge to smile came over him. But he knew that would be frowned upon, so he stood stony-faced.

An hour earlier, the seven men had finished a secret meeting with no minders or note-takers, not even a servant to pour the tea. In power since November, the Standing Committee's first gatherings had been perfunctory administrative affairs. But today's meeting had been the first to test whether Jiang had correctly judged where the numbers and the will of his comrades lay.

Although technically one of the most junior of the seven, Jiang had led much of the debate around the carved wooden table, outlining his plans as the Minister for Propaganda.

He had been pushing hard for China to take an aggressive stance against the United States and its new President. The declaration of China as a currency manipulator was an insult that needed to be met with unshakeable resolution.

Jiang had known that the President was with him, as was one other. What had mattered was whether he could secure a fourth vote.

He was determined to push the committee into taking a hard line with the West. If he succeeded, then, for the first time in several decades, it would signal the nationalists were back in charge. It was Jiang's firm belief they should send a powerful message to any nation that did not afford China the respect it deserved.

His opening monologue had analysed America's weakness: a military fatigued by a decade of war, a faltering economy still staggering from the financial meltdown. The US Government's hand was losing its grip and its people were dismayed.

And China was growing more powerful by the day. The delegations of heads of government, financiers and industrialists from around the globe were evidence of a shift in the world order. Wealth bought military might: China would soon launch its latest nuclear-powered submarine to patrol the disputed waters of the East China Sea.

Tomorrow, a front-page article in the *People's Daily* would denounce America's financial attacks on China as part of a plan to contain its surge to pre-eminence. It would declare that China would not sit idle while its interests were threatened.

Jiang had told his comrades that America had made a critical strategic error and that it was an opportunity that should be seized: immediately and forcefully.

'We need to press our advantage now, with all the means at our disposal – diplomatic, military and business – to put pressure on the United States,' Jiang had said. 'We need to force it to publicly retreat from its pledge to pursue us as currency manipulators. If we can make the superpower take just one step back it will be a massive symbolic victory. A turning point in our history. A sign that China is now powerful enough to bring the US to heel. If they so much as blink, we have won.'

Jiang had studied the faces of his six comrades, trying to gauge whether his argument was cutting through. Two places to his left, Wu Weifang had coughed to indicate his intention to speak.

'My young friend is getting ahead of himself.' Wu was the oldest member of the Standing Committee and his opening remark was designed to make Jiang sound like an impulsive teenager. Wu was in charge of anti-terrorism and national security and despite his age was considered to be the most liberal of the magnificent seven.

'China must not make the mistake of the West and rush into battle, as the United States did in Iraq and Afghanistan. Patience is our ally. Daily we are growing more powerful but now is not the time to provoke a conflict. What if we misjudge? If we are forced to retreat, this Standing Committee will lose face and credibility early in its tenure. We should push back, of course. But let's temper our response and bide our time.'

'Age does bring wisdom … for some, Comrade Wu.' Jiang had locked on the elder statesman, his words laced with sarcasm. 'But we have waited for more than a century. Generations of our countrymen have lived and died in humiliation. I do not intend to join them. If we listen to you, we will be debating for another hundred years.'

It had been a risky play. Wu was highly regarded. But Jiang judged that others shared his impatience to demonstrate China's strength. His intention was to snatch power by isolating dissenting voices. He made his move.

'I believe that these extraordinary times demand the President's leadership.' He'd spoken slowly, turning to each member of the Standing Committee. 'I propose we establish a new National Security Committee which will direct the military and the police, with the President as its chair.

'Its aim will be to focus all our energies on responding to this unprovoked act of aggression. The committee would, of course, include Comrade Wu, as it will absorb his responsibilities. I propose that I be the third member because to prevail we will need to harness and direct the nationalist sentiment of our people.'

No one had spoken as the committee digested the audacious bid to strip Wu of his responsibilities and to hand unprecedented power to the President.

Wu had turned and pleaded with his leader.

'Comrade Meng, what is proposed is unwise. It is best that the seven of us deal with these matters and keep the arrangements that have worked so well for our predecessors ...'

The President had silenced Wu with a dismissive wave of his hand.

'I believe Comrade Jiang's proposal shows a wisdom well beyond his years.' Meng's words had been a deliberate rebuke to

Wu, and acted as a warning to any committee member swayed by his argument.

'We did not provoke this confrontation, the Americans did. This new President is determined to humiliate us, to contain our growth. If we step back, America and its lap-dog Japan will step forward. Wavering will be seen as weakness: by our enemies and, as importantly, by our people. The question is are we, are you, strong enough to seize this opportunity. I propose we vote on Comrade Jiang's proposal. Right now. And I support it.'

The President had raised his hand and searched the room for compliance. Jiang's hand had joined his leader's, and had been followed by the Party Secretary's. And, as the tension in the room had risen, slowly, so had a fourth hand. The chair of the central committee for Discipline Inspection had completed the majority.

Jiang had smiled, the long hours of preparation had not been wasted. Wu's voice would mean nothing on the new all-powerful National Security Committee, as he and the President were of one mind. This committee's plans would be settled before it met.

And when it acted, the world would shudder.

In the early evening, Jiang met President Meng. Alone.

'Have you organised the next steps as we discussed?' Meng asked.

'Yes, sir.' Jiang pushed a piece of paper across the desk. 'This is a map of our proposed expanded air defence identification zone. As you can see it covers the Diaoyu Islands. We will demand that any commercial or military planes that intend to fly through it lodge their flight plans with us.'

'The Americans will have to test it.'

'I believe they will. We will be ready.'

'But there will also be other steps, on the water?'

'Yes, sir, as we discussed. But, of course, not by us.'

'We must be careful. We cannot afford a full-scale confrontation with our more powerful enemy. Instead, my friend, the assassin's mace is our weapon. We do not need to defeat the giant in battle but to wound and neutralise it.'

Jiang nodded. The President continued.

'And call the North Korean Ambassador. I am sure Korea can be a useful partner in this enterprise.'

'Of course, sir. Anything else?'

The President searched his younger comrade's face. He had been expecting some news on another project and took the fact that the information had not been forthcoming as a bad sign.

'Zero Day. How is it progressing?'

Jiang looked down at his papers, as if seeking a file note. He'd expected the question but had hoped for better news before briefing his leader.

'It is proceeding, sir,' he eventually said. 'But you know better than anyone that it is our most sensitive program. We have an operational issue that has yet to be resolved. We are moving more slowly than we'd hoped, but I am confident Zero Day will proceed. As planned.'

The President sensed some hesitancy, but decided against pressing further.

'Very well, Mr Jiang. Remember, a tiger moves with stealth-like steps. We must leave no trace. No trace.'

CHAPTER FOURTEEN

Canberra

His eyes were piercing and black; his face, flanked by a crop of luxurious grey hair, bore a hint of a smile and a poise that carried across more than two hundred years. Joseph Banks was a man of wealth and influence, a child of the Enlightenment, whose innate intelligence was evident in this masterful portrait.

'What do you think of him, Harry?' Charles Dancer spoke with soft appreciation, not turning to face the journalist but keeping his gaze on the painting on the National Portrait Gallery wall. 'He was one of the true fathers of this nation. He invested his wealth without rancour and was a man of intellect and vision.'

Harry Dunkley tilted his head to suggest he was appreciative rather than baffled.

'He was a giant of his age.' Dancer turned sharply, his gaze as intense as that of Banks. 'And so superior to the pygmies who rule us now, don't you think?'

Dancer left the question hanging, inviting a response.

'Charles, I didn't realise you were such a student of the arts.' Dunkley filled the void. 'The dark arts maybe, but not fine arts.'

'Very droll, Harry. I wanted you to soak up the history. You need to be able to put everything I'm about to tell you in perspective.'

Dancer gestured at the painting. 'Banks was a guardian of his age as we are guardians of this age, keepers of an ephemeral flame. Our role is to hand on a better nation. To look to the long term, for the common good. Not to be captives of the moment, of the latest fad.' He spoke with quiet resolve. It was nearing 10.30am and the gallery was yet to fill with the bustle of tourists and locals.

Dancer clearly loved this place. Dunkley, too, was fond of the gallery, but the work that moved him was on the other side of the room. 'Come with me.' It was his turn to reveal his favourite.

There, in the middle of the back wall, were two bronze busts by Benjamin Law, commissioned in the mid-1830s. The first, of an Aboriginal man, was as proud and sure as the image of Banks.

'Wurati, the chief of Van Diemen's Land.' Dunkley stood close to the bronze, wondering what the man had been feeling and thinking when the piece was set. Wurati's face bore no trace of the pain to come.

'His people would be all but exterminated by "visionaries" like Banks. And beside him is another.' Dunkley stepped across to stand beside the bronze of a woman.

'This is his wife, Trukanini, long thought to be the last of her people. Benjamin Law cast Wurati first, regal and strong. But the statue of Trukanini, made just one year later, is very different: downcast, tragic. She knows what the white man's arrival means. Maybe that realisation was dawning on the artist, too, that the nation Banks envisioned would be built on the bodies of another people.'

Dancer had viewed the busts before, but he studied them and their inscriptions afresh.

'True, Aboriginal dispossession is the Original Sin of settlement. I am sorry for that,' he finally said. 'But it was inevitable. If it had not been us it would have been the French, the Dutch or the Germans. History does not stand still, Harry. The lesson from your art tour is that powerful people survive, and the weak are enslaved or murdered. I don't intend to be on the side of the weak.'

Dunkley wasn't sure about Dancer's agenda. But he needed to settle one of his own.

The death of their friend Kimberley had brought the two together. They'd forged a working bond and shared a grudging respect. But Dunkley suspected the relationship was as flimsy as the Toohey Government's grip on power.

'Why didn't you return my calls?' Dunkley challenged the diplomat. 'You promised to help track down Kimberley's killer. You know I can't do it on my own.'

'Harry, please, let it go.' Dancer was examining the next portrait. 'It's a futile quest. It wasn't a single person who killed Kimberley, it was the ideology of an evil state. You should never have got her involved; neither of you was equipped for the task. You were innocents wandering into a war.'

Their conversation was interrupted by the giggling of a nearby couple.

'Let's go for a stroll, Harry.' Dancer led Dunkley into an adjoining gallery.

'So why did you call now, Charles?'

Dancer fronted a portrait of Lachlan Macquarie, a man described in his native Scotland as the 'Father of Australia'.

'Harry, I have wrestled with this … with what I'm about to tell you. My career has been about protecting the realm, without the public knowing about it. Almost everything I've ever done will never be known, recorded only as a part of this nation's large library of secrets.'

'That is as it should be. Unlike you, I believe that nations need secrets. Bismarck knew that the sausage grinder of the state was best kept from public view. Traitors like Julian Assange would be jailed if I had my way.'

Dancer turned to face the reporter. 'But when a state is led by fools, sometimes the people need to be stirred. It's now clear that this government is not just incompetent, it's dangerous.

'It's blinded by Chinese wealth and intellectually crippled by its determination to stay in power. It can't be moved by wise counsel behind closed doors because the only thing that motivates it is public opinion. So the public needs to be jolted awake, to be warned that it's sleepwalking into disaster.'

'What "disaster"?' Dunkley's voice held a sniff of annoyance.

Dancer was examining a poorly constructed painting of the brilliant but headstrong explorer Matthew Flinders.

'This government has absolutely no idea what it is dealing

with and how dangerous its rise is. It foolishly believes you can separate Chinese commerce from Chinese politics. But it's bartering with this country's soul. It's betting that there will never come a time when we will have to choose between prosperity and our traditional security pact with the United States.'

The passion flared in Dancer's eyes.

'China can never be a true and trusted friend, not now, not ever. Each step towards it is a step away from our real friends. And into a very dangerous future.'

He had stopped pretending an interest in the art and had turned all his attention on Dunkley, taking a step towards the journalist. His voice became more intent.

'You know that now, Harry. Kimberley's death has taught you that much. If anything it's perhaps given you a perspective you never had. I've been reading your opinion pieces. They've been very good.'

'Well thanks, Charles.' Dunkley stepped around the intelligence officer and continued to inspect the Flinders portrait. 'We at *The Australian* always aim to please the powers that be. And that only occasionally includes governments of the day.'

'Of course you do.' Dancer's laughter echoed around the empty room. 'And I can see that the government's feelings towards you are just as mixed. Anyway, let me tell you a story. Off the record, of course, and with absolutely no trace back to me.'

The reporter nodded, and the two men kept walking. The ancient code – between a source and a scribe – would be honoured.

'Thank you. Okay. Harry, did you hear about the body that was dragged out of the lake four days ago?' Dancer didn't give the reporter time to respond. 'He was an Asian man, aged in his thirties, and he had no ID.'

'Sorry Charles, but I've been a tad too busy with national politics to focus on local life. I vaguely recall some mention on local radio, though.'

'Yes, the police called for assistance in identifying him. At first, our man was a real John Doe, as the Americans say, an unidentified corpse fished out of the lake after a group of school children spotted him.'

Dancer dropped to *sotto voce* and Dunkley stepped closer.

'But he was a Chinese national. Part of a team that is building the new Chinese embassy.'

The reporter was starting to get the tingle that came with the hint of a cracking yarn.

'Was he an embassy official, Charles?'

'Well, yes and no. And that is part of the problem and the point of this sorry story. When Catriona Bailey was prime minister, she ticked off on a deal that allowed the embassy to be built in complete secrecy with an entirely Chinese workforce. Dozens of them were flown in on diplomatic visas. The site is off limits to everyone; not even unions or local government safety inspectors are allowed in. Only a select number of local suppliers can come and go but they are whisked in and out under close watch. Of course we've sent people in under the guise of being contractors, but frankly, Harry, that site is a black box to us.'

Dancer was beginning to get animated.

'No prime minister with this nation's best interest at heart should ever have agreed to sign off on a project like that. And now it appears we may be paying a high price for Bailey's desperation to please Beijing.'

An elderly couple appeared, looked into the room for a moment, consulted a map of the gallery and then turned to try to find whatever it was they were searching for. A few heartbeats after they disappeared Dancer picked up the theme.

'Bailey's replacement, Martin Toohey, is just as bad. He's asleep at the wheel and his government is wilfully blind to the threat from China, especially from cyber-espionage and warfare. We've tried to warn them. The real and present danger this nation faces has been pressed home by officials at National Security Committee meetings. We've even shown the Prime Minister evidence that his own emails have been hacked, along with everyone else's in Parliament. And what have they done to defend themselves? Nothing. The government doesn't seem to care that Australia is being attacked every day in the virtual world by a country that poses as our friend in the real world. Our man, we think, was trying to alert us to the extent of that threat.'

'Did this John Doe have a name?'

'Yes. Lin An, but we don't know much more about him than that.'

'So do you know what he was up to? Or why he went for a swim?'

'We're not certain about anything. But we think he was trying to defect.'

'How do you know that, Charles?'

'Because we found this in his gut.'

Dancer discretely opened his right hand. A USB memory stick lay across his palm.

'Jesus!'

'Indeed. I wanted to show you this, just to assure you there is potentially a very big story about our man in the lake. We're still analysing the material, and, no, I can't give you too much at this stage. But I reckon you have enough to get started.'

Dunkley took out a small pad and pen from his shirt pocket.

'Yep, but I'll have to get a few notes.'

'Of course, but let's keep this brief.'

A few minutes later Charles Dancer turned and sauntered off, leaving Dunkley to appreciate a gallery of Australian sporting icons, and the mystery of the body in the lake.

CHAPTER FIFTEEN

Canberra

A pair of white pillars embossed with gold numerals – the number '25' – frames a steep driveway. There is nothing else to tell guests they've arrived at the Commonwealth Club.

Because if you don't know where it is, you aren't meant to be there.

Set on a gentle green rise overlooking Lake Burley Griffin, the Commonwealth is a reminder of an imperial past, one governed by strict and immutable rules. The grubby affectations of modern life are banned. Exchanging business cards is forbidden, menu prices are banished, and no cash ever changes hands. In the sedate surrounds of the dining room, the mobile phone is taboo.

Moneyed men had been refused membership because here the currency was power.

But the four men who'd gathered in one of the club's discreet rooms on this long summer evening had no doubt that they belonged. It was just one of their many certainties. They carried an unshakeable conviction that they were the sentinels of prosperity and freedom, mandarins who could outwit and would outlive the longest serving politician.

They called themselves the Alliance, an homage to the security pact between Australia and the US. Indeed it was the rock on which this grouping had been built, but its edifice was under threat. As power shifted from the West to the East, more quickly than they could have imagined, the meetings of the Alliance had taken on a more urgent edge.

They saw themselves as defenders of the realm, and in fact were largely responsible for Australia's national security, their CVs reflecting the close bonds forged with Team America.

Air Chief Marshal Jack Webster was Chief of the Defence Force and a decorated former pilot. He'd flown sorties during Gulf War I, when he'd been attached to the Third Marine Wing during the infamous 'Highway of Death' attack on retreating Iraqi forces. Webster retained the physical hard edge of a man thirty years his junior and his square-jawed demeanour screamed 'Don't-fuck-with-me'. Few did.

David Joyce, Secretary of the Department of Foreign Affairs and Trade, was a former Ambassador to the United States.

Thomas Heggarty, Director-General of the Australian Secret Intelligence Service, the overseas network of spies, had studied at CIA headquarters.

And domestic spymaster, Richard Dalton, had clocked up a year on exchange at the FBI. The Director-General of ASIO –

the Australian Security Intelligence Organisation – could still mimic a Virginian accent on call.

But now a new world order threatened to destabilise decades of collaboration with the Stars and Stripes. The security pact with America was under threat as the Toohey Government wrestled with the rise of China, embracing the communist power in ever-closer economic and political ties.

Just how close became clearer when the US Ambassador to Australia, Brent Moreton, strode into the meeting, late and very pissed off.

Moreton nodded curtly to the four mandarins as he took his place beside Webster, throwing back a neat Scotch before slamming the table with his open palms. 'Gentlemen, we've got a fucking big problem.'

The envoy outlined the bones of a briefing he'd been given by one of his trusted Labor sources. 'Your prime minister is about to strike a deal with China that will make your country beholden to it. Forever.'

Webster, miffed at being out of touch, leapt in. 'Brent, how do you mean "beholden"?'

'Toohey plans to sell off a gas-field in the Northern Territory to the Chinese in a desperate bid to buy votes for his re-election. The strategic stupidity of it is … just mind-blowing.'

The Ambassador gripped his chair. He was having trouble controlling his usually implacable manner.

'He is selling off your farm, gentlemen. And he doesn't understand that once he announces the deal, he will be a wholly owned subsidiary of China Inc. His political survival depends on them paying up. He will temper every action and every statement to ensure this deal holds until he gets to the other side of the election.'

Moreton rose and theatrically pounded a fist into his open palm, leaning towards the stunned mandarins. 'This will hover over Australia like the blade of a guillotine.'

Webster searched for a response. But it was Joyce who leapt into the fray.

'The Japanese will go crazy,' the DFAT boss said, incredulous and angry. 'They've been begging us to sign an energy security pact for years. It's their number one concern. They're already convinced we've abandoned them for China.'

Other doomsday scenarios played out.

'So we're going to set up a Chinese platform just off Darwin.' Heggarty began to imagine the possibilities offered to any spy chief worth his salt. 'If I was running China's Ministry of State Security, I would turn it into a listening post. Our ears for the entire region to our north are based at just three places: Cocos Island, Bamaga and Shoal Bay. Every one of them will be compromised and the Chinese could listen to every call from Hobart to Broome.'

The Defence Chief finally spoke. He was horrified. 'The range of our Jindalee over-the-horizon radar is a lot more than 3000 kilometres. Imagine what China could do? Jesus, they could monitor every RAAF and Qantas take-off and landing. And we plan to base more troops and more kit up north.'

'And more marines,' Moreton chipped in. 'They could monitor every movement, every joint exercise.'

Dalton saw the platform as an evil ark. 'Well,' he said, 'when ASIO is asked for coordination comments for the Cabinet debate, we'll red flag it as a grave security risk.'

'Don't be so fucking naive, Richard. You won't be asked. None of us will be.' Webster was on his feet. 'This government is paranoid about high-level leaks and with good reason. Who among us would trust anyone in that Cabinet? Toohey won't talk to any but a select few before announcing this sell-out to China as a done deal.'

'So if they won't seek our advice, what are our options?' Dalton asked, reflecting the frustration of the room.

Webster was staring out the window as the lake caught the last glow of the sunset. He turned back to the room, placing a hand supportively on the Ambassador's shoulder. 'This can *never* be allowed to happen.'

CHAPTER SIXTEEN

Canberra

Gnarled fingers danced over a battered keyboard, attempting to coax a must-read yarn from a tangled mess of background material, off-the-record quotes and join-the-dots supposition.

Harry Dunkley had sold this exclusive hard, providing his editor with the barest of outlines, promising to file early enough to allow News Corp's lawyers time to hook their claws into his copy.

It was a four-coffee-down sort of day. The time read 3.07pm on his MacBook Pro and Dunkley figured he had an hour, maybe one and a half, of scribbling and polishing before he'd hit 'send'.

This was no run-of-the-mill yarn. Not the usual 'scoop' hand-delivered by a press secretary patsy on behalf of some malicious MP intent on inflicting damage on a colleague or enemy. Or both.

Dunkley had taken delivery of plenty of 'exclusives' that had fallen off the back of the proverbial truck. Words repackaged to appear on the front page the next day. All very neat and tidy. Thanks for the scoop. Now fuck off.

He stretched and scratched a left shoulder that was itchy and dry, much like the weather on this smouldering Canberra day. He checked a notepad, flicking through several pages of shorthand. He'd negotiated a verbatim quote from a 'senior intelligence source', and this was critical to getting a legal tick without his copy being gored to death.

His hand massaged a face that hadn't seen a razor for forty-eight hours.

Dunkley liked to joke that he had a good head for print. He wasn't interested in joining those prima donnas who pranced around Sky News or ABC News 24, seeking to build their profiles as 'political analysts'. One day, the press gallery might well be one giant TV studio. Journalists would be wandering around with cameras strapped to their heads, delivering commentary in real time. Every story would be 140 characters long.

The ether was already full enough of bullshit. *This* was what he lived for. The thrill of the chase, the scent of a big splash that would cut through the vapid nonsense that passed for news these days.

Okay, now for the lead. Plenty of drama, plenty of grunt, make it tight, and make it sing.

The body of a man dragged from Canberra's Lake Burley Griffin has been identified as one of a small army of workers flown in to build China's new embassy.

All the workers on the highly secretive building are Chinese nationals travelling on diplomatic passports and the site is immune from local laws under a deal struck with the Labor Government.

Little is known of the dead man, Lin An, prompting intelligence officials to voice their concerns that the embassy site might pose a national security threat.

The mysterious death comes on the back of a spike in Chinese-based cyber-espionage against Australia.

The Australian has learned that Cabinet's National Security Committee has been briefed twice in the past six weeks on 'specific threats' from Chinese cyber-units.

And the emails of key government figures, including the Prime Minister, are understood to have been hacked. US intelligence officials alerted their Australian counterparts and provided evidence that China was the source of the attacks.

Worried intelligence officials have accused the Toohey Government of being 'asleep at the wheel'.

The project's secrecy has also prompted concerns over worker safety. Union and ACT Government representatives are barred from the site and there appears little they can do to ensure no one is injured or killed.

Jesus, that should get their attention.

Dunkley sat back and studied his handiwork. Thirty years in the hard news business and he still got a thrill when it all came together, when the usual grind of daily journalism gave way to a big delicious fillet of prime news.

This was a news story that mattered and could make it onto the international stage. If it wasn't legalled to death.

He checked the time: 3.18pm, and there was still no response from the PM's office. He'd gone to them an hour ago with a series of questions. This was too big a story for him to simply ring the press office at a quarter to six and demand an instant response.

He rechecked his notepad, wondering if he had missed some vital piece of information. He'd already written around six hundred words. It would bump out to seven hundred, once the flacks in the PM's office stopped panicking and actually scripted some bullshit response.

Dunkley's mobile rang. It was Eleanor Todd, the PM's hard-boiled senior press secretary, who, mercifully, had replaced Dylan Blair six months ago, bringing some much-needed grunt to the role.

'Hello mate. You calling to invite me to the Lodge for dinner?'

'Hah, very funny, Harry. You know why I'm calling. Listen, I'm about to send you a formal response but, um, can I ask, off the record, if you don't want to take a breather on this one?'

'I don't think so, Eleanor, not unless you're telling me I'm completely off track – and I don't expect you're about to do that?'

'No mate, but Harry, we're dealing with a pretty sensitive matter here, national security and all, and, ah, well it would be nice to be able to walk you through it, the nuances and the consequences, if you go to print. Not me personally, but someone very senior. Maybe the Attorney?'

'Danny Maiden? You are kidding, Eleanor. In the three years he's been Attorney-General, he's barely grunted in my direction. He's a pumped-up Melbourne rich kid who fluked his way into a senior ministerial role and who now thinks he's God's gift to fucking democracy.'

'I'll take that as a "no" then. Okay Mr Dunkley, have it your way. Response being emailed to you now. '

'Love you too, Eleanor. See ya.'

Dunkley hung up and waited. He liked Todd, a former senior political reporter who'd brought maturity to the Prime Minister's office after replacing Blair, who was young, good-looking and rumoured to have bedded more women than were paid-up members of Emily's List. But who knew diddly squat about actual journalism.

Half a minute later, he received an email marked 'Eleanor Todd, Senior Press Secretary, Office of the Prime Minister.'

'Via Beijing,' Dunkley joked.

He opened the email and started reading. She had copied his questions to the top.

Is the government aware that a Chinese national who recently drowned in Lake Burley Griffin is linked to the new Chinese embassy site? Is the government aware of what this man's role was?

Has the Toohey Government been made aware of potential cyber-attacks by China against key Australian facilities, including the email systems of the Prime Minister and other senior ministers?

Ms Todd's response was straight out of the 'give 'em nothing' school of political bluster.

Harry, you can quote a spokeswoman for the Prime Minister on the following:

As a matter of long-standing principle and practice, the government does not comment on specific cyber-related incidents, investigations or operations. However, improving cyber-defence is a top national security priority for the government which is also pro-actively engaging business and the wider community.

The Prime Minister's National Security Strategy released on 23 January identifies defending our digital networks through integrated cyber-policy and operations as one of our key priorities over the next five years.

The government will also be fast-tracking plans for a new Australian Cyber Security Centre, to be built in Canberra.

Marvellous, Dunkley thought. I'm about to go into print on a huge political yarn and the government thinks a lick of spin will demonstrate everything's under control.

No wonder they're in so much strife.

He called up his story and fed the lines in, reasonably high up to appease the lawyers.

But then he added a quote from a 'senior national security official' that would trump the PM's bland PR bull.

'We are one step away from cyber-war. And yet this government seems intent on chasing China's cash at the expense of our national sovereignty,' the official told *The Australian*.

'Beijing is launching daily cyber-attacks against us, and yet Mr Toohey says nothing. When will the government learn that you can't appease a dragon?'

Dunkley read the draft a final time before checking his watch again: 4.12pm. He lined up his editor's email, cc-ed it to his chief of staff in Canberra, and then hit 'send', watching a story that he had lovingly crafted over the past two days disappear.

He leaned back in his chair, a self-satisfied grin creasing his face. Then he wondered just how many prying eyes would read his sparkling prose before it was published online at midnight.

CHAPTER SEVENTEEN

Canberra

It was the Ides of March, spring but still cool.

He lifted his finest purple robe above the dirt as he crossed the cobbled street. A rider slowed his horse as he recognised the pedestrian, and dipped his head in homage.

The familiar shape of the Theatre of Pompey hove into view. The Senate was in session and Caesar was due to address it.

As he strode towards the theatre, Tillius Cimber called out to him beseechingly.

'Caesar, please … I ask you again to consider the fate of my brother. I have gathered signatures from some of Rome's finest citizens pleading for his return.'

The emperor dismissed him with an imperious wave. 'I have told you before. The matter is settled.'

The petitioner's face hardened to a snarl as he dropped his scroll and dragged down Caesar's tunic, pinning his arms to his sides.

Within seconds the emperor was engulfed as a dozen conspirators emerged from the shadows, striking at his unprotected flesh with their blades.

The searing pain as the metal tore into his body.

One face leered from the crowd, plunging his dagger deeper than the rest.

'*Et tu, Brute?*'

With his final breath the emperor whispered three defiant words not recorded by history. '*Non occides ambitione.*'

Catriona Bailey's eyes flashed open as the nightmare shook her awake. The face of her murderer was still vivid.

Her heart was racing. The nightmares were becoming more frequent. Even in waking the hallucinations were sometimes so real that it was hard to separate dreams from reality.

Bailey's doctor had warned her that this might happen when she'd demanded a radical course of treatment to speed her recovery: a dangerous cocktail of Stilnox and Prozac.

'I strongly advise against it,' he had said. 'Yes, it might see a rapid improvement in your physical condition but you risk destroying your mind. There are a host of possible side effects and you could do permanent damage.'

She had dismissed his concerns.

Now, in her waking hours Bailey could feel her body growing stronger. But sleep became a torment. And, sometimes, reality blurred.

'I had to do it, you know.'

Martin Toohey's voice startled her. He stepped from the shadows of her hospital room.

Why?

'Because you risked everything.'

You will pay. Soon.

Toohey's face vanished into the dark, and Caesar's last words echoed in her tormented mind.

You can't kill ambition.

CHAPTER EIGHTEEN

Canberra

Nguyen Thi Mai Loan – 'just call me May' – pulled the latest copy of *Foreign Affairs* from her satchel as she crunched into another muesli bar. The whip-smart graduate student was pulling the graveyard shift, alone. It was 5.05am and a long night was nearly over.

She wondered whether eminent diplomatic careers usually started like this, waiting for dull consular calls to replace lost passports.

Bugger.

Her computer screensaver had kicked in during the few minutes she'd been distracted. She hit a keyboard button to refresh it. Then she froze.

TEN CHINESE FISHERMEN OCCUPY SENKAKU ISLANDS

A tremor shot down her spine as she digested the Reuters newsflash.

'Holy fuck,' she said, in an accent minted in Sydney's outer west.

Before being accepted into DFAT's prestigious graduate program, Nguyen had finished a PhD on the Chinese military. Part of that involved wargaming scenarios that might escalate into armed conflict between China and the US. This was straight out of the textbooks.

Even the name of these benighted islands was a source of dispute. Japan called them the Senkakus, while China hailed them as the Diaoyu.

They were five uninhabited islands and three barren rocks lying around two hundred nautical miles southwest of Japan and the same distance east of China. The largest was just a tick over four square kilometres.

In the history of mankind, had there ever been so much dispute over such a useless pile of rocks? she wondered.

Both countries claimed the islands but Japan administered them and they had been an increasing source of tension ever since oil had been discovered nearby in 1968. But the bilateral relationship hit rock bottom when the Japanese Government bought three of the islands from a Japanese family that had held their title. Asserting government control was supposed to reassure the Chinese that no one was about to do anything rash. That was not how the message was received.

The official Chinese response had been blunt. Its Foreign Ministry said Beijing would not 'sit back and watch its territorial sovereignty violated'. Relations had not improved when Shinzo Abe had been re-elected as Japan's Prime Minister, a man Beijing viewed as a dangerous nationalist whose instincts would be to try to contain China's growth and, likely, move to undo Japan's constitutional constraints on its defence force.

Recently the *People's Daily* had described the bilateral relationship as 'politically cold and economically cool'.

Then, without warning, the Chinese had escalated the dispute by inventing what it called an 'air defence identification zone' covering the islands. It demanded all aircraft flying in the region lodge flight plans with China or face 'emergency defensive measures'.

So far, despite bluster from the US and Japan, there had been no breach of the airspace but no one believed things would hold for long without China's resolve being tested.

So the fishermen's occupation meant only one thing: it was a government-sanctioned act of aggression. No matter how China's Foreign Ministry would spin it, the dragon was testing its power, daring the West to confront it or retreat.

Nguyen digested the news and what it meant. Less than a minute after viewing the newsflash she was on the phone to her boss. After seven rings his croaky and cranky voice barked: 'This had better be good.'

She wasted no words. 'Boss, ten Chinese fishermen have raised the red flag over the Senkakus.'

Three heartbeats later Adrian Carmody was wide awake. 'I'm on my way. I'll call the Secretary.'

An hour later the DFAT crisis centre was alive with a dozen senior officials poring over each shard of news. Secretary David

Joyce had called in the PM's chief of staff. Around the globe similar departments were abuzz, no matter the time zone.

George Papadakis was dressed in a tracksuit and wore the expression of a man who believed international and domestic events were conspiring to make his life hell. And he was beginning to take it all personally.

Joyce's mood was grimmer than usual. He was studying a cable and muttering. 'The bastards, do they really think we are fools?'

'So, what do we know for sure, David?' Papadakis and Joyce had been friends for years and Papadakis wasn't fazed by his mate's dog days.

'We know that ten Chinese fishermen went ashore on the largest island just before 3am, Beijing time.' Joyce hadn't lifted his head from the cable he was reading. 'The island is called Uotsuri Jima by the Japanese and Diaoyu Dao by the Chinese.'

Joyce put down his papers, took off his glasses and looked at the line of clocks on the crisis centre wall.

'If the timing seems odd, George, consider this. The fishermen announced on social media that they had taken the island within minutes of landing. They were well-organised because Reuters had a newsflash out inside five minutes. That meant it lobbed into the US just after 2pm. Very decent of them. It ensures that every network has plenty of time to make sure it leads the evening news.'

He handed his friend the cable he had been studying. 'Here's a one-page summary of the story so far.'

The brief began with an official statement from Beijing. The People's Republic did not sanction the actions of the fishermen but its leadership 'understood the genuine affront that all its citizens felt at the illegal occupation of Chinese land by a foreign power'. The government could not be expected to contain 'the nationalist zeal' of a handful of its people.

It would work with the fishermen to try to get them to quit the island voluntarily, as a demonstration that China was a good international citizen. But China's claim over the island stood and the incident only served to highlight the need for a rapid resolution.

It didn't wash with the Japanese, or anyone else, who knew that, at the very least, the occupation had an official sanction.

The Japanese statement fairly shook with rage as it castigated China for an 'act of aggression'. It called on the Chinese Government to remove the fishermen within forty-eight hours and carried a barely disguised threat: 'Japan does not rule out taking unilateral action to bring this invasion of its territory to an end.'

By contrast, the US State Department had issued a tempered response, calling for calm. It trotted out its long-held line: that the US did not have an official position on who owned the islands.

However, America recognised that Japan administered the islands and that any attack on them would trigger the US–Japan bilateral security pact.

'But this isn't an attack or an official act of the Chinese Government, is it, David?' Papadakis had some admiration for China's deft hand.

'That's the beauty of it,' Joyce said. 'The fishermen have asserted China's claim and given Beijing distance from it. Of course their government sanctioned it and, probably, organised it. But we can't prove that. So now the ball is in the court of Japan and, most importantly, the US. What they do next is crucial.'

Joyce had served in China and had risen to become Ambassador to the United States. Papadakis thought him the pre-eminent Australian diplomat of his age. This is what Joyce was the master of, looking at the pieces on the chessboard and analysing what was going through the players' heads. Then calculating a perfectly executed move of his own.

'And, George, never forget that any government, dictatorship or democratic, is also playing to a domestic audience. This move is also an exercise in stirring Chinese nationalist sentiment, and focusing it outwards.

'Most people in the West don't understand how important public opinion is in China. They see a dictatorship and imagine it has absolute control over the masses. It doesn't. Tiananmen Square proved that public anger can turn inwards, on the government.

'So the role of the skilled propagandist is to harness and direct the people's mood. And whoever is the brains behind this knows his audience well. These fishermen will become national heroes and this cause will be elevated to the top of the nation's agenda. That will force the weak-kneed in the Chinese administration to side with the hard-liners. They have stirred the hornets, and they're headed our way.'

Papadakis looked at the wall map of the East China Sea with a growing sense of dread. 'So how will the US respond?'

'That is tough. My guess is State will want to fartarse around drafting crafty statements while the Pentagon will demand a measured but proportionate and decisive response. And in the mix will be Republican firebrands in and out of Congress who think that a proportionate response is to nuke Beijing. The question, George, is what will you do?'

'Try and stay out of it.'

Joyce's face hardened.

'You might be able to buy a few weeks but you can't keep doing that forever, George. This is a tough choice but the US is our ally. China is testing us. You might think that you can walk the tightrope between these powers but you can't.'

Papadakis thought of the months that had gone into his plan to dig the Toohey Government out of its electoral hole. It relied on Chinese finance. He just needed to nurse that deal to the other side of the election. He needed to buy time.

'Is it weak to want peace? Our country's prosperity, your kids' jobs – they depend on peace and doing business with China. We need to use our unique position to urge China and the US to see that escalating this dispute is in no one's interest. The bloody Yanks started this whole mess anyway when that redneck idiot in the White House declared China a currency manipulator. Why kick a fucking hornets' nest?'

'Everyone wants peace, mate.' Joyce was bent on trying to get Papadakis to make a stand. 'And I think we will have peace but it won't be easy as the big powers come to a settlement. But we can't allow China to keep throwing its weight around with its neighbours or there will be no end to it. No one respects weakness.

'Leaving aside who started it, my advice is to fall in behind the United States when it decides to act. The Chinese are not going to stop doing business with us in the long run. They need us as much as we need them.'

'Your advice is noted but it's the short run that worries me.' Papadakis picked up his notes and started heading for the door. He wasn't about to be backed into a corner by Joyce. He took another pace then stopped.

'Before I brief the PM, what's our own intelligence telling us?' he asked.

Joyce frowned and ran his hands through what remained of his hair.

'There's a Collins class submarine in the area and it can see the camp set up by the fishermen,' he said. 'Hopefully it can also see the subs from China, the US and Japan that no doubt are there. The waters around that island will be like Hoddle Street at peak hour. The last thing we want is for a sub that we claim only patrols Australian waters to surface two hundred nautical miles off the coast of China.'

Papadakis groaned. 'Don't say that, David. Knowing our luck we'll have rear-ended a Chinese sub by lunchtime.'

CHAPTER NINETEEN

Canberra

Edward 'Ted' Spencer adjusted the black Jawbone on his wrist, rubbed a sore calf muscle and drew in several long breaths.

Fourteen minutes. Flat chat.

That was today's challenge.

Like most spooks, the Deputy Director-General of the Australian Security Intelligence Organisation was a fitness junkie, as proud of his physical prowess as he was of his intellect. Every second morning, close to 5.30am, Spencer would make the gruelling trek up Mt Ainslie, a couple of kilometres east of Civic, Canberra's city centre. The uphill route was 2.2 kilometres – a winding path that climbed 250 metres in elevation.

A light breeze tripped around the back of the Australian War Memorial.

Spencer inhaled deeply once more then pushed his 44-year-old body into a steady breathing pattern as he prepared for a jog that was as much mental therapy as physical exercise. The spymaster didn't have the luxury of indulgent lunchtime runs around Lake Burley Griffin, like so many pen-pushers. Instead he would flog himself till he cried, so that by the time he reached the peak, he would be gasping for oxygen.

But that was okay; he lived by the maxim that pain was weakness leaving your body.

The first hint of sunrise was lifting the gloom as Spencer made his way through three gates, getting into stride. He passed two women with a pair of eager labradors, and one of the excited dogs veered across his path without warning.

'Morning,' he said curtly.

He was nicely into rhythm now, softly mumbling a tune from his youth as he climbed the first set of stone steps, taking them two at a time, before reaching the first corner. An older man in a rugby jersey was on his way down, the two nearly colliding in the semi-darkness.

'Whoa … sorry.' Spencer was making good ground despite feeling as though he was running an obstacle course. He was nearing the end of the middle section that stretched over five hundred metres or so. The lights of Canberra Airport came into view, flickering in the distance.

He turned into the final stretch, a punishing kilometre that culminated in a series of killer stone steps. Ignoring the pain and a twinge in his left knee, he left the steps behind and leaned into the final climb – a twenty-metre path to a metal barrier.

He'd made it, although not as fast as he would have hoped for. Fourteen minutes and twenty-three seconds.

He quietly chastised himself as he gulped the fresh morning air. He grabbed at his sides, gingerly making his way towards the large flat area that offered a stunning view across Canberra's parliamentary triangle to the Brindabellas on the horizon.

The city sparkled, its streetlights illuminating a maze of arteries just coming to life. He lapped hungrily from a water tap, careful not to swallow too much. His breathing was returning to normal. He stretched and contemplated a quick set of twenty-five push-ups on one of the four timber tables placed along the concrete strip.

He stopped. Something wasn't right.

Spencer's eyes scanned to the right, then to the left, then straight ahead. At first it appeared nothing was amiss. Then he gazed upwards, his eyes fixing on the aviation beacon that sat on top of a high metal pole. It was out.

Bloody hell.

He checked the time: 5.50am. The approaching rush hour meant that a dozen or so planes would soon be arriving or departing from Canberra Airport. And while he wasn't sure of the navigational role performed by this beacon, Spencer decided to alert the crew at Airservices Australia.

He reached for his mobile, which he carried at all times, and called into the National Operations Centre at Airservices HQ in the Alan Woods building, near the heart of Canberra's CBD. He knew a few of the overnight staff, including the supervisor Gary McDonald, a veteran of the aviation bureaucracy.

After four rings, McDonald answered, abruptly.

'Ted, good to hear from you.'

'Gary, the beacon on top of Mt Ainslie, it appears to be—'

'Mate, forget the beacon. The whole fucking show is down.'

CHAPTER TWENTY

Canberra

Martin Toohey scratched absently at a prickly chin and adjusted his Geelong jersey, upping the pace slightly and silently enjoying the laboured breathing of his walking companion. The Prime Minister was halfway through his daily constitutional, a brisk thirty-minute walk, and was determined to make every step count.

'I want to reach for the stars with this one, George. I really do.'

The PM turned to his chief of staff, George Papadakis, a man who until recently had harboured a near pathological fear of physical exercise. But a medical check-up had given Papadakis a fright and for the past few weeks he'd joined his friend and boss whenever the two were in Canberra together.

It was a chance not only to walk off the previous night's dinner but to plot and scheme, to hatch a plan that might revive the dire fortunes of the Toohey Government. Or, more likely, to debrief on the latest disaster.

In a week, Toohey would address the National Press Club and his speech would attempt to reboot the government and set the tone for the election year.

'We've got to turn things around next week, George, otherwise we'll be well and truly rooted.'

Toohey desperately needed a big cut-through statement. He wanted a speech that would stand the test of time, that would resonate through the ages like Paul Keating's famous 1992 Redfern speech which had so magnificently captured the torment of Australia's indigenous community.

The two men were walking by the edge of Lake Burley Griffin, passing the toilet block outside the Southern Cross Yacht Club, a quarter hour from the Lodge. It was 5.55am.

Two bodyguards walked ahead while a white security car, with two more guards inside, tracked a discreet distance behind. The national capital was still layered in darkness; sunrise was a half-hour off but the first hints were just beginning to paint the horizon.

Papadakis grunted as he contemplated the climb back up to State Circle.

'I know boss, I know.' He squeezed the words out between wheezing pants. 'James has got a first draft ready for you … to look at later this morning. He's taken me through a few sketches … and it isn't bad. Plenty of grunt for the comrades … and a great mental health plan for the base. Future lies to our north … the looming Asian century … the innovative hub of Asia … that sort of stuff. Our best Treasury man is working on the numbers in strict confidence … word is that everything is fiscally sound … which is good. Jesus, Martin, can you slow down just a touch …'

The PM glanced across to his friend and confidant, smiling as he eased off, allowing him to draw level. Neither man looked a picture of fitness but the competitor in Toohey enjoyed the rare feeling of superiority.

'Sorry George. I get a bit carried away sometimes, don't I? That's what you love about me though, right?' Toohey playfully danced around Papadakis, giving his chief of staff a light jab to the arm as he skipped ahead.

The PM didn't notice that his senior security man had stopped until he was right next to him. A look of urgency was furrowing the big man's face.

'Boss. We got to move. To Parliament. Just got a call from the office. We have a crisis.'

George Papadakis put his mobile into a locker bearing his name then punched a six-digit code into the pad by the security door. It slid open revealing an airlock and another door leading to Cabinet's hi-tech situation room.

The Howard Government had dismissed a 'Sit Room' as indulgent but Catriona Bailey had embraced having her own Washington-style bunker, just metres from her office. So taxpayers had spent $35 million building her one.

That had caused a storm at Senate hearings with one Coalition senator describing the room as an extravagance built to 'feed the *West Wing* fantasies of the Labor leadership'.

Seventy-two thousand dollars had bought two long 'integrated' tables that abutted each other in the centre of the room, with inbuilt computers and communications systems. Each of the thirty German-built Wilkhahn 'FS' armchairs, covered with specially ordered green leather, had set taxpayers back $3000.

Huge plasma television screens covered the entire length of both of the room's long walls. The screens were run by technicians in the nearby communications room. Mostly they were used for teleconferencing; there were secure locations in all the state capital cities where a minister or official could go to be beamed into the Sit Room. A dozen embassies and high commissions around the world were also fitted out for secure videoconferencing.

By convention the politicians sat on one side of the table, and the defence, police and intelligence officials on the other. But only the politicians had voting rights. The officials were there to offer expert advice.

Lining the walls behind the main table were rows of chairs for other advisers. And, just as in the Cabinet room, there was a chair in each corner for a notetaker. Every word spoken was logged; each person at the main table was fitted with a microphone.

George Papadakis took his place just behind the PM's chair. He loved the Security Committee meetings here because this was the real work of government and it was in this setting that Toohey shone.

If only the public could see how he performs when it really matters.

Toohey never wasted time, kept the meetings focused, issued orders that were clear and set realistic goals.

Now the Prime Minister strode into the room carrying a bundle of papers, the chatter about the table dying as he sat down.

'Welcome, everyone. Okay, what do we know? Eliza?' Toohey nodded to the head of Airservices Australia.

'Just before 6am this morning the entire air-traffic control system on Australia's east coast went down. For thirteen minutes every plane in the air vanished from our sight.'

Eliza Stubbs paused as the plasma screens lit up, displaying a map of Australia overlaid with a sketch of the air-traffic control network.

'The TAAATS system controls twenty-three radar towers, mostly on the east coast. There are two centres, Brisbane and Melbourne. So the network's split north and south, with Brisbane controlling the northern zone, Melbourne the southern.'

The image changed to a flow chart showing Airservices' security hierarchy.

'In each centre there are forty-two consoles, divided into groups to cover different sectors. And there are multiple backups to ensure a system failure cannot shut the whole show down. When the primary system in Melbourne failed at 5.47am the duplicate system swung online automatically. It failed. So did our third layer of defence in Melbourne. We immediately moved to the contingency plan. There are ten consoles in Brisbane which are configured to take over from Melbourne in the case of catastrophic failure, and vice versa. When we switched them on, the system froze.'

The room was silent and Stubbs continued.

'Prime Minister, there is a one in ten million chance that all this could happen by accident. Chillingly, the crash occurred just before the 6am curfew in Sydney was lifted. So international and interstate flights into Sydney were starting their approaches to Kingsford Smith.

'We made radio contact with every plane and told them to hold their course if they were still en route or to switch to a pre-ordained emergency holding pattern if they were preparing to land.

'At exactly 6am all our systems returned.'

Stubbs' face was grey and there was a slight tremble in her voice as she finished.

'Prime Minister, we have no idea how it happened.'

Toohey tapped his pen on the desk as he digested the explosive news.

'Ted,' the Prime Minister turned to the ASIO Deputy Director-General who ran Intelligence Coordination, 'what do you think?'

'Well, the official line has to be we don't know – because we don't,' Spencer said. 'But I know what it looks like. This is an attack, not an accident. And because it was so contained I can only assume it's a shot across our bow. Someone is letting us know they own us.'

That observation resonated with the worst fears of the room.

'Who?' The Prime Minister scanned the brass, braid and suits across the table. 'Who would do this and why?'

Thomas Heggarty, head of the Australian Secret Intelligence Service, spoke. 'It's just about impossible to pin this stuff down. It could be a bored teenager in a bedroom in Tokyo. It might be a group of anarchists like Anonymous. But … I don't think so.'

Heggarty studied the layers of backup that had to be disabled to cripple Australia's air-traffic control system.

'Something this sophisticated has to be state sponsored. And the disturbing thing is that this isn't trawling for information. This is an act of aggression. If this was happening in the real world under the old rules and someone had bombed these installations we would immediately declare it an act of war.'

Heggarty looked down to a note from a previous security committee meeting.

'We can't be sure who did this, but Prime Minister, you will recall our discussion on the massive increase in cyber-attacks on the US since it declared China a currency manipulator. We also know that there have been several attacks on US banks where the intent was not just to steal but to bring systems down.'

'Sure,' Toohey said. 'But we have good relations with Beijing. I have publicly called on the US to moderate its language on China. We have also, deliberately, been very guarded in taking sides on the Senkaku Islands dispute.'

'That's what we say, Prime Minister,' Heggarty continued. 'But yesterday the Chinese would have noted that the first rotation of US marines arrived in Darwin. Two hundred men from Lima Company, Third Battalion, Third Marine Regiment. As you know they are here to stay as part of the US pivot to Asia and their ranks will swell to 2500 over time. They were welcomed by the US Ambassador and the event knocked crocodiles off the front page of the *NT News.*'

David Joyce, the Secretary of Foreign Affairs, interrupted. 'Yesterday the Chinese Ambassador made a pointed reference to the marines' arrival at a function I attended. He said it appeared Australia had made an interesting choice. When I pressed him to elaborate he pointed to an editorial from the arch-nationalist paper the *Global Times* that, intriguingly, was reprinted in the *China Daily*. It is in your papers.'

Toohey flicked through his briefs. It was a front-page editorial.

AUSTRALIA COULD BE CAUGHT IN SINO–US CROSSFIRE

Apparently, Australia aspires to a situation where it maximises political and security benefits from its alliance with the US while gaining the greatest economic interests from China. However, Prime Minister Toohey may be ignoring something – Australia's economic cooperation with China does not pose any threat to the US, whereas the Australia–US military alliance serves to counter China.

Australia surely cannot play China for a fool. It is impossible for China to remain detached no matter what Australia does to undermine its security. There is real worry in Chinese society concerning Australia's acceptance of an increased US military presence. Such psychology will influence the long-term development of the Australia–China relationship.

Toohey wasn't surprised that the *Global Times* would take such a hard line. The paper was the Chinese equivalent of Australia's radio shock jocks, always shaking its outraged nationalist fist at the world. But he knew enough about China's leadership to know Beijing was sending a serious message when this red-ragging rhetoric was reprinted as an editorial on the front page of the leading English-language daily.

'How many of you believe that the blackout was a warning shot from China?' he asked.

Every official raised their hand.

'Who is certain?'

All the hands went down.

'We can't go on maybes. Ladies and gentlemen, this is now your number-one priority. Throw everything you have at it. We need to know what happened. Who did it. And how we can stop it happening again. We'll meet this afternoon at two, sooner if there are any developments.'

Toohey began to gather his papers.

'Before you leave, Prime Minister,' the Chief of the Defence Force, Jack Webster was speaking, 'we haven't addressed the serious situation in the East China Sea, which you mentioned in passing earlier.'

Toohey could see the usually cocksure Defence chief was choosing his words diplomatically and wondered why a matter that wasn't on the agenda was being raised. He settled back into his seat.

'Yes, go on.'

'I think I speak for all agencies when I say we need to stand firmly beside Japan and our ally the United States. When they act we need to act with them. Our one statement so far has simply been to call for calm. We have to speak with a stronger voice.'

Toohey ran his eyes along the line of officials. 'You guys been workshopping?' His tone was sardonic.

'That's our job, sir.' Webster met the Prime Minister's gaze with an icy stare. 'And to offer our professional advice. Our advice is to back our friends and the alliance that has served us so well.'

Toohey weighed his reaction and tried to calm his rising anger.

'You're right on two counts,' he said. 'We, the Security Committee, do need to discuss this issue and I do need to take firm action.'

He took a breath and took a plunge.

'Your advice has been noted. But it is my decision. So I want the officials to clear the room. This is a debate for committee members only.'

No one moved. No one could believe what was being asked. Only the Cabinet had been invited to stay. Even Papadakis looked stunned.

'Ladies and gentlemen,' the Prime Minister's voice was cold with authority, 'the military types among you should understand the difference between a request and an order. I said go. And I meant now.'

CHAPTER TWENTY-ONE

Canberra

'No queue jumpers, Dunkley.'

The journalist turned to be greeted by the greasy smirk of John Bossini.

It was 8am, a terrifying time for an old-school print journalist to be charging into the working day. But Harry Dunkley was on the hunt for a good yarn and his source, a chief of staff to a Cabinet minister, had suggested an early-morning 'off-the-record' chat.

Dunkley hadn't expected a coffee queue snaking around the cramped interior of Aussies Cafe and spilling outside. Fifteen minutes for a flat white and now this, stuck next to a former Liberal minister who'd been forced to walk the plank after being caught out fiddling his entitlements.

Like many retired parliamentarians, Bossini continued to suck on the teat of public generosity, supplementing his indexed pension with work as a 'strategic consultant' to several of Australia's best-known blue chips.

The two eyed each other suspiciously.

'Harry, good to see you're still standing. By the way, I've told you I don't like you calling me "the disgraced former minister" every time I'm mentioned in your columns. It's not good for me or the Liberal Party. I'm federal vice-president now, you know.'

Christ. It's too early to engage with scumbags.

'Ease up turbo. Tell you what, John – I'll ask Wikipedia to change its description of you, the one that goes, "Bossini's fall from grace came after he was forced to pay back $25,000 for wrongly claiming entitlement while taking his family on a vacation to Disneyland".'

'Oh, and this from a reporter who invents so-called Cabinet "leaks" and then has the audacity to put an exclusive tag on it. Spare me mate, spare me.'

Dunkley sighed and turned away, sizing up the queue and calculating how many minutes of his life would be spent with this lowlife. His eyes wandered around the unique parliamentary nook.

Aussies sat at an intersection of corridors in the secure area of Parliament. It was an epicentre of deal-making and, like a small airport lounge, a hub for people on the move.

The cafe's lease included a roped-off area with room for a dozen tables inside. Weighty steel-and-glass doors opened to an attractive courtyard where patrons could enjoy their coffee al fresco. Lovely at the moment, but only the bold ventured out in sub-zero winter temperatures.

Today, with the circus in full swing, every table was occupied. Lobbyists mingled with political staffers who ogled pretty young parliamentary aides who giggled at security hulks who glanced menacingly at anyone straying into their orbit. Journalists circled like starved seagulls around any minister trying to steal a few minutes of peace.

Aussies' owner was Dom, a first-generation Italian–Australian who invariably sported a brightly coloured Ralph Lauren polo-shirt. Dom was Parliament's father confessor, privy to the secrets of caffeine-needy staffers and MPs. He was as trustworthy as a vault, and the searching questions he occasionally lobbed showed a deep knowledge of politics.

The queue had barely moved and Dunkley toyed with the unthinkable.

The Trough?

No, Dunkley would rather skip coffee than retreat to the staff cafe on the other side of the building. His phone buzzed in his pocket. He took it out. There was a message full of cryptic promise.

'Ten minutes. Usual place.'

It was another source, a trusted source, who only mentioned 'usual place' when he had something juicy. Dunkley abandoned his miserable companion.

'Well, great to see you, John. Keep up the good work for democracy.'

Bossini scowled.

Dunkley fended off a few barbs from his gallery colleagues as he meandered through the crowd towards the Members' Hall, texting his coffee date. 'Mate, your turn to stand in the queue. I'll join you in twenty.'

After fifty metres, the corridor Dunkley was following widened to an expanse that bridged the gap between the House and Senate chambers. At its centre was a square pool made from a single piece of South Australian black granite. High above, a skylight revealed the massive flag flying above the Parliament, its image reflected in the glossy blackness of the pool.

Dunkley chuckled as he recalled the Parliament's architect explaining the thinking behind the small pond.

The sound of water trickling through the pool prevents the conversations of Members of Parliament from being overheard.

Except it was a thoroughfare. There were better places to share secrets.

Dunkley walked to a little-used lift, just past a glass walkway that led to the Senate chamber. The doors slid open and he hit 'M'.

Fifteen seconds later, a mechanical voice announced 'Mezzanine' and he stepped into one of Parliament's legendary spaces.

Few people ventured to the meditation room to meditate. Few even knew where it was. A small plaque declared the room was set aside for religious observance or quiet reflection. But most came here for illicit sex.

Several cubicles offered a measure of privacy, and Dunkley walked towards the furthest one. He contemplated a dubious stain on the blue lounge within, wondering if a DNA swab would link it to any minister.

A minute later, the lift doors opened again. He tensed then relaxed as a familiar shape emerged.

Brendan Ryan dumped himself on the lounge beside Dunkley. Over the years he'd morphed from a source for the journalist to almost a friend. He was finally in the job he'd always craved, Minister for Defence. Time was short.

'No notes, no tape. Just memorise.'

Jesus. Who's been fucked over now?

'NSC met half an hour ago. Earlier this morning, just before curfew finished, air traffic across Australia went down. Planes were flying blind, international and domestic. It could have been a disaster but thankfully all landed safe. No one else in the media knows. It's all yours.'

'You're kidding? How long was it … air traffic … down?'

'According to Airservices, it was thirteen minutes. Exactly.'

'And there was no warning?'

'That's not the way it works when you want to launch a cyber-attack.'

'What?'

'A cyber-attack, Harry. An act of aggression. C'mon, get with the agenda. Looks like someone in Beijing has decided that hacking into the PM's emails was just a warm-up.'

Dunkley glanced at Ryan, noticing a steady tap of his index finger. For a seasoned political assassin, he seemed tense.

'You suspect China was behind this?' Dunkley asked. 'What proof have you got?'

'Harry, we ain't 100 per cent, but the view around the room – in the NSC – was that China's the most likely culprit. Oh, and Harry, because I know you are super-careful in checking detail and fact, you might like to know that Tom Heggarty, head of

ASIS, reported an increase in cyber-attacks by China since the US declared it a currency manipulator.'

Dunkley was trying to break it down into a series of mental dot points, wishing he could write down a few notes.

'Brendan, this is dynamite. I'll work on it during the day, file for tomorrow's paper.'

'Mate, this is a twenty-first-century attack; you live in the 24/7 era. No, this is for your digital readers. They've got to get something for paying their subscriptions to Rupert. A lot of planes were involved and you can't be sure this story won't break elsewhere.'

Dunkley weighed his options. He hated publishing online without verifying every last fact. He could fight, but Ryan might give the yarn to someone else.

No, he'd knock this into shape and file asap, much as it pained him to give his competitors entree to the story before the evening presses rolled into action.

An hour later, *The Australian*'s website splashed with a stunning exclusive.

CYBER-STRIKE: AUSTRALIAN AIRSPACE UNDER ATTACK

Urgent investigations are under way into a suspected cyber-attack that shut down Australia's air-traffic system for thirteen minutes this morning.

The Australian can reveal that Prime Minister Martin Toohey hastily convened a meeting of Cabinet's National Security Committee to consider the unprecedented assault.

It is understood the Melbourne-based centre that controls the southern air space across Australia went 'black' just before 6am.

Several figures in the NSC – including Thomas Heggarty, the head of Australia's overseas spy agency, ASIS – are understood to have pointed the finger at China as the most likely source of the attack.

A spokeswoman for Mr Toohey refused to confirm that NSC had even met. But another member of the top-level security committee confirmed Cabinet ministers and intelligence heads had been called to the meeting around 7am.

One senior source, familiar with the NSC discussion, said, 'There was real fear in the room, and all roads lead to Beijing.'

CHAPTER TWENTY-TWO

Canberra

'Steady on the powder, love, you'll have me looking like a drag queen.'

Bruce Paxton was his usual gruff-and-grumble self, but he had a soft spot for the ABC's makeup artist.

The former Defence Minister had stepped into the press gallery bureau to be interviewed – and the ABC was buzzing on a high-octane loop of commentary sparked by Harry Dunkley's story.

Reporters were pumping out reaction to the extraordinary news that Australia's air-traffic control system had been attacked.

The call had gone out for talking heads and Paxton was happy to oblige as it allowed him to fill two of his favourite roles – discussing national security and pissing on Labor's bloated carcass.

He was still a member of the ALP, but in name only. Paxton had recast himself as a dissident. He was now Mr Dial-a-Quote and his bareknuckle assaults made even Mark Latham sound like a voice of restraint.

'Hi Bruce.' As Paxton entered the studio, ABC News 24's political editor, Lyndal Curtis, looked up briefly from her notes. 'We'll go live in two minutes.'

Paxton sat impassively as a small team fussed around the studio, wiring him up while makeup gave his face a final dab. When it was time to play ball, he would not disappoint.

'Lyndal, the cyber-security white paper the Toohey Government released in January was a sad joke. It offered no new money to fight on the twenty-first-century frontline and simply rebadged programs that were already funded.'

Curtis shot back.

'So you are blaming the government for this?'

'My oath, I blame them. I wanted Defence to focus less on its big-ticket toys and more on the main game. Cyber-hacking and warfare are real threats. All Martin Toohey wants from Defence is to strip out a couple of billion to prop up his Budget. And he put Brendan Ryan in charge – what a mistake! He's a diabetic in a lolly shop. Ryan spends too much time sucking up to Washington and not enough looking after our national interest, Lyndal.'

Paxton was on a roll and Curtis lobbed another inviting question.

'Do you believe, as the national security team is reported to believe, that China is responsible for this?'

'Look, if you believed everything the brass said about China it would be banged up for dressing up as a dingo and taking Azaria

Chamberlain. It could have been anyone, and remember, this is a cyber-attack, not hacking, which is usually the Chinese go. The point is we need better defences and we don't have them.'

Curtis shifted tack to the standoff in the East China Sea.

'Well, on that, you won't get a cigarette paper between me and the PM, Lyndal.'

Paxton had long argued that it was high time Australia rethought its alliance with the United States and had been critical of Japan's determination to isolate China. The future, as he saw it, was for Australia to draw back from the US and encourage it to share power in the Pacific.

'I see that the Prime Minister has said that Australia has no view on the ownership of the islands and has urged all sides to act with care and solve the problem diplomatically.'

Paxton leaned forward and tapped his prosthetic left hand on the oval table.

'Let's not forget who started all this, that Tea Party tool Earle Jackson. He decided to base his presidency on an ill-conceived attack on China using US financial clout. I think the Chinese have every right to respond. In any event, this fishermen's convention on the Diaoyu Islands is not sanctioned by Beijing.'

'You mean the Senkaku Islands,' Curtis corrected him.

'No I don't.'

It was some of Paxton's finest work. He ambled into the bureau feeling chuffed. As a sign that his handiwork had hit a nerve, the hallway outside the ABC was crammed with journalists from other networks, desperate for a Paxton grab they could call their own.

He was happy to repeat the performance but kept it tight. A ComCar was waiting on the other side of Parliament to whisk him to another appointment.

Fifteen minutes later, he'd arrived at the Thai embassy in nearby Yarralumla. He usually baulked at diplomatic functions but had struck up a good relationship with the new envoy. And a decent feed was on offer.

'See you here in an hour, Bill,' he said to his driver.

Like most of Canberra's diplomatic estates, the Thai embassy was designed to reflect its nation's architecture. The buildings had steep, elegantly curved and tapered roofs, made for a hot, wet climate.

The fragrant smells of coriander, spiced beef and sweet sauces tantalised Paxton as he passed an outdoor marquee. But he made a beeline for the drinks waiter, snatching a Hunter Valley white as he scoured the crowd for friendly faces.

Oh shit!

Ali Bakir, the Palestine Liberation Organization's apparently permanent representative in Canberra, was in close orbit. Paxton used to joke, when he was Defence Minister, that Bakir was a small bore, but could be used with lethal effect. Today, though, the last thing he wanted was a dissertation on the evils of the Jewish State.

He turned towards trestle tables laden with food, grabbed a plate and edged his way into the queue. 'The dim sum are delicious,' a woman remarked.

He loaded his plate and carefully manoeuvred his way through the crowd with his head down until he guessed he was a safe distance from Bakir.

A gentle, familiar laugh. He froze.

It couldn't be.

He searched the crowd and there she was, in a tight circle of admiring envoys – laughing in that way that men found intoxicating.

The last time he'd heard that sweet beautiful sound was at the St Regis in Beijing. He'd just called room service, from memory.

She caught sight of him, dipped her head and turned, expertly exiting the conversation, leaving disappointed diplomats in her wake.

'What are you doing here?' Paxton's urgent whisper was part question, part rebuke.

'Good work for my government, Mr Paxton. I arrived just over a month ago.'

She smiled and old feelings stirred.

'It's nice to see you, Bruce.'

Weng Meihui's hand brushed his arm as she removed an imaginary piece of cotton from his suit.

'And you. And … us?' Paxton surprised himself with his last words.

'That is for another day,' she said, another small ripple of laughter cutting like crystal through his heart. 'For today there is someone you need to meet.'

Weng guided Paxton to a man standing a few metres away.

'Mr Paxton, this is my husband, the new Ambassador, Tian Qichen.'

CHAPTER TWENTY-THREE

Washington

The white folder bore the Presidential seal, a strip of bold red cut across its centre highlighting the black capitals that declared the contents 'CLASSIFIED'.

Earle Jackson scanned his copy of the Morning Summary and frowned. The US President loved a good horror story but this was terrifying. And all too real. It seemed as if the whole world was on edge, bad news overlapping ever more dire headlines.

The overnight watch team in the White House Situation Room had compiled a list of international flashpoints. The Middle East was its usual basket case. Baghdad was ablaze with daily suicide bombings, and the growing tide of Syrian refugees from the civil war was swamping Lebanon and other nervous neighbours. In Thailand the public was venting its anger while South America's incessant drug war was taking a heavy toll.

But it was the Pacific, the geographic arc that stretched from the Arctic to the archipelago of Indonesia, that troubled him most.

In the weeks since he had declared China a currency manipulator, a wave of real and virtual reprisals had washed like a tsunami from East to West.

China had reasserted its claim over 80 per cent of the South China Sea. But it was in the East China Sea that the real danger loomed.

The fishermen who had invaded the Senkaku Islands were Chinese folk heroes – the English-language *China Daily* had dubbed them the Diaoyu Ten – and Beijing was offering no solutions on moving them.

It had taken an enormous effort to restrain the Japanese from retaliating. They had agreed to wait, for now, but only after the US promised to issue a strong declaration in the United Nations in support of the Japanese being recognised as the 'administrators' of those troublesome rocks.

The US President had been harangued by Japan's Prime Minister in a personal call. Shinzo Abe had made it crystal clear that his patience was running out. It was time for the US to show that its core alliances mattered. It was time to act. 'Weakness is provocative,' Abe had said, quoting Rumsfeld. 'And nothing is more provocative than a weak White House.'

The North Koreans, predictably, had decided to reboot their nuclear program and pull out of the five-party talks. The insane hermit kingdom, no doubt at the urging of the Chinese, was planning to test another missile that would track over South Korean airspace. The South was demanding more sanctions but that was being blocked in the UN Security Council by China and Russia.

There were reports that Chinese nuclear submarines were patrolling the waters near Hawaii and the Commander of the Pacific Fleet was demanding the right to engage 'the enemy' if the U-boats entered US territorial waters.

Through the portals of the internet, all-out war was raging as cyber-warriors armed themselves with ever more potent weapons. The number and scale of cyber-attacks on America and its allies had exploded, ranging from the frivolous to the dangerous. Government websites had been shut down by denial-of-service attacks; Wall Street's computers had been compromised, causing a run on US blue chips until trade had been suspended. And in Utah, a sewage spill into a local dam was being blamed on hackers who apparently had infiltrated the local water utility's SCADA operating system. In Washington, the Pentagon was reporting thousands of attempts a day aimed at cracking its formidable defences.

Jackson slurped a mug of cocoa and looked around the Situation Room, wondering if JFK had felt as impotent during the Bay of Pigs crisis in '61.

No, for all his faults, JFK never felt impotent.

It was Kennedy who had established the Sit Room following that disaster. A half-century later, the forty-fifth President was charged with mapping a path to sort out the mess that he'd helped create.

The surprisingly small room was crowded with nearly twenty people including the Vice-President, a former Governor of Dakota whose favourite pastime was hunting buffalo with a prized bow-and-arrow.

National Security Adviser Patrick Denton had been a more sensible appointment. The career diplomat was a rarity in Washington – he possessed impeccable Republican credentials and had enjoyed a stellar career in the State Department, that viper's nest of bleeding-heart Democrats.

Denton filled the long pause in the meeting caused by the President's demand that he be allowed time to properly digest the Morning Book.

'Mr President, we recommend a two-track response. We should make a stronger statement in support of Japan over the Senkakus. And we have to back that with action. We need to do something in the real world that reasserts our position as the dominant power in the Pacific and one that won't be played for a fool. Not to act only emboldens China and it will invite another move designed to test our resolve.'

Denton knew this would play better with the President than the rest of his advice.

'But then, sir, we need to offer an olive branch to China over the currency war. We have to settle things down and seek a return to normal diplomatic relations.

'No one wants a conflict, and if things keep tracking the way they are going, the chances that either we or the Chinese will miscalculate are large. And sir, to be blunt, America is in no shape for conflict in the Pacific. We need time to regather ourselves. We need to press the reset button.'

Jackson scanned the room, wanting to avoid the hard decision for a moment. He picked out Dick Hargreaves, another southerner and the four-star general who ran both the National

Security Agency and Cyber Command. NSA was the world's largest intelligence agency, listening to every whispered secret on the globe. And Cyber Command was the nerve centre for America's elite computer warriors.

'Dick, what do you think? How are we going to get around the Great Firewall of China?' The President chuckled at his little in-joke as if he had invented the term, jolting the room into forced mirth.

'Mr President, the number of cyber-strikes from China has gone off the charts. We are certain they have infiltrated – or at least positioned themselves ready to strike – key civilian and military targets. And Cisco is reporting a number of unidentified attacks on Tier 1 ISP networks which we suspect are coming from our red friends.'

Jackson snorted. 'Our red friends? Now that's an oxymoron if ever I heard one.'

'Yes Mr President.' Hargreaves continued without losing a beat. 'We have not been sitting idle on this matter either.'

He lifted a bound folder onto the desk and opened it.

'Sir, Operation GENIE has managed to insert a number of weapons behind enemy lines, behind the Great Firewall, as you put it. In short, we have broken into some of China's military and civilian networks and placed covert implants within them. Those bugs will allow us to hijack computers and steal data. Or destroy it. I have a full brief here.

'China knows some of its systems are compromised. But we are certain they have no idea how deeply because we have developed hardware, called "Quantum", which allows us to jump the gap to computers that are not connected to the internet. We can now access, or bring down, some of China's most sensitive systems using covert radio waves. It is our most secret and lethal weapon.'

The general was clearly pleased with the capabilities of his computer army, but ended on a sober note.

'In short, our homeland is vulnerable to a serious Chinese attack – but Beijing understands that retaliation would be swift and very, very potent. It depends on how much damage we are both prepared to inflict on each other.'

Jackson ran his finger around the inside rim of his mug, collecting a rich foam of chocolate-coloured milk. He plunged his chubby digit into his mouth, his signature move, disgusting at least half the people in the room.

'So what you're telling me is that we're in a classic stand-off. Jesus, it's the old American versus Commie mutual self-destruction scenario, ain't it? The goodies against the baddies.'

'Well sir, that is essentially correct.' Hargreaves thought the analogy trite but decided to leave it. 'China knows that we could do serious damage to its economy, to its infrastructure, through our cyber-weapons. But equally, they could unleash a cyber-attack on us that would do significantly more damage than 9/11. And Mr President, there are no rules of engagement in cyberspace. Once it starts in earnest there is no telling where it will end.'

Jackson knew he couldn't avoid addressing the central question forever. He had to decide whether to press ahead with his plans to continue the currency war by imposing trade sanctions on China or seek some kind of negotiated settlement. And over the last few days he'd finally seen the wisdom of tempering his actions. This escalating fight was consuming all his administration's energy and his domestic agenda was being swamped.

'Ladies and gentlemen, I need a few moments alone. Can you give me the room?'

The request came as a surprise but the brass and the bureaucrats dutifully obeyed their commander-in-chief.

With the room emptied, Jackson picked up the phone and dialled the one man in Congress he feared.

For Morgan McDonald ignorance wasn't bliss, it was a career.

The Republican congressman, known universally as Big Mac, firmly believed that too much information got in the way of clear decision making and, judging by his success, his constituents agreed.

As a teen McDonald had been horrified when his musical hero Elvis held his 1973 Aloha concert in Hawaii. In protest at the King's decision to perform outside continental USA, McDonald had burned his Elvis collection. His mother had counselled, 'It's still America, honey,' but that rang hollow to Big Mac's suspicious mind.

He had been a founding member of the 'Birthers' who claimed Barack Obama's birth certificate was a forgery. When a TV news anchor presented him with hard evidence that Obama was born in Hawaii, not Kenya, he immortally replied: 'Well Hawaii is not really America.'

That quote had gone viral and the Hawaiian Governor was apoplectic. But he was a goddamned Democrat so it went down a treat with Big Mac's base.

McDonald caught the Tea Party wave, and rose to become leader of the House. When it came to foreign affairs he joked that he had never owned a passport and was reluctant to get one.

Big Mac neatly divided the world into allies and foes: at home and abroad. An ally did what you told them. Foes were everyone else. He liked to quote the Bible to back this view.

'Hell, Jesus said, "If you aren't with us, you are against us."'

Since the fall of the Berlin Wall, McDonald had been convinced that no state would ever again rival American power. But he watched the rapid rise of a new breed of communist in the East with growing dismay. And Beijing was more cunning than Moscow.

Wolves who've wrapped themselves in the sheep's clothing of capitalism.

Big Mac was deeply offended by what he saw as China's manipulation of the market. While America had written the rules and exported wealth and freedom to the far-flung corners of the globe, the communist state was gaming the system and building wealth to export its malign influence everywhere.

And they have us by the financial balls.

Beijing now owned more than a trillion dollars of US bonds and, in Big Mac's view, held the American economy hostage. He'd been staggered to learn that China might rise to become the world's largest economy by 2030. He wanted to bring the Reds to heel, before it was too late.

We have seventeen years to corral this beast or it will kill us.

Big Mac became obsessed with stunting China's rise. He encouraged a two-pronged plan, which he'd developed with a trusted few cronies.

The first step was containment. Big Mac supported the creation of a new strategic block that included the USA, Japan, the Philippines, Taiwan, Indonesia, Malaysia, India, Vietnam and Australia.

Publically he called it the Asian Area of Cooperation and Peace, but privately it was the 'Dog Collar'. He would surround, isolate and choke the beast. As part of this pact, the US would respond to any incursion into the territorial waters of treaty members.

Despite some early promise, work on the treaty had stalled. So Big Mac set to work on the second prong of his plan: confrontation. He had confided it in a well-received secret briefing to his Pentagon pals during the Presidential election campaign.

'We need to goad China into a fight with America before it acquires sufficient military strength to be a real threat. If it believes we are frustrating its financial growth, it will lash out as Japan did at Pearl Harbor. Once it does that, gentlemen, you need to argue that America should respond with devastating force.'

He had crafted the President's threat to declare China a currency manipulator and would ensure that his friend followed through. For too long, the US had been weak in the face of growing Chinese provocation and it was time to strike back.

'I don't want my kids to live in an America where everything is stamped "Made in fucking China".'

Some of his confidants worried that the US couldn't afford a long war, that Iraq and Afghanistan had demonstrated that it couldn't occupy a foreign country. Big Mac dismissed such weakness with a standard response: 'We ain't gonna occupy them, son, we gonna nuke 'em.'

And if that meant the end of the world through nuclear war?

'Well son, then that's God's will. And remember your Bible. The end of the world will bring about the second coming of Christ. Jesus will sort through the corpses and bring the Christians to eternal life. If that is to be, then I will be proud to be the disciple who made it happen.'

Big Mac was at his desk when the call came through. He listened for less than a minute, then exploded.

'Goddamn you as a coward, Earle Jackson. We made a deal. You made a sacred pledge to the American people. You will keep your promise no matter how hard the road seems. You will impose tariffs. You will bring China to heel. You will restore the empire. For if you do not, I'll give you four years of hell.'

CHAPTER TWENTY-FOUR

Canberra

Tian Qichen angrily pointed at the small group opposite the front gates of his embassy.

'Why are they still here? Pestilence.' The Chinese Ambassador spat out the words as his late-model BMW turned out of the driveway, the protesters just metres from his window.

Three women and a man camped beneath a trio of banners accusing China of harvesting human organs and other abuses.

'Falun Gong has no right to be here.' Tian had arrived in Canberra five weeks earlier, excited at the prospect of becoming his country's representative in Australia. But he struggled to understand the country's tolerance of troublesome minorities, like the one that was a permanent fixture outside his embassy.

For the past decade, successive ambassadors had lobbied prime ministers and other figures in power to remove this embarrassment. Now Tian turned to his political counsellor. 'I want them gone within a month.'

His deputy nodded wearily, knowing the request was futile.

The Ambassador flicked open a briefing note. He was heading to Parliament House for his first formal meeting with Prime Minister Martin Toohey.

The most important item was finalising the 99-year lease over the Northern Territory gas-field. The resource was valuable, but more important was the unambiguous signal that would ricochet across the Pacific when the deal was signed. Australia would be crossing a Rubicon by allowing effective foreign ownership of some of its key resources. This southern land would be tied, ever closer, to the economic apron strings of China. The deal would bind the two nations in a long-term strategic embrace.

Tian looked out the window as the car purred up the road that climbed the outer edge of Parliament House. He smiled.

How will the United States and Japan respond?

Tian wondered why Australia clung to the American alliance like a national security blanket. The dependence was personified by the presence in Darwin of a battalion of US marines. That was also on his list.

As the BMW pulled up outside the ministerial wing, the PM's deputy chief of staff, Richard Andrews, was waiting.

'Mr Andrews, very nice to see you.'

'Welcome, Mr Ambassador. Nice to see you. Please, this way.'

It was a short walk to the Prime Minister's office and the Ambassador was ushered straight in. Martin Toohey and George

Papadakis were waiting and effusively welcomed Tian and his counsellor.

'Mr Prime Minister, the President sends his best wishes,' Tian began. 'And I hope that my time here will be as successful as my predecessor's was.'

Toohey had prepared a welcome gift – a package of a rare green tea. He offered it to Tian.

'Your favourite, I'm reliably informed. I've bought some for us to share in our meeting today.'

Toohey pointed to the tea service on the table placed between two comfortable chairs.

'Ah Mr Toohey, your spies have done good work.'

They laughed as they eased into each other's company.

'Please.' Toohey motioned to the lounge. 'I apologise for the weather, Ambassador. Must be a difficult change after coming from your winter.'

'I have been through much worse. Three years in Egypt prepares for you for even the most extreme heat.'

'Ah yes, that was the experience of our soldiers too – during World War II.'

'Yes, I imagine they would have suffered. I have read of the exploits of your 6th Division in battles with the Italians in Egypt. They fought with the British and they fought well.'

Toohey was impressed. This Ambassador had done his homework.

Tian continued. 'Australian soldiers seem to make many expeditions to fight in foreign wars. But since the Second World War, always with America: in Vietnam, Iraq and Afghanistan.'

It was the neatest of verbal transitions, a move worthy of a chess grandmaster. Toohey had offered an opening and Tian had taken it, pivoting the conversation to the American alliance.

'Well, we are out of Iraq and in the process of withdrawing our troops from Afghanistan,' Toohey countered. 'They'll be out of that place by year's end. And then? Well I fret for that country's future, I really do.'

'Its future will be like its past, Prime Minister. Lawless. Tribal. Violent. It has driven out invaders for centuries. The British and the Soviets could not hold it, so why did the US believe that it could?'

Tian took a sip of his green tea, nodding approval at its familiar taste.

'But the Americans have a new interest. In Asia. And they will have a much warmer welcome in Darwin.'

This was the main game. Toohey had been expecting it.

'Your country should not fret the small stuff, Ambassador. Australia and the United States have shared joint military exercises for decades – and never has that encroached on our relations with your wonderful country. At times, we've told the Americans they've overstepped the mark – I remind you of John Howard's speech to the Asia Society in New York in … when was it … 2006? Washington did not take kindly to that.'

Tian put down his tea and looked up at the large map of the world on the southern wall.

'You are right, of course, Prime Minister. But the strong economic and trade links we have built are no threat to America, while an increased American presence in the Pacific could be interpreted as a threat to us. You can understand that some of my colleagues might be concerned about a build-up of US troops in Darwin and increasing joint military exercises. Some don't necessarily view that as being the action of a country that is seeking a special relationship with China.'

Toohey sipped the green tea. It was bitter.

My move.

'And countries seeking that special relationship need to be fully open and transparent with each other. We are concerned about a recent, serious security breach of our air-traffic control systems. There are signs that point back to China.'

Tian was impassive as he leaned forward to return his cup and saucer to the table.

'Yes, I have read the reports in *The Australian* newspaper. It seems it has a very negative view of our government.'

Toohey laughed, genuinely.

'*The Australian* has a very negative view of *my* government. Believe me, you get better press than I do.'

Tian's face held a trace of a smile. 'But it seems that some in your government believe we are acting as aggressors. It does disturb me that China is so often blamed without evidence. All countries are at risk from cyber-attacks. We believe the United States is behind many security breaches in our own systems.'

After several more minutes of moving verbal pawns about the table, Toohey decided to open another delicate line of inquiry.

'We are also concerned about the rising tensions in the East China Sea. As you know, we take no position on who owns the disputed islands and have simply called for calm. But we are concerned about the potential for this fishermen's occupation to be … misinterpreted … and to get out of hand.'

'Prime Minister, my government thanks you for your temperate response on this matter. You will appreciate that, just as you cannot control your newspapers, we cannot be held responsible for the zeal of some of our citizens. We are working on removing the fishermen but they have become very popular at home. We ask for patience and believe the matter can be resolved.'

Toohey knew a long discussion on the disputed rocks would go nowhere. Besides, he was keen to nail down some outstanding issues concerning the proposed gas deal.

'Mr Ambassador, happily most of our dealings are about issues of friendship and mutual benefit. We are very excited about the Northern Territory gas hub and George and I would now like to discuss the details with you.'

Tian beamed. 'May I say that my superiors in Beijing view this agreement as a sign of a new maturity in our relationship.'

Twenty minutes later, Toohey and Tian ended what had been a mostly successful meeting.

'Mr Ambassador, I would be honoured if you would be my special guest when I give the speech at the Press Club announcing the agreement.'

Tian clasped his hands as a smile creased his face. 'Of course, Prime Minister, I would enjoy that. Very much.'

The two men rose and shook hands. As the Ambassador departed, Toohey turned to his chief of staff.

'Well, what do you think? How did I go?'

'About a draw, I'd say. Got a bit interesting at the start but the two of you brought it back on track pretty well. You never know, you may actually get to like him.'

'I do like him, George.'

'But do you trust him?'

The PM gazed out at the courtyard's summer haze.

'About as much as I trust any member of Cabinet.'

CHAPTER TWENTY-FIVE

Canberra

Tears streamed down Catriona Bailey's pallid face as she looked at the empty plastic cup resting in her trembling hand. It had taken all of her formidable willpower to lift it to her mouth and drink.

It was a liberation. After twenty months on life support Bailey had been unshackled: from the ventilator that kept her lungs pumping; the catheters that drove her circulatory system; and the oxygen that flowed through the tracheotomy in her throat.

She was propped upright in her hospital bed, drinking alone and unassisted. That simple act had been a daydream just a few weeks ago. She put down her cup and slowly practised flexing and unflexing her fingers.

The slightest of movements made her feel powerful, alive.

Bailey recalled the moment she had awoken in hospital after her stroke. It was so horrifying she'd thought she was having a nightmare. She could hear the doctors, nurses and visitors come and go from her room, could feel the weight of her body on the bed, the sheets that covered her and the tubes that cut into her. But she could not move, see or speak.

When I realised it wasn't a dream I thought I would go mad.

She'd heard the whispered conversations, the doctors who'd measured her life in days and discussed harvesting her organs. And the sound of that hated voice. Martin Toohey. Visiting with a posse of his gormless ministers.

She would never forget the poisonous words he'd uttered when they were alone – 'You selfish bitch.'

That's when she'd decided to fight. To recover. To rise and destroy him. The thought of revenge had given her the will to live.

The first miracle had occurred only days after that encounter when the Melbourne specialist had removed the gauze from her eyes and realised that she could see and was alert. The simple act of being able to blink her eyes meant Bailey could communicate.

The second miracle was the technology that could turn her eye movements into words on a computer screen and transmit them around the world. That meant she could work and continue her love affair with the public.

My people.

Bailey had lived out every moment of her life in public. She maintained an almost continuous Twitter stream. But only the very observant among her two million followers would have noted that recently she had stopped talking about every minute change in her condition.

And as her health rapidly improved, she'd restricted visiting access to just her chief of staff.

When I return no one will see me coming.

'Eight thousand fucking words!' Brendan Ryan shook his head as he scrolled through line after line of the pedestrian prose that marched off the *Guardian*'s online features page. The typically pseudo-intellectual babble carried the byline 'Catriona Bailey' and the headline: TOOHEY CAN BRING PEACE IN THE PACIFIC.

It began, as articles by Bailey almost always did, by quoting herself. 'In 2008 I coined the term "the age of non-polarity" to describe a world dominated not by one or two states but by dozens of actors'.

It then rambled on through bloated sentences of tortured syntax, each stuffed with academic and Biblical references, historical analogies and a dozen more verbal selfies before it got to the point.

> We live in a dangerous time where the two largest actors on the
> world stage are locked in a rapidly escalating battle over who will
> build the international frameworks of the twenty-first century,
> frameworks that will replace the settlements struck and maintained
> by the United States after the Second World War. Both China and
> the United States are wrestling for the pen with which to write
> those settlements. I fear they might see the sword as being mightier.

Another thousand mind-numbing words on, Bailey stirred Australia into her witch's brew of an argument.

Australia can use its privileged place as one of the United States' oldest allies and China's most reliable energy supplier to broker peace between the behemoths of the world stage by leveraging its role as a creative middle power.

Then came the *coup de grâce*, the point Bailey knew would run in the news and cause maximum grief.

On my advice, Prime Minister Martin Toohey has been masterful in ensuring Australia does not get trapped into taking sides in the East China Sea islands dispute. But he can, and must, take a larger role. He must use our middle power status to immediately engage in shuttle diplomacy between the major powers to bring about an enduring peace and an agreed international framework in the Pacific. Or a 'Pax Pacifica', as I like to call it.

As a political professional Ryan had a grudging admiration for Bailey. She was an evil genius. She knew her 'shuttle diplomacy' line would be parroted by the media the next time Martin Toohey stuck his head up for a press conference. Like all of Bailey's advice it sounded reasonable but it was designed to put Toohey in an impossible position. If he demurred he would be portrayed as missing an opportunity for peace. But if he was mad enough to agree it meant he would be out of the country for weeks on end during an election year. And that would cruel the minute chance he had of winning the poll.

Who am I kidding, he might as well go. Jesus Christ couldn't raise this party from the dead.

164

Ryan had orchestrated the coup that snatched the prime minister's mantle from Bailey and he was still proud of it as a clinically brilliant political assassination. But he had been very disappointed in Toohey. He was a decent man but the public saw him as a devious back-stabber. Far worse in Ryan's eyes was that Toohey liked grand, expensive, centralised social planning. That cost money the Treasury didn't have and so he racked up debt and cut deeply into other areas, particularly Defence.

Ryan had plotted to bring down the former Defence Minister and left-wing fool, Bruce Paxton, in an effort to try to stop cuts that he believed were a threat to national security. But it had been futile. The Prime Minister was determined to bribe his way back to power and Defence was simply a cash cow to be milked.

Maybe losing the election was the best thing that could happen? What Ryan didn't want was to lose so badly that political recovery would take a generation.

He scrabbled in his desk drawer for a bar of chocolate as he tried to conjure a plan that would keep his party viable.

I'd back anyone against Toohey now as long as they could save some furniture.

'Minister?' His personal assistant was at the door.

'Yup.'

'The Prime Minister's chief of staff is here.'

The familiar stocky frame of George Papadakis ambled into the office and sat down with a thud. As usual he was carrying the weight of the nation.

'Do you have any Scotch?' Papadakis asked theatrically.

'George, it's barely lunchtime.'

'Heroin then. I've just come from a meeting with the Chinese Ambassador and can't face any more green tea. And I need something to dull the pain of trying to keep this shambles of a show on the road.'

Ryan liked Papadakis and didn't envy his job but he was disappointed that this member of Labor's Right and old-school Treasury hard-head hadn't managed to rein in his profligate boss.

'I've got headaches of my own, mate. ERC wants more cash from Defence and we're down to the bone. As I've said many, many times I'm now concerned that we are compromising national security and—'

Papadakis held up his hand.

'Brendan, I know. I've heard your complaints many times and I have said, many times, that everyone has to take a hit. And you know that the mental health plan is close to the PM's heart and probably our only hope of victory at the election.'

Ryan had known he'd get no joy from Papadakis but simply wanted to underline his growing concerns.

'So mate, apart from liquor and hard drugs, what's on your mind?'

'It's your political brain I need. You know how much the PM values your judgement, you're one of his trusted few. These leaks are killing us, Brendan. We expect them from the party, even Cabinet, but we're now being white-anted by someone in the intelligence community. The leak from the NSC is intolerable.'

Ryan rocked back in his chair and swung round to face the window.

'George, you know as well as I do that leaks are one of the symptoms of a government in decline. Leaks from the administration are as good as a death knock. If we can change our fortunes, then we might get back some semblance of order.'

Papadakis checked his watch and started to rise from his chair.

'I know. I just needed the walk. And a shoulder to cry on. Thanks Brendan.'

'Hey, have you seen the *Guardian* feature by Bailey?'

Papadakis slumped back in his seat and groaned.

'No. What does the Zombie Queen want now?'

'She says Toohey should engage in shuttle diplomacy to ensure world peace.'

Papadakis was massaging his temples as he got up.

'Cocaine, that's what I need. I'll go find someone in the NSW Right. One of them's bound to be a dealer.'

CHAPTER TWENTY-SIX

Canberra

In the distance, the mountains were a tapestry of green and violet. The Brindabellas were majestic under a sky of startling blue broken by tufts of cotton white skating across the city horizons.

From the top of Red Hill, Bruce Paxton soaked up the capital's western sprawl. Suburban estates straight off the Masterton assembly line were baking in the late afternoon sun, replacing pine plantations bulldozed to make way for Canberra's growing population.

The city was greener than he'd expected after this summer from hell. Arterial roads carried loads of post-school children and harried mums, high-vis tradies and brow-beaten cabbies. But the byways wove in and out of the land's natural contours and suburbs vanished beneath the rising green of trees.

'Can you believe that a lot of Australians hate this place?' Paxton turned to Weng Meihui, also transfixed by the view.

'In my city there are few trees and the sky is black with smog,' she said. 'I love the space and the clarity of the air here.'

They walked the few metres to the bar, thirsty for a drink and conversation.

She is ageless.

Paxton wrapped his right hand around a chilled glass of white and glanced at her face. A nervous smile.

Why has she come back into my life? Now? After all this time?

The MP was cautious. He wanted to play it cool, despite himself. It had all seemed so convenient, that she would arrive. Unannounced, but not unwelcome.

His first instinct had been 'This means trouble'. But now, as evening fell, the memories came flooding back. Of nights wrapped in her tantalising, impossible embrace. His Chinese temptress.

She teased him with a smile. 'What are you thinking, Bruce?'

'Well, don't mock me, but there's a line from a song I just love, by a bloke called Eric Clapton. Bit of a guitar god. Anyway, he sang about a woman looking "wonderful tonight". And …'

She leaned over and gently took his hands.

'Why don't you fix the bill?'

The key turned and the door to his apartment opened. His flatmates – two Labor comrades from South Australia – were both out and he'd taken the precaution of doing a bit of cleaning up.

'So, here it is, the castle. Not much, but I like it. And the TA – travel allowance – covers the rent.'

She sensed his apprehension, and gently stroked his arm. 'Just relax,' she reassured him.

He bent to the CD player and flicked through a messy pile.

Jesus, fucking Nirvana?!

He chose a Michael Bublé compilation instead. Personally he couldn't stand the smug Canadian crooner but women, he was told, loved him. A soft-flow tune played, something about a woman making him feel young.

Now, that's appropriate.

He turned and leaned into her tight body, hungrily meeting her lips, that familiar scent of musk and milk.

'It's been a—'

'Shhhh.' She cut him off as her fingers skilfully played with a row of buttons, releasing his shirt and easing it to the floor.

He stood in his singlet, arms crossed self-consciously.

'And off with that, too.'

Her small and nimble fingers reached firmly beneath the hem of the singlet, and she pulled it up so insistently that he had no choice but to raise his arms above his head.

The cloth covering his eyes, he started with sweet surprise as he felt her soft, warm lips press again upon his own rougher mouth. She kissed him long and lusciously, and he luxuriated in her familiar yet exotic scent. Finally she released him, and he quickly shed his remaining clothes, all body consciousness lost as he urgently drew her to him.

Kissing all the while, he unzipped her high-collared dress and allowed the silken sheath to fall to the floor. They tumbled together onto the bed, hands eager upon one another. Hovering above her, he admired the taut lines of her body, tracing an ardent line from her lips, down between her exquisite breasts and onto the silken small of her stomach.

Just a second's hesitation and his fingers drew lower. He circled and teased until she could bear it no longer, then he slowly took her.

They made love in a languid embrace, lacking the urgent heat of the last time they had met in Beijing. But it was somehow more intense, more connected; they built carefully and inevitably to her climax and, soon after, his own sweet release.

Her fingers traced circles in his chest hair while she rested her head on his arm. The last vestiges of the day had disappeared, and her stomach purred with a mild hunger.

For the first time, she noticed a few sun spots on his neck.

'You need to take care of yourself,' she said, triggering a grunted response.

'Why darling? Who's coming after me now?'

'No Bruce. I mean your skin.' She dabbed a small red blotch under his chin. 'There.'

'Oh that. Too many years in the outfield, waiting for some bastard to hit the ball my way.'

Weng looked perplexed.

'Cricket, my love. Only game in the world that can last five days without a friggin' result.' He laughed at the sheer bloody idiocy of it.

Weng eased her body up on a pillow. 'Sounds like a meeting of the People's Congress. It can last five days, sometimes six, and all they do is rubber stamp what has already been decided. The current Standing Committee is the worst we've ever had.'

Paxton had never heard Weng speak this way; normally she offered nothing but slavish praise for her masters.

'You're sounding a touch bolshie, Mei. Things not going so well for you out here?'

She raised herself on both elbows, suddenly serious.

'Bruce … sometimes …'

Her voice softened and he noticed the slender trail of a tear.

'Mei … what is it, my love?'

She sighed. 'Sometimes … No. Often I question what I have become. What I have done for my state. I used to believe in it and that made what I did bearable. But now I fear my country is lost. And I am lost with it.'

Paxton leaned over and smoothed a lock of hair from her face.

'Well, you're not lost, you're with me. And I know what you are, Mei. I have always known. I didn't delude myself that you were attracted by my charms. But I've never told you anything that would compromise my country.'

'I know. Maybe that is why I love you.'

Paxton held her close as she continued.

'If I had my way, I'd replace all the generals and apparatchiks with the smartest graduates from the universities. Then I'd allow them to open China to the outside world, to really let a thousand flowers bloom. But President Meng … well, he seems intent on withdrawing into some nationalist past. We are regressing.'

Paxton could empathise. For the first time in many years he was questioning his own commitment to the great cause. He had played the loyal ALP footsoldier for nearly four decades and had never recoiled from a fight.

From the time he'd signed up as a member of the Rockingham branch in Perth, his dues paid by the Building Workers' Industrial Union, he'd obediently followed every instruction. He'd never questioned orders to do over some useless prick, some political dropkick, some reprehensible turncoat. He didn't mind the battles with the corporate bloodsuckers, of course. They were fair game. Blowing the top off a big industrial stink and watching halfwit bosses fall to pieces – well, that was good sport. But it was when he was ordered to strafe his own bruvvers – another union thug or a Labor mate – well that's when he got shin-splints. Not that he'd ever asked to be substituted.

He'd copped his fair share of shit too, losing his hand in an industrial 'accident', and then losing his family as they lost interest in a schemer who spent more hours than were healthy on the red-eye to Canberra.

All the time he was climbing the greasy pole, eyes firmly on the prize. And now? He'd been fed to the wolves a year and a half ago, and for what? He'd broken no laws. Sure, he'd built a slush fund with some Chinese cash but who in politics had clean hands when it came to that? He'd been dumped because the government was too weak and too gutless to fight.

'I believed in a great cause, the Labor Party. Believed we could change this country for the better, follow in the footsteps of Hawke and Keating, build a stronger and fairer Australia. I believed we were united in the common good, taking on all those mugs and hillbillies who tried to shoot us down.

'Australians used to believe in us too, that we would make a difference, that we cared about the little guy, that we were the enlargers who wouldn't leave them behind. Now? I'm not sure what we stand for anymore. We seem to spend most of our time apologising for cock-ups. And when it does get hard … well, we usually cut and run.'

He paused and gazed at his Chinese princess.

'What went wrong, Mei?'

She kissed him. Gently.

'We got older,' she said. 'Now I have to go.'

CHAPTER TWENTY-SEVEN

Canberra

The three-car convoy swept into the National Press Club, the prime ministerial limousine, C1, sandwiched between a pair of gleaming white security vehicles.

Several guards jumped from the cars into action, taking up positions on either side of C1. Advisers hurriedly grabbed notepads and iPhones.

On a soft leather seat, protected by bullet-proof glass and bodyguards trained to kill, Martin Toohey wrestled with the knot of a silk tie that was refusing to behave. Finally, he slipped off his seatbelt.

'Okay George, time to rock-and-roll.' The Prime Minister gave his chief of staff a friendly pat on the arm.

Near the entrance a gaggle of environmentalists was protesting against what they saw as a pitifully low carbon emission target. One was dressed as a polar bear in a suit that looked as if it had been knocked up by his mum. A bedraggled koala lurked without menace. Both were suffering in the heat, and having trouble with the scansion of their chant.

'Five … five … will not keep us alive.'

Papadakis thought they were the ones endangered by climate. Practically no one watching the evening news would have the foggiest idea what the protest was about, he mused.

'Clowns,' yelled Maurice Reilly, the Press Club's no-nonsense CEO. Reilly, who in a previous life had helped enough wayward AFL players overcome their troubles to earn a sainthood, was taking no chances. He personally shepherded the PM and his entourage into the club's newly renovated premises.

The PM admired the two-and-a-half-million dollar overhaul of a building that had hosted every prime minister since Fraser. 'I like these renovations, Maurice,' Toohey said. 'But you do seem to have a thing for brown.'

The club was packed with journalists, lobbyists, bureaucrats and the Labor faithful. Toohey's office had primed the media with snippets from his speech billed as a game-changer. More than that, this was the Grand Final.

Strategically, the Chinese Ambassador was seated at the main table, causing a flurry of activity among the snappers.

'Switch your phones to silent.' Reilly's directive reminded the room that Toohey's speech, just minutes away, was being broadcast live across the nation, on the ABC and Sky News.

In his seat, Toohey took a final gulp of water, brushed at his suit sleeve and gathered his speech notes. He walked to the podium and scanned the room as the NPC's president, Laurie Wilson, made the introductions. The applause was generous.

'Thanks Laurie.' Toohey got straight into stride.

'This election year is a contest for the future. A contest between the builders with the vision for a twenty-first-century nation and the wreckers who lust for power for its own sake. And who will drag us back to the past.

'Our mission, Labor's mission, is to build a better Australia, to build the jobs of the future and to invest in a fairer country.'

Toohey's opus was laid out as a series of steps. Each would be a news story in its own right. Toohey would make some admissions of fault in an effort to consign error to the past. Then there would be a run of headline moments that culminated with the big bang announcement.

The first declaration guaranteed a headline on its own.

'So that we are not dogged with speculation for the rest of the year, today I announce that the election will be held on Saturday, 14 September.'

There was a sharp intake of breath at the working press tables followed by frantic scribbling. Twitter went into overdrive. #EDay.

This was unheard of, a prime minister giving away the natural advantage of keeping the election date a secret up until the last moment. But it was just the start.

'A decent nation cares for those who cannot care for themselves. No one in our community is more vulnerable than those with a mental disability.

'Just last week in Penrith, I met Jody, a young single mother with three children. One, Michael, has a severe disability. Jody is only twenty-four and Michael's needs are so great that she has to care for him day and night. She does not have any family to offer respite.

'She told me that she lies awake at night worrying about what will happen to her son when she can't take care of him anymore.

'A fair Australia, a just Australia, a decent Australia, lends people like Jody and Michael a hand.

'So today I announce the most sweeping reform to mental health care since Federation. My government will legislate this term to secure the future of Jody and Michael and the thousands who struggle each day with this silent epidemic.

'Ladies and gentlemen, the Mental Health Justice Act will provide universal and lifetime cover for those, like Michael, who need our support.

'It will also provide generous respite care for mothers like Jody.

'This will not come cheap. In 2018, the first full year of the scheme, it will cost $6 billion a year ...'

At this point, the economic writers lowered their heads and began to scribble. Toohey could see it on their faces: here we go, yet another unfunded promise by Labor.

But the PM was ready for the pointy heads.

'... but it will be fully funded, through savings already booked from Defence, and by a unique agreement with the People's Republic of China.

'This afternoon the chief executive of Sinopec and I will sign a heads of agreement concerning the Medusa gas-field off the Northern Territory coast. The Medusa is the largest known gas reserve in the world.

'The agreement will give Sinopec a 99-year lease over the site. In addition to the usual company taxes and royalties, it has agreed to an immediate down-payment of $10 billion and yearly leaseholder payments of $1 billion every year thereafter. All of that money will be put in trust to build a war chest for the Mental Justice package.

'So, $11 billion will flow from next financial year, after Sinopec signs the lease. We expect that to be finalised by late August.'

On the floor in front of the stage, two tables of working press sat stunned. They were used to observing the first rough draft of history – but this was epic.

Toohey was building to his punchline which was aimed straight at Labor's core supporters. As he did he noticed several of the journalists picking up their mobiles and checking messages that had flashed onto their screens.

Probably their editors gobsmacked by my plan.

'This program is Labor to the bootstraps. It tends to the weakest by leveraging our nation's bounty. And it delivers jobs. Ten thousand jobs in the construction phase and a thousand permanent jobs thereafter. It cements our place as an energy superpower and it builds even stronger ties with our neighbours in this Asian Century.

'Only Labor has the plan to deliver a fair go for Australia. Help for the weakest. Jobs for the rest. Prosperity for all.'

The Prime Minister finished his speech to rapturous applause. He acknowledged it with a nod and took a drink of water, readying himself for the queue of questioners.

'Thank you, Prime Minister, for that truly important speech,' Wilson said. 'We now turn to questions from the press gallery. The first question: Jonathan Robbie from Channel Nine.'

Robbie cradled the microphone and wore a smug smile.

'Prime Minister, fantastic speech. But I have just received extraordinary news. Catriona Bailey has tweeted a picture of herself. She's been taken off life support. Here ... can you see the picture? What is your response?'

That unspeakable cow.

'Jonathan, I could not be more delighted to hear that the Foreign Minister seems to be making a miraculous recovery. I am, quite literally, speechless. I look forward to seeing her soon.'

The next question was from News Ltd's Tom Shapiro, a young gun with a high opinion of himself, training to be a head-kicker.

'Given the Foreign Minister's close links with China, will she play a big role in helping to make sure this deal is sealed?'

'Tom, I'm sure she will have a role to play but this deal will be sealed. By me. My office has all the necessary plans in place.'

Andrew Probyn, the *West Australian's* feisty political correspondent, was on his feet.

'PM, the Foreign Minister has just tweeted congratulating you on picking up one of the ideas that came up at her 2020 forum. Is that true?'

You little Pommy prick!

'Andrew, more funding for mental health was a recommendation from the forum but I think you'll find that the detail of this plan is far wider in scope than anything that has come before. And, if I might take some credit for this, there is a big difference between having an idea and sealing a deal.'

The next three questions were all about Bailey, the gallery ignoring the detail of Toohey's tour de force.

Finally, Laura Tingle, the political editor from the *Australian Financial Review*, got the call and Toohey knew she hated Bailey at least as much as he did. She was also a serious economic journalist.

'PM, you've skated over an important element in funding this plan. The briefing notes suggest that by 2025 your funding model will be $1 billion a year short of paying for itself. And you plan to lift the Medicare levy to fund the shortfall.'

We hoped that would be a footnote, not a focus.

'You're right, Laura. The difference will be funded by lifting the Medicare levy by a modest 0.25 per cent. But that will not happen until 2020 and, even then, it will only add a few dollars a month to the costs of an average family. Again, I stress that cost will not come for seven years. I think you will agree, Laura, that is a modest charge for a safety net that will give everyone peace of mind.'

Phones were starting to light up again on the working press tables.

The final question was from Paul Bongiorno, Ten's veteran political correspondent.

'PM. Bruce Paxton has just put out a press release saying he is quitting the Labor Party to sit on the crossbenches. Will that jeopardise the passage of your bill?'

Fuck me drunk, can't I have a second of clear air?

'Well, Paul, that is a surprise. But Bruce Paxton has spent his life trying to improve the lot of working men and women and I would be staggered if he did not see the merit in this plan. I will be seeking a meeting with him and briefing the other crossbench MPs soon.'

And with that the Prime Minister stepped down from the podium, ignoring the gift of a Mont Blanc pen and honorary Press Club membership.

A day that promised triumph and glory had turned to shit. Again.

CHAPTER TWENTY-EIGHT

Canberra

It's dubbed the 6pm index, a few minutes of primetime torture that can test the bravest.

Every night the Prime Minister and his inner sanctum would gather around a bank of television screens to see how they'd fared on the commercial networks.

Tonight was a disaster.

The Seven network led with 'exclusive' footage of Foreign Minister Catriona Bailey sitting serenely in a wheelchair, flanked by a deeply tanned neurosurgeon from Brisbane.

The network had a special relationship with the former prime minister, forged over her years of appearances on its breakfast program, *Morning Glory*.

'This is close to miraculous. I've never had a patient show such steely determination to recover,' the neurosurgeon said. 'And, let me emphasise this, very few people suffering from Ms Bailey's condition ever get off life support. We hope that soon the Foreign Minister will be able to talk.'

On Nine, Laurie Oakes had scored an interview with Bruce Paxton, who was declaring his intention to be yet another thorn in the side of the Toohey Government.

'I will treat every bill on a case by case basis,' Paxton advised. 'This government had better not take me for granted.'

Ten lacked the other networks' audience clout so its bulletin, an hour earlier than the big two, had no exclusive, but Hugh Riminton reported that the Prime Minister's speech had been 'overshadowed' by the breaking news on Bailey and Paxton.

At 7pm, the ABC led with the 'serious reservations' being expressed by the Queensland and Western Australian governments about the gas hub plan. Both feared the Commonwealth's intervention would jeopardise projects planned for their states. And both were making noises about a vague constitutional problem that neither would elaborate on.

'What crap!' spat Papadakis. 'We have all the legal power we need to proceed in the Territory.'

'Mate,' Toohey sighed with the resignation of a man with low expectations.

'The longer I'm in this job, the more I wonder whether I have any power at all.'

Melbourne

The Toorak tram rumbled by as Matthew Sloan hustled along the footpath with the frantic resolve of a man who was late.

'Fuck those professional bores.' Sloan swore under his breath as he wove between footpath saunterers conspiring to add more delay to his journey.

He had hated every minute of the Multicultural Communities Council meeting he'd just endured. Typically, minutes had piled into wasted hours in the drone of self-important speeches. The conclave of complaint was supposed to be done by six, leaving him ample time for the 7.30 dinner rendezvous. It was now 7.50.

If only the public could gaze inside a Member of Parliament's life.

While the perception was of a life of privilege and taxpayer-funded travel, in truth the diary of an MP was larded with tedious speech nights and vapid community events. And meetings. Constituents, complainers, urgers and spivs all demanding time to whine. Meetings with hopelessly divided groups, like the Multicultural Communities Council, to which the application of liberal amounts of precious time usually failed to resolve even the most trivial of issues.

But then there were the moments he lived for, the hidden pearls that made his job worthwhile.

As chair of the Parliamentary Joint Committee on Intelligence and Security, Sloan had access to some of the nation's deepest and most sensitive secrets.

It also meant he was feted by every embassy and enjoyed junkets across the world to meet with counterparts in exotic lands. He'd just returned from the US, where he'd been given a personal tour of Langley by the new head of the CIA. A framed photograph of Sloan arm in arm with the Director now graced his office wall.

He was now within smelling distance of Bacash, one of Melbourne's best eateries and Sloan's favourite restaurant. He loved the slate-grey interior, the crisp white tablecloths, the dutiful, uniformed staff, and the exquisite menu. He could already taste the char-grilled calamari with chorizo.

Waiting for him at a corner table was Blake Cornwall, the political counsel at the United States embassy in Canberra. Dressed in a sharp dark-blue suit, Cornwall could have been a top-flight banker or lawyer waiting for a client. Instead he was effectively America's number-one operative in Australia, the CIA's eyes and ears who could even pull rank on the Ambassador when it came to the big calls.

He rose to meet Sloan with an exaggerated handshake.

'Sorry, sorry, I'm late. Held up at the last event by a group of blowhards,' the MP apologised.

'Don't worry about it, Matthew.' Cornwall spoke in polished Bostonian tones. 'I've already ordered some entrees, the one you like, and a decent bottle of white. It's really great to see you. How's Mary?'

'Really well. And she wanted me to pass on how touched she was when the Ambassador wrote to her after her mother died.'

'He was deeply saddened to hear about it, Matthew, deeply. As he often says, the bonds between our nations are so deep that we are essentially family.'

'Very true, Blake, very true. And you know there is no stronger friend of the US than Australia.'

'Is that so?' Cornwall's smile vanished, his face turned to stone and his voice dropped.

'Then what the fuck are you pissants playing at in this gas deal with China?'

Sloan was stunned. He struggled to compose himself.

'Blake, err … it's an economic compact, it's …'

'It's a sell-out. Yet another sign from your government that the old alliances are fading. You have forgotten who your friends are. Do you really believe that this region would be peaceful if we hadn't done the hard defensive yards? I went to the trouble of getting you a briefing from the head of the NSA. Do you know how rare that is? Are you so stupid you missed the key message? Make no mistake on how this is being viewed in DC. By everyone. Hell, even the State Department and Pentagon agree: you're giving us the bird and we aren't about to sit quietly while you guys rat on us.'

'What do you mean, Blake … ending security agreements?'

'Use your imagination. And enjoy your dinner. Alone. I've ordered and paid. You guys should be used to that.'

Cornwall threw his napkin on the table as he rose and left.

Sloan sat crumpled, unable to eat. He fumbled for his mobile and hit the speed dial number for the PM's chief of staff.

'George, we are in serious strife.'

CHAPTER TWENTY-NINE

Canberra

CABINET SPLIT ON CHINA DEAL

The Australian's splash was designed to erect a tombstone on the policy Martin Toohey and George Papadakis had meticulously crafted over the previous three months. A report on the mental health package was relegated to a pointer off the front to page 5. Predictably, the national broadsheet had instead seized on political divisions within the government over the gas mega-deal.

A 'senior source' claimed most of Cabinet had been kept in the dark on the details of the package. There was deep disquiet about 'selling off the farm' to the Chinese and serious concern about how the proposed deal would be received by Australia's neighbours and its ally-in-chief, the United States.

The chief of staff had barely slept. Papadakis had left the office after watching a *Lateline* interview with West Australia's Colin Barnett, who was in meltdown. The Premier of the resource-rich state had accused the Commonwealth of stealing potential Chinese investment money and issued threats of a Constitutional challenge.

Throughout the long evening, Papadakis had been peppered with disturbing calls.

In Melbourne, his close friend Matthew Sloan had been monstered by the CIA's chief spook. The Secretary of the Department of Foreign Affairs and Trade had been shirt-fronted by what he described as a 'hysterical' Japanese Ambassador at a charity ball in Parliament's Great Hall. The South Korean consul had ear-bashed the Minister for Trade and suggested that Labor had placed Australia on a perilous course, one that could jeopardise a planned free-trade agreement. Even the Israelis had briefly lifted their eyes from the Middle East to give their American friends a diplomatic hand. This time, it had been delivered with their usual shovel-to-the-head bluntness to a hapless Parliamentary Secretary.

Toohey stuck his head around Papadakis's door, holding his iPad.

'You know, I miss the old paper version of this rag because right now I'm off to the bathroom.'

'What the fuck do we do now?' Papadakis asked in despair.

'We stick to our guns, mate. This is a good program. You and I know that. We can't be knocked off course. So, what are your plans?'

'Well, maybe I'll tune into Alan Jones and get his calm, considered view on the foreign investment side of this. Just so my spirits can soar with the eagles.'

CHAPTER THIRTY

Canberra

Seven black letters. A shadow from the past now branded on the nation's soul. Vietnam.

Harry Dunkley slowed as he passed the monument to a decade-long struggle that marked the moment when folk, young and old, began to lose faith in government.

His LandCruiser lumbered north on Anzac Parade, late in the morning. Three bronze diggers, dressed in their combat kit, stood amid a stand of poles representing the dead from another Asian conflict. Korea.

He looked back to the road. Straight ahead, the striking facade of the Australian War Memorial drew close, its copper-green dome set against the moss-and-emerald forest of Mt Ainslie.

What is it about this shrine to the dead that I find so compelling?

The reporter had spent countless hours at the Memorial

absorbing the tragic history of a young nation that had lost too many to the horrors of war. It never failed to move him.

Charles Dancer had called again and asked that they meet in the First World War gallery, just off the main entrance. When Dunkley arrived Dancer was contemplating a white landing boat, scarred with bullet holes from the day it approached the beach at Gallipoli.

'Imagine it, Harry ...' Dancer tried to conjure up century-old spirits. 'The boys in this open boat. And they were boys. The hellfire raining down on them. The noise. Friends dying around them. Yet they go on, driven by a sense of duty. To their country. To each other.'

As he turned to drive his message home, Dunkley could see this place also moved the flint-hard intelligence man. He was beginning to get a sense of what drove Dancer: he saw himself in the long line of warriors who'd guarded the nation.

'Never ever forget the sacrifice made over generations to ensure this country's stayed free,' Dancer stressed. 'People like Keating argue that the First World War wasn't our fight. Well, sometimes a fight chooses you. And the boys who died in that war perished in the belief they were fighting for a good cause.

'Their country, their friends, their way of life and maybe even quaint old notions of Empire. Those are things worth fighting for, Harry. Their sacrifice was noble and should be venerated. We can't look back from this distance and judge them. If they were following the wrong cause, it's the politicians and generals who should stand condemned by history. The footsoldiers were honourable men. Heroes.'

Dunkley walked to the bow of the boat to examine one of the ragged holes where a bullet from a Turkish Mauser had ripped through the metal of the hull, just above the waterline.

'You're sounding quite sentimental today, Charles. I like military history lessons. But I suspect that ain't the reason you called me here.'

'It's not history, Harry. War is always with us. It's sometimes hot, sometimes cold. Sometimes you see it and sometimes it's a secret war with invisible trenches. Right now the frontline is just over there.'

Dancer turned and pointed south, in the direction of the new embassy being built by the Chinese. He pulled a small handful of prints from his jacket pocket.

'Have a look at these, Harry. And yes, they are yours to keep – and publish.'

There were three photos, all aerial shots taken from directly above the new Chinese embassy compound.

'Jesus, how did you get these, Charles? A spy satellite?'

'Hardly.' He smiled. 'That kind of technology is a bit expensive. Actually, Defence finally put that RAAF hot-air balloon to good use. We tried a few times before the winds were on our side. It drifted right over the embassy site, and the Chinese were none too happy.'

Dunkley flicked through the crisp colour pics, each showing a different aspect of the embassy compound. In one, three men in white overalls were shovelling inside a deep trench. A black pipe was being laid down the middle. The work looked difficult and dangerous.

'I'm assuming these guys don't have their union cards.'

'Very funny, Harry. I suspect you're right. The Chinese appear to have brought their OH&S habits from home. But we've had a close look at the work and, coupled with other pictures and information I can't share, we believe that site will mostly be used as a communications hub. It will gather and distribute intelligence.'

Dancer moved to examine a glass case displaying some of the hand weapons used in the First World War. He seemed quite taken by a vicious-looking trench knife that married a wickedly sharp blade with a knuckle-duster handle.

'Inventive.'

'Brutal,' Harry replied.

'Well, if I'd been in the trenches I would have wanted one of those. Each war calls for new and better weapons. And in the current war our man in the lake was well-equipped for battle.'

Dancer had lowered his voice and Dunkley stepped closer to the case.

'As you know, Lin An came to Australia on a diplomatic passport; his occupation was listed as construction worker. Turns out he was a cyber-spy, one of China's best. He was attached to Unit 61398, an arm of China's People's Liberation Army. Its headquarters have been tracked to a building in Shanghai.

'Harry, that building is the source of thousands of cyber-attacks launched by the PLA against dozens of countries and numerous corporations.'

Dunkley had read reports on the growth in China's cyber-armies. He also knew that cautious governments and corporations were reluctant to admit to security breaches. So people were in the dark about the scale of the problem – and whether it was driven by states, criminal syndicates or thrillseekers.

'Charles, I'm no great shakes on computing but can't you hack into a system from anywhere in the world? Like those teenage nerds who bring down New York banking systems from their bedrooms?'

Dancer tapped the glass case holding the array of weapons.

'All these things are harmless, you know, Harry. Here behind the glass. They're made with deadly purpose but only become dangerous when they're wielded with deadly intent. But if I were to smash the glass, pick up a gun, load it and point it at you? Well, you'd get a whole new perspective on the weapon.'

Dancer squatted beside the case and pointed out a long-barrelled pistol near the bottom of the display.

'I'd pick that one, by the way. It's a variant of the German Luger that came out in 1917. The Parabellum M17. It can hold thirty rounds. Beautiful. You have to admire the Germans.'

'What's your point?'

Dancer rose in a swift fluid movement that belied his fifty-nine years.

'Computers are just another weapons system. To be dangerous they have to be operated by someone with evil intent. To be deadly they have to be able to defeat the trenches and castle walls we build to defend ourselves. Our most precious secrets are very well defended. To get at those, Harry, you need someone to open the door.

'Lin An's memory stick reveals that the Chinese have managed to crack some of our most secure communications. Not everything. But given he was trying to defect, I assume the USB was just a taster. God knows what the Chinese have. If Lin An hadn't jumped the fence we would be none the wiser. And we still have no idea where the hole in our defences is.'

Dunkley pondered the menacing contents of the display case.

'So someone has broken the glass and is about to use our own weapons against us?'

'It would appear so. And the glass was broken from the inside.'

The next day, Dunkley's story ran prominently on page one, above the fold, accompanied by a trio of sharply detailed photos.

SNAPPED: CHINA'S SECRET SPY MISSION

China's new embassy in Canberra is a sophisticated spy-base that poses a direct threat to Australia's national security, senior intelligence officials fear.

A series of photographs, obtained exclusively by *The Australian*, reveals the secret construction works that will form part of a hi-tech eavesdropping hub.

The Australian has also confirmed that the Chinese official who drowned in Lake Burley Griffin this month was a high-ranking cyber-spy. Lin An, aged in his thirties, has been identified as a member of the Shanghai-based cyber-command centre, Unit 61398.

It is understood Mr Lin was planning to defect and was carrying information that suggests China has compromised some of Australia's deepest secrets.

Officials say former prime minister Catriona Bailey ignored National Security Committee advice when she gave China the go-ahead to build its new embassy with an imported workforce.

Martin Toohey re-read the story as he subconsciously fiddled with the knot of his Armani tie. George Papadakis recognised the sign that his boss was agitated.

'How come Dunkley knows more about our intelligence than I do?' the PM thundered. 'And why is it that someone in the intelligence community has decided to parade their concerns on his front page? That's a crime. If they have a beef, why don't they come to me?'

Papadakis gave voice to what they were both thinking.

'Maybe they're not on our side.'

CHAPTER THIRTY-ONE

Melbourne

Even before she'd stepped out of her St Kilda apartment, Alison Cox suspected the gods were conspiring against her. The day had started badly when her Remington flamed out. She'd had the hairdryer less than a week and wasted fifteen minutes searching for its warranty slip.

It was closing in on 7am and she scurried to catch a 122 tram. A half-hour later, she was juggling a half-eaten croissant and a coffee as she waited for another tram to Docklands.

The ANZ's Melbourne office was the headquarters for the bank's information systems. Cox was Manager, Network Behavioural Analysis – a job title that took a fair bit of explaining at dinner parties.

'We are the new vault walls,' she would say.

A small team was under her watch, charged with ensuring that tens of millions of dollars in daily transactions were secure.

She'd been hired six months earlier, as part of a big push to bolster ANZ's defences against cyber-criminals.

It was nearly 7.45am when she walked into her office and the overnight traffic flows were being analysed by her team.

She examined the summary sheet. 'Volumetric flows are normal.'

An hour and a half later, as Cox was convening her first meeting of the day, the first sign of trouble appeared. It was 9.11am when her team identified a spike in traffic on the internet banking system. It was manageable.

Two minutes later, her phone buzzed. 'Alison – my office, now please.'

Wendy Chang was ANZ's high-powered chief information officer, a brilliant analyst recruited to overhaul creaky security systems.

'What's happening with this uptick in traffic?' She was pointing to a graph on one of her computer screens that was blinking madly.

'Not certain at this stage, Wendy. It's certainly a big increase; we are monitoring and trying to isolate it now.'

'Okay, keep me posted. Thanks.'

Cox walked back to her office, stopping briefly to talk with a colleague about Thursday night drinks. The chat was interrupted by her deputy.

'You need to see this, Alison. It's going haywire.'

It was 9.45am. ANZ's internet banking system was being bombarded with wall-to-wall requests.

Customer service was starting to receive irate phone calls as frustrated customers tried and failed to log on to the bank's internet system, bogged down by a massive increase in traffic.

Cox's phone rang – it was her boss, and she wanted her back.

'What's going on?' Chang asked.

'It looks like a denial of service attack.' Cox furrowed her brow as she stared into the system diagnostics readout on her screen. 'And it's massive. Our computers can't keep pace. If it amps up anymore they'll start to shut down.'

'God!' Chang had been at the bank for only a year and in that time had seen very few real cases of internet sabotage. She was taking no risks.

'Okay, I'm convening a high-priority incident team. Alison, I want you and Grant in the meeting room. Five minutes.'

Chang swung around to her computer. She clicked on her email, shaking out the stress in her shoulders before composing a note to ANZ senior management.

High Incident Alert.

It appears that the bank has been hit with a cyber-attack.

The first signs were logged just after 9am.

High volume of requests on internet banking.

Customer service has slowed.

Looks like a distributed denial of service attack. Lots of 'bots'.

Not sure of its origins.

My team is monitoring and seeking to rectify.

I will issue another HIA at 11am.

Wendy

It was now 10am. Chang had convened her security team. There were six in the group and each had been through countless cyber-drills and exercises.

But this was the real deal.

'What's the latest on traffic volumes?'

Andy Taylor had the data, and flicked across his iPad screen till he found the exact figure. 'It's up 189 per cent on daily average. We're adding extra capacity but it's not ... doesn't appear to be working at the minute ...'

'Wendy ...' Cox leapt into the conversation. 'I've just had an alert from credit card transactions. They're in trouble, too.'

It was compounding. Chang was now seriously worried. The ANZ was under attack.

'Okay, give me a minute.'

She walked into her adjacent office and picked up her phone. She dialled '1' and waited a brief moment.

'John, we've got a big problem. You know we've been hit with a 'denial of service' attack. It's getting worse.'

John Griffith had been ANZ's chief executive for the past eight years. He'd kicked off his career more than thirty years earlier as a teller in the Queensland rural centre of Roma, rising through the ranks to become one of the highest paid CEOs in Australia.

'How bad, Wendy?'

'Internet banking has slowed and some portals are down. Credit card transactions are also reporting massive increase in traffic volumes and they're not coping. We're adding extra capacity where we can ... but John, I'm not sure the systems are going to cope. I've got a high-priority incident team in place;

they're next door now, and we're trying to identify and isolate where it's coming from. Hold on, just one sec, John …'

Chang turned towards an ashen-faced Cox who was holding up her iPad. She put the phone down and moved closer to see the information on the screen.

To her surprise it displayed a map of the Asia-Pacific region and a small blinking light was pulsing on a city to Australia's north.

Shanghai.

Canberra

George Papadakis's afternoon was shaken by an urgent call from the ANZ chairman.

'George, I'll be brief.' Ken Donaldson was agitated.

'In fifteen minutes we'll be issuing a formal statement to the ASX. It will announce that all of our systems have been shut down due to a technical issue with our servers. None of our customers will have access to their accounts or credit cards for the next twenty-four hours. We'll assure people that their money is safe and that normal service will resume as soon as possible.

'Now, George, I'm about to tell you something in the utmost confidence. Our systems have been attacked. We've been forced to shut them down. And we're genuinely concerned that if this news gets out it will shake customer confidence. I don't need to tell you what a run on the ANZ would mean for the entire financial system.

'We're trying to trace the origin of the attack but that's very hard as whoever is behind this has recruited zombie computers from around the world. But we know this much. It's very sophisticated and our guys believe that only a state would have the resources. Everyone here in Melbourne is pretty sure it's coming from China.'

Papadakis raced into the Prime Minister's office.

'PM ...' Papadakis was breathless. 'PM ... the ANZ is shutting down internet banking ... a massive cyber-attack ... they think it's coming from China.'

Toohey looked exhausted.

'And I just got off the phone to the head of the stock exchange. It's suspending trading twenty minutes early and blaming it on some vague computer malfunction. It's not true. Their computers were overloaded by a denial of service attack. They think it's China too.'

The two men grappled with the bombshell.

'First air-traffic control, now this.' Toohey broke the silence. 'What could we have done to piss off the Chinese so much that they would do this? It just doesn't make sense.'

Papadakis responded cautiously. 'Well, I'm guessing. But we trumpet the US alliance, and then allow American troops on our soil. This while relations between the US and China are about as bad as they have ever been. Maybe it's a warning.'

'And we're supposed to do what? Just roll over and cop it? Christ, I do that every day in this place. I'm jack of it. We need to send a message of our own.'

Toohey thumped his desk.

'Martin, what can we possibly do to cause them any kind of grief? And this is the important bit, mate – what can we do that's deniable?'

The Prime Minister turned to his trusted lieutenant and smiled.

'George, get me the CFMEU.'

CHAPTER THIRTY-TWO

Canberra

The steel handcuffs dug into the soft flesh of wrists shackled to a medieval wooden truss. Leather straps bound his ankles, stretching his pale body into a naked 'X' framed in a rectangle. Livid red marks striped his back.

Jonathan Robbie was used to being flogged by parliamentarians but this was very different.

A riding crop lashed the journalist's buttocks, delivering a small dose of pleasure and plenty of pain.

'Arrrhhh!'

'Scream, bitch!' yelled his tormentor, whose ardour was growing with each whack.

Emily Brooks was a study in dominatrix chic. Thigh-high black boots tapered to six-inch, silver-encased stiletto heels. Rock-hard muscles met a taut arse, bare save for the sliver of a lipstick-red leather thong. Her toned and tanned torso was also bare and a black studded bra scarcely contained breasts that seemed too pert for her forty-eight years. Her hands and arms were encased in over-the-elbow gloves that neatly matched the none-too-subtle shade of the thong. A studded dog collar circled the Opposition leader's neck.

Brooks paused to admire the criss-cross pattern she'd imprinted on her lover's flesh and searched for a patch of unmarked skin. She found her spot and delivered a diagonal welt from right hip to left thigh with, perhaps, an excess of enthusiasm.

'Shit! That really hurt,' yelped her increasingly unwilling accomplice. The pair had agreed on a safe word before the sex play began and now Robbie decided to tap the mat.

'Kittens!' he squealed.

'Oh, has the little petal had enough?' sneered Brooks. 'I was just getting warmed up.'

'I know, my love, but we did discuss this.' Robbie was struggling to get his hands free. 'You know I'm uncomfortable with the handcuffs. I prefer rope or stockings, so I can get loose if I have to. Right now I feel ... well, trapped.'

'Don't you trust me, sweetie?' Brooks purred close to his ear.

The answer was no. He was terrified. The tingle of excitement had turned to a shiver of fear.

'Of course I trust you,' he lied. 'So "Kittens", my dear. Let me down.'

'But I can't do that just yet, Jonnie. I have something I wanted to talk about. And a special treat.'

'You want to chat? Let's get a coffee.'

'I needed your full attention, dear. I was very disappointed with your story on our asylum seeker policy. I thought it was a bit unfair. You made me sound like a monster.'

'Well, threatening to use the navy to sink asylum seeker boats is a touch extreme. I was tame by comparison with the others.'

'But you know I wouldn't do it. I just think we need to show some real steel to ensure no one makes that terribly unsafe journey. Sometimes what seems like cruelty is really the best way of saying I love you. So I'm disappointed in you, Jonnie ... but, don't worry, you'll get your special treat anyway.'

There was a dull buzz as something battery-powered was switched on.

'What's that?' Robbie's heart was pounding. 'What are you doing?'

Brooks strayed into his view with her hands behind her, looking at once both fearsome and coy.

'Just a little something I found in Fyshwick.' She slowly pulled her hands from behind her back, revealing a breathtakingly dangerous-looking sex toy.

'No, dear, no,' Robbie pleaded. 'You can't be serious. And this isn't funny. Kittens' ... Kittens' playtime is over now!'

'My dear, playtime has just begun.'

'Nooooooooooooo!'

CHAPTER THIRTY-THREE

Canberra

Dean Hall dubbed it Operation Trojan Horse. The local head of the militant building union had been dreaming of this sweet moment for a year. Everything had been planned to the minute.

The Chinese embassy site had been off limits to the Construction, Forestry, Mining and Energy Union, and that chafed. Instead the Chinese had shipped in their own labour – on diplomatic visas – to build their new headquarters behind a wall of secrecy. Several aerial photos showed, though, that the Chinese had a low regard for workplace safety.

What fucking building site would wrap razor wire around its perimeter?

The Chinese had banned Australian workers from the site; not even the ACT's chief building inspector had been allowed to run the ruler over it. The gates were only ever opened to foreigners when the Chinese took delivery of building materials. This morning, the embassy had organised a delivery of blue metal. The supplier had been instructed to be at the front gate at 9.30am precisely. It was now 9.26.

The truck pulled up and the driver sounded the horn. The gate was unbolted and one of the Chinese security guards emerged. He recognised the driver but motioned in Hall's direction and shook his head.

'He comes in while I unload, mate,' the driver shot back. 'New union rules.'

The goon looked suspiciously at Hall but went back to the gates and pushed them both open. The diesel engine rattled into gear and the truck rolled fifty metres inside the wire.

The union chief yelled into his mobile. 'Trojan Horse is go, go, go!'

The tarp covering the tipper was thrown back and twelve fearsome organisers leapt into action. Two ran to the gates and held them open while the rest fanned out across the compound.

Once the gates were secured a small convoy appeared from a hundred metres away, led by Channel Nine's live links van. Harry Dunkley was in the next car with a News Corp photographer.

Hall waited until the cameraman was out of the Nine van and rolling before he grabbed the loudhailer. It squealed into life.

'This site has been declared black!' he yelled. 'We believe there are serious breaches of occupational health and safety on this site and we're here to ensure that's rectified.'

A few Chinese workers tried to intervene but they were hopelessly outgunned.

A chant broke out from the brothers who had unfurled a giant CFMEU banner and were standing defiantly under its proud sail.

'Aussie jobs! Aussie jobs! Aussie jobs!'

Dunkley spotted a tough-looking Chinese national on the edge of the melee. He was dressed in a suit and talking into his mobile.

'Ray, take a few pics of him, please,' the reporter called to his snapper.

He edged closer, determined to try and ask a few questions while the union bovver boys were playing havoc with the bewildered Chinese workforce.

'Hey, mate! You got a moment?'

The tough guy shot Dunkley a lethal look with his jet-black eyes. Then he saw the snapper and turned and walked quickly into one of the half-finished buildings.

After thirty minutes of mayhem, Hall called the union members together for one last show of strength. And a pic fac for the cameras.

'We, the CFMEU, will never allow standards to be compromised. Too many workers have been hurt, even killed, in the ACT during the past few years due to lax occupational health and safety standards. The Chinese Government should get this message: You play in Australia under our rules.'

The dirty dozen cheered and offered some last-minute fist-shaking for the cameras. Then they climbed aboard the tipper. A sandy-haired thug tilted his head to the skies and began to sing.

The workers' flag is deepest red
It shrouded oft our martyred dead ...

Just over a kilometre away, Martin Toohey and George Papadakis watched as the protest played out on Sky. They'd brushed off a minister's tap at the door as they sat engrossed in the Prime Minister's office.

'Do you think he knows that China actually has a red flag and that it's already a workers' paradise?' Papadakis asked.

'I think the irony is lost on him.' Toohey couldn't recall when he had last enjoyed Sky's political coverage so much.

'The Chinese won't be happy about this,' Papadakis said.

'George, how can we be held responsible for the actions of a militant union?' Toohey couldn't suppress a laugh. Victories had been few and far between. 'Believe me, the CFMEU will be happy to take all the blame ... and the credit. They'll be printing T-shirts with "Hall's Heroes" stamped on them before the end of the month.'

Papadakis shook his head in admiration. 'So, Prime Minister. The Senkakus have come to Yarralumla. Nice work.'

CHAPTER THIRTY-FOUR

Canberra

The clip of shoes on the hard polished floor announced the arrival of Chinese Ambassador, Tian Qichen, in the R.G. Casey building. He was greeted by a junior official waiting at the reception desk.

'Mr Joyce is expecting you, Ambassador.'

Tian offered a weak smile and nodded for the underling to lead the way. He was in no mood for banter. In his briefcase was a démarche: the highest form of official complaint from a foreign embassy to a host government. He'd been instructed to hand-deliver it to the Secretary of the Department of Foreign Affairs and Trade and to protest in the strongest possible terms against the invasion of Chinese sovereign territory by union thugs. Australian–Sino relations were at their lowest ebb since Catriona Bailey had delivered a lecture in Mandarin to Peking University students lamenting the treatment of Tibet.

In his fourth-floor office, DFAT secretary David Joyce, armed with an official statement from the Prime Minister's office, gazed through expansive windows to Parliament House, just up the hill, as he waited for the diplomat.

Joyce had known Tian for years. He'd performed his professional duty by welcoming the Ambassador to Australia with a Sunday evening barbecue at his Forrest home. He quite enjoyed his company.

But the Secretary knew this encounter would be bruising.

'Ambassador, very nice to see you. I hope you and Ms Weng are enjoying your first weeks in our country.'

Tian said nothing but placed his black briefcase theatrically on Joyce's desk and flicked its two locks open. Reaching inside, he removed a letter. A single sheet of paper was embossed with official Chinese Government letterhead.

'Mr Joyce, I am sure you are aware of my government's strong displeasure concerning yesterday's events. They were unacceptable. Needless to say, they have done nothing to help negotiations over a free-trade deal.'

He glanced at the official letter as if seeking guidance.

'The embassy site is contaminated; its role has been compromised. The Chinese Government is demanding another block of land suitable for our new building.'

Joyce had his own piece of paper, stamped with the Australian crest and signed by Martin Toohey. He decided to match Tian's theatrics and read some of it aloud.

'The Prime Minister says he regrets the incident and notes that the "actions of the workers were not sanctioned by anyone in government". But as a Labor prime minister he understands "the genuine affront that all decent union officials" would feel at what they saw as "illegal work practices on Australian soil by a foreign power".'

The Ambassador immediately recognised the wording. It was almost a carbon copy of the language used by Beijing to describe the occupation of the Senkaku Islands by the Chinese fishermen.

Joyce lowered the paper and looked over his half-moon glasses at Tian.

'As for the land, Mr Ambassador, that is not within my gift. I will pass on your request to the Prime Minister and the National Capital Authority. But you should be aware that diplomatic land in the capital's dress circle is in short supply.'

The Ambassador responded carefully. 'I came to Australia hoping to build on our excellent relationship, one that has proved very beneficial. The Prime Minister's announcement on the gas deal was evidence of this deepening friendship.'

'And we want to continue to enjoy a good relationship,' Joyce said. 'But, to be frank, some in our government believe that the recent attacks on our aviation and banking systems originated in China. If so, they would not be the actions of a friend.'

Tian looked out at the Parliament building, its enormous flag stretched full in the late afternoon breeze.

'It is ironic, Mr Joyce. If what you say is true about the invasion of our embassy, then this truly is a land where the workers run the government.' He turned back to the Secretary. 'I thought that was my country, not yours.'

CHAPTER THIRTY-FIVE

Canberra

Our man in Canberra Dunkly on fire. Must be in line for Gold
Walkley. About time.

The fact Rupert Murdoch had misspelled his name couldn't dent
Harry Dunkley's pride at featuring in a tweet from the great man.
The reporter had been delivering a regular supply of white-hot
scoops for the *Oz*. Earning a commendation from News Corp's
global chief was icing on a very tasty cake.

Harry had almost morphed into the very thing he loathed –
a celebrity journalist – and was in fierce demand with voracious
television and radio networks, always on the lookout for new talent.
He'd become a darling of 2GB with the Sydney radio station's hosts
clamouring to have him on their programs to buttress the network's
'Fortress Australia' mentality. Alan Jones had even asked him to

front a 'Buy Back the Farm' campaign he was planning to launch the following week, an invitation Dunkley had politely declined.

Jones had then dangled a bigger carrot.

'Harry, I'm backing a new party – Australia First – that will run candidates in every electorate at the September election. C'mon, you can be part of this – even become prime minister,' Jones had told him over tea and cucumber sandwiches at his apartment overlooking Circular Quay.

Again, Dunkley demurred.

But it was true that public opinion was turning. The Lowy Institute's annual poll on Australian global attitudes showed that the nation was becoming more suspicious of China.

Dunkley's stories were tapping into the lizard-brain fears of Australia. Old prejudices stirred. The internet was alive with the worst of the human spirit. Dark anonymous forces had established a blog with a subtle title: 'The Yellow Peril'. Its motto? Revive White Australia.

Dunkley fretted about the extreme end of this debate. In every interview he repeated the mantra that he was 'not anti-China'. But in his reflective moments he was pleased to be at the vanguard of those sounding the alarm over the rise of the communist nation and the shift of power from West to East.

And when he was honest with himself, he knew what was driving him.

They killed Kimberley.

He tugged a jacket over his shoulders and put a protective arm around his girlfriend as they left the Dendy cinema in Civic.

It was closing on 9.30pm and Celia Mathieson had insisted on seeing the latest Ryan Gosling flick, an escapist fantasy that he'd found vapid.

'I liked it, Harry. Yeah, it wasn't *War and Peace*, but so what?' Celia suggested a quick bite at one of the restaurants along Bunda Street, but as they peered into Wagamama they saw the staff putting up the 'Closed' sign. It was an all-too-familiar scenario in the national capital, which still lacked the big-city vibe of Sydney, Melbourne, even Brisbane.

Still, the silken touch of Celia's blouse as they strolled along the spine of this pretend CBD was compensation enough. Their relationship was still in its early phase: a few movies, a nice dinner, a picnic on the lake, several overnight stays in her Kingston apartment and a handful in his untidy pad.

Tonight offered similar promise.

'What about a drink, Cel? Cube should be open.'

'Ooh, you are being adventurous, old man. Didn't think you liked gay bars?'

'Ease up. I'm not your typical boring middle-aged hung-up male.'

She stopped and swung in front of him, blocking his path as she hooked a long lingering kiss on his lips. 'We'll see about that, Harry.'

He was entranced, caught in her web, exposed to the prying eyes of a city that traded on gossip.

Right then and there, though, the rough-and-tumble journalist, the ace scribe whom Uncle Rupert thought was God's gift, couldn't give a flying fuck.

215

CHAPTER THIRTY-SIX

Canberra

The pink brush with ivory inlay swept across her raven-black hair, fixing every strand in place. A whiff of perfume – musky vanilla – roused a memory. Her first time with Bruce, some three decades ago … they had been so young, and hadn't known how precious and fleeting that gift was.

In the confines of her room, Weng Meihui dabbed on makeup with the skill of an artisan and frowned. She turned on a harsh light and directed its glare towards her slender throat.

She was in her early fifties and still alluring to men. But this southern light troubled her. It revealed too much, highlighting every hint of age.

Weng was unsettled.

How long will I be of use to them?

The State had raised her, schooled her, trained her, employed her, housed and cared for her. She was lucky; she'd been chosen for her intellect as much as her physical appeal. And she had repaid their faith, every time, without question.

No man was her hero, and she was no one's servant. She was flint-tough, sharp-minded and had used her quick wit more than a few times to escape difficult situations.

There were two soft knocks at the door. 'May I come in?'

He was here. Her consort. Her partner. Their choice. Tian Qichen entered without waiting for her response.

'I was pleased when I heard that you would be accompanying me to Australia. How are you enjoying this place?' he asked.

She was unsure how to answer. After all, it had only been a matter of weeks and the assignment, still in its early stages, was not without its challenges.

He sensed her hesitation and stepped in to break the silence.

'Your mission with the parliamentarian has gone well. Beijing is pleased.'

She smiled.

Of course they are.

'Yes, I am quite happy that he decided to sit as an independent in the federal parliament.'

'Did he take much convincing?'

She hesitated. There were things that she needed to keep to herself.

Yes, he was a willing accomplice.

He repeated the question. 'Did he take much convincing?' He'd moved closer, bringing with him a faint smell of mint and wax.

'No, not much at all. He understood that sitting as an independent would allow him to leverage that position and to put pressure on the Prime Minister. And remember, he is no special friend of the Americans,' Weng said.

'No, of course not. Not a special friend.'

Tian looked around the room as if searching for something. He turned back to her.

'You have feelings for him?'

Weng felt a tinge of shame.

'Of course not. This is my … profession.'

'And I have always admired you for that. You are very skilled and much respected.'

He moved even closer and reached out to stroke her hair. 'You are very skilled … and very beautiful.'

'You are kind.' Weng turned to face him and smiled. 'But I am getting old and the light in this country does me no favours. Soon my country won't have any use for me.'

'You are being too hard on yourself.' He clumsily reached out to grasp her hands.

'Don't.' She pulled away, feeling nothing for him, surprised at the cold slap of her voice.

His face hardened.

'As you wish, Ms Weng.'

She rose from her chair and looked down as she walked past him to the bathroom.

'Please, Ambassador, close the door on the way out.'

CHAPTER THIRTY-SEVEN

Sydney

The dashboard lights of the Mercedes SLK softly lit Elizabeth Scott's face as she negotiated the sweep left onto Manly Road. It was late and the call, though unexpected, had been welcome. They'd arranged to meet in a carpark near Orso Restaurant, just off the Spit Bridge and a short drive from her Manly home.

Scott had come close to quitting Parliament after being dumped as Opposition leader eighteen months earlier. Her husband had begged her to return to business, where she had made her fortune.

But Scott could not bear admitting failure. She believed she still had plenty to offer and was the best person to lead the Liberal Party, which was being dragged hard to the right by the odious Emily Brooks.

Redemption in the mainstream had come slowly for Scott, though she'd found to her surprise that she'd been quickly taken up by the luvvies of the Left, who saw her as the civilised face of conservative politics. These were the same people, of course, who had pilloried her every move when she'd actually led the Liberal Party.

What had really liberated her was being on the backbench. Better still, her willingness to act as a commentator on her party and leader had put her in high demand with the media. Now, eighteen months after her demise, opinion polls showed she was among the most recognised and popular politicians in the nation.

Scott had learned brutal lessons about politics and she did not intend to play fair. She would exploit her wealth and had engaged a private investigator to comb through her rival's life.

Now the PI claimed to have hit paydirt.

Crossing the bridge, Scott turned left onto Parriwi Rd and into the carpark. She pulled up her convertible alongside a smart-looking Ford.

Thank God someone still buys Australian.

A middle-aged man limped from the car. His demeanour and clothing bore the unmistakable stamp of the ex-copper. He opened the passenger's door of the Mercedes and climbed in.

'Very nice set of wheels. I'm obviously not charging you enough.'

'Hah!' Scott wasn't in the mood for small talk. 'What do you have for me?'

'Gold. Pure unadulterated gold.'

'Photos?'

'Better. Video.'

'What? How did you …? No, don't tell me how. Just tell me what.'

'I'll tell ya, love. I saw some strange shit in my time at Vice down the Cross but this makes *Underbelly* look like an episode of *Lassie*.'

CHAPTER THIRTY-EIGHT

Canberra

'Welcome to the best Japanese restaurant in Canberra, Harry; great to see you.'

Akito Mori's familiar shape framed the doorway. He was officially listed as the counsellor for public affairs at the Japanese embassy but Dunkley suspected he was the station chief for Japan's spy agency, the Cabinet Intelligence and Research Office, or Naicho.

'Akito, nice to see you too. Sorry I'm late. I hope you got my messages.'

'Don't mention it, just make sure you sign the visitors' book. That is the one thing His Excellency cares about.'

The book lay open on a table in the entrance hall of the Ambassador's residence. Harry had inscribed his name in it many times. He had become firm friends with the previous Ambassador when the two had conspired on a series of stories that had infuriated Catriona Bailey during her first trip overseas in 2008.

Ambassador Satoki Tenaka was waiting in the informal dining room, a glass of champagne in his hand. Dunkley smiled as he greeted the diplomat.

'Apologies, Your Excellency, I was held up at work.'

'Harry, you know it's Satoki.' The Ambassador bowed his head slightly as they shook hands. 'If you keep calling me Your Excellency, I will fear you have forgotten my name.'

Tenaka was of middle height and the flecks of grey in the thick hair framing his boyish face were the only hint of his more than sixty years. Like his predecessor, Tenaka had a storyteller's capacity to make the complexity of the world understandable. Dunkley looked forward to these dinners because he always learned something useful.

After several minutes of chatter about family and work, Dunkley asked Tenaka to revisit a story he had told before, from his years as a junior diplomat in Singapore. The journalist wanted to have the history of China's rise clear in his head.

'The Chinese were fascinated by Singapore in the late '80s and early '90s and there were many delegations from Beijing,' Tenaka said. 'Deng Xiaoping was contemplating how to manage the growth of China. In Singapore he saw a state that had everything he wanted: one-party rule; no effective opposition; and, apparently, little corruption. But most important was the social harmony that was ensured because the people were wealthy. And that was the bargain he decided to strike with the Chinese people: "We will make you rich and you will obey us".'

The Ambassador had exchanged his champagne for sake and he swallowed a mouthful from a delicate cup.

'So far it has worked, but the Chinese are always wary of their people. They know they are one mistake away from internal unrest. So they need an external enemy to ensure the people focus their anger outwards.'

'And although we focus on the rhetoric aimed at the US or Australia,' Dunkley said, 'Japan is the country China has its major grievance with.'

Tenaka put down his cup.

'We fought two wars in fifty years between 1894 and 1945,' he said. 'In the first we humiliated the Qing Dynasty and became the major power in Asia.'

The Ambassador took off his glasses and rubbed his eyes, as if he was recalling a personal, painful memory.

'The second war was from 1937 to 1945. We occupied China and … many terrible things happen in war. Some in China think the Americans ended the battle too soon and that China's war with Japan is not settled. There is an anti-Japanese museum in Beijing and although we have apologised many, many times for the … excesses … it will never be enough for some.'

Dunkley had more than a little sympathy for China's anger. He had been horrified by what he had read about the Japanese occupation and the pictures of countless corpses.

'Perhaps as many as twenty million Chinese died.' Dunkley knew he was treading on sensitive ground.

Tenaka put his rimless glasses back on and met Dunkley's gaze.

'As I said, war is a terrible thing. More than two million of my people died in the Second World War. Over 200,000 died when the two atomic bombs were dropped. But America would argue that they ended a war that would have claimed many more lives. Was what they did right, Harry Dunkley?'

That was a question Dunkley had contemplated many times: can brutality be justified for a greater good? He had no answer, just more questions.

'So is it just history that's driving this new nationalistic push from Beijing?' he asked.

'No. A large part of it is driven by economic concerns. China's growth is slowing. If the people do not feel the benefits of growth they will see only its costs, like huge damage to the environment and displacement. And they will become restless. Then there is the direct competition between our two nations for energy.'

Tenaka motioned that the journalist should stir some more wasabi into his soy sauce to go with his sashimi, but Dunkley declined. Tenaka shrugged.

'So this new leadership embodies three things: a real and deep sense of grievance expressed as a determination to retake China's role as the centre of the world; and, on an immediate practical level, maintaining a reliable energy supply and ensuring its people are controlled and directed.'

Dunkley had spent enough hours at the Japanese Ambassador's table to know that the ill-will between China and Japan wasn't a one-way street. Japan's foreign policy was aimed at getting the US to use its power to box China in and restrain its growth.

'But Japan has its own grievances with China, doesn't it, Satoki?'

'Japan is only eight hundred kilometres from China. We can feel it. Its rubbish washes up on our shores; its pollution stains our skies. We have economic problems of our own and our key concern is also energy. Since Fukushima, things have got much worse. We have to import 75 per cent of our fuel. So we need secure suppliers, like Australia, and we need secure trade routes. Those routes run through the East China Sea. A rapacious China threatens all that. Never forget, there are two powers in East Asia, Harry, and they are rivals.'

As usual, Mori had deferred to his boss and remained silent for much of the meal. He finally spoke.

'Things are very bad in the East China Sea, very bad. China is testing us. And we have the views of our own people to consider. We cannot be seen to retreat from Japanese land – it would bring down the government.'

Dunkley didn't doubt it. Tenaka dabbed his mouth with his napkin and pointed to a world globe on the mantelpiece that showed Japan and China facing outwards.

'And, thanks to the internet, the front line in this conflict is the whole world, as you point out in your many fine articles. But to be frank we are very disappointed with the response of your government both to the provocations we have suffered over the Senkakus and the virtual attacks on your own homeland. We wonder if China's wealth is blinding Australia's government to the very real and present dangers.'

Mori lowered his voice. 'The battle in Australia isn't confined to the internet. We were most interested in the pictures you published after the union raid on the new embassy. Do you remember this man?'

He handed over an enlarged version of the picture Dunkley had asked his snapper to take of the be-suited man inside the construction site.

'Yes, I remember him. He clearly wasn't mixing concrete. And he scarpered when I tried to front him.'

'We know him. He is attached to the Communist Party's Commission for Discipline Inspection. It is a secretive internal investigation unit that interrogates and disciplines party members. It operates independently of the police and is known for its brutality. This man is a Communist Party stormtrooper, Harry. His only role is as a torturer and a killer. So why is he here in Canberra?'

Harry looked long and hard at the picture.

'I have no idea.'

'Well,' Tenaka said, 'as you say. He's not here mixing concrete.'

It was very late when the Ambassador saw Dunkley out. Tenaka motioned to the visitors' book as they walked through the entrance hall to the front steps.

'Did you sign my book?'

'Yes, Your Excellency.'

The two men laughed and as they shook hands Dunkley had one final question for the Ambassador.

'Will there be a war?'

'We hope not, Harry. But we are planning for it.'

CHAPTER THIRTY-NINE

Sydney

It was like stepping into a sauna fully clothed. Sydney's steamy heat engulfed Paul Mahoney as he emerged from the air-conditioned cool of the Great Southern on Thomas Street.

His mood was as dark as the schooner of stout he'd left, half drunk, on the bar.

A screech of tyres snapped his introspection.

'Look out fuckwit!' Mahoney slammed his hand down on the bonnet of a petrol-blue Subaru WRX as it swerved, dangerously close, running a red light and playing chicken with a crowd of pedestrians on the busy Chinatown street. The driver proffered a one-finger salute as he sped off.

Mahoney shook his head and continued his trudge back to the ABC's head office at Ultimo. Typically he was angry. Angry at the inner-city obsessions of his employer and its employees. Angry that he had moved from Canberra on the promise of a bright future in TV only to find himself back on the treadmill of radio current affairs.

And he was pissed off with himself for being angry, knowing that others would kill to have his secure job in one of the last bastions of serious journalism.

It was Friday afternoon and he'd hoped to slope off for a long lunch only to be dragged back by a radio producer demanding that he file for the ABC's flagship drive-time current affairs show, *PM*.

'But I told you, Sasha, I don't have a story,' he complained.

'And I told you, Paul, right now I don't have a show. So get your arse back here and find one.'

'Bastard,' he'd said, after he was sure she had hung up. He'd left two of his colleagues propping up the bar. They worked for *Four Corners* and their story had gone to air on Monday, so they were in a week-long wind-down before the hunt for another yarn began.

Both had been full of what they saw as the most recent management travesty.

The broadcaster had been given millions to set up a fact-checking unit, and with space at a premium it had usurped rooms from the children's show *Giggle and Hoot*. The outraged kiddie producers weren't good at sharing and demanded new digs. Management had rolled over and decided to punt them up to the third floor, taking valuable space from *Four Corners*.

The multi-award-winning journalists were incensed at being ordered to hand over precious real estate to a blue owl and a clown, so the ABC's HR unit, People and Learning, had been hauled in to mediate.

That was bad enough, but all hell broke loose when the *Giggle and Hoot* team discovered they would now have to share facilities with their hated *Play School* rivals. Soon, several nasty incidents had been logged with mediators and open warfare broke out after a damaging leak that was being sheeted home to Rhys from *Play School*.

James Jeffrey, the acerbic wordsmith behind *The Australian's* 'Strewth' column, was on the receiving end of a corker of a yarn. The puppeteer behind the blue owl, 'Hoot', had suffered a recurrence of a nasty case of RSI. It had flared during a wrestling match with a *Play School* producer over the ownership of half a packet of Scotch Finger biscuits.

As a result the puppeteer could no longer move his arm to the right. Which, effectively, meant that Hoot's neck was partially paralysed. The puppeteer blamed his injury on ABC mismanagement, demanded compensation and refused to stand down. He called in the union to ensure the show's script was modified around his disability.

Human resource bureaucrats now vetted every *Giggle and Hoot* script, enforcing an order that Hoot never look to the right.

The conservative commentariat lapped it up. A missive from management warning of serious consequences for leaking lobbed in Jeffrey's inbox thirty seconds after it had been sent, marked 'Strictly Confidential'.

The unsavoury dispute escalated with the kidnap of Big Ted. He was discovered ritually hanged in the boy's loos with the menacing note 'You're next, Jemima' pinned to his yellow fur.

That image brought a smile to the face of Mahoney as the ABC building hove into view. 'It could only happen here,' he thought.

As he entered the *PM* workspace in the first-floor newsroom, his phone rang. It was a number he hadn't seen in the months since he'd left Canberra.

'Elizabeth Scott, what use do you have for a retired gallery hack?'

'Now Paul, you know you were always one of my favourites and I know you can be discreet,' she purred.

Mahoney knew the tone. He was being courted for a favour.

'Well, I hope you've got a story because I have a deadline that's just an hour away.'

'Oh, I do. But you didn't hear this from me.'

'Sure, what is it?'

'In twenty minutes a video will be posted on YouTube. I'm going to give you a headstart simply by telling you where to look. The Radio National version of *PM* will have an exclusive.'

'I'm intrigued.'

'You will be more than intrigued. And, my dear, you'll owe me.'

Mahoney's mood improved immeasurably. And it soared when he saw the surprisingly graphic images of Emily Brooks and that Channel Nine grub Jonathan Robbie.

Oh, to be able to use the pictures …

Once again, he longed to work in the bright lights of television.

CHAPTER FORTY

Washington

Big Mac wiped the crumbs from his lips and lifted a sheaf of papers. 'Nancy, how do I look?'

'Like a leader going into war, sir.'

Morgan McDonald was preparing for a press conference in the Capitol building and had been rehearsing the script with his press secretary. The Republican House leader was fired up, ready to rumble.

He clapped his hands loudly, a habit that came to the fore when the adrenalin was flowing. Like now.

The Tea Party – the group of dissident, far-Right-wing republicans that McDonald controlled – was in revolt and he wasn't about to make life any easier for President Earle Jackson.

He would teach that son of a bitch what it meant to go limp-wristed.

'Right, team. Let's roll.'

Big Mac led his entourage to the media conference room, a hundred metres from his office.

It was nearing 4pm, and the press corps was getting restless, needing to prepare evening bulletins and newspaper articles.

Oh my, I am popular today.

'Ladies and gentlemen, thank you for coming.'

McDonald used to hate the press, particularly the liberal media who'd given Nixon, Reagan and Bush Mk 1 and 2 such a hard time. Obama, by comparison, had been shown easy street even though his damned healthcare package threatened to bankrupt the Stars and Stripes.

In Big Mac's eyes, the *New York Times* was America's *Pravda*.

But he'd learned the importance of forging a good working relationship with the media to ensure his political message was spread as widely as possible.

'Okay ... ready, fellas? Today I am here to announce that I am calling on President Jackson to take decisive action to ensure the United States can live within its financial means.

'America is a great world power. Our friends overseas need us now more than ever. But a weakened United States, beholden to the foreign dictates of countries that don't share our values and beliefs, cannot be allowed. That's what being in debt to the world means. As leader of the House Republicans, I will do everything within my power to ensure the US remains a force for good.

'When the President calls for the debt ceiling to be lifted, I appreciate that he believes he is acting to repair the damage inflicted on this country by the Democrats. But we can't do that without getting an assurance that big cuts to government spending are planned.

'Yes, I know the deadline to resolve this, in order to prevent a government shutdown, is drawing close.

'So tonight I will call the President and offer him a ten-point plan. This has been thrashed out with other right-thinking Republicans. It is a sign of goodwill, that we are willing to compromise.

'But we will not compromise the supremacy of the United States in world affairs. I urge my friend Earle Jackson to reconsider his weak stand on Chinese currency manipulation. If he doesn't, then, ladies and gentlemen, all bets are off.'

Several hours later President Jackson delivered a foreign policy speech to the Right-wing hawks of the American Enterprise Institute. He began with some domestic house-cleaning.

'My friends in Congress are right when they say that we should not live beyond our means. But they are wrong to try and starve this government of funds. I will bring down the deficit but that can't be done overnight.

'I have taken a call this evening from my ol' friend Big Mac … sorry, the House Majority leader, and I have agreed to sit down and discuss his ten-point plan to try and find a way to bring Washington to heel. I pledge myself to this: government will be smaller. I am happy to report that the House Leader will be coming to the White House in the morning for talks on how we can bring about this historic change. As a sign of goodwill, he has offered to pass the debt-ceiling legislation through Congress tonight.

'So, as friends do, Big Mac and I have had our disagreements. But there is one thing where we see eye to eye: the United States of America should bow to no one.

'I will be honest and say that there are many voices in my government who are urging me to back off on my demand that China play by the international road rules. They say that we should accommodate the rising power in the East. But if we let China push us around now, what will the future hold? If I step back, China will step forward and, in the end, we will retreat right across the Pacific.

'So I make another pledge tonight. I will do everything in my power to ensure the best possible relationship with the Chinese leadership. I do believe that we can live together.

'But I will not kowtow to Beijing. Given China has done nothing to increase the value of its currency, I will be putting a plan to Congress to impose tariffs on a range of Chinese goods. It will begin with motor vehicles and television sets, but the longer China refuses to act the more I will increase the scope of the tariffs.

'And tonight, in a sign of solidarity with our good friends in Japan, I have ordered two unarmed B-52s to fly over the Senkaku Islands. I also reaffirm that Japan is the rightful owner of these islands, now and forever.

'God bless our ally Japan. And God bless America.'

CHAPTER FORTY-ONE

Beijing

Jiang Xiu pulled back from the TV screen and smiled. The Americans were practically doing his job for him.

What does Jackson think he's doing? Is he that big a fool?

The Minister for Propaganda had been urging his comrades to take an even more assertive stance. Some on the Standing Committee were still sceptical and were counselling restraint. But Jiang had been deploying all official channels to ensure his aggressive message was disseminated as widely as possible.

It was working. The *People's Daily* had become almost as strident as the *Global Times*, renowned for its anti-Western tirades. Chinese nationalist spirit was stirring. Anti-US and Japan sentiment was bubbling nicely.

Online attacks against the US President had already been trending on China's own version of Twitter, Weibo. And now Earle Jackson had made a fatal error.

Jiang could not believe that Jackson had declared Japan the 'rightful owner' of the disputed islands. It was likely that this was a slip of the tongue because it was not the official position of the United States. But words were missiles in diplomacy and Jiang had already ordered CCTV's general channel to run that grab on a continuous loop. It would be used to whip up public outrage.

Just as astoundingly, Jackson had telegraphed his next move. A worthy general did not do that. Jiang assumed the B-52s would make their pass over the islands at night. That gave him all day to urge his comrades into action.

All of China was watching. After today all of the world would be watching. He picked up the red phone. A female voice answered within two rings.

'I need to see the President. This morning. For at least fifteen minutes.'

Three hours later, Jiang was led into the Hall of the Purple Light within the Zhongnanhai complex – the real seat of Chinese power. As always he marvelled at the stately architecture, and relished the rich history of the compound that had hosted many communist leaders since Mao.

Here, the past intersected with the future. An official led him into a splendid room of Qing dynasty furnishings. Their beauty papered over a dark stain on Chinese history. It was the last remnant of the Qing who fought and lost the 1894 Sino–Japanese war, signing the unequal Treaty of Shimonoseki that ceded control of Taiwan to the Japanese. That had led to the annexation of the Diaoyu Islands.

The Middle Kingdom must never allow itself to be pushed around by inferior countries.

President Meng was concluding a meeting with several senior financial advisers, and Jiang waited patiently before being ushered into his suite.

'Mr President, you have seen for yourself that the United States is determined to try to stifle our legitimate territorial claim over the Diaoyu Islands. Now they threaten to send war planes into our airspace.

'Nothing we have done comes close to such provocative action. We cannot back down. We cannot display weakness. Our people need to see that our resolve is firm.'

The President clasped his hands. He had trained Jiang well, but the next steps were the most dangerous of all.

'Comrade Jiang, I know that you are anxious to see China rise, as I am. But we must not overreach. We cannot be seen to be the aggressors. Our response must be proportional to the affront.'

Jiang signalled to an assistant, standing by the doorway, to join them. He placed two folders on the table.

'Mr President, I have a proposal for you to consider.'

CHAPTER FORTY-TWO

Western Pacific Ocean

Emanuel 'Manny' Sanchez pushed forward on the throttle and felt the surge of power as eight Pratt & Whitney TF33 engines spat into action.

Four hundred and fifty thousand pounds of aviation muscle lumbered down the runway on the mission signed off by President Jackson just two nights earlier. It was time to demonstrate support for one of the United States' most trusted friends.

It was late February and the easterlies were prevailing over the Pacific island of Guam, one of America's largest non-mainland military bases. Three hours to the north, a small outcrop of rocky islands had become the touchstone in an increasingly fraught political dance.

The US and China were at each other's throats, neither willing to cede ground as the battle between capitalism and communism reached fever pitch for the first time since the demise of the Soviet

Union. A visit to Beijing by the former Secretary of State Henry Kissinger had failed to pacify the Chinese who believed they – not the Japanese – had a rightful claim to these resource-rich grounds. Several well-credentialled analysts in Washington were suggesting a new Cold War might be developing.

Sanchez was wearing his 'sanitised' flight suit, the one with the badges of his beloved 69th Bomb Squadron hidden away, a precaution against identification if he was shot down. Two and a half years ago, Sanchez had taken a break from flying to complete his staff tour at COMTHIRDFLT in San Diego, responding to his wife's request following the birth of their son, Emanuel Jnr. But the role of Air Training Exchange Officer had failed to quench his need for high-stakes flying action. He'd sought a return transfer to the 69th within a year.

Now, back in the B-52, he felt for the reassuring grip of his 9 millimetre, and turned to the sky.

It was pushing 2200 hours and the B-52 would climb east out of Andersen Air Force Base before turning north-west. Major Sanchez felt every crack in the 11,200-foot runway as the BUFF cranked towards 155 knots.

'Tommy. You ready, brother? Black hole ahead.' Manny Sanchez spoke with the larrikin ease of an experienced pilot who lived by the motto: Work Hard, Play Harder. He and his co-pilot, Tom Danville, had flown many times out of Andersen but those first few moments when the island's visual markers gave way to the black of the Pacific could still be disorienting.

'Yeah, Manny. Let's do this.'

The two pilots were joined in the cramped cockpit by Sam Meserve, the E-Dub. The electronic warfare officer was the butt of many jokes as the crew used humour to alleviate the tension of long flights to dangerous places. Meserve served another useful purpose – he was the in-house cook.

Tonight's mission was scheduled for just under seven hours. Two B-52 bombers would fly, unarmed, to the disputed islands where they would engage in a simulated weapons drop over the largest, Uotsuri Jima. They would then return to Guam, arriving at a scheduled 0500.

Sanchez listened as radio navigator Jim McCowan chatted with the step desk, taking in the latest weather forecast. Fine and light winds. The radio crackled as air-traffic control issued final instructions. 'ICER One Two. Climb and maintain nine block 10,000.'

Sanchez lifted the proud veteran of the skies from the tarmac, muttering a silent prayer as a single bead of sweat tracked down his back.

Huan Tun-jen impatiently paced the bridge of the *Changchun*. The newly minted ship of the People's Liberation Army Navy should have been further out in the East China Sea by now.

But the Luyang Class II Type 052C destroyer, commissioned just a month earlier, had been hampered by problems with its Ukrainian-made gas turbines. The engines should have been propelling the *Changchun* along at nearly 30 knots.

Instead, it was cruising at a modest 22. Huan was battling to contain his frustration. This mission was critical.

Twelve hours earlier, Ding Haichun, the political commissar of the PLAN's East China Sea Fleet, had rung with strict instructions. The *Changchun* would sail from its base at Zhoushan City where mechanics had been working around the clock. The engines should have been fixed. But time had run out and Huan was commander of a vessel whose speed was no better than China's outdated cruisers.

Not that he was anticipating conflict on the ocean itself. This mission would rely on the vessel's Active Phased Array Radar system and its ability to track enemy targets to a distance of 150 kilometres.

Manny Sanchez scanned his instrument panel, the steam gauges that had barely changed since the late '50s. He liked to explain to novices that BUFF, the affectionate name used by B-52 crews, stood for Big Ugly Fat Fucker, laughing at the comic crudity of an airframe that would be ninety-four years old at its scheduled retirement in 2046.

A flip-down computer screen gave him a read-out on their position, the GPS-aided moving map offering a picture of the globe. It also told him the last known positions of Chinese airframes, something he sensed would come in handy.

The FENCE check was perfect. The BUFF was flying at M.84, just over 600 mph. They were at FL28, the legal limit for an airframe that is non-reduced vertical separation minimum (RVSM) certified.

They were two hours out of Guam. Flying conditions were good and Sanchez would shortly declare 'due regard' with Tokyo Centre, allowing the plane to climb to 34,000 feet.

They would maintain contact with Tokyo. Up to a point.

Flying 'due regard' meant that Sanchez and his crew, and the other B-52 flying one mile behind and one thousand feet above, could do whatever was necessary to accomplish the mission.

The lead radar technician on the *Changchun* picked up the first blips of the American planes at 0032. He jotted down their position before relaying the information up the chain of command.

Huan was told three minutes later. The aircraft were approaching the largest of the Diaoyu Islands and the radar nav had placed them at 25°46′N 123°31′E.

Despite the public declaration by President Jackson, Huan was still mildly surprised by America's blatant disregard for Chinese sovereignty. The *Changchun* was positioned fifty kilometres west of the Diaoyus, now sailing at 19 knots. The commander knew his instructions to the letter.

He checked his watch. In fifteen minutes, he would issue the first warning. Then he would log the position of the two enemy planes with the mainland.

'Sam, I'm looking forward to that chicken.'

Manny Sanchez appreciated good food and he liked to give the E-Dub a lift when he could. Staying positive was good for morale, but he knew the food would have to wait until the B-52 was heading home to Guam.

The two bombers were closing on the Senkaku Islands, their mission running smooth as silk. In a quarter-hour, they would begin the simulated mission over Uotsuri Jima. Thirty minutes of training exercises, then the return to Andersen. The mood was quiet and serious.

They were flying FL34, the thinner air allowing the planes to nudge up to M.88. Sanchez wanted to slow the BUFF in a few minutes, though, once they began their bombing exercises.

Just then, the E-Dub patched in. 'We've got early warning radar, Manny. Chinese.'

Sanchez wasn't surprised and he wasn't fazed.

The BUFF would maintain its position despite China's attempt to knock them off course. He had his orders. They weren't carrying munitions, they were in international airspace, the communists could go to hell.

Huan took the call from the mainland at 0049. The aircraft had ignored the early warning signals, as he'd expected. Such arrogance.

He placed the *Changchun* on a full war footing and waited for further instructions on the red phone.

Just over 140 miles away, two of China's fourth-generation fighter jets, Shenyang J-11s, raced down the Ningbo runway. It would take them just fourteen minutes to intercept the enemy, to show the Americans that the world's most populous nation would no longer be pushed around by an arrogant imperial power.

'Motherfuckers!' Sanchez couldn't believe the Chinese fighter would make such a reckless move.

The two jets had appeared on the radar eight minutes ago, maintaining a discreet distance on either side of his plane, and out of visual sight. But he had been warned about Chinese aerial cowboys and one of the jets had broken formation to fly across the BUFF's airzone.

It was pure intimidation. Dangerous and irresponsible.

'He's flashing his wings.' Sanchez radioed through to the B-52 accompanying him, barking instructions to abort the training mission.

It was time to apply the speed brake, taking the BUFF over the falls. He dropped power and pushed the yoke forward. He applied the brake and buckled in for the rollercoaster ride that would take them almost into negative Gs.

The BUFF would descend 4000 feet in a blink. And then?

Sanchez called back to Andersen. He was pulling out of the mission. He'd follow instructions and fly an oval-shaped race-track for a few minutes, then turn for the safety of home.

He wouldn't risk a dogfight with an enemy who was clearly dosed.

'Time to leave. Tommy, let's bring this plane around. Nice and slow.'

Flying thirty thousand feet above the East China Sea, being pursued by a reckless daredevil from the PLA Air Force – that really wasn't in the training manual.

Manny Sanchez briefly closed his eyes, conjuring up an image of a laughing, trusting, loving three-year-old boy. Then, for the first time in a long while, the pilot reached for the cross around his neck and offered a silent prayer to the heavens.

CHAPTER FORTY-THREE

Canberra

Martin Toohey massaged his temples, trying to fend off the stress that was building in this early hour.

Christ! Is this how wars start?

For once, the screaming headline on news.com.au matched the gravity of the story, and Martin Toohey's apprehension grew with every word.

SECONDS FROM WAR: US, CHINA IN MID-AIR STOUSH

China and the United States came within moments of disaster last night in a high-stakes game of brinkmanship over the disputed Senkaku Islands.

Chinese warplanes confronted two unarmed B-52 bombers, a move that military experts said put the two powers one mistake from war.

Pentagon officials claim a 'reckless' act by one of the Chinese fighter planes forced the B-52 pilot to take emergency evasive action to avoid collision.

The Prime Minister flicked through the daily briefings on his desk. It was 6.20am and the leader's office was pulsing with the energy of forty staff.

In his office next door, George Papadakis looked more worry-worn than usual as he leafed through the same high-level briefings that had been prepared by the Office of National Assessments. They offered ominous warnings that the US–China standoff could be the flashpoint for a regional confrontation.

He glanced up at a monitor on his office wall to note that Toohey had arrived and was hard at work. Papadakis had a special camera trained on the PM's desk. Not even the Australian Federal Police were given access to it. He bundled up his papers, grabbed his coffee mug and walked the short distance to greet his friend.

'One mistake now and this will go completely pear-shaped,' he said.

'Yeah, it isn't good.' Toohey still had his head buried in the briefs. He looked up and took off the reading glasses he wore in private, rubbing the bridge of his nose.

'I gave the Canadian Prime Minister a call last night before this latest bloody escapade and he thinks Earle Jackson is the most dangerous President in our lifetime. The Tea Party has him by the balls and he's an ugly mix of stubborn and stupid.'

'And the Five Eyes intel is starting to paint a pretty chilling picture of this new Chinese leadership.' Papadakis pointed the PM to a file in his papers marked 'Analysis of the Standing Committee'. 'The President relies heavily on the head of his Propaganda Department, Jiang Xiu. He turns out to be an ultra nationalist.'

Toohey pulled out the brief and read its four pages. 'Gee … we've managed to bug the leadership's phones.'

'Well, not us specifically, but the Americans have been pretty successful at getting a fix on the President – what he's contemplating and plotting.'

'Question is, where does that leave us? I don't want to get drawn into a pissing competition with the two biggest dicks on the planet.'

'But we might not have much choice in this, Martin. The Americans will expect us to roll in behind them.'

'Mate, we can't afford that. We have to try and keep this dispute at arm's length. Just say enough to keep the Yanks happy and not so much that we piss off the Chinese.'

Papadakis rolled his eyes. 'That will take a level of skill that we haven't yet displayed.'

'Well, we'd better get this right. Our future actually does depend on it. We'll keep our position non-committal for as long as we possibly can. I intend to nurse this gas-hub deal to the other side of the election. Even if it evaporates the day after it.'

'And if we can't manage that? If conflict breaks out?'

Toohey leapt from his seat with a ferocity that startled Papadakis.

'Then, George, I will be a leader during a national security crisis. I will use fear to make the Australian people think twice before they change government. I'll win this election fair and square … or I'll use every dirty trick in the book. Just like my fucking opponents always do.'

Papadakis was shocked and disturbed. For all his faults Toohey usually kept his cool. Now even that was breaking down.

A knock on the door interrupted a tense silence. 'Prime Minister, the Greens leader is here to see you, for her scheduled 7am meeting.'

Toohey groaned.

'From the absurd to the absolute fucking ridiculous.'

Kiirsty Stanford-Long was in her early thirties, a political vixen who'd schemed her way to the helm of the Senate's balance-of-power party. She was statuesque and shiny and had one of the Parliament's sharpest tongues. In another life, Toohey might have found her alluring.

But he despised Stanford-Long's holier-than-thou approach to politics, so typical of this party of wowsers, environmental flat-earthers and do-gooders. Meetings with her always reminded Toohey of Whitlam's barb to the Victorian Left: 'You are pure in the way that eunuchs are pure.'

'Prime Minister.' Stanford-Long offered her hand. 'Thanks for seeing me, I know you have a very busy schedule.'

'Well Kiirsty, nothing is more important to me than the Mental Justice Bill and I hope that we can rely on your support. The numbers will be tight and this is the kind of initiative that this country needs.'

'Martin, I'm delighted by the bill and the Greens have always supported legislation that seeks to improve the lives of

Australians. Of course we support it, but I think that we have a historic opportunity here for more sweeping reform.

'As you know, Prime Minister, one of the biggest contributing factors to depression is the abuse of alcohol. The Mental Health Commission's latest report was quite explicit on the link between excessive drinking and the growing number of people seeking help.'

Toohey could feel it coming: a Greens boondoggle that would, no doubt, nail him to the cross of a dog of a policy.

'What do you have in mind?'

'We have a once-in-a-generation chance to take the lead here, as we did with the plain packaging of tobacco.'

Stanford-Long lifted several sheets of paper from her bag.

'We've been working on this in the party room and with the help of the preventative health agency. It's bold. And, I am sure, will be popular. Here, have a look at some of these pictures.'

The Prime Minister gazed down at what he hoped was a mock shot of a bloodied corpse lying across a car bonnet, beneath three words blasted in large, prominent font.

DRINK. DRIVE. DEAD.

Toohey rubbed his brow, sensing a headache building. 'Let me get this right. You want me to plaster every can of beer and every cask of wine in Australia with graphic shots of dead people. So every night when people sit down to relax with a harmless quiet ale they can be reminded that I've ruined one of the few pleasures they have left. That should go down a treat in marginal seats.'

Stanford-Long wore the expression of a pet cat that'd been chastised for bringing a dead rat into the home.

'I'm disappointed, Prime Minister. I thought you would see the wisdom of this. The bottom line is: we want this as part of the mental health package. Without it the job is only half done. We are not going to support a bill that locks in failure.'

Toohey's temper was rising. 'That's what you said when you opposed our first emissions trading bill and allowed the global warming sceptics in the Opposition to argue that not even the Greens thought it was any good. Because of that we lost a once-in-a-lifetime opportunity to get bipartisan support for action on climate change. That's what I call locking in failure.'

The Prime Minister paused and took a deep breath before continuing.

'Kiirsty, can I remind you that the last brainwave the Greens had – and that we foolishly accepted on the advice of closet activists in the Department of Health – was to ban foods with high salt content.'

Toohey was reliving what was clearly a painful moment.

'The problem was that the salt level was measured by every 100 grams. Unfortunately that saw Vegemite pulled from supermarket shelves. For a bloody month! No one eats 100 fucking grams of Vegemite on their toast! No one! That's half a jar. Oh, and remember the tabloid headlines when it was discovered there was a black market in the stuff: "BOOTLEG KIDDIES".'

Toohey was getting red in the face and Papadakis briefly worried that the PM might be getting too much salt in his diet. But he was just warming up. He stood up and began to pace the room. Stanford-Long was shocked into silence. For once.

'Oh, and then it got out that you and your mates in Health had been exchanging emails about kids' exercise. You proposed, and they entertained, the idea that we ban all contact sport for under-eighteens.

'And who found out about that? Who got the leak? I'll tell you who. Ray fucking Hadley. He only built his fucking first career on calling fucking football and his second fucking career on fucking me. It was the perfect storm. And the first thing I knew about it was when the shock jock broadcast it.'

Papadakis considered intervening. But Stanford-Long was flint-hard and was not going to be bludgeoned into changing her mind. Toohey could engage in bluster but she had what he needed. The numbers.

When Toohey finished shouting, her response was icy.

'Thanks for the history lesson, but both of those reforms would have succeeded if you hadn't gone to water. And the country would have been better for it. We are not turning on this. I look forward to your considered response.'

Stanford-Long gathered her papers and bag and stormed out. Papadakis turned to a still-fuming Toohey as the door slammed.

'Have I ever told you how much I admire your masterful way with women?'

CHAPTER FORTY-FOUR

Canberra

Emily Brooks had achieved what she had always courted. Worldwide fame. The online footage of her cavorting with journalist Jonathan Robbie had gone *Gangnam-Style* viral.

Snippets of the sex tape had also aired round the clock on Australian TV. The images had been discreetly blurred, but what was left to the imagination only made it worse.

The warning at the end of every introduction was guaranteed to draw a crowd: 'The following story contains graphic sex scenes that might offend some viewers.'

Towards the end of each replay it became apparent, even through the blurred images, that the man wasn't having such a good time.

'Noooooooooo!'

Online there were no constraints and the images were paraded in their uncut glory. On Twitter #SpankMeEmily had become the top trending Australian topic for 2013.

Inevitably, the creative sexual escapades of two mostly consenting adults had been distilled to one predictable phrase: 'Bondage-Gate'.

The Left-wing blogs were ablaze with anger at the hypocrisy of a leader who had made so much of her Christian values, but had been caught *in flagrante delicto*. Despite the Left's profound commitment to advancing women's rights, when it came to Brooks all bets were off. Blog sites were littered with lewd and sexist references to the Opposition leader.

Fairfax couldn't get enough of the story and the News Limited tabloids were in overdrive.

But *The Australian* decided to use the issue to launch one of its regular jihads on the ABC. It focused on the public broadcaster's 'ethics' in breaking the story when the media had traditionally avoided peering into politicians' private lives. An *Oz* editorial thundered that the story was driven by 'a blatant Left-wing bias that infects the entire organisation'.

Channel Nine was in a position almost as uncomfortable as the one that its manacled reporter had endured. It couldn't ignore the story and yet its Canberra-based attack dog had a starring role. Its news stories focused on Brooks and referred only fleetingly to 'television journalist Jonathan Robbie'. The network was also forced to put out a statement saying that Robbie was taking extended leave to recover from a lower back injury.

For Seven and Ten, 'Bondage-gate' was proof that, somewhere in the universe, there is a God. They camped outside Robbie's Deakin home and tried to doorstop him whenever his 1971 orange and black VH Valiant Charger pulled into the driveway.

But the real gold was mined when an eagle-eyed ABC crew, Dave McMeekin and Nick Haggarty, spotted Robbie's unmistakable muscle car at the Deakin shops. Both hated Robbie from long days spent working with the bad-tempered and arrogant reporter in pool crews on overseas trips.

Their camera was waiting as Robbie emerged, decaffeinated soy cappuccino takeaway in hand, from a bustling Cafe D'Lish. McMeekin was shooting, Haggarty was carrying the sound boom and firing off questions.

'Jon, have you got a moment?'

'Piss off you bastards.' Robbie pushed past the camera.

'Mate, can you relive the experience for us ...' Haggarty was grinning like a schoolboy.

'I've got nothing to say and you guys are invading my privacy.'

'It's a public place and ... hey, why are you limping?'

'I'm a sick man.'

'We know, we saw that online.'

'Leave me alone, I have nothing to say.' Robbie lifted his pace but was clearly labouring. It was a long walk to the Valiant but the two hardened professionals had no trouble keeping pace under the weight of their gear. By the time Robbie was fumbling with the keys at the car door he was breathless and angry and the camera was a metre from his face.

'Does that kinky stuff hurt?' Haggarty was running out of questions that could run on prime time.

'Fuck off you vultures!' Robbie screamed as he slammed the door, upending the nancy-boy coffee he'd left on the roof. The V8 roared to life and its tyres squealed as he reversed and the crew retreated. Then, the footage would show, he appeared to veer towards the camera as he took off, laying down more rubber as he straightened at the last moment before extending his arm out the window, offering the middle finger of his right hand in a final defiant salute.

News of the encounter reverberated through the gallery even before the crew had arrived at Parliament. The ABC's pool-sharing arrangement meant that its partner, Ten, would have access to the footage, but not Seven.

When word of the pictures reached Seven's chief of staff, Craig Sullivan, he sprinted across the corridor from his office to front the ABC's chief of staff, Simon Johnson.

'Simes. I beg you. I beg you, mate. Let us have it.'

'No.' Johnson was enjoying the rare opportunity of having something he knew Sullivan couldn't live without. Several long minutes of bartering ensued before Johnson relented.

'Okay, but next time I want something from you, remember this moment,' Johnson said. 'And we're bugging these shots.'

That meant the ABC logo would run on the pictures given to Seven, something the commercial channel's management hated. But Sullivan knew his bosses would love the pictures.

'You're killing me, mate.'

Emily Brooks was also under siege. The initial response from her office to the outside world had been stony silence. Brooks was determined to follow the ancient political dictum: 'Don't explain, don't complain and never resign.' But in the long run, saying nothing had not been an option.

The first step had been to issue a statement raising the possibility that the pictures had been doctored. Her footsoldiers were dispatched to sell this line, with disastrous results. No one believed them. Experts were paraded across every television and radio program, every print outlet, to testify that the images were genuine.

Next, the Opposition leader's press secretary, Justin Greenwich, had been urged by Brooks to spin the story.

'How the fuck do I explain this away?' Greenwich had muttered to a colleague. 'Houdini couldn't escape those images. They're keeping me awake at night.'

Greenwich was in awe of Brooks's toughness and calmness under pressure. Although she had forged a reputation as one of the hardest politicians ever to walk the corridors of Parliament, she rarely lost her temper with her staff, no matter how bad the day. She was not panicking now, refusing to resign and adamant that her party would have to sack her if it wanted her gone. Together they devised a plan that might save Brooks's political skin.

Brooks would make a statement to the Parliament. The advantage was that she wouldn't have to face questions from the media. The downside was that she would have to face the scorn of the House of Representatives. She could not lie. And she would be beamed live to the nation, as when she announced that she would seek the House's indulgence to make a personal statement, the networks decided to carry it live.

The chamber and its galleries were full when Brooks strode in with her carefully prepared speech. In the end she and Greenwich had decided that the best form of defence was attack. She would cast herself as the victim and only address the tricky question of her bondage session in passing.

Brooks began by theatrically turning on the press gallery, pointing her finger at representatives of each media outlet.

'J'accuse you … and you … and you …' Brooks thundered. 'You seek to stand in judgement of me: as judge, jury and executioner. Today I open my own court and you are indicted. You are charged with a criminal invasion of privacy and the gross abuse of your privileged role as journalists. Our democracy has been damaged by your desperation to damage me.'

Brooks put on her glasses and turned to her speech like a QC checking a brief.

'Let's begin with the facts. I am a single woman in a relationship with a single man. We are consenting adults. I have broken no law. What was done occurred in the privacy of my own home. People can make their own judgement about what they have seen. All I ask decent Australians is to consider how they came to see it.'

Brooks's voice was strong and her hands steady as she turned the pages of her speech.

'Someone broke into my home. That is a crime. Someone installed not one but two video cameras in my bedroom. That is a crime. Someone videotaped me without my knowledge and then distributed the images without my consent. All those things are crimes. I ask the Australian people: how would you feel if the same thing happened to you? How would the members of this House feel?'

Brooks's eyes wandered slowly around the chamber, searching out those with more interesting private lives.

There was a nervous shuffling. Some MPs who had been riveted by the Schadenfreude of Brooks's discomfort found pieces of paper that, all of a sudden, demanded urgent attention.

'But those crimes pale beside the complete moral bankruptcy of the media.' Brooks eyeballed the journalists in the gallery just a few metres above her. 'You trafficked these stolen goods and then you had the gall to demand that I, the victim, be made to stand trial.'

Brooks had memorised the final paragraphs of her speech and addressed the chamber with a confident air.

'But I will not be lectured to about morality by the media or my opponents. I will not. And after today I will not be answering any more questions about my private life. If asked by the media about it, I have plenty of questions of my own about their role in a series of crimes. I have asked the police to investigate. Politics is a hard business and I play it hard. I expect no more or less than is expected of others.'

It was a bravura performance and a throaty 'Hear, hear' followed Brooks as she gathered her papers and swept out.

After the speech the corridors rang with gossip as MPs of all political persuasions appraised Brooks's performance and her prospects. Even her enemies were impressed by the audacity of a speech aimed at morphing her from villain to victim. There was a grudging admiration, too, at her shifting the attack onto the media, something all politicians and most of the public enjoyed.

But some Coalition MPs told their Labor mates that they thought her leadership was doomed.

'We'll let Brooks take all the hits on opposing the mental health bill and then we'll dump her and have a new leader for the dash to the election,' one Coalition plotter said. 'Say what you like about her, she's tough. Elizabeth Scott would wave the bill through even though we can't afford it.'

For the first time in ages, Martin Toohey and George Papadakis looked forward to the evening news. The PM had ordered snacks and a good bottle of red. They were ready for showtime.

'Hurry up, George; you'll miss the start,' Toohey hollered at 5.58pm.

Papadakis bustled through the door to the opening strains of the Seven News theme. The sting promised extended coverage of 'Bondage-gate'.

Toohey and Papadakis rocked with laughter at the opening. Commercial TV news stories usually run for ninety seconds, but a staggering three minutes was devoted to Robbie's encounter with the ABC.

'Stick that up your arse!' Toohey yelled at the television and then laughed himself red at his own wit. Wiping tears from his eyes he turned to Papadakis.

'I've always hated that little shit and, no matter what happens to Brooks, this is the end of him. He'll never be able to set foot in the gallery again. The ABC just paid for itself. Let's give them more money.'

The next story, covering Brooks's speech, wasn't as good.

The Opposition leader had shown steel and pulled off a great performance in the most difficult of circumstances.

The third was a collection of vox pops, and opinion was split on whether Brooks should go. But everyone agreed Robbie was a grub. 'Like all journalists,' one woman added.

When the fun on Seven ended after ten glorious minutes, Toohey ran through the tapes of Nine and Ten. He switched to SBS live at 6.30. The entertainment only ended after the ABC's *7.30* devoted twenty minutes to the affair, including a side-slapping defence of Brooks by her deputy, the dour National Party leader, Charles Mayfield. The best exchange was, as always with Mayfield, unwitting.

'It's you lot at the ABC that should be ashamed,' Mayfield raged. 'You've been whipping this up into a frenzy.'

'Would you like to rephrase that?' a poker-faced Leigh Sales replied.

7.30's last story examined the reaction of the Christian lobby and it was clear many were struggling to defend Brooks, although the word 'forgiveness' was used a lot. Toohey was sorry when the program finally moved on to other news.

'How do we keep this going?' The Prime Minister, the usual whipping boy for the nightly news, wanted to drag out the Coalition's pain.

'We could have a few of the more crazy-brave MPs and senators drop some inflammatory remarks,' Papadakis said. 'We'll get the Victorian Right's online stooge to post some really appalling stuff. Ah, and Martin, there are all those fake Twitter accounts the national secretariat manages.'

Toohey had been schooled in the art of union 'shit sheets' since his early years in Labor and knew the best stuff needed imagination and flair.

'Yes, yes, all that. But we need something that will really bite. I know, get someone to call Robbie Swan and get the Sex Party to come out and say it applauds Emily Brooks for making bondage acceptable. And that as a result of her good work he hopes to see the basics of it taught in high school. That kind of third-party endorsement will screw with her base.'

Papadakis frowned at his boss.

'Sometimes you scare me, Martin.'

Toohey wasn't listening.

'And Black Ops, George. We don't want our fingerprints on it.'

CHAPTER FORTY-FIVE

Honolulu

'Thank you, Mr President. I will do that, sir. You have a good day.'

Aubrey W. Holland bristled with anger. His men, on a peaceful mission in international airspace, had been provocatively shadowed and put in harm's way.

The admiral's fury had been heard all the way to the White House.

From his base in Hawaii, the Commander of Pacific Command controlled an area spanning half the world: from the blue waters of the US west coast to the western border of India. From Antarctica to the North Pole.

Within an hour of the B-52s returning to their base in Guam, shaken after their run-in with the Chinese fighter jets, Holland had issued a robust statement. It was just after 9.30am in Honolulu.

'The actions of those Chinese pilots were unnecessary, unprofessional and showed a lack of experience,' he'd thundered.

'As a leader I find it impossible to believe that they were not acting under orders. China is growing more aggressive by the day. It now claims most of the South China Sea and is involved in territorial disputes there with Vietnam, India and the Philippines. In the East China Sea it is threatening South Korea and Japan. Most of the world's trade passes through these waters.

'It has the posture of a country that is spoiling for a fight. It is now up to the leaders of all free nations to decide if they are prepared to let China rule the international waterways.'

Holland had personally briefed the President. He liked the steel that Earle Jackson had put back in America's spine. The admiral believed that it was overdue for the US to assert its rights of free passage on the high seas. Jackson agreed.

In a few hours time the President would hold a press conference. And he wasn't promising words, he was promising action.

CHAPTER FORTY-SIX

Canberra

Soft turquoise wings sketched on satin skin, a pair of butterflies in hidden places, a stencil of forbidden delight. Pixie dust mingled with stars in tiny constellations across a smudge of black.

Harry Dunkley allowed his eyes to linger on the soft curve of her hip until every centimetre had been traced. Then he fell back onto a pillow, hands clasped behind his head, feeling guilty contentment after a night with his lover.

He mentally did the maths as she quietly lay on her stomach, her arms folded beneath the pillow.

You're in way over your head, Dunkley.

Celia Mathieson was gorgeous, feisty, whip-smart – and twenty-two years his junior.

He wondered what the social media wowsers – the Twitter mullahs who loved to stand in judgement – would make of this liaison.

They'd hand me to the lynch mob.

But fuck 'em. This was 2013 and if he wanted to sleep with a 32-year-old then the self-appointed morality police could go take a running jump.

Besides, he'd made enough sacrifices as he'd pursued his career. A marriage that had never got out of second gear had broken down; his ex, Belle, had taken refuge from the national capital, escaping to Sydney, then Byron. She had never come to grips with his selfish commitment to political reporting, his 'fucking obsession with that fucking paper'.

His relationship with his daughter had also turned fractious. He'd all but ignored Gaby during the difficult final year of her degree, a double arts major at his alma mater, Sydney University. He'd nearly missed her graduation, arriving half an hour late and with the academic jamboree in full swing.

He wondered how she would respond to her dad having an affair with a woman a handful of years older than she was. He could hear her reproach in his head.

Disgusting!

Maybe it was better to keep his beautiful sleeping muse a secret. Besides, the only people who counted in this arrangement were the two of them. He was fifty-four and Celia was several months shy of thirty-three.

So she was perfectly capable of deciding whether to throw herself, butterfly tattoo and all, into this relationship.

She isn't Lolita, for Christ's sake.

He checked his watch: 7.56am. It was a Wednesday and there was plenty to get on with. If only he could drag himself away from Ms Butterfly Wings.

He slipped out of bed and into the kitchen, filling the kettle. He was contemplating listening to *AM* when his mobile rang, and he swiftly answered it before it woke Celia.

'Good morning, Harry.' It was a voice he didn't know.

'Hello. Who is this?'

'Someone who'd like to meet with you. Alone.'

'I usually like to know who I'm meeting.'

'I can appreciate that, but I think you'd find our conversation interesting – and useful. Let me just say, I think Ben Gordon would probably appreciate it too.'

The mention of his friend's name triggered a familiar surge of emotion in Dunkley. Remorse. Guilt. Sadness.

Then there was a different feeling as a deft hand teased his lower torso, urging him back to bed. He turned to Celia, putting his index finger to his mouth.

'Okay Mr Anonymous. Where and when?'

'Hansel and Gretel Cafe in Phillip. I'll meet you there in, say, forty minutes, around 8.45.'

Dunkley felt a soft tug on his arm, a whisper of encouragement.

'Yep, okay ... but can we make it an hour please?'

'Certainly, Harry. I'll be wearing a blue-and-white checked shirt, glasses, sandy hair. Look forward to meeting you then.'

The Mazda 3 was a sporty number with leather seats and a sound system to die for.

Dunkley loved revving Celia's vehicle around Canberra's quiet streets, although he was careful to avoid the city's myriad speed cameras. He squeezed the car into a parking space in Prospect Court, just around the corner from the coffee shop.

He was a few minutes late, checking his watch as he weaved past three ambling tradies. It had been a while since he'd visited Hansel and Gretel. As he entered, a harried-looking woman was helping an elderly man struggling to grip a coffee cup with arthritic hands. 'Dad, it won't bite,' she said with a hint of annoyance.

He spotted the sandy-haired man with the checked shirt, his head buried in a copy of that day's *Australian*.

Carefully, the man folded the broadsheet before offering Harry a cautious smile, beckoning the reporter to join him.

'Harry, nice to finally meet you in person. Trevor Harris.' A freckled hand stretched out with a firm grip.

'Coffee?'

'Flat white, thanks.'

As Harris motioned to a waitress who'd just emerged from the small kitchen, Dunkley struggled to place him in Kimberley's circle of friends.

'Let me make it easy for you, Harry. I was Ben's immediate boss at DSD when he died … was killed. What was it? Eighteen, twenty months ago?' Harris shook his head with genuine regret written on his face.

'Kimberley's boss? What's your role at DSD?' Dunkley probed.

'So you call Ben "Kimberley"? I never really got the hang of that.'

Harris placed their order and continued.

'Well, my former role was head of the Scientific and Technical Analysis branch. I spent quite a bit of time there, at DSD. About ten years all up. But I've been out of the agency coming up to six months now.'

There was a hesitancy in Harris that hinted at a larger story.

'Why did you leave?'

'Variety of reasons, a touch too complicated to discuss right now. You know the agency's in the process of being reorganised and will be integrated into the broader intelligence framework?'

'Yeah, I've heard some stuff about it, although the secret society of spooks isn't really my speciality.'

'Really? I've read several of your recent pieces in *The Australian*. That article about the "Challenge of the Dragon" was quite perceptive, I thought. And well informed.'

Harris was fishing for his intelligence sources and that was something Dunkley never discussed. He drew on his flat white, smiled and took a moment to soak up the cafe's ambience.

The dark chocolaty aroma of freshly roasted arabica hung in the air, blended with the scent of nuts and the glacéd fruit that Hansel and Gretel was renowned for. He and Belle had been regulars at the company's original outlet in Manuka, introducing Gaby to the pleasure of frothy milk when she was tiny. The memory brought on a momentary pang of nostalgia.

'So why am I really here?'

Harris clasped his hands and shifted his gaze to his coffee before looking directly at Dunkley.

'Harry, first things first. I don't want to get into trouble, I don't want to breach the Secrets Act. I am most definitely not a whistleblower. But you need to know some things about our dead friend.'

He stole a quick glance around the cafe. No one was close enough to hear them over the background clatter. Still, Harris was taking no chances, and leaned further towards Dunkley.

'You only have part of the story of Ben's death. When I was informed of it, I assigned a colleague to close down his IT profile. It's usually a straightforward task – access the person's files, download any unfinished business to a common user hard drive, provide a report to management. To me. That sort of thing. But Ben's profile was stubbornly hard to access. That's when I took over the task. Personally.

'Some interesting stuff came floating out. I found a gmail address that he'd set up. You recall the email that Ben sent you, the one that referred to "shades of '75"?'

Dunkley looked blank. 'No, can't say that I do.'

'Really, Harry? Ben sent you and another of his friends a very similar email – about twenty minutes apart – on Thursday, August the fifteenth, 2011.'

'Sorry, but I honestly don't recall receiving any email like that. I mean, I get literally dozens of the buggers each day, but I reckon I'd remember something Kimberley sent me, particularly so close to when it happened. She was killed three days after that.'

Harris shifted in his seat, seemed to reflect for a moment, and then reached into a green shopping bag. He took out an A4 sheet and placed it between them.

'Here it is.'

Dunkley was about to pick up the document when a shrill voice interrupted. 'Another coffee for you two?'

The waitress, wearing a black dress with a silly-looking apron embroidered in lace, stood with pen poised. She was just doing her job, but Harris shot her a dark look.

'Yes, same again.'

Ms Gretel took the hint and scurried away, allowing the reporter to read the succinct email.

Harry

Starting to look like shades of '75. We really need to talk.

Call me

Kimberley

The two men looked at each other. Harris spoke.

'Well, Ben sent it. I found it and made a copy. He meant you to have it and he sent it from a private account, so I'm not breaking any rules by giving it to you.'

Dunkley read the note several times before speaking.

'What does it mean?'

'Well, Harry, maybe it means you've been looking in the wrong direction.'

CHAPTER FORTY-SEVEN

Canberra

A film of dust confirmed that the box had been undisturbed for a while, dumped in a corner of Harry Dunkley's cluttered garage. He'd all but forgotten this carton filled with bits and pieces recovered from Kimberley's apartment. As the executor of her estate, Dunkley had settled her will and filled the box with the items left to him. None had appeared to be of much value.

Had he, in his absent-minded grief, sought to consign its contents to history? Maybe. But now, eighteen months later, Dunkley had a reason to prise the box open.

Shades of '75? What was that about?

He carried the box into his flat and sliced the tape sealing it with a sharp kitchen knife.

'Open Sesame!'

Celia had brewed a fresh pot of filter coffee and joined him at the dining table with two mugs. Dunkley worked his way through the top layer of job-related letters and files, a public service manual – *Ethics in the Workplace* – and piles of Christmas and birthday cards.

He examined each item in turn and continued digging till he reached the layer of books lining the bottom of the carton. Richard Dawkins's *The God Delusion* was there, and a couple of tomes on Asian art. Wedged tightly in a corner was a paperback version of Paul Kelly's *The Dismissal*.

Dunkley turned to Mathieson who had picked up a bundle of Kimberley's old birthday cards.

'She was obsessed with the Whitlam Government and hated John Kerr and Malcolm Fraser with a passion,' he explained.

Celia had found a couple of cards from Dunkley and was smiling at the inscriptions.

'Malcolm Fraser's not so bad; he's the only Liberal I like.'

'Believe me, in 1975, you would have hated him.'

'Waaay before my time, grandad.'

Dunkley tensed at the reminder of the difference in their ages and looked more closely at the well-thumbed book. It had been bookmarked with an old plastic pass card at the opening page of a chapter titled 'The Security Crisis'. Mathieson gently kneaded Dunkley's shoulder as they both leaned in to read two words scribbled in the page's margin.

Reg Withers.

'Who's that?' she asked.

'Reg Withers? He was the leader of the Senate when the Coalition blocked supply. Fraser's upper house henchman during the crisis in '75.'

Celia opened up her MacBook, keen to find out more.

'He was a minister under Malcolm Fraser but apparently got the bullet and never forgave him for it. Surly-looking type, if you ask me. Harry, pass me that card ...'

Dunkley pushed the plastic bookmark across the table as he began to read the chapter's opening paragraphs. Like most political animals he found the Dismissal intriguing and somewhat unbelievable. But he'd forgotten the questions raised at the time about the role of the CIA in Whitlam's downfall.

'In the days preceding 11 November there were two major upheavals in Australia's system of government. The first was the political and constitutional crisis which covered the newspapers and engulfed the country,' Kelly wrote.

'The second was a security crisis that centred on the United States' communications base at Pine Gap near Alice Springs and the cover of American CIA agents operating in Australia. Only the tip of the security iceberg was ever apparent.'

Dunkley shivered.

'"Shades of '75."'

Then, it hadn't been the Chinese accused of meddling in domestic politics. It was the Americans. And they'd been charged with helping to bring down a democratically elected government.

'Harry?'

Dunkley looked up from the book. Mathieson was turning the card over in her hand.

'This is a crypto card. It's one part of a series of keys that you need to get into a highly secure Cloud archive.'

'A what? Can you speak slowly and in words of one syllable?'

'Sorry old man, I forgot.'

'Okay, that's twice now. You don't need to be nasty, miss.'

'The Cloud is a huge memory bank. Anyone can store documents in it. It means that you don't have to put everything on a hard drive and can access it from anywhere in the world. It's dead simple, Harry. Even you could do it on Google.'

Mathieson chuckled and Harry narrowed his eyes.

'Three times.'

'But this is much more secure. It plugs into the side of the computer and I'm pretty sure it works with Amazon Web Services. But I'll need the other keys – a username and a password – to get into it.'

'Well, let's have a look, Cel.'

Mathieson pulled a card reader from her computer bag and plugged it into one of her MacBook's USB ports. Then she pushed in the card and called up the Amazon Web Services page on her browser.

Dunkley was always amazed at the speed with which this digital native could navigate a world he found alien.

A few moments later a page opened with two empty boxes in it. The cursor blinked in the top one. Mathieson looked pleased with her handiwork.

'Okay, so far so good, but we don't know the username.'

Dunkley pointed at the handwritten words on the page. 'Yes we do.'

Mathieson typed 'Reg Withers' into the box, and hit the tab. The cursor jumped to the lower rectangle.

'Any idea of the password?'

'Not a clue.'

'Well, you don't get too many chances.'

Dunkley rifled through the book to see if Kimberley had left another handwritten key. There were none.

'For Christ's sake, Kimberley! I'm not Miss Marple.'

He turned to the front cover.

'Try "'dismissal'".'

Mathieson typed in the nine-letter word. 'The password you entered is incorrect' flashed in red.

'Bugger.'

'Next?'

'What else could it be?' Dunkley slapped his thigh as he rose from the chair. '1975? Kerr? Gough? Try "Whitlam" …'

Again, the computer flashed 'The password you entered is incorrect' and this time it added 'You have one more attempt before this account is locked'.

'How long will it be locked?' Dunkley looked anxiously at Mathieson.

'I don't know, depends on how secure Kimberley wanted it to be. Could be five minutes. Could be an hour. Could be a day. Could be forever.'

Dunkley looked skyward. 'Jesus wept, Kimberley! You could have given us a few more clues.'

'Well, short of divine intervention, we better make this one work.'

Dunkley tried to put himself in Kimberley's shoes. She knew everything about the Whitlam Government and its dramatic fall.

He turned and went back to the computer, staring at the two boxes that stood between them and Kimberley's trove. 'Reg

Withers' filled the first. A Liberal senator who'd eventually fallen foul of Fraser. A West Australian tough guy. Loved to throw his weight around …

Dunkley's face lit up.

'Cel, try "toecutter".'

'You sure?'

'Yes.'

She tapped out the letters carefully.

T-O-E-C-U-T-T-E-R.

The computer whirred for a second. And then the gates opened.

CHAPTER FORTY-EIGHT

Canberra

The six ceramic panels sparkled in the artificial light. The ode to an ancient landscape now marked by the furrows of agriculture and scarred by industry ran the width of Parliament's Mural Hall. 'The River' was Martin Toohey's favourite piece of art in this democratic cathedral, and he found it both humbling and inspiring.

'It's called "The Dreaming", isn't it?' A rich American baritone broke his concentration.

'Brent, good to see you. I wasn't expecting you here. I didn't know that Australian art was your thing. And no, that's a common mistake; it's called "The River".'

The Prime Minister turned to shake the hand of the US Ambassador, noticing at the same time that a small group was gathering on a nearby podium, meaning that he'd soon be required for official duties – the opening of an exhibition of Pacific Rim art.

'Ah yes, of course, I can see that,' Brent Moreton said. 'And I'm no culture vulture, I'll admit that, Martin. But it pays to fly the flag – particularly when the Office of the Prime Minister requests your presence at the cutting of a ribbon.'

'Oh, I didn't know you'd be leaned on to attend this event. Sorry.' The two men smiled.

'Don't worry about it, Martin,' Moreton said. 'Besides, I wanted a chance to have a quick chat. About something important.'

'What's on your mind? Presumably not the virtues of Polynesian art.'

'No, Prime Minister.' Moreton stepped in closer. 'I wanted you to hear this from me first. The President plans to call you today, at 11am, if that's convenient.' Moreton didn't pause for confirmation.

'The United States is stepping up military plans for the East and South China seas. We want our allies to back us and, in some cases, share the burden.'

Toohey knew he was about to cop a curve ball from the baseball-loving envoy.

'As part of the US pivot to the Pacific, the President will invite you to forward-base Australian forces on Guam. It would be a tremendous gesture of support for the alliance. It would open a raft of possibilities for joint training and allow a rapid response to natural disasters.'

The PM had been blindsided. He was still digesting this bombshell when one of his aides motioned to him to join the group on the podium.

'One minute, Jenny, please.'

He turned back to Moreton. 'You're telling me the President will ring me in two hours and ask that Australia send soldiers to Guam?'

'Well, not soldiers specifically. We were thinking of a squadron of your Super Hornets which are already inter-operable with our forces there.'

'Well, my friend, we do that and the Chinese will go ballistic. And I use the word deliberately. I have to go now but I can tell you that my initial reaction is a firm no.'

Toohey turned, retrieving a wad of notes from a folder handed to him by an adviser.

Moreton touched the PM's sleeve, halting his progress. 'Well, you might like to reconsider that, Prime Minister. Because the President will formally announce his plan for a new Pacific partnership at a press conference in the White House. In four hours time.'

Thirty minutes later, Toohey thundered into his office, hitting a call button with unusual ferocity. 'George!'

His chief of staff arrived seconds later. 'Oh good, I'm glad you're back, I've got those papers for the Cabinet meeting—'

'Forget Cabinet. The United States of god-forsaken America wants us to put planes on Guam to give the Chinese the idea that it's building a coalition of the willing, just in case they get any funny ideas.'

'Shiiiitttttt! Where did this come from?'

'Moreton shirt-fronted me in the Mural Hall; told me Jackson will publicly invite us to help them with the regional heavy-lifting to bolster the US presence in Guam. '

'And if we don't?'

'The public declaration is designed to make this an offer we can't refuse. It doesn't pay to piss off the United States. But the Chinese will crucify us. They must know that.'

Toohey closed his eyes and exhaled. He wore the mantle of national leadership with great pride, but at times like these it threatened to exhaust and overwhelm him.

'The Americans are trying to drag us into war, their war, again.' The Prime Minister offered his friend a weak smile as he slowly shook his head. 'George, they've got my balls in a vice.'

CHAPTER FORTY-NINE

Canberra

'Jia, I'll be back in a short while.'

Weng Meihui skipped out of the embassy into the Canberra afternoon glare. She was keen to avoid the stares of the Falun Gong protesters across the street and lowered her head as she turned left towards the lake.

Her hands gripped a small bag containing a paperback: Tim Winton's *Cloudstreet*. She'd borrowed the novel from a colleague, Xiu Linjiang, to read on the plane from Beijing, taking his word that it contained 'great insight' into the Australian character.

How she had enjoyed the foray into the lives of two working-class families, desperate and dirt poor, drawn together by their daily effort to survive. It had reminded her of stories her mother told of growing up in the backstreets of Lhasa, the Tibetan capital, following the 1950 'liberation'.

She was returning the book and was keen to see how Xiu had

been faring in the month since he'd arrived from the northern winter to work at the new embassy compound, installing communications equipment, he'd told her.

The compound was only four hundred metres from the embassy, but the workers' accommodation was very different to the luxury Weng enjoyed in her suite. They were housed in dongas and makeshift cabins, and kept under virtual house arrest.

Security had been further tightened since the drowning death of Lin An and the invasion by the Australian union thugs. The workers' weekly movie night at the embassy had been cancelled and communications with the homeland curtailed.

'A secure China must come first,' the Ambassador had told Weng when she'd voiced concerns about the workers' loss of amenities.

Now she walked up the curved driveway off Alexandrina Drive as a cement-mixer rumbled past. The gates were open and she waved to the security attendant.

'Hello. I am Weng Meihui.' She flashed her official pass and looked around the busy site, taking in the drilling, clinking, hammering and shouting as a dozen workers laboured in the baking sun.

The attendant looked at her suspiciously, as if he was surprised to see a woman, particularly the Ambassador's wife.

'Xiu Linjiang. Where will I find him?' Weng asked pleasantly.

'He's not here, madam.'

'Where is he?'

The attendant shuffled nervously. Weng sensed something was amiss.

'Mr …' She checked his pass. '… Wong. Tell me where Xiu is, please.'

'Madam, I don't know. Please, I am just security on this gate.'

'Where is his room then? I want to return a book.' She took the paperback from her bag and showed it to him.

He blinked, a nervous twitch. He pointed to a group of huts about eighty metres away. 'That one at the end,' he finally said. 'Upstairs.'

Weng walked into the compound, ignoring the wolfish stares of three labourers who were shovelling dirt into a long trench.

So this is where the union thugs did their business.

She arrived at the two-level cabin and had begun to climb a set of external stairs when an agitated worker came up behind her, asking her to stop.

'Madam, I don't think it's a good idea. Please.' His voice had a pleading edge.

'I just want to drop a book off to Xiu Linjiang, the man who arrived here four weeks ago.'

The man's voice softened. 'He's not … he's not here.' He was clearly nervous.

'Well, I'll just drop off the book.'

'I don't …' His voice trailed off, as if he was keeping something back.

She kept walking up the stairwell, impatient now to complete her errand. There were two rooms on the upper level, the names of the occupants written in texta on the beige-coloured walls.

Xiu's name was on the furthest room, along with those of his two room-mates: Dong Mao and …

284

She froze. The third name was unmistakeable. Lin An.

She was starting to understand why the security guard and the worker seemed worried. She entered the room. It smelt of antiseptic. There were three bunks and each had been stripped of its sheets.

Weng placed the book on a bedside table and was turning to leave when she stopped. There was a small wardrobe made from flimsy-looking timber against the far wall. She walked over to it and opened the door.

Empty.

'Weng. Why are you here?'

His voice startled her. She turned. Zheng Dong loomed in the doorway.

'That book, Zheng. Xiu lent it to me. Do you know where he is?'

'He is gone.'

'Where?'

'Home, for good.'

'Why?'

'The compound has been compromised. His work has been suspended.'

'And the other one who was here?'

'Same.'

'And did either of them know what happened to Lin An?'

'No.'

'How do you know, Zheng?'

'Because I asked them.'

CHAPTER FIFTY

Canberra

Line after line of meaningless code. A jumble of computer-generated hieroglyphics, inverted numerals, symbols and squiggles. None of it, not a single word, made any sense.

Kimberley, give us a fucking break.

Harry Dunkley's eyes ached as he tried to digest the mystifying mess. He felt like he was in a maze, with all the fun squeezed out.

'So, what do you make of this?'

He looked forlornly at Mathieson, hoping that her IT expertise would allow them to crack the next nut. She whistled and was wide-eyed in her appreciation.

'Harry, your friend didn't want to make it easy.'

'Yeah. Kimberley never liked to do things by halves. The question is, can you make sense of it?'

'I can do anything with the right level of persuasion.' She

nudged him light-heartedly. 'But seriously, Harry, I don't know. This is a big job and decryption is not my speciality.'

Celia took a sip of Diet Coke. She had a newfound respect for Kimberley, who was clearly more than just a pretty – albeit dead – face.

'This is going to take serious time, Harry, just to get to first base. Obviously she wanted this stuff deep in the ether.'

CHAPTER FIFTY-ONE

Canberra

The long table was set just for two. Hewn from a single ancient teak tree, it was made for formal functions, to impress large groups of dignitaries with the size and strength of the new China.

Tonight's intimate setting only magnified Weng Meihui's sense of isolation. The Ambassador had insisted on dressing formally for this full moon dinner in a dark suit and tie, a spit of grease in his hair. Weng had thought about wearing a casual outfit but had reconsidered. The consequences of offending him were too great.

She'd spent weeks in this strange country, trying to adapt to its quirky customs and habits. It was hard, dry, confronting, beautiful. She knew she could learn to love this land of open spaces.

But something she could never enjoy were the dinners alone with her 'husband'. He had demanded they maintain their marital facade, warning her that prying eyes were everywhere.

She was practised in the art of small talk, usually able to beguile even the most boring of men. But Tian was her greatest challenge – tedious, narrow-minded, controlling.

Recently a darker edge had invaded their dinners. He desired her, and that made their relationship increasingly awkward.

His first advances had been amusing as he fumbled to find the words he hoped would entice her to his bed. But his veneer of charm had evaporated when she'd resisted. Privately, he became aggressive and occasionally crude. He could remove all pretence of being the dutiful husband in a moment. And that scared her.

Tonight she would be her charming self. She was troubled by her visit to the compound. Troubled and frightened.

No one could shed light on the fate of Lin An's room-mates. She'd discreetly sounded out a secretary who made travel arrangements for the workers from China. 'I know nothing, Madam Weng,' was the curt reply.

A curtain of silence had fallen. The State was capable of much. She suspected the men had been brutalised, but why?

Had they, too, sought to escape the compound? Were they even now hiding in this bland city?

'Good evening, Mei.' His sudden appearance startled her. He reached for her hand and gently squeezed it.

'Good evening, Qichen. It's nice to see you. How was your day?'

'Productive, my dear. Productive and satisfying. We are making good progress on the latest trade talks despite some difficulties over Australia's defence ties.'

He motioned to the butler. 'A whisky, neat, and wine for Ms Weng. Now.'

Weng had not planned to drink alcohol, but did not contradict the Ambassador. She was after answers. Wine would at least help lubricate the conversation.

'And you, my dear, what have you been doing with your time today?' Tian asked the question with a slight smile.

How much has he been told?

'I had a good day. The plans for the exhibition are progressing well and I had coffee with several other partners. Miss Lindwall from Britain, and Mrs Toffey from Canada. Nice women and, like me, fairly new to this city.'

'Ah, that is good, that is good. Yes, the diplomatic community likes to look after their own. We are all strangers together, I guess.'

Tian contemplated his whisky. He looked back at Weng, took a step toward her. 'And you paid a visit to the compound, I hear.'

'Yes. The architecture is very nice.'

'The architecture? I had no idea of your interest in building design …'

'It is something I have been intrigued by … for some time…' Weng was stumbling. He was toying with her. She felt herself blushing.

He motioned to the table. 'Shall we?'

Weng took her place, the butler pulling her chair out from the table.

'Thank you.' Her smile masked an inner trembling.

Tian lifted his chopsticks and sampled an appetiser of salmon and rice. He ignored the offer of wine and fixed his gaze on Weng.

'Mr Zheng tells me you have an interest in Mr Xiu and his whereabouts.'

'He lent me a book. I was returning it. An Australian book, *Cloudstreet*.' Weng tried to sound calm and conversational.

Tian dragged a thin bone from his mouth, placed it on the side of his plate.

'I sent a cable to the Office today about your visit to the compound. The Commander will ring tomorrow on the secure phone.'

Where is this heading?

She nodded as she gripped her wine glass. A clatter from the kitchen startled her. A slight sweat stained her neck.

'You know ...' Tian considered his words. 'There is a good opportunity for us to make something of the next few years, together here in Canberra. The task is to follow the instructions we have been given. I don't recall you being asked to become an inquisitor, my dear.'

She tensed as he leaned towards her.

'I could make life here very difficult for you, Mei. Or very good. It is your choice, my beloved wife.'

She had known too many men like Tian. When they couldn't get what they wanted through charm, they used blackmail. Or violence. They deluded themselves that this was power, when their desperation for sex made them weak.

Weng had spent her life gathering loose words from these men and knew her power over them. They swelled with pride after a conquest and paraded like pumped-up peacocks. And they talked.

White light from the full moon washed through the room. Tian lit a cigarette and blew smoke across the bed. He looked satisfied with himself. Smug and pompous.

'My dear, would you care for a drink?'

'Yes, a cognac would be nice.'

'Of course.'

Weng smiled at his absurd nakedness as he strutted across the room and poured two drinks from a shell-shaped bottle. His weak chest, pot belly and reed-thin arms and legs were obscene in the moonlight.

No doubt you think you're handsome, pig.

The brown liquid jiggled in the glasses as he returned to bed.

She leaned on his arm. 'I was just returning a book, you know. My curiosity got the better of me.'

Tian gazed out the window at the moon. 'It is best not to ask questions about things of which you know little.'

'Of course. I was just concerned.'

Weng knew she was on very dangerous ground. Tian's desire was tinged with contempt and when, inevitably, his lust was sated her life would be expendable. Those who sell their souls have always looked down on those who sell their bodies. She hoped her meek response would invite an answer that his arrogance could not resist.

'Those men failed in their duty. Lin An escaped and threatened the entire operation. An operation vital to our state. Known only to a trusted few.'

Her fingertips traced a line down his face.

'You must be one of the trusted few to be in charge of this very important mission.'

He snorted proudly. He was content.

She pushed a bit harder. 'And those men? What happened to them?'

'They are gone.'

'Home?'

'No, just gone. Anyone who fails in this mission will meet the same fate.'

Tian turned to face her.

'And that includes you and me. Our leaders were displeased by the attack on the compound. We considered aborting the project but there is no sign our enemies know what we are doing. The rewards will be great.'

'What rewards?'

The Ambassador gently ran the back of his hand over her breasts, sweeping upwards. His fingers rested on her neck. And tightened.

'You understand so little. You steal small secrets one at a time from feeble men. My mission is to know everything. That building will be our gateway to the West, to everything that they know. And Mei, we are already in.'

CHAPTER FIFTY-TWO

Canberra

The voice was steeped in '60s soul and drove through the earbuds. She loved Adele, this British chanteuse who sang of fickle hearts and fractured relationships.

Celia Mathieson turned up the volume and bounced into stride. She'd shared a drink with a friend at Old Parliament House, and now faced a short walk up the hill. It was closing on 7pm. She'd arranged to meet Harry in his office and was tingling with excitement.

It had taken her a whole day to untangle just one of the documents in Kimberley's cloud, translating a mountain of IT mumbo-jumbo. There were still dozens of documents to unlock. She had a couple of pages of text and little idea what it meant.

Still, it was exhilarating to be working on a cloak-and-dagger project. She'd dashed off an email to Dunkley and couldn't wait to see his reaction when she unveiled it.

Harry,

Eureka! I've cracked the code on Kimberley's cloud! Am having a drink with Annie and will bring up the booty tonight.

See you soon

Cel

PS. What is the Alliance?

The sun was low and the evening chatter of birds was rising as Mathieson walked towards Parliament. Both houses were in session and there was a big story brewing about health reform. As if she cared.

Politics meant little to her, particularly after the government – this 'caring' Labor Government – fed Julian Assange to the lions.

Harry had ridiculed her description of the WikiLeaks' founder as a 'freedom fighter'.

'Supreme narcissist, more like it,' he'd fired back.

Oh Harry …

A band of exercisers was jogging up a grass-covered slope and a few tourists were still wandering around the forecourt fountain as she crunched across red gravel to the building's front doors. Mathieson ignored the main entrance and skipped down a set of stairs on the left. At the bottom she pushed her way through a stainless-steel door to the security station known as Point One. Only pass-holders could enter this checkpoint, the only one staffed 24/7.

Mathieson scratched around for her pass as a bored security attendant watched *Sky*. Her bag and phone passed through the security X-ray. She followed, walking up a set of stairs to a pair of concertina doors that folded open as she approached. Beyond, a passageway opened to a vast tunnel system: a labyrinth of concrete and cables.

Mathieson loved the underground network of roads, one of the building's many secrets. During the day it bustled with a small army of technicians, chefs, labourers and tradies who kept the Parliament functioning. But it emptied at night.

It was so easy to get lost down here that there were two lines painted on the floor, marking the way to the nearest lifts. A green line hooked left to the House of Representatives while red ran to the Senate.

Mathieson knew there was a longer path to a lift that emerged outside the News Corp bureau on the second floor. But it wasn't marked and she'd lost her way once before. Tonight she would follow Harry's advice. 'Stick to the red line'.

Her footsteps echoed along a concrete roadway as she passed locked storerooms, pallets of goods, parked electric cars and mysterious passageways.

'Level two,' a mechanical female voice announced when the lift arrived on the second floor.

The gallery was abuzz and Mathieson passed the boys from the *West Australian* slinking off home.

She walked the long corridor to the News bureau, arriving to find Dunkley under the pump. He barely lifted his gaze, stabbing at the computer, word after word after boring word.

'Deadline, honey. Sorry.'

Oh great, I bust a gut to get this stuff and he's wrapped up in a ho-hum story.

'Sure, no probs. I can wait. What's the story anyway?'

'Harry, they need it now. Please.' The shrill voice of Leonie Willacy, the bureau's harried chief of staff, rang out.

'Yeah, it's coming, give me a few mins, just got to tidy up something.'

'Harry, don't mean to hassle but can you give me an ETA?'

'Cel, sorry but I've got to write a comment after I finish the splash. Reckon I'm another hour; forty minutes, at least.'

'Sure.' She touched his arm. 'Well, could I just have a few minutes of your time to discuss you know what?'

He looked up, a felt-tip pen in his mouth.

'Can't stop right now. I know I told you I'd be done and dusted by 7.30 but ... well, Toohey's in deep trouble. His mental health bill is line ball. And they've called an all-nighter.'

He shrugged, hoping Celia would sympathise with his plight.

She wanted to, but didn't. She'd been so excited by her progress with the files and had been dying to share her find with Harry. She felt ridiculously disappointed and suddenly exhausted.

'Oh Harry, for fuck's sake, I've spent the best part of today getting this stuff ready for you and you can't even spare me a few minutes ...'

She threw an envelope on his desk.

'I'll see myself out.'

'Cel ...'

No time for others. Takes me for granted. Christ, I'm sounding like Mum.

She was fuming as she strode out, as angry with herself as with Harry.

Close to tears, she was not in the mood to see anyone and headed towards the nearest lift.

'Basement,' the female voice intoned.

Three floors down, she entered the bowels of Parliament. A pungent rotting smell was being driven by a cold air-conditioning draught.

These were unfamiliar surrounds. She needed to get her bearings. These tunnels must follow the building footprint. So turn right, and walk to a road flanking the western edge. Then down the length of the building and right again, back to Point One.

There was something unsettling about this part of the underworld. Many of the lights had been switched off and pools of darkness loomed over openings in the passageway, to both the right and left.

She paced one hundred metres down the corridor. It closed to nothing.

Bugger you, Harry Dunkley. I should have stayed out drinking.

She retraced her steps to the lift, and stopped.

Okay, you've done this before. I must hit a road that goes north. Soon.

Her pace quickened along a dim corridor, passing a row of odiferous bins.

A mechanical bang bounced off concrete walls. She stopped. The tick of a clock above. It was 7.38pm.

She looked around for any sign of life. Nothing.

Get a grip, Celia. Anyway, I've got my phone.

She checked. No reception.

Slowly, she started walking again, drifting to the centre of the corridor to avoid the dark alcoves and recesses. 'No Entry' signs flanked her on either side.

Above her, a tangle of cables and pipes snaked along the ceiling, the arteries of the building.

An intersection loomed. East Terrace.

This is it.

The corridor was curved and dark. She couldn't see the end. Just a small green and white 'Exit' sign in the distance. The lonely clip of her heels on concrete echoed eerily. She turned at the sound of a vehicle reversing, its mechanical beep amplified in the quiet, but saw nothing.

She turned back. Something was wrong. Two massive fire doors had swung shut, blocking her path. She reached for her phone. It showed 'SOS only'.

A tingle of fear shivered through her.

Taking a deep breath, she pushed hard against the heavy metal barriers, forcing them open. Ahead, black shadows. Had she triggered an alarm? The exit sign was maybe seventy metres away. She had a choice: walk through the gloom or return again to the lift.

The globe above flickered, then darkness engulfed her.

CHAPTER FIFTY-THREE

Canberra

George Papadakis had a PhD in economics and knew every nuance of the market economy. A former Treasury boffin, he had a peerless understanding of the complex algorithms of the nation's finances. But when it came to the simple maths of counting parliamentary heads, Dr Papadakis was lost.

That job fell to Alberto 'Burt' Crespo, Leader of the House and one of the best number-crunchers ever produced by Labor.

'Jesus, Burt, there are only one hundred and fifty MPs, why is this so hard?' Papadakis was flustered.

'Well, George, there aren't one hundred and fifty, for a start.' Crespo always carried a pad and was constantly making lists to keep track of the shifting sands of crossbench support. A pen was permanently lodged behind one ear.

'Bailey has been out of the equation for twenty months,' he explained. 'So that's one hundred and forty-nine. And since we bludgeoned the Tories into agreeing to pair her vote, the starting point is one hundred and forty-eight.'

Papadakis was determined to focus: the government's future relied on passing the mental health bills. Negotiations had stalled. In the last few hours Martin Toohey had declared that Parliament would sit until the bill was done.

Angry MPs had rescheduled their Thursday night flights home. Debate and procedural manoeuvring were raging in a House that would probably sit all night.

'Okay.' Papadakis took a deep breath. 'One more time from the beginning.'

'We started this term with the Coalition and us locked on seventy-two votes each and there were six swinging votes on the crossbench: one Green and five independents.' Burt looked up from his pad and Papadakis nodded.

'We got the support of the Green and three of the independents to get seventy-six votes and form government. But after that every other vote has been negotiated on a bill-by-bill basis.'

'With you. Go on.' Papadakis knew that was the easy bit.

'But we had to supply a Speaker, and he only votes when there is a tie. That's why we got a Coalition MP to rat and sit in the Chair. On any important tie, he always votes with us, but that's rare. On most bills, having him in the chair just strips one vote off them. So after that they had seventy-one to our seventy-two, with seven swinging votes.'

This was where Papadakis usually lost focus. Because behind each of these bland numbers was a long and usually painful story.

The deal to get the Speaker was a prime example. They'd been lumped with one of the most unsavoury MPs ever to park his arse on the green leather of the Lower House. Labor's chances of survival rose in Parliament but fell in the electorate.

'George, are you with me?' Burt nagged.

'Yep, yep. Continue.'

'But then we lost Bailey. And the Coalition refused to pair her. For a while things were grim. But she whipped up public opinion and forced the Tories to grant her a pair. So on a good day we have our seventy-one, plus the Green, plus three independents. Which is seventy-five. And they usually get seventy-two when you add the independents who support them and subtract one to cover Bailey.'

'Excellent.'

'But then we lost Paxton to the crossbench.'

Papadakis rubbed his temples. Crespo was on a roll.

'Actually, I think we'll get Bruce. He's a genuine left-winger and thinks mental health is a matter of social justice.'

'That's great.' Papadakis's face brightened slightly.

'The Greens on the other hand—'

Papadakis interrupted '—are extremist jihadists who are about as ready to compromise as Al Qaeda.'

'Yep, if they don't get plain packaging of alcohol, their MP will vote against the bills.'

Crespo flicked through the pages of his pad and frowned. He was a brilliant parliamentary strategist and had managed to herd the Lower House cats so well that the government's legislative program rarely missed a beat. But this bill was proving harder than most.

'But then there's the bad news.'

'That last bit wasn't the bad news?'

'No. All through that we still had the numbers. Right now, we have seventy-three at best, but so does the Coalition. Support from the crossbench is going to cost us. One of the independents is threatening to abstain and the others are shaky. George, the Speaker is wavering. His electorate's up in arms about the deficit and this is a big call on the public purse. And they hate the China deal. A tie means we lose.'

'What about the rest of the crossbench menagerie?'

'Well, George, that's where it gets complicated.'

CHAPTER FIFTY-FOUR

Canberra

Harry Dunkley had been hammering the keyboard solidly since Question Time, knocking out a splash, an inside lead and a 40-centimetre comment.

He was buggered, famished and in need of a drink. Or three. Most importantly, he owed Celia an apology. Finally, he closed down his PC.

'See ya tomorrow, Leonie. I'll be in early to monitor the vote in the House – can you make sure someone updates for online?'

Oh shit …

He'd nearly left the bureau when he remembered the envelope Celia had thrown on his desk.

It was lying under a notepad and recorder. He shoved it in his leather bag, reaching for his mobile to call his girlfriend, mentally rehearsing a well-worn apology.

Five rings and a familiar voice. 'Hi. You know the drill. Leave a message for Celia. Bye.'

Bugger.

'See ya Harry, which way d'ya reckon it'll go?'

Phil Coorey wore his usual look of mischief as he shuffled along the gallery corridor. The *Financial Review*'s chief newshound was tough competition and Dunkley wasn't in a sharing mood.

'Don't know, mate. We'll find out tomorrow, I guess.'

'Tomorrow? Too late Dunk. I've already called it. The government by one.'

Dunkley pushed the lift button, eager to escape Parliament after a twelve-hour shift. As the doors closed, he pulled out the envelope.

'Notes from the Cloud' was written along the top of the first page.

He scanned the first few lines. It was mainly practical stuff, explaining how Celia had decrypted several megabytes of Kimberley's parting gift to the world.

Hey, that is interesting.

A roll call of former mandarins jumped off the page. Leaders of Australia's defence and security establishment, going back decades. The names of several former US Ambassadors, too.

All under the one heading.

The Alliance.

Three minutes later he was sitting in his four-wheel drive in the Senate carpark. He turned on the interior light to read the rest of the material. His hands told him he needed a Scotch.

Celia had done great work and Dunkley was keen to atone for his tardiness.

He started the LandCruiser and reached for his phone, hitting the 'redial' button as he drove out into the night.

'Hi. You know the …'

Celia, don't do this to me. I'm sorry.

He eased the Toyota around Parliament Drive and turned into Kings Avenue. He was five minutes from her apartment in Kingston, a nice place in the new Foreshore development that Daddy had bought. Celia had moved in when she'd returned to Canberra six months ago, ignoring her father's plea to move back home.

She'd given Harry a key to the place a few weeks back, when it appeared their relationship was becoming more than just lustful obsession.

He turned right at National Circuit, past the Department of Prime Minister and Cabinet until he hit Brisbane Avenue. He veered towards the lake, flicking Celia's number again.

'Hi. You know …'

Dunkley cursed himself.

Hell hath no fury like a woman …

Except he hadn't scorned her. He'd simply been engrossed in knocking out a strong front-page yarn for the newspaper that had employed and sustained him for the past twenty-something years. He would make it up to her.

Is there a florist open this time of night?

No. And wilted carnations from the servo wouldn't do the trick. An apology on bended knee and praise for her detective work? Besides, they had work to do. Celia had uncovered material that would lead them – where?

The address was Kingston dress circle: Eastlake Parade. Third floor, views over the lake, tastefully furnished, fridge full of decent plonk, comfy bed. What more did a man need?

He opened the door, gently calling her name.

The lights to the apartment were on and the CD player was pumping out some Gen Y nonentity. And the entire place had been royally trashed.

She was curled up on a lounge, pale and scared. Her eyes were red-rimmed and she barely registered when he leaned down to kiss her cheek.

'Celia, what happened? Are you okay?'

Harry Dunkley hated coming to her parents' flash Forrest residence on two counts: her father, Roger, was just a decade older than he was, and Harry had touched up the pompous bureaucrat more than once.

But tonight Dunkley had swallowed his pride. A dozen calls to Celia's mobile had gone unanswered, and he'd arrived at Mathieson Manor just after 10pm.

'A beer, Harry?' Roger Mathieson was trying to be civil for the first time since he'd become aware of Dunkley's relationship with his daughter.

'Thanks ... er ... Roger. That would be great. Much appreciated. Have you called the police?'

'Yes, they came and went in a half-hour.'

Dunkley knelt by Celia's side. She looked washed out and had barely said a word. She was trembling.

Her brother sat on a facing lounge, glaring through unfashionably long hair. Clearly, the family was pinning the blame on the journalist for whatever had happened.

Suddenly Celia gave off an exaggerated sigh and sat up. She pointed to a brightly coloured canvas covering most of one wall, an opus by one of the Nungurrayi clan.

She whispered, so quietly he nearly missed it, 'He knew about it.'

Finally it was just the two of them. The rest of the Mathieson family had gone to bed, leaving Harry and Celia alone.

She was still subdued, avoiding his gaze. He was hungry for information but unsure how hard to push her. She reached for the safe grip of his hand.

'It was cold, Harry, cold and metallic. He placed it on my throat, not hard, more as a warning. I could barely see. I thought ...'

Her voice trailed off.

'Go on Cel, tell me what happened.'

'Well, I stupidly took the lift near the *Age*'s office, down to the basement. I was pissed off with you, didn't want to see anyone.'

He stroked her arm encouragingly.

'I'm walking along, trying to get my bearings, thinking I was heading the right way. Then, all of a sudden, the lights went out.'

She shuddered. 'Then he was there. Right beside me in the dark. His voice was ... so ... so calm and evil, as if he did this for a living. He told me if I screamed again it would be the last sound I made. I believed him.'

Celia reached for a whisky. It seemed to fortify her a little.

'He knew about what I'd been doing, Harry. The Cloud. The download. Everything.'

She was looking straight into his eyes.

'Go on,' he said.

'I was petrified. I saw an exit light down the hall, but he was blocking my way – he had a calm fury that scared me to pieces. He came right up to my face and that's when he mentioned the Nungurrayi. Oh Harry, I nearly … I mean that painting … he knew my family … I can't …'

Celia began a quiet sobbing again. 'I'm sorry. He knows too much – about me, us, my dad. I can't go on. Not with this. Not with you.'

CHAPTER FIFTY-FIVE

Canberra

Emily Brooks dropped her head into her hands and ran her manicured nails through her coiffured hair.

'I hate the fucking National Party.'

She had once said that nothing a politician could do would surprise her, but eighteen months as Opposition leader gave lie to that boast. The astounding news from her press secretary had again recalibrated her tragically low expectations of her colleagues.

'So he checked himself into hospital. Which hospital?'

'Canberra Hospital.' Justin Greenwich had taken a call moments earlier. 'He claims he's suffering nervous exhaustion and won't be able to vote.'

Dallas Bairstow was a New South Wales National Party MP who had spent his tender years as a boarder at Sydney's St Joseph's College. That was two strikes against him before he swung a bat in Brooks's eyes.

Bairstow had all the afflictions that came with both his creeds. He was an agrarian socialist who was deeply suspicious of markets and foreign investment. He never saw a government dollar that couldn't be spent on subsidies for the bush. And he was a bleeding heart. In Brooks's eyes, his only redeeming feature was that his years in a Catholic boarding school had given him a pathological fear of homosexuality and he was vehemently opposed to gay marriage.

'So, Justin, why is he really in hospital?' Brooks made a note to ensure the Trade portfolio was taken from the Nationals, should she ever become prime minister.

'The Nats tell me his electorate has the highest rate of mental illness in Australia and that his people love Toohey's bill. He says he can't vote against it.'

Brooks grabbed her mobile, searched its contacts and punched the name of the Nationals' leader.

'Charles? Emily. Don't talk, just listen. Get your deputy and get a private car. Drive to Canberra Hospital. Find that weasel Bairstow. Bring him back. Then don't let him out of your sight until after the vote.'

Brooks paused as the National leader's protest could be heard through the earpiece of her phone.

'I really don't give a rat's arse how you do it. Just do it.'

She hung up and threw the mobile down in disgust.

'Okay, let's assume all our own numbers hold on this vote. Who else have we got?'

Greenwich stared at his dog-eared notebook and chewed the end of his pen.

'Well, the Manager of Opposition Business assures me that, if pushed, the Speaker will use his casting vote with us on this one. But it won't come to that. Counting Bailey's pair, no matter how you cut it, I reckon we come up one vote short.'

Brooks drummed her nails on the desk.

'Pull the pair,' she spat.

Greenwich pleaded with her. 'Boss we can't. We were crucified in the media the last time we did that. You had to make a grovelling apology. And if the vote is tied, the Speaker might still rat on us. So we'd lose twice.'

Brooks shuddered at the memory; she hated having to apologise for anything.

'Justin, let me make this clear. I am not opposing this bill just to make Martin Toohey's life a misery. I'm doing it because the nation can't afford it. Toohey's racking up the national credit card and the bill will fall due when he's well out of politics. What is proposed is far worse than just an attempt by Labor to buy itself another multibillion-dollar indulgence in luvvie heaven. I would oppose the breathtaking stupidity of ceding Australian territory to China even if the billions it raked in were being used to build the landing pad for the second coming of Christ.'

Greenwich added one to his column.

'Well boss, if we do that, and if the Speaker holds, we win. But at what cost?'

CHAPTER FIFTY-SIX

Canberra

It glistened in the warm evening, this keeper of dark secrets, an artificial waterway neatly dividing the capital.

Canberrans either lived north or south of Burley Griffin, and too many, for Harry's liking, argued pointlessly over the merits of their postcode.

Dunkley played with the volume on the car radio as he gazed out at the troublesome waters. The night was quiet, but far from relaxing. The songbirds had gone silent; a few night creatures rustled in the bushes.

The memory. Two decades ago, he'd watched as an English tourist was hauled from the lake at this very spot. The man had become entangled in wire netting that fenced in the swimming hole used during Canberra's warmer months.

While the lifeless form was being dragged from the enclosure, Dunkley had peppered an irritated constable with questions.

He'd just been doing his job, a reporter on the make. But as he'd driven away in a photographer's car, he'd realised that he'd barely paused to think about the poor dead Brit.

That's when it had struck him like a thunderbolt: he had lost his compassion, his empathy. He'd become a hard-nosed scribe, caring only for the story. Callous and selfish. He'd lost his soul.

Here, at this lake. The devil's lake.

NewsRadio punctuated the night air. Parliament had descended into full-throttle chaos as the government and opposition traded kidney punches.

'Mr Acting Speaker, the Honourable Member is a grub …'

'Order! Order!'

It was closing in on midnight and Dunkley gazed past the pontoon and across the sheet of uninviting water. Having seen the damage to Celia's apartment, he wasn't in a hurry to go home. He needed to make sense of the past few hours, of the violence that had been unleashed. He felt alone, rushing headlong into danger.

His fists pushed against the vehicle's roof, his body tense.

Think mate, think.

He needed to put together the pieces of the puzzle. The ones he could see.

Eighteen months earlier they'd been working on a story about Bruce Paxton. Dunkley had been following leads that pointed to the Chinese. Kimberley had apparently uncovered another strand. Then she was killed.

Now Celia had been threatened after she'd unlocked some of Kimberley's secrets.

This was a story people were willing to kill for.

He needed to delve deeper into this murderous affair. He owed it to Kimberley, Celia, even to the unfortunate Englishman.

He also needed help. He checked the time. It was late, but the fearful never sleep.

He fumbled for his phone, scrolled through his contacts, and punched on a recent addition.

It was a ramshackle apartment on the edge of the Yarralumla shops. Trevor Harris had been forced to downsize when his marriage collapsed. It was still lawyers at ten paces, but she'd kept the house and he'd taken refuge in this man cave.

It was spacious and messy: a trio of surfboards in baggy covers leaned against a wall while some serious-looking hiking equipment was heaped in a corner. Two leather lounges fronted each other and a coffee table was layered in magazines – *Men's Health, GQ, Esquire, FHM.*

Harris selected some tunes on the MP3 as he explained that his oldest son, Drew, was using the apartment as part-home, part-storage shed. 'I've told him to come and go as he pleases, which he does.'

Dunkley nodded. He only wished Gaby would visit occasionally.

'Beer, Harry? Oh wait on … looks like Drew's taken the last one. Bugger.'

'No problem. I'll take whatever you've got.'

Dunkley had arrived ten minutes earlier feeling self-conscious. Harris was hardly a best mate.

'Sorry to barge in at this time of night.'

'That's okay. I don't sleep that well and, anyway, I'm running behind on a consultancy job.'

'Look, I appreciated our little chat the other day. In truth, I'm not sure where to go with this, Trev. But before we go any further, can I ask why you contacted me?'

'I thought long and hard before I did. I didn't know how much I could trust you.'

'Yeah, I felt the same way.'

'Well Harry, maybe it's time we both took a risk.'

Dunkley leaned forward and clinked his glass of red against Trevor's tumbler.

'Cheers to that, mate.'

'I don't think you appreciate how this game works, Harry. I worked for the signals directorate. We scoop up information from everyone. We work with similar agencies around the globe. Mate, we have bugged the planet. If we get interested in you, you have to assume that every move you make is being logged. Your mobile phone is a tracking device. We can turn it into a listening device. Every time you send an email, use an ATM, splash out on a credit card or surf the net for porn, we know.'

Harris nestled his glass between his hands.

'Harry, everyone marvels at what technology can do. They think it liberates them. But we've become slaves and chained ourselves to Big Brother.'

Dunkley thought of conversations he'd had with sources. How many had been monitored?

'Trev, you're making me nervous.'

'You should be nervous.'

Dunkley needed to delve into Harris's past.

'So why did you leave DSD?'

'As politicians say, mate, that is a very good question.'

'Do you have a good answer?

Harris put his glass down. He thumped the arm of the lounge twice.

'I was Ben's boss. He had access to some of the most highly classified material in the country. The means to tap into phones and computers. Usually if someone in that position dies in suspicious circumstances the intelligence community is all over it. That didn't happen.'

'Are you saying it was a cover-up?'

'I'm saying they didn't even do the basics. They didn't ask the usual questions. There was no inquiry. I kept pushing for one and was told the intelligence community was satisfied with the police report. It was made very clear to me that I should just let it drop. '

'But you couldn't, Trev?'

'No. And in my own time, and in my own way, I began to look more closely at what Ben had been doing. He had been accessing deeply sensitive material on our system and was covering his tracks along the way. And he was very good at it.'

Dunkley smiled. 'Kimberley always bragged that she was one of the best in the business.'

'Almost as good as me, mate.'

'So what did you find?'

'I found myself on the dole queue. I was made redundant, with no explanation.' Harris paused. 'So what have you got?'

Dunkley pulled out the plastic crypto card.

'I've got this.'

A pair of iMacs purred into life.

'I prefer to have two running, an old habit from DSD days,' Harris explained.

Dunkley perched on a leather dining chair he'd dragged across the room.

The page opened on a file of encrypted documents. Harris smiled in professional appreciation.

'I trained that guy well. He put some serious effort into making this a hard nut to crack. I'm sure I can open them but that's going to take some time. Let's have a look at what your girlfriend discovered.'

The two read in silence. It was quite a tale.

It was the late '60s, the height of the Cold War. Vietnam was escalating and Whitlam was making inroads into the national consciousness as a would-be prime minister.

A small cabal of Canberra mandarins was fretting at the prospect of Gough winning the 1969 election. So they formed a group, the Alliance – its name a salute to the security pact that was their sacred text – and began to meet regularly with the serving American Ambassador.

Names that had long vanished from the public gaze came tumbling out of Celia's summary.

* William Marshall, a former head of Foreign Affairs who'd served several stints in Washington during an illustrious career that stretched back to the agency's tenure as 'External Affairs'. The Queen had gonged him for 'public service leadership'.

* Nathan Martin, a top-line spook, once the head of Australia's domestic spy agency, ASIO, and then its foreign cousin, ASIS.

* Richard Althurst, who'd logged three decades at or near the helm of Defence, through to the early '90s. He'd been rewarded with a plum job as Australia's Ambassador to NATO.

* Darcy Guinness, another mandarin with feet in the intelligence and defence camps. He was stationed overseas for a decade before his appointment as head of ASIO from 1977 until 1984. Howard had considered appointing him Ambassador to the US after his '96 victory but had apparently been talked out of it.

* Gavin d'Alessio, a former paratrooper who'd turned Defence into a fearsome budget-gouging machine. The second-generation Italian courted controversy when he later snared lucrative contracts with several global 'gunrunner' firms that he'd dealt with as head of the military.

* Thomas 'Bulldog' Charlton, an infamous public service chief who'd floated in and out of Foreign Affairs during a forty-year career. He was renowned for stonewalling when parliamentarians came snooping on even the most trivial matters.

'Wow, quite a line-up, Harry. Very impressive. They would have sunk some dollars into the Commonwealth Club.'

'Sounds like a cult, dreaming up coups over G-and-Ts, all very cloak and dagger. But how does it link to the present?'

'That, my friend, is another very good question.'

CHAPTER FIFTY-SEVEN

Canberra

The first hint of dawn washed into the House of Representatives, a shimmer of light on a scene of parliamentary chaos.

For fourteen brutal hours the Toohey Government and Bailey Opposition had fought a war of attrition over the mental health reforms. The chamber, where the nation's laws were debated and written, may as well have been washed in blood. MPs were tired, emotional and impatient to escape the capital. A roster of speakers had struggled to keep order amid the pandemonium.

The previous afternoon, a successful ploy by the government's Manager of Business, Burt Crespo, to suspend standing orders had forced the MPs to stay. The Labor warhorse had delivered an impassioned speech, declaring, 'no one in this place should sleep soundly in their beds until this nation lives up to its duty of giving justice to the mentally ill'. But while Crespo had the numbers and the guile to ensure the House kept sitting, he didn't yet have sufficient backing for the legislation.

Labor had pulled every procedural trick in the book and filibustered the debate to keep the chamber running. Behind the scenes the Prime Minister and his team fought to cobble together an alliance that would deliver victory. The Manager of Opposition Business was counter-punching, trying to terminate proceedings as Emily Brooks schemed to kill the final vote.

Frantic whips from both parties had struggled to keep their unruly teams in check. Dallas Bairstow had been dragged back from hospital and was under house arrest in his office, with a Liberal and a National MP assigned to escort him to and from the toilet.

Every Labor MP had been instructed to stay awake and within a brisk four-minute walk of the chamber, as failing to make a division before the doors were locked could spell disaster. Unfortunately it was harder to stop exhausted and homesick MPs drinking and some of the small-hour speeches had been train-wrecks.

Around 4am there'd been a near disaster when the bells rang for a division and an eagle-eyed whip told Crespo that one of his charges was missing.

'Who?'

'Xavier Quinn.'

Crespo rolled his eyes.

'Of course.'

There were no prizes for guessing what the over-sexed Education Minister was up to, but the question was where? He should be able to hear the bells from anywhere in the building. Except …

'The Meditation Room!' Crespo yelled, unnerving nearby MPs as he sprinted from the chamber.

Crespo had been a useful rugby league centre in his youth and he hit full pace as he dashed along the glass-walled corridor that led to the marble-floored Members' Hall. He fixed his eyes on the call buttons of a little-used lift.

He hit 'UP' like an Olympic swimmer ending a race as he counted down the moments he had left to capture the errant minister and drag him back before they were both stranded on the wrong side of locked doors.

Elephant 200, elephant 199 ...

Once inside, he pressed the 'M' button and moments later a soothing recorded female voice intoned 'Mezzanine'. The next female voice he heard didn't sound so relaxed.

'Yes! Yes! Xavy ... ohhh!'

Crespo recognised the voice as belonging to Quinn's twenty-something press secretary, the latest in a long line. Happily they were so overcome with lust that they were disporting themselves within reach of the lift doors. Equally conveniently, the position they had assumed made it relatively easy to disentangle the MP.

'Hey! What the ... I'm busy!'

It must have been the adrenalin. Somehow Crespo managed to manhandle Quinn into the lift before the doors closed, leaving a startled press secretary hitching up her knickers in their wake.

'By my count you have eight seconds to get that thing back in your pants,' Crespo wheezed as he leaned on the elevator handrail for a breather. 'And when those doors open you keep pace.'

'Ground floor,' the mechanical voice rang.

'Run, fuckwit!'

Crespo had hold of the libidinous minister's jacket as the two hurtled across the marble hall, with Quinn trying to haul up his fly without inflicting permanent damage. That wasn't such a success.

'Arrgghh!' Quinn stumbled as their footsteps echoed in the glass-walled corridor just metres from the doors. Crespo yanked on his lapel and the MP managed to keep his footing.

The two men collapsed into the chamber just as the sands on the four-minute hourglass ran out. The bells fell silent. The Speaker intoned: 'Lock the doors.'

In the Prime Minister's office the night was proving as expensive as it was long. The smell of a desperate government is like the scent of blood for a shark to a crossbench MP. And, like all commodities, the cost of a vote rises with the level of demand.

George Papadakis was charged with keeping a running tally of the promises as five of the seven crossbench MPs cycled in and out. At 5.30am he, Martin Toohey and Crespo took stock. The Prime Minister had handled the negotiations and was exhausted but pleased with himself.

'I think we're just about there, aren't we, Burt?'

Crespo had checked and rechecked the undertakings as the numbers shifted through the night. He nodded.

'Right now, if everyone holds we have seventy-four votes to their seventy-three. So there will be no reason for the Speaker to have to use his casting vote. But if anything changes, if anyone goes missing and there's a tie, then he assures me he'll vote the bill down.'

Toohey turned to Papadakis who was nervously shuffling a small pile of notes and looking every one of his fifty-six years.

'Didn't we even try to get him, George?'

'PM, as I said, I went round to his office and personally invited him to chat with you. He made some joke about not wanting to be swayed by your charms and repeated that his electorate would rebel if he supported the bill. Almost nothing would sway him.'

'Almost. You're holding out on me, aren't you?'

'It was absurd, I'm sure he was joking.'

'What did he want?'

'Ambassador to the Holy See.'

'And we can't do that?'

'Not if you want to retain a shred of dignity. But after tonight I'm sure dignity is also on sale.'

Stung, Toohey changed the subject.

'And what did Paxton want?'

'Nothing.'

'Nothing?'

'Yep. I visited his office at about 2am. He said he was voting with us because he believed in the bill and would I mind pissing off because he'd found a replay of the drawn VFL Grand Final in 1977. He said it was his favourite game for two reasons: the drama of the draw and knowing that Collingwood would lose a week later.'

Toohey made circles with his finger on the rim of a glass balanced on the armrest of his burnt-orange lounge chair.

'So what's the damage?

'After the Tasmanian left ten minutes ago with his pockets stuffed full of cash, the bill for this little exercise topped one billion dollars over four years, Martin.'

Papadakis didn't hide his distaste for the vote auction. He knew Toohey also felt sullied. The Prime Minister gulped a mouthful of water and wearily put the glass down.

'It's a small price, George; we're making history here. Think of the legacy.'

'I will. But I'm also thinking about the bill I will leave my grandchildren.'

Toohey was starting to wriggle in his seat. Papadakis knew it was a signal he was tiring of the debate. The Prime Minister went fishing for a compliment.

'But George, the great negotiator sealed the deal again.'

'Martin, you can win over anyone when you give them everything they want.'

The government called on the vote at 7.22am and 147 exhausted MPs and a weary Speaker trudged into the chamber. The public galleries were packed with people who had come from across Australia to cheer the landmark reform. Several activists were ejected when they called out 'Shame on you, Emily Brooks' as the Opposition leader entered.

Toohey looked across the table that separated him from Brooks, caught her eye and glanced towards the Speaker. They rose and walked into the small space behind his chair, out of range of prying cameras.

'Emily, trust you had a good night.'

'And you, Martin.'

'We have the numbers.'

'It looks that way.'

'You should back this bill, Emily. This is a historic reform that would really benefit from bipartisan support.'

'It's billions we don't have and I will never support it.'

'As you wish. But this will be popular and I will make you wear your opposition like a crown of thorns.'

'Do your worst. Oh, and Martin. If this vote goes down I will count it as a want of confidence in your government and begin calling for an immediate election.'

Before he could answer, she had turned and walked over to the Manager of Opposition Business who was standing nearby. Something was up. As Toohey returned to his seat he heard the Speaker's call on the Third Reading vote.

'All those in favour say "Aye".'

Labor roared 'Aye' in unison.

'Those opposed say "No".'

The Coalition benches rang with 'No'.

'I think the ayes have it.'

'The noes have it,' called a group of Liberal frontbenchers.

'The House will divide. Ring the bells for four minutes.'

The clerk turned over the first of the three hourglasses that sit between the dispatch boxes on the table separating Government and Opposition. The Prime Minister was transfixed by Brooks, just metres away. He knew how hard she had fought to stop this bill and yet she was laughing with some of her frontbench colleagues. He motioned to Crespo, who was a handful of paces away and talking to the whips.

'Burt, do we still have the numbers?'

'Yes, just. By one. Seventy-four to seventy-three. Why?'

'Something's up, Brooks is too relaxed and was making threats about what she'll do if we lose.'

'There's no way. With Bailey out and her vote paired, seventy-four wins it.'

'Burt. That's it! Who's Bailey's pair?'

'Melanie Alexander.'

'Is she in the chamber?'

Crespo hoisted himself up onto the green leather frontbench and searched the faces of the Opposition. Then he saw her, tucked away in the National Party end of the chamber known as 'Cockies Corner'. With the pair withdrawn the vote would be tied, and the Speaker's casting vote would see the bill defeated. The Liberal MP's unexpected presence in the House had doomed Toohey's landmark reform.

Crespo jumped down beside Toohey and caught the eye of the Manager of Opposition Business, then hissed in a stage whisper, 'You rat.'

Toohey grabbed his arm. 'Stop the vote.'

'I can't. The division's started.'

'But they've broken the rules.'

'There are no rules. It's a convention, a matter of honour. And they have none.'

Brooks smirked. Toohey's shoulders sank and he slumped forward on the table. He turned his head to the hourglass and could see his dreams running out with the sand. In less than a minute, his treasured bill, and Labor's last hope of redemption, would be lost.

It was the change in the chamber chatter that made him look up. The gossip of the MPs began to wind down and heads were turning towards the rear doors that led to the Members' Hall.

There, framed in the light, was the silhouette of a wheelchair. Toohey wondered if it was a protester. Then there was a gasp of recognition from one of the Labor MPs near the door.

'Catriona Bailey.'

The chatter faded to astonished silence as the Foreign Minister's electric wheelchair glided across the threshold as the hourglass ran empty.

'Lock the doors,' boomed the Speaker.

The public galleries exploded in applause and cheers echoed ever louder despite the Speaker's protest.

The messiah had risen.

CHAPTER FIFTY-EIGHT

Canberra

It was a dangerous and symbolic location. But there were no safe places now. Her every movement was being monitored.

So she had chosen Nara Peace Park deliberately, ignoring his pleas for somewhere more secluded.

The park edged down to the lake. It was a short distance from the Chinese embassy with its secretive sister compound taking shape behind the razor wire. Weng Meihui had ventured several times to this lush square since arriving in Canberra, marvelling at the grace of its pagodas and stone sculptures.

Japan's Nara had forged a sister-city relationship with the Australian capital two decades ago and presented this small themed garden, featuring two of the largest stone lanterns ever built in Japan, as a gift to the people of Canberra. The lanterns symbolised the robust relationship between Australia and one of its largest trading partners – which also happened to be China's historic enemy.

He arrived late, sweating under the white-hot glare of a midday sun. The ComCar had dropped him off behind the Hyatt. He was dressed in a charcoal suit, white shirt and a tie of bold yellow.

Very handsome today, Bruce.

Paxton surveyed the garden suspiciously. A handful of women were pushing strollers along a stone path, engaged in the carefree banter of mums with a rare bit of time on their hands.

A park attendant, dressed in a khaki uniform, was fiddling with a sprinkler, trying to redirect its spray towards newly laid turf.

They met and embraced. He pulled back quickly.

'Relax, my darling,' Weng whispered in his ear. 'Of course they are watching. They expect us to meet. I want to make it easy for them to see but not hear us.'

She led him down a wide path to a gazebo where they took a seat on a timber bench. To the unsuspecting, they were a normal, loving couple stealing a moment.

Weng leaned into him, nestling her head on his right shoulder, dropping her voice.

'I'm scared, Bruce.'

Paxton looked down on her black hair.

'Why?'

'The Ambassador is suspicious of me. He caught me asking questions about two men.'

She sighed. Paxton reached out to hold her shoulders, lifting her gaze to his.

'What did you want to know about these two men?'

'They were room-mates of Lin An, the man who drowned in the lake. They are both dead, although I'm sure they had no choice in deciding their fate.'

Paxton's head was spinning. Three Chinese men dead.

'How do you know about this, Mei? When do you think they died? And why?'

'He told me, the Ambassador. He was warning me. I don't know all the details.' Weng straightened and pushed away. She looked careworn. 'Lin tried to defect and died in his escape. Nothing was handed back when we retrieved the body. But he is – was – one of our best cyber-minds and he could have placed a lot of information somewhere. And knowing the man who questioned Lin's roommates, I assume they died at his hands.'

Paxton gazed out at the surrounding parklands: Canberra at its orderly best. The heat had deterred the luncheon crowds. Mothers shielded their children from the sun. The lake was tranquil, several yachts trying to catch a few wisps of breeze.

And in the midst of this, just a few hundred metres away, two men had been murdered.

He shivered.

'Do you think he might hurt you?'

'Yes Bruce, I know he will.'

Paxton drew her close again as he absorbed the horrifying news.

'We could call in the police, Mei, or I could make an official complaint through Foreign Affairs. '

'Your government will not take the risk of offending mine. If there is a controversy the State will drag me back. And if I'm sent home I have no future.'

He looked at her tenderly. 'Perhaps you should consider defecting.'

'Where could I ever go, Bruce?'

'Look, I'm no great friend of the Yanks. But I'll give them this. They don't have any problem standing up to China. I know their defence attaché well. We could get you out of the country. Soon. Mei, you would be a coup for them.'

She started to sob quietly. He held her tight, ignoring a couple walking past the gazebo just a few metres away. He needed to protect his angel.

They would make plans to get away. Yes, the risk would be great, but the risk of doing nothing was far greater.

'And maybe if you go to America I could join you.'

Weng nestled into his embrace, resting her head on his shoulder. For the first time in days she felt safe.

CHAPTER FIFTY-NINE

Melbourne

'Saffy, what's your favourite colour?'

'You know the answer Jimmy: green, green, green.'

Saffron Burgess and James Saville sat a few metres apart in front of a bank of computer screens flashing lines of technical data.

They were two of Vodafone's leading security boffins, paid to monitor the beating heart of the telco's vast mobile network. Burgess, a computer science graduate from Sydney's UTS, had punched her way to the top of the notoriously blokey culture. She was now one of the senior members in Vodafone's network operations centre, based in Melbourne.

Saville was her boss, a street-smart IT buff who had joined Vodafone back in the '90s, shortly after the British-based firm had secured Australia's third mobile phone licence. He was closing in on his fifty-eighth birthday and was known affectionately throughout Vodafone as T-Rex.

Each day, they and their team monitored the cellular base stations and network for hiccups, ensuring that customers got their dollars' worth.

The last two years had been the toughest in memory, a series of network crashes earning the ire of customers and management alike. Saville knew the real reason behind the outages – a failure to invest by the Scrooge-like board.

But that didn't stop the executive team giving him a kick up the backside every time they went to red.

'Have you been to that new laneway bar, Jimmy? The something Institute?'

'C'mon Saffy, those places are for you young types. Besides, Anna and I try to walk every night around the bay. Clears the head after—'

Saville pulled up quickly. 'Uh oh, we've got orange in the west.'

He traced his finger along a row of data to a pulsing circle that had suddenly changed colour: green to orange. That meant an overload of data traffic on one of the gateways.

And that meant customer access to the internet on mobile phones would be cut off.

'We got a position on this yet?' Saville asked his offsider.

'No. I'm trying to locate it right now. Looks like it's on the coast, just south of the CBD.'

Saville punched a series of buttons, trying to get an accurate picture of the network traffic levels. Something was amiss. A swift response was crucial if they wanted to avoid further outages.

'Mandurah, Jimmy.' Burgess spat out the name.

'Jesus, I thought we'd spent decent money upgrading those gateways down to Margaret River. Okay, let's divert some of this traffic to Rockingham.'

Garden Island, WA

The military band stood poised, waiting for the conductor's signal. As the first strains of 'The Star Spangled Banner' rang out, Aubrey W. Holland raised his right hand to his breast, eyes trained on the unfurled beauty of the American flag.

The four-star admiral had been appointed Commander of the US Pacific Command just under a year ago. This was his first official visit to HMAS *Stirling*, the Australian navy's main base on the west coast.

It was just after 11am and an early sea breeze was softening a blazing summer's day. Holland had arrived in Perth the previous evening, and had several days of meetings lined up, primarily to discuss a series of joint naval exercises. He was also hoping to catch up with several old naval buddies, including an Aussie mate he'd met during his first tour of duty to Vietnam in '72.

It reminded him of San Diego, this naval base; the sparkling waters and friendly personnel. A small flotilla of vessels was moored at the dock, undergoing routine maintenance while their crews enjoyed several days of shore leave.

'Admiral, this way sir.' He was guided up the gangplank of HMAS *Perth*, the youngest of the navy's fleet of ANZAC frigates, commissioned just seven years ago.

It was impressive, a descendant of the warship that was sunk by the Japanese during the Battle of Sunda Strait at the height of World War II.

'The commander is waiting for you, Admiral.'

'Thank you, sailor.'

Holland was ushered into a plush boardroom, lined with photos of the ship and its crew. A waiter poured coffee as the admiral waved away a plate of pastries.

Michele Miller bounded into the room, flanked by an aide. She'd made history when appointed to command the warship in 2007, the first female sailor to do so. Holland considered her an impressive addition to Australia's naval elite, although her absence at his official welcome had been a tad mysterious.

'Nice to see you, Commander.'

'And you too, Admiral. You look well, sir. Sorry I missed the anthems. For some reason, Vodafone has decided to shut down our internet coverage. Again.'

Melbourne

Saffron Burgess straightened, pushing her ribcage and lower back forward to untangle the knot of her muscles. The pressure was building.

A small network hiccup had grown into a more serious problem. She and James Saville had tried to isolate the outage but it had spread. Orange lights were flashing across her screen and Saville was increasingly frustrated at the time it was taking to put in place back-up systems.

'Christ, I thought we had this covered,' he said, his voice rising in volume.

Mobile internet connection was out of action from Fremantle to Augusta, hundreds of kilometres away. Vodafone's customer service lines were being overrun by scores of irate punters unable to access Google or Facebook.

More disturbing was the inexplicable claim that some punters couldn't make phone calls.

The data and voice systems were strictly separated. Voice was carried through radio waves, and data through internet IP.

Vodafone's diagnostic systems showed that the voice lines were fine.

Something didn't add up.

It was a PR nightmare and the operations centre was being harassed by management to get things right, pronto.

'We can't divert all this traffic to Perth. It will overload the network,' Burgess said.

They'd been joined by Dave Taylor and Ross Hopkins in the operations centre, the four of them tasked with rescuing Vodafone from an expensive and embarrassing meltdown.

Saville studied the network plan, a series of orange lights now flickering their warnings.

'Have we got a fix on the problem here?'

'Not yet boss,' Burgess fired back.

A team of technicians had already been scrambled across the south-west of Western Australia, but the remoteness and huge distances meant it would be hours before all the problems were diagnosed.

'Another one down, boss.' Hopkins delivered the bad news without a glimmer of emotion.

'Shit, where this time?' Saville asked.

'Down at Albany, bottom of the state.'

'Right, so we've got problems from Freo right along the coast, and inland hundreds of kilometres.'

Burgess looked up from her screen. 'And it's about to get a whole lot worse.'

'Why?'

''Cause we've just gone to red.'

Patrick Fitzgerald's patrician voice boomed out of the speaker-phone. Since arriving from Britain two years earlier, the Vodafone CEO had spent endless hours defending the company's reputation.

'A new era of network investment and improvement,' had been his mantra, against claims the company was the telco equivalent of the Leyland P76.

But this was his greatest challenge. Vodafone's network in the west was collapsing and his technical crew had failed to isolate the problem.

Twitter was in overdrive – #notfunnyvodafone was starting to trend. The company was fielding media calls from local radio stations, while irate customers were flooding its Customer Care hotline.

The CEO was in a black mood. He'd ordered an emergency meeting of the crisis incident response team. They were scattered around Australia, patched in via conference-call technology.

'James, what's the latest?'

'It's not good news, Mr Fitzgerald. The IP network in the west is seizing up. We're scrambling to divert traffic but the network is showing signs of system overload.'

'Have you got a fix on the source of the problem, James?'

'We're working on that, Mr Fitzgerald. I've got three of my team trying to isolate the source and I hope to have an answer within a few hours. But there seems to be a problem with our control-plane diagnostics. The read-outs don't match the calls we're getting.'

The CEO rubbed his eyes and sighed. Loudly.

'Not good enough, James. I want a report in half an hour. The problem must be solved. Network outage means bad publicity means loss of customers and revenue. Fix it. Now!'

Pumped-up Pommy prick.

Saville was livid. He'd been flat chat for the last four hours on this crisis and his CEO was treating him like an intern. It was always the same with the Brits. They sent out favoured sons who thought they'd lord it over you, only to find out that running a mobile network in Australia was much tougher than it seemed from a distance of 17,000 kilometres.

'Saffy, you got the latest read-out for me, please?'

Saville was determined not to lose his cool. His team had managed to stabilise the number of outages but he was worried about a report just handed to him by a network analyst.

'Vodafone network hit with 1.5Gbps D-Dos. UDP-based attack. Some form of botnet used, originating from India via Russia.'

340

Christl

That alone meant Vodafone was in deep, deep trouble. He'd never experienced a botnet attack but, like most tech-heads, had read the literature. He knew how easy it was to buy a swag of infected computers and train them on a target.

The victim, this time, was Australia's third largest mobile phone network.

That kind of attack would explain the loss of data but not of voice connections. Something else was wrong on the system's internal control plane. The adversary had got behind the firewalls.

'Jimmy, line four for you.'

He picked up the phone. It was Sam Vasoukis, the PR head calling from Sydney.

'Hi Jim, got a minute? We're in deep do-do. Channel Nine's called. Not good, mate, not good.'

'Sam, what exactly is the issue?'

'Sorry, Jim.' Vasoukis sighed loudly. 'I just got off the phone from the executive producer out of Sydney. They're going to air with a story on us. They reckon we've been hacked into … by the Chinese.'

Canberra

Martin Toohey swept into the secure Cabinet Situation Room, a phalanx of advisers in tow. His mood was toxic. He was supposed to be entertaining a group of schoolchildren as a favour for an old Labor mate.

Instead, the National Security Committee had been summoned following Nine's 6pm bombshell. Toohey was furious.

The company had made no effort to warn the government and he'd instructed his Minister for Communications to put a bomb up Vodafone.

The other television networks had swung into spoiler overdrive, attempting to play catch-up on a massive story that had serious implications – for Australia, for the Toohey Government, for relations with China.

He had adopted a cautious approach to these cyber-attacks – until now. The court of public opinion was turning swiftly against the Chinese and the PM knew that he would be collateral damage if he didn't take firm and decisive action.

As he took his usual seat he glanced around the room at his National Security Committee team. Every face was bleak.

'Right ... what have we got?'

Attorney-General Danny Maiden was on a video link from Melbourne.

'Prime Minister, Vodafone has confirmed that it was the target of a highly sophisticated D-DOS attack. That's "distributed denial of service". This one was lethal. Usually when the network overloads, they shift traffic between gateways. Each time the technicians tried that, the D-DOS point of attack shifted. No one in the company has ever seen anything like this before. But there was another, more disturbing, aspect to this.'

'What's that, Danny?'

'The attack should have only brought down data. This one also cut off voice.'

'Can they explain that?' Toohey asked.

'They think their control plane – that's the highly protected management system that runs the whole show – was infected by malware. An email opened by the CEO several weeks ago spread a virus. The D-DOS attack triggered it. Their systems were spitting out incorrect readings. Every move they made only exacerbated the emergency. Eventually they shut themselves down.'

Toohey demanded answers from the room. 'How many Vodafone customers are there in Australia?'

He was met with stony silence.

The PM turned to his chief of staff. 'George, how many are there?'

'Too many, Prime Minister – and most of them vote.'

The PM exhaled. The fallout would be devastating.

'Danny, are they back online yet?'

'Yes, they're limping back to full capacity, and the damage is restricted to the Vodafone network.'

'No, Danny. The most popular television network in the country has linked this attack to our largest trading partner. Every other media outlet is following. The damage is much greater.'

Toohey turned to the Defence Minister. 'Brendan, has the signals directorate any clear idea who was behind this?'

Brendan Ryan picked up a briefing note he'd been handed just moments earlier.

'Well, PM, we're still analysing it. DSD has no doubt that the last two cyber-attacks, on air-traffic control and the banking system, originated in China. But I note that the Vodafone attack originated close to the naval base at Stirling. And it happened just as it was welcoming the US Pacific Commander.'

Toohey looked at the leaders of his national security agencies.

'Gentlemen, I asked you once before if you thought China was behind these attacks. Have you any doubts now that Beijing masterminded them?'

'No sir.' Jack Webster, Chief of the Defence Force, answered for all. 'Not one of us.'

'Well then, we are effectively under attack. If I don't respond I will be failing in my duty to defend the nation.

'So we will send a squadron of planes to Guam. We will tell the Americans and the Chinese that they are being sent for "joint exercises".'

Toohey turned to his chief of staff. 'George, I want Ambassador Golding called back from Beijing "for talks". I want the strongest of messages sent to the Chinese Government. I will announce these measures after this meeting.

'We won't let Beijing screw us over anymore.'

CHAPTER SIXTY

Canberra

The diplomatic red carpet had been rolled up. The usual pleasantries had been dispensed with. There was not even the offer of a cup of tea.

'Prime Minister, thank you for seeing me at short notice. I will not waste your time.'

It was just the two of them in the office: not even a notetaker. Neither of them sat down.

Tian Qichen cleared his throat. 'My government is very displeased with your decision to send Australian war planes to Guam.'

Toohey stood ramrod straight, his ruckman's build towering over the Ambassador.

'And I am very displeased, Ambassador, that my country has come under cyber-attack – not once, but three times in the last month. And we're talking serious, damaging, potentially fatal attacks,' the PM responded.

He motioned to a sheaf of papers. 'My national security team says there is no doubt the attacks were launched from China. Frankly, I'm baffled. I have no idea what we've done to prompt this.'

Tian was equally resolute. 'Prime Minister, we deny it absolutely. You have no evidence that China is behind any of this. The Vodafone strike was routed through Russia and India, according to your own media reports. China does not attack its friends.'

'Ambassador, the evidence is overwhelming. Our best security analysts are now convinced that China – officially or otherwise – is behind these attacks. Beyond that, your country has been increasingly aggressive since the beginning of the year. You have behaved maliciously towards your neighbours in the South and East China Seas. Japan is Australia's good friend.'

'And China is your major trading partner, Mr Toohey. You don't seem to value our relationship as highly as I thought.'

'We value it greatly. But we are not going to have our silence bought as you seek to shift the balance of power in the Pacific. I've been a good friend of China. I've publicly called on the US to exercise restraint and accommodate China's peaceful rise.'

Toohey fiddled with the knot of his tie before continuing.

'But your provocations make restraint impossible. If I'm to be forced to choose between trade and peace, then I choose peace. I ask you: withdraw the fishermen from the disputed islands. Close down the Air Defence Identification Zone. Propose talks to end this conflict before a fatal mistake is made. If China does that, I will ensure no Australian warplanes leave these shores.'

Tian bristled. 'China is not the aggressor in this conflict. We find ourselves surrounded by hostile forces. We are merely defending our territory, as you would defend Australia. America is determined to keep us boxed in.'

'I'm sorry you feel that way, Ambassador. But while you hold these positions I am bound to protect what I see as the interests of my nation. We will support our friends. And that shouldn't be taken as an act of aggression.'

Tian held Toohey's gaze as he unclipped his briefcase and reached for an envelope that he handed to the Prime Minister.

'This is a letter nullifying the heads of agreement between Sinopec and your government, Prime Minister. China will search elsewhere for gas.'

Toohey had been half-expecting this response, but still wore the look of a man who'd just glimpsed his own mortality.

'I was assured by you, Mr Tian, that dealing with a Chinese state-owned enterprise was no different to dealing with any business from any country. You lied.'

CHAPTER SIXTY-ONE

Canberra

The Defence Minister's office was a salute to the best military hardware that money could buy.

Two models of the F-35 Stealth fighter, locked in a mock dogfight, stood next to a plastic Collins Class submarine. An air-warfare destroyer, just over a metre long, had pride of place on a coffee table.

As Harry Dunkley passed through the outer office, he recalled that Brendan Ryan had once confided to him that he'd never aspired to be top dog. No, the only jobs he ever craved were 'powerbroker' and 'Defence Minister'.

Now he had both.

Ryan always found time to meet with Dunkley. Harry was one of a select few in the gallery whom the minister courted.

'Thanks for seeing me, Brendan. It's been a crazy few weeks,' the reporter said as he was ushered into the inner sanctum.

'Sure has, Harry, and we're a long way from done yet. Anyway, you called this meeting and we don't have much time. So what's on your mind?'

Ryan chewed into a donut and washed it down with a swig of Coke Zero.

'I want to chat, off the record, about some stuff that's come into my orbit.' Dunkley began. 'You remember my friend Kimberley, who was killed. Well, she was working on some important stuff just before she died.'

'Yep. I remember it well. We had a long conversation and I think we agreed that the Chinese were involved.'

'We did. But now I'm not so sure.' Dunkley coughed. 'Mate, what's the weirdest stuff you've come across as minister?'

'Christ! In Defence? There's stuff that we did in Vietnam that's still not declassified. So if you're looking for weird shit, you've come to the right portfolio. But what's your point?'

'I'm not sure I have a point, but I want to run some stuff past you to see if it makes any sense.'

The minister gulped his Coke and nodded.

'So, here's the thing,' Harry said. 'I've got indications that the Americans have done some interfering in Australian politics. Deeper and for longer than I would have imagined.'

'How so?' Ryan was stony-faced.

'A group of mandarins was at the core of it. Senior defence and intelligence people in this town. I've got a list of names – old names – who were effectively running a shadow government in league with the US embassy. It stretches back to before Whitlam.'

'Harry, let me play devil's advocate. You're telling me that some former bureaucrats were talking to American ambassadors about how Australia is run and defended? Isn't that their job?'

'Brendan, this looks to be more than friendly fireside chats. I'm talking the real deal here. These guys have been interfering – quite maliciously – to get their own way.'

'That's a serious accusation. What have they done? And what evidence do you have beyond a list of names?'

'Well, we've got—'

'Hang on. You said "I" before and now you're saying "we". Who's working with you?'

'Don't worry about that, mate, just hear me out. Okay, so I came across some material that had been placed on a computer Cloud. You know what that is?'

'Stuff on the internet, like the stories that say there was a second gunman at the Kennedy assassination.'

'No mate, stuff that a top-line security analyst uncovered – not long before she was killed.'

'Kimberley? How did she come by this material? Did she steal it?'

'You and I know each other pretty well, Brendan, we trust each other. How she got the material matters less than whether it's fair dinkum.'

'How she got it actually matters a lot, but let's get back to my main point. What's this secret society doing and what hard evidence do you have?'

'Mate, there's the list of top-level officials – departmental secretaries and the like – who were part of this secret society. It

350

includes former heads of ASIS, ASIO, Defence. And, like I said, US ambassadors …'

'Oh, and who else? Robert Mugabe? The Pope?'

Dunkley ignored the jibe.

'They called themselves the Alliance. The whole thing stretches back forty years. Remember Whitlam's speech to Parliament after he was shafted? He belled the cat. The Yanks were behind his demise. It's just that your mates mythologised the great man by claiming he was a victim only of Fraser's duplicity.'

'Harry, don't lecture me on Labor history. Whitlam did have reason to be angry. The Yanks did get more involved than they should have.'

'I told you eighteen months ago the Yanks were worried about Paxton, and they had every right. He was the Defence Minister and was cavorting with a Chinese spy.'

'So of course the US kicked up a stink. They share intelligence with us. And yes, sometimes they get a bit pushy. But you're asking me to believe they were part of a shadow government running Australia. That, my friend, is a world-class conspiracy. Show me your evidence. Isn't that what your editor would ask?'

Dunkley was firm. 'I have evidence but I can't share it yet. I ain't gonna stop, Brendan.'

Ryan ran his hand over a plastic M1 Abrams tank, rubbing dust from his fingers.

'Harry, you know I have the greatest respect for you. And I do remember that conversation. Vividly. I told you about America's concerns. You didn't seem to think it was such a big deal then.

Because it wasn't. And I told you that I feared our former PM was a Chinese spy, and you accused me of peddling fiction.'

Ryan started fiddling with the model's cannon as his tone softened.

'I'm sure you'll have something that will turn out to be a story. You always do. But if you came here hoping that I'd be able to confirm this … extraordinary tale … you're out of luck. It's all news to me.'

The parliamentary bells started to ring. The Senate was dividing. Ryan glanced at his watch.

'Listen mate, I have to go, but look, I have a real story for you, one ready to print. I know you hate leaving here empty handed.'

He reached into a drawer and pulled out a sheet of A4 paper. Dunkley could only make out the words 'UMR Polling'.

'Harry, you can't have this or look at it. But I'll tell you what's on it. Usual rules, no reference to government sources – but you can report the ALP has been road-testing Catriona Bailey in marginal seats. Twice in the last fortnight. One in Sydney's west, the other in Brissie. A nice coincidence with her return to Parliament, don't you think? And, my friend, the Foreign Minister is rockin' in the suburbs.'

CHAPTER SIXTY-TWO

Canberra

Martin Toohey could feel the noose tightening around his neck.

Within hours of his showdown with the Chinese Ambassador, Sinopec released a statement saying the Northern Territory gas hub had been shelved 'for the foreseeable future', citing finance problems.

It was another lie, but one Toohey would be forced to mimic to cover the crumbling relationship with Australia's largest trading partner.

The immediate problem was summed up in an AAP wire story. With the gas deal off, the rivers of gold to fund Toohey's ambitious social program had evaporated.

TOOHEY'S MULTIBILLION-DOLLAR BLACK HOLE

Chinese energy giant Sinopec has scuttled plans to build a gas hub off the Northern Territory, sabotaging the Toohey Government's hopes of using the project's cash to fund mental health reform.

The landmark legislation scraped through the Lower House last week, with the stunning return of Foreign Minister Catriona Bailey tipping the balance in the government's favour.

Sinopec's decision is the latest disaster for Prime Minister Martin Toohey, with Ms Bailey's return reigniting leadership speculation.

One Labor MP described the Sinopec bombshell as 'the sound of the coffin lid being dropped on Toohey's carcass'.

The PM turned as he heard the sound of the door opening behind him.

'It's bad,' Papadakis said as he entered. 'I've been taking soundings with Caucus and the vultures are circling. I've got the secretary in the Environment Minister's office across the hall from Bailey's suite keeping watch. There's a traffic jam of suckholes down there. I've asked Brendan Ryan to start counting our numbers.'

'Does he have any idea how they stand?'

'It's close. If the Right holds we might hang on but you know better than me that nobody really controls the numbers in leadership ballots. There's no block votes, just alliances of convenience. A cross-factional group is working with Bailey. Apparently they call themselves the Cardinals.'

The PM rolled his eyes. 'Really?'

'Really. You couldn't make this shit up. These people read too much Dan Brown. If only they put their vivid imaginations to good use.'

Toohey turned back to his computer and flicked through some of the dozens of articles that had been written about Bailey's 'miraculous' return. From the moment she'd glided into the chamber, Toohey knew her gravitational pull would suck all the light from his mental health reforms. But her reception had staggered him. News stories on her rare recovery, heroism, selflessness and courage had plastered the papers, the airwaves and online.

One pointy head at *The Guardian* had even dubbed Bailey 'Mother Courage', dredging up the title of the 1930s play by Bertolt Brecht. Whatever she was called, Bailey and her plotters were a real and present danger.

'If she wants it, she's gonna have to blast me out.' Toohey thumped the desk. 'I'm not getting spooked into calling a ballot based on plotting and whispering. They'll need signatures to force a Caucus vote. Let's see which mother has the courage to put their name to that.'

Papadakis nodded. 'Anything else, PM?'

'Yep. Tell Brendan to get down here so we can go through the numbers. I'm not making any calls or that will leak too. And when we're done with that, there's the minor matter of World War Three brewing on our doorstep. We might want to discuss that at some point. I'm afraid the Yanks are about to do something that we'll all regret.'

There was a knock at the door and Eleanor Todd opened it a fraction.

'PM, you got a minute?'

'Yep, George and I were just finishing.'

Todd pushed the door open and leaned on the frame.

'PM, I thought I should let you know. The *Financial Review*'s been in touch with Standard and Poors. They're threatening to review our AAA credit rating if we push ahead with the mental health reform.'

'It would be easier spinning for Big Tobacco. Brooks is now so toxic she should come with her own health warning.'

Justin Greenwich ended the call to his girlfriend and scrolled forlornly through dozens of messages.

We're rooted.

Greenwich was a Liberal careerist who had risen from the ruck of Victorian state politics to make it to the big arena of Canberra. He'd arrived just as the Howard Government fell and had been the media minder for three opposition leaders in six years.

It was the job almost universally acknowledged to be the most thankless in politics. He saw his role as the whipping girl's underpaid understudy. Years of ritual flogging at the hands of the media had hardened his hide. But he had never seen anything like this.

The decision to deviously revoke Catriona Bailey's pair would have been hard to spin on any day.

But to do it and then lose the vote ... Gandhi couldn't survive that.

Liberal Party focus group testing showed it had cemented the community's many concerns about Brooks. 'Deceitful, heartless bitch' pretty much captured the mood of the mob.

Brooks had even been canned by radio shock jocks and the Right's online cheerleaders. All agreed that she should have been an unbackable favourite at September's election, but instead she was a drag on the Coalition's strong polling.

Let's face it, we were dead when the bondage video came out.

Greenwich picked up a media release he intended to get framed, to commemorate the moment when the Opposition leader hit the point of no return.

SEX PARTY BACKS BROOKS

The Australian Sex Party will campaign for the re-election of Emily Brooks in her Queensland seat of Moncrieff.

Sex Party leader Robbie Swan said the party would direct preferences to the Opposition leader in her Gold Coast electorate. Local sex workers would person every booth and hand out how-to-vote cards.

'She has done more to make bondage mainstream than *Fifty Shades of Grey*,' Mr Swan said. 'That should be rewarded.'

CHAPTER SIXTY-THREE

Yokosuka

'Sir, it's PACOM. Line Five. Admiral Holland's office.'

Frank W Vinson looked up from his dinner, placed his cutlery on the table and rose to take the call.

The one-star admiral wiped his mouth with a white napkin, embellished with 'FWV', and turned to his two dining companions. 'Gentlemen, 'scuse me. You keep eating though, that beef is good.'

The naval veteran was commander of Carrier Strike Group 5, an eight-ship flotilla whose flagship was the USS *George Washington*, one of ten nuclear-powered aircraft carriers that sailed under the Stars and Stripes.

The carrier was a floating colossus, measuring three football fields bow to stern, and twenty stories high. Two fourth-generation nuclear reactors could keep it steaming for eighteen years without refuelling.

More than 5000 crew crowded inside. In the heat of combat, its four steam-driven catapults could sling one of its seventy-five planes into the air every twenty seconds. Each was a deadly war machine.

In blue water the *George Washington* was a giant hub radiating deadly spokes. Its Super Hornets prowled the sky, guided missile cruisers *Shiloh* and *Antietam* defended the sea, and destroyers *Curtis Wilbur* and *Fitzgerald* the water beneath. Two nuclear-powered attack submarines, the *Tucson* and *City of Corpus Christi*, lurked ahead and the oiler USNS *Tippecanoe* tagged behind, carrying jet fuel and other supplies.

Vinson commanded an armada that combined more military muscle than most nations could muster. Moored in Japan, it was the only forward-based US carrier strike group, projecting American power to China's doorstep. When it sailed, it sent an unmistakable message: we rule the waves.

It was 7.10pm in Yokosuka, which made it just after midnight in Hawaii. Something was biting.

Vinson opened his office door, flicked on the light and manoeuvred around a narrow space to his desk. He sat in his leather swivel chair and pushed a button on his phone.

'Sir, how are you? It must be early in Honolulu. This must be serious.'

Admiral Holland's appointment as Commander of the Pacific Command was a popular choice; he was a former aircraft carrier leader who'd been awarded the Distinguished Service Medal.

'Frank, you sound chirpy, or maybe I'm just damn tired. But you're right, this isn't a personal chat. I've already talked with

PACFLEET and the Seventh Fleet Commander, but wanted to speak directly to you.'

Vinson had been expecting a call, but not from the man who commanded all US forces over half the world's surface. But he was ready: his group had been 'working up' to put to sea for days. They could sail within eight hours.

'Sir, what's my mission?'

'The President has ordered you to sail into the Taiwan Strait. He is determined to reassert America's right of free passage through international waters. I want you on the move by midday tomorrow.'

It was an extraordinary command. And it was high risk. Sending one of America's nuclear-powered warships into the disputed waters was akin to throwing a flaming rock at a swarm of angry wasps.

'Aubrey, that is quite a move. What are my rules of engagement?'

There was a slight pause before Holland spoke. 'You are to do what it takes to sail from one end of the strait to the other, north to south, and return to port.'

'What is my posture, sir?'

'Condition Zebra. I want you battle ready. Combat aircraft flying, electronic warfare systems up on all vessels.'

It was an extremely aggressive way to enter the strait. The Chinese electronic eyes would see a strike group ready for war.

'And if there's an incident? Do I escalate, or de-escalate?'

'You do what you have to to complete your mission.'

Vinson was disturbed. The strike group was the safest, and

most formidable, on the open sea. He would be placing his crews in harm's way in contained waters, within reach of all the PLA's weapons.

If the group got into a fight they would face an overwhelming force with nowhere to retreat. But there were larger strategic considerations. Any miscalculation by either side could quickly spiral out of control. An accident could be misinterpreted and spark a regional war. Or worse.

'Sir, you know better than anyone that there are no protocols covering an incident at sea between the US and China.'

'I appreciate that, Frank. If something happens I can't pick up the phone and tell Admiral Leng Sha that we have no intention of picking a fight.'

'So all they can do is read our body language through their radar.' Vinson wanted his reservations underlined. 'And it will be screaming that we have kicked open the doors on the toughest bar in town armed with a broken bottle.'

'Believe me, I understand all your concerns.' Holland sounded weary. 'And they are reasonable. But I have my orders and you have yours.'

'Yes sir.'

'Thank you, Frank. Detailed orders and rules of engagement will be sent through asap, usual channels. Your trip will be announced by the Secretary of Defence on *Good Morning America*. Now, m'boy, I'm going to get some shut-eye.'

Vinson sat back and exhaled. It had been four years since America had sailed one of its carrier groups through the Taiwan Strait. That had nearly ended in disaster.

The USS *Kittyhawk* had been shadowed by a Chinese attack submarine and destroyer, triggering a twenty-eight-hour stand-off.

This would be very different: a deliberate, public swagger through China's front door designed to show the world that there was only one superpower.

That really was taunting the dragon.

The admiral lifted a framed photo on his desk. His wife, Judy, still gorgeous despite the years, flanked by their extended family. The commander's diaspora. He loved this clan, and they loved him back.

He pulled a pad from the desk drawer and started making notes. He would follow his orders to the letter, even if the thinking behind this decision was hard to fathom.

Beijing

The outdoor broadcast vans from China Central Television had arrived early. A crowd of several hundred Chinese was already gathered on Liangmaqiao Road outside the Japanese embassy. They carried nationalist flags and chanted anti-Nippon slogans in the freezing Beijing morning. They were mainly young, enraged – and sanctioned by the State.

Ambassador Ito Sanetomi gazed down at the growing mob. Six months earlier, more than a thousand marauding Chinese had demonstrated outside these same walls against Japan's rightful claim to the Senkaku Islands. He recognised several faces as three vans of Chinese riot police arrived.

'Asumi, I want all embassy staff to the central meeting room in ten minutes, please.'

The ambassador was taking no chances. Last September's protests had triggered a wave of violence against Japanese consulates throughout China, incited by inflammatory banners that declared 'For the Respect of the Motherland, we must go to War with Japan'. A Toyota van had been torched – a pointless reprisal.

Now that the United States had decided to sail the *George Washington* through the Taiwan Strait, he would take no chances. All staff except for emergency personnel had been ordered to leave.

A crash drew his eyes to a mob who'd separated from the main crowd and were trying to scale an embassy fence. They were being forced back by riot squad officers. The defence was holding, for now.

But the ambassador knew this mob – and crowds like it throughout China – would only grow and become more aggressive. Sanetomi was anticipating a recall to Japan. He'd received a cable to say that he should expect such a directive if the situation worsened.

He'd ordered his wife to pack and prepare their two children. As he looked out at the violence below, he longed to breathe the peaceful air of his beloved Tokyo.

Jiang Xiu carefully studied the material in front of him, erasing several words that he found distasteful. He blanched at one sentence that was excessive, but otherwise he was pleased with the work.

China's Central Propaganda Department was in full swing and Jiang was barking instructions to a team of senior editors who'd gathered in his Beijing office.

'I want this out through the 50 Cent Party. Now!' The communist giant was mounting a public relations offensive against the West and Jiang needed every piece of his propaganda arsenal primed and ready to roll. The 50 Cent Party was an informal network of bloggers paid a pittance to echo the party line.

'Ming! Ming!' he shouted at the editor of *China Daily*. 'When will this be online? Why the delay? Come on, let's move.'

Jiang studied the latest briefing from the CDP's Bureau of Media Statistics. It was sobering. The United States and Japan were winning the international propaganda war – he was starting well behind and at a big disadvantage. He did not expect to be able to quickly overcome the inbuilt jealousy and antipathy towards China in the international media. But here in the homeland he commanded the headlines and he could not afford to lose, even for a moment, the people's support. What had Mao said? 'Politics is war without bloodshed.'

This war would be fought – initially at least – through the internet, in newspapers and on television screens. He must not fail.

A woman entered his office, placing a mock-up of the *China Daily* front page on his desk. She smiled, seeking his approval. Mao had once said that women hold up half the sky. Yes, but they were not the ones to lead armies into battle. He ignored her, grabbing the galley proof.

The headline was striking: CHINA AND DPRK IN NUCLEAR PACT. *Yes, that is good.*

The article outlined plans by China to assist North Korea with its peaceful nuclear expansion. An official spokesman for the Foreign Ministry outlined how the cooperative deal was designed to help North Korea generate the next phase of its nuclear power industry.

'All of this has been done within the framework of UN and Chinese laws,' the spokesman said.

The article went on to say that China was opposed to proliferation – but Jiang knew this line would be ignored as the West absorbed the story's tenor.

The Middle Kingdom would meet acts of aggression by its enemies with unflinching resolve.

'Xiu!' He turned to a familiar voice, that of Bo Gangmei, a long-time friend who, like Jiang, had worked hard to earn promotion through the party hierarchy. Two months ago, Bo had been appointed editorial supervisor at Xinhua, the official Chinese news agency. His appointment had been strictly on merit, but this had not stopped a range of underground and dissident outlets from reporting his friendship with China's chief propaganda officer.

Jiang had told him to ignore the jibes. They were fuelled by petty jealousy and, besides, several of the critical ringleaders had been jailed.

Bo had been working on a top-secret project. Jiang pulled out a chair for his friend, eager to examine the details before they were released to the world.

'Oh! Very nice, Gangmei, very nice.' He read over the article to be released through Xinhua again.

China has advanced plans to sign a historic military cooperation agreement with the Democratic Republic of Fiji. The two countries are expected to formally enter the agreement within a month, allowing the People's Liberation Army to conduct formal exercises with the Pacific nation.

Fijian Prime Minister Commodore Frank Bainimarama is due to arrive in Beijing in a fortnight when he is expected to sign a pact with President Meng. China has also agreed to increase aid to the Pacific nation. This will reduce Fiji's reliance on Western countries, like Australia, which have been increasingly hostile to the island nation.

Jiang was satisfied. The evidence on the streets showed he had correctly read the mood of a people determined to see their country rise again.

America's decision to send the *George Washington* into Chinese waters was as predictable as the sunrise. Those fools in Washington had stumbled into the trap. Everything had been focused towards enticing the US to make an aggressive play. It had worked.

Now the world was watching. If the superpower retreated, China would make that giant leap forward.

And the world would shift on its axis. Forever.

CHAPTER SIXTY-FOUR

Canberra

The newspapers lay unfurled across the kitchen table. Harry Dunkley cradled a cup of tea and munched on a piece of toast. He was in his element – the familiar black stain of newsprint on his hands.

His exclusive screamed from the front page.

LABOR'S SECRET BAILEY POLL

Martin Toohey's leadership is under siege with Labor secretly road-testing Catriona Bailey as an alternative prime minister.

Internal party polling, details of which have been obtained exclusively by *The Australian,* reveals the Foreign Minister could save a swag of marginal Labor seats.

The polling confirms Ms Bailey – who made a triumphant return to Parliament last week – is far more popular with swinging voters than Mr Toohey.

> The Prime Minister's grip on power was yesterday rocked by the collapse of his multi-billion-dollar Northern Territory gas deal.
>
> Critically, the polling shows that Labor could be returned if Ms Bailey was prime minister when voters go to the polls on 14 September.
>
> Labor has been testing Ms Bailey's support in the key electoral battlegrounds of western Sydney and Brisbane.

The journalist knew his splash would ignite the simmering leadership speculation and dominate today's political drama. He'd already fielded calls to appear on Sydney and Melbourne radio.

He glanced at the other front pages as the blare of the *AM* intro sounded on Radio National.

Tony Eastley plunged into Dunkley's story off the top.

'We now cross to our chief political correspondent in Canberra. Sabra Lane, I understand there has been an explosive development in the story leading the front page of *The Australian*.'

'Yes Tony, just minutes ago I took a call from Labor's national secretary, Gerry Tighe, who demanded air time. He's on the line now. Mr Tighe, good morning, I understand you say this story is an invention.'

'Good morning. Yes it is. I admit Labor's struggling. Our numbers aren't good. But the story in *The Australian*, Sabra, is pure fabrication. I never usually discuss internal polling, but I can tell your listeners that Mr Dunkley's so-called scoop is 100 per cent wrong ...'

'In what way, Mr Tighe?'

'Well, *The Australian* reports so-called internal party polling on Catriona Bailey. I can say this: we have not done any such polling. Dunkley has simply made it up.'

The online vultures started circling immediately, driven by a hatred of Murdoch and old media. In just a few hours, the press gallery veteran had become the Antichrist.

The social media lynch mob was whipping itself into a frenzy, words laced with poison and relish. But the outrage spewed well beyond the twitterverse. Cabinet ministers were telling senior gallery figures that *The Australian's* star scribe was a dead man walking.

'Dunkley's about as popular as Alan Jones at a Destroy the Joint meeting,' one female minister told a Fairfax journo, eager to plunge the knife into the News Corp hack.

In Parliament, the Toohey Government had suspended standing orders so its chief head-kicker, the Minister for Education and failed marriages, Xavier Quinn, could take a baseball bat to Dunkley. For fifteen ugly minutes, the South Australian MP laid out the case against the Murdoch employee, every word protected by parliamentary privilege.

'Politics is a tough business and we, in the government, respect the role that the fourth estate plays in holding those in power to account,' Quinn said. 'But this so-called journalist – this Murdoch journalist – has crossed the line between reporting the news and being an activist.

'One of my colleagues calls Dunkley "the player" – and it's an apt description. For on this occasion it appears he was intent on sabotaging a democratically elected government.'

Ease up, turbo. I got some polling figures wrong, okay? Toohey's still fucked. And I was set up.

The Greens and the independents were predictably linking the story with News Corp's alleged persecution of the Toohey Government and the forty-third Parliament.

'The "hate media" has overstepped the mark yet again in its unprincipled desire to bring about regime change,' Greens' leader Kiirsty Stanford-Long had told reporters.

In his office, the journalist sat helpless as the assault on his reputation intensified. On the twittersphere, #DunkleyDoneFor was trending.

He'd desperately tried to raise Brendan Ryan, the man who'd fed him the figures and later verified the thrust of his now discredited scoop. There was no answer and his office said the minister would be busy all day.

His character was being shredded. Still, he could hardly complain. He'd built his career on being the hardest hitter in politics. He never shied from a tussle and worried about the diminishing pool of journalists willing to get their hands dirty.

'If you want to play in the big league, you've got to be prepared to take more hits than Joe Frazier,' was his advice to young guns arriving in Canberra.

This was no boxing contest, however. It was more like a one-sided UFC bout – and he was on the ground taking whack after painful whack.

'Hey Harry, how ya going? Want a coffee?' Ben Wakefield, *The Australian*'s irrepressible online journo, was hovering.

He liked Ben but it wasn't caffeine he needed.

'No thanks, comrade. Appreciate it, though.'

Wakefield was one of the few colleagues to have sauntered over to see how he was faring. As if he should have been surprised. That was the nature of the press gallery. If you were on top of your game and filing scoop after scoop you received grudging admiration – but if you slipped up, look out.

The bared fangs of jealous vipers were frightening.

His phone buzzed. It was Celia, the first time she'd rung since the big fright. He was heartened to see her name flash on his phone, but now wasn't the right moment to talk to her. He let the call go to voicemail.

Dunkley's mouth was dry and his head was pounding.

Two minutes later, his phone rang again. And this time he had no choice about answering.

'Harry …'

His name rolled out of Deb Snowdon's mouth. *The Australian*'s editor sounded as if she'd been lined up against a wall. As Dunkley would later discover, for the past thirty minutes she'd been camped on level five of the News Corp head office, trying to salvage the career of her political editor.

Mahogany Row, as the executive suite is called, is not a place for the faint-hearted. It's where Murdoch editors go to be executed – usually about a week after the mogul has left Australia.

'Hey Deb, how ya going?'

'Terrific, Harry, couldn't be better.'

'Well, that's good.'

'So, here's the plan …'

371

It wasn't so much a plan as a defensive ploy, designed with one thought in mind – heading off a threatened media inquiry.

'I want you to take extended leave, Harry, a long holiday. I'll get Helen to look after the details. How much leave have you actually got?'

'A heap, Deb. But—'

'No buts on this one, Harry. The suits need a sacrificial lamb. And mate, just in case you've forgotten, we're bleeding cash and don't need to be picking fights with management – not unless we're 100 per cent certain that we're right. And on this … well, the phrase "overplayed his hand" springs to mind.'

The reporter took a deep breath. He was about to be benched for the first time in a long and previously illustrious career – and it hurt.

'Harry, I'm sorry. I truly am. But things are fraught with the government. And yeah, we're not going to back off, but it will be bloody hard to prosecute the case against this lot if you don't fall on your sword. This way, we can say that when serious mistakes are made we will act.'

'Wow, Deb, that does sound like I'm being fed to the wolves. Guess all those award-winning scoops really count for something, hey?'

'Don't get started, Harry. You know I'm your biggest fan, but mate, these are fucking difficult times and none of us are … well, indispensable.'

'So I'm dispensable?'

'Yes Harry, don't make plans to come back.'

CHAPTER SIXTY-FIVE

Canberra

Harry Dunkley was alive, but only just. He lay sprawled on a mess of a bed, staring at an upturned tumbler.

The day was half over, and he was trying to remember – through the dusty thud of a hangover – how he'd walked through these gates of hell. His mouth tasted of dirty copper and a faint scent of nicotine hung in the air.

Strange. I don't smoke.

He leaned across to pick up his watch, glancing it off the table and onto the floor.

Fuck, I just want the time.

It was a Thursday, sometime in March. 2013. Beyond that, he didn't have much of a clue. Then it slowly started to come back, thoughts he'd tried to drown in a lake of tequila. He sat up, a little too quickly, knocking his brain off its fragile mooring.

The previous day he'd been thrown to the wolves. News Corp's over-anxious management had discarded their gun political reporter.

The fallout was spectacular. The Toohey Government, desperate and nearly friendless, had leapt on his gaffe with relish. And when they came hunting for Dunkley's carcass, the brave company that he'd fought for had given him up without a moment's hesitation. On yer way, cobber.

Of course they'd tried to spin his sacking as something else. They'd toyed with the idea of Harry taking a 'sabbatical' or embarking on a 'special project as part of a strategic realignment'. A 'long and well-earned rest' was considered, too.

But the cold hard reality was that he had been turfed out by a bunch of back office pretenders who wouldn't know a breaking yarn if it smacked them in the mouth.

Like other newsbreakers, Dunkley had been under constant pressure to bowl up stories that would cut through, sell newspapers and lure punters to cash-starved websites.

He did it better than most – but News couldn't afford a wide-ranging media inquiry.

'You want to know why fewer people are buying papers? 'Cause you bastards have got rid of all the decent reporters,' he'd told one executive who spent his days watching his back.

Bugger them all.

He dragged himself into the kitchen, searching for something to ease the John Bonham tom-toms playing paradiddles in his head. Three Nurofen scratched at his throat as he reached for a chair, ignoring the mobile phone ringing somewhere in his flat.

Christ, you don't have the stamina for this anymore.

He'd drunk himself into a stupor of self-pity and self-loathing and was paying the price.

'All right, all right …'

The phone was ringing. Again. Someone was determined to get through.

Alcoholics Anonymous?

He stumbled into the lounge room and retrieved the device from beneath a cushion on the couch. Eight missed calls.

The SMH *offering me a job?*

Not likely. They'd cut to the bone and the word was Fairfax management wanted another hundred editorial staff gone to balance the books.

He flicked through the list. No Caller ID. No Caller ID. Celia. Jack, his brother. Celia again. He would talk to her, but his wounded ego screamed not yet. He continued to scroll down the calls. He stopped: Trevor Harris.

Wonder what he knows?

Dunkley eased himself into the shower, tilting his head as a tsunami rained down on his sorry skull. He stayed like that for five minutes, ignoring the nausea, until he felt half human.

Moving gingerly, he wrapped a threadbare towel around his shoulders.

C'mon sunshine, you'll live.

His head still hurt but he was determined to look the world in the eye. Kind of.

After dressing in jeans and an unironed shirt, he picked up his mobile. He pressed redial on one of the calls and waited a few seconds.

'Trevor. Harry Dunkley. How're you going? Feel like a coffee? Great. Hansel and Gretel in thirty.'

The cafe had attracted a decent lunchtime crowd, and Dunkley secured the last remaining table, next to a glass room-divider. He scanned a menu before ordering a double shot, his first for the day. His head still ached, but it was manageable pain. Like listening to Eminem with Celia.

A couple at a nearby table shot him a glance, exchanging conspiratorial whispers.

Yes it really is me. Mr Bring-Down-the-Government.

Harris was running a few minutes late, but that was fine. He had all day, and the day after. The waitress had just delivered his coffee when the former DSD analyst strolled through the door, gazing around the busy cafe before spotting Dunkley.

'G'day. How are you?'

'Not bad, Trevor. Well actually, let me rephrase that. A tad dusty. Last night was a big one.'

'Yes, you look a little worse for wear.' Harris was not about to paper over the bleeding obvious. He signalled to a waitress, ordering a long black before turning back to Harry. 'Have you registered at Centrelink yet?'

'Hah, not yet. Thought I'd wait a day or two.' Dunkley smiled with a not-a-care-in-the-world bravado. He hadn't even contemplated the dole until Harris mentioned it.

'So, you've taken the rap, Harry. Big time. I read about it in the *Canberra Times* – they seemed to quite enjoy writing about your ... er ... downfall.'

'Yeah, you find out who your mates are when the chips are down. I was thinking about offering myself up for a public flogging, but just about every bastard in this town would want to take a swing.'

'I guess that's the unfortunate nature of your business, the political world. It's tough and unrelenting. It's very human to revel in the misfortune of others. You obviously did your job well, and there are plenty wanting to give you a whack now that you've ...' He stalled.

'I know, mate. I fucked up. Overreached. Was fed a dodgy bit of polling. Wrote it up. Hard. Front page of the broadsheet that matters. It was wrong. I was set up by a trusted source. And I've been executed. End of story.'

'I don't think so, Harry.'

'You don't think what?'

'That it's the end of the story. For you, that is.'

Dunkley appreciated the remark. Compassion had been in short supply.

Harris fiddled with his mug of coffee. He looked anxious.

'Harry, I need you to trust me.'

'I'm not sure I can trust anyone anymore, Trevor.'

'I can appreciate that, but I'm going to trust you.'

Harris drained his long black and looked round for the waitress. He appeared to be struggling for words and Dunkley knew from long experience that the best course was to stay silent.

'Harry, when I came to you the first time I was simply handing over an email you were supposed to have. Then I said I would look at documents encrypted on Ben's Cloud. At no stage did any of that break the commitments I've made to keeping this country's secrets.'

Dunkley prodded. Gently.

'Has that changed, Trev?'

'What's changed is what I've found out. I've unlocked many of the documents that Ben hid on the Cloud. Harry, he stole some of this nation's most sensitive files. That is a crime. Trafficking it is a crime too.'

The shatter of glass on polished concrete made Harris swivel. An errant child had swept a cup onto the floor and a mother was fussing with the shards. Harris bore the look of a man who felt his every word could be overheard. He dropped his tone.

'They are all top secret. AUSTEO: Australian Eyes Only. On top of that, Ben pieced together information from a host of classified sources to build a picture of the Alliance. If I speak to you about any of it, I am breaking the law.'

The analyst's face was agonised as he wrestled with his conscience.

Dunkley understood better than most the fine line that people are forced to walk between what is ethically 'right' and legally 'wrong'. He felt the public interest was best served by letting the sun shine on government. Folk like Harris thought secrets were essential to keeping the nation safe.

'What's the price of *not* telling me what you've found, Trev?'

'I'm not really sure. Perhaps my soul. I don't believe in God but I've always strived to do what I believe is right. I fear that if I stay silent, Harry, I'll be protecting people who see themselves as above democracy.'

'That's a big call, mate. But I suspect you might be right.'

'You already know part of the story, Harry. The Alliance was set up in the late 1960s when the Americans and our defence and intelligence establishment began collaborating, sometimes against the Australian government of the day. It had a hand in Whitlam's fall. But it didn't end there.'

'It's alive and kicking. RIGHT. NOW.' Harris emphasised the last words with two thumps of the table.

'You have the old membership list. Ben pieced together the current one. By his reckoning the Alliance is now led by Jack Webster.'

'Webster? The defence force chief?'

'Yes. And it's an impressive list. Also on it is Brent Moreton, the serving US Ambassador, the Secretary of Foreign Affairs and the heads of ASIS and ASIO. Oh, and one Labor politician, Brendan Ryan, the Defence Minister.'

The list fell on Dunkley like a slap that snapped him awake. His eyes cleared as he saw how the jigsaw pieces assembled into a picture. It confirmed what he had suspected since his polling story had been disavowed. He'd been lied to, done over, to stop him from exposing this powerful cult.

'Trevor, you've taken a risk. Now I'm about to take one. To do something I've never done before. And that's reveal a source. Brendan Ryan was behind the story that broke me.'

'I suspected as much.' Harris nodded. 'But thanks for the vote of trust.'

Dunkley caught his breath as he glanced around the cafe. A table of tradies was engaged in banter about women, cars and beer. Two young office workers held hands as they shared a pastry and the first shy blushes of a relationship.

Australians who worried little about how their country worked. Imagining in their apathy that the people they voted for ran the nation.

And in their midst, two outcasts drawn together by the murder of a friend that pointed to an extraordinary conspiracy. If they stood up and shouted what they knew they would be considered insane.

Yet Dunkley knew in his bones it was true. That everything he had believed in, right until that moment, was a myth.

The journalist rubbed his eyes and tried to compose himself.

'How do they work?' he asked.

'Harry, you have no idea how deeply embedded our defence and intelligence community is with America. You're a well-informed man, but did you know that B-52s based in Guam regularly fly training missions to the West Australian desert and drop live bombs? And did you know that the distance from Guam to that patch of Australian sand is the same distance as Guam to Beijing?'

Dunkley shook his head. It was news to him.

'Well, the Chinese know. And what do you think they make of that? And do you really have any idea what Pine Gap is used for? Among other things it watches every missile launch and nuclear test from North Korea to India. It's a vital cog in the US war machine.'

Harris kept glancing about as his voice dropped to a whisper.

'For all intents and purposes the Australian defence establishment is an outpost of the US. Our generals and admirals like it that way. They call it interoperability, but it's really integration. China knows that. Is it any wonder they question our politicians who claim we can be an ally of the US and not pose a threat to them?

'Most of the time all our defence establishment has to do is nudge the government of the day into line. Buying US military equipment. Ensuring that we can't operate with anyone else. Telling politicians that we need to go to war for "alliance maintenance". And governments, for the most part … well, they are happy to comply. Even to think it was their idea.

'But sometimes the establishment needs to make a radical intervention, like in '75. And right now the Alliance is feeling so threatened it's decided to declare war against its own.'

Harris reached under his chair for his green shopping bag and removed a document, placing it in front of Dunkley. It was marked AUSTEO.

'Jesus, Trevor.'

'Indeed, Harry. Read it.'

The cafe had emptied out, but Dunkley glanced around before he turned the cover sheet and exposed a three-word heading: THE LUSITANIA PLAN.

The document outlined how a 'false flag' operation could be mounted in cyberspace. The plan was to stage a series of attacks on one nation's infrastructure routed through a third country in an attempt to hide the adversary's true identity. Potential targets included dams, electricity grids and traffic systems. But three specific targets leapt out: air-traffic control, banks and mobile phone networks.

'Shit!' Dunkley could feel the blood pumping in his temples as he struggled to digest the document's explosive implications.

'Harry, the attacks on Australia might not be coming from China. Maybe the Alliance is trying to shunt the government back into line. If Toohey believes China is the adversary, that forces him back into the arms of America …'

Dunkley finally realised the role that he'd been playing in this great game. He wasn't a journalist. He was their stooge.

'And, Trevor, if every attack is reported as coming from China, then a government that didn't act would be seen as weak on national security. The people would turf it out.'

Dunkley knew he had been played by Ryan. But there was one other who had hung him on the hook.

CHAPTER SIXTY-SIX

Canberra

A red wall topped with gold-rimmed black tiles and a sliver of blue sky formed the background of Yue Minjun's famous painting. But it was the stark foreground that had first drawn Elizabeth Scott's attention.

Eight identical Asian men were divided into two groups of four. Those on the right were stripped to their underwear, while the others trained invisible rifles on them.

Scott loved Chinese contemporary art, but it was the title that really appealed: 'Execution'.

The print hung in her parliamentary office, a stark reminder of her brutal dispatch as Opposition leader.

She pondered tweeting a picture of it today, as her executioner, Emily Brooks, took her place up against the wall. The aborted attempt to fix the numbers on the mental health vote had buried her.

But there could be no gloating in public and precious little in private. Scott had assumed the rebirth of her popularity would guarantee the return of the Opposition leader's mantle. Her party had other ideas.

'The troops see you as too left wing.' The South Australian Liberal MP Steve Pitt had been walking the corridors. The ballot was at 11am and things looked terminal.

'How many by your count?'

'Twelve.'

That tallied with her own assessment, and she was shocked by how risibly low it was. She had loudly declared she'd be a candidate, so there would be plenty of humiliation to go around this day.

Scott wondered again why she didn't quit.

'Out of the eighty-eight Liberal MPs and senators, only twelve will back me. Who are the other seventy-six morons voting for?'

'They want someone new. And after experimenting with a wet from New South Wales and a dry-as-dust Queenslander, there's a strong mood for a Victorian. The one thing everyone keeps telling me is they want "a safe pair of hands". Bruce Landry seems the most likely.'

Scott shook her head. 'The guy's a cardigan-wearing dill. My twelve-year-old labrador has more energy and appeal.'

'Well, maybe we need a drover's dog.'

The routine slaughter of Opposition leaders is much like putting down a sick kitten: unfortunate, but ultimately a kindness.

Before the suffering ends, though, there are media rituals that must be observed. Political death is a spectator sport in Australia and approached with the anticipation of a footy grand final.

The commercial television breakfast programs had moved their anchors to Canberra for the day, setting up marquees outside Parliament. Sky and ABC News 24 had been cycling politicians, journalists, analysts and anyone else who could string a sentence together through their studios. The major print bureaus had rolled their Sydney and Melbourne-based heavy hitters into town, and when they weren't crafting portentous opinion pieces, they were acting as network commentators. Radio talkback was filling the airwaves with chatter.

Security in Parliament House had been relaxed to allow cameras and journalists access to a junction of corridors about fifty metres from the Opposition party room. The burble of live TV and radio crosses echoed through the building.

Excitement was rising. There was speculation, growing by the minute, that two leaders might fall before this day was done – something unique in the one hundred and twelve years of Federation.

Martin Toohey was resisting a call for a Caucus ballot. But a rumour was circulating that a petition was being organised for a leadership spill.

Ten minutes before the Liberal Party ballot, the first MPs and senators began running the media gauntlet.

Then the combatants arrived, faces fixed, acolytes in tow, to a barrage of shouted questions.

'Ms Scott, Ms Scott, do you have the numbers?'

'We'll see.'

Bruce Landry had firmed as the favourite. Dull, but solid as a rock. He also had recent, real-world business experience, chairing a Victorian water business and turning around its fortunes.

Given it was a state-owned corporation and Landry had donated his board fees to charity, the job fell well inside the rules for MPs.

'Mr Landry, can you win it?'

'Whatever happens, I hope it's for the good of the party and the country.'

Finally, Emily Brooks appeared. Alone. An act of defiance from a woman who'd been subjected to so much humiliation and ridicule. Determined to show her spirit was unbowed, she smiled as she passed the salivating media pack, camera motor drives clattering through five frames a second.

'Is it over, Ms Brooks?'

'While there's life, there's hope.'

Justin Greenwich absorbed the broadcast, transfixed, camped in the Opposition leader's office.

'Say what you like about Emily Brooks, she makes Thatcher look like Tinkerbell.'

CHAPTER SIXTY-SEVEN

Canberra

It was like walking onto the set of *Gone with the Wind*. Sweeping lawns cut by a circular driveway led to a grand Georgian-style manor, replete with white-latticed windows set in a red-brick facade.

Bruce Paxton half-expected to see Scarlett O'Hara promenading on the lush grass.

The United States embassy had been built to evoke the best of America on foreign shores. Its grace. Its beauty. Its power. Since 1943, it had stood near the symbolic heart of the national capital, a few hundred metres from Parliament. Like the nearby Israeli embassy, its perimeter walls were heavily fortified. Two uniformed marines guarded the entrance, day and night.

Every Fourth of July the embassy's manicured turf hosted hundreds of guests. But today, on the spot where hot dogs and Budweiser were usually served, two men sat in deep and private conversation.

John Kowalksi stubbed out his cigarette on the sole of his shoe and turned to face his Australian friend. 'Bruce, I'll say it bluntly. Why should we fly your Chinese mistress to the United States?'

Standing just over two metres tall, Kowalksi was the defence attaché, a former Navy Seal who'd served with distinction in the first Gulf War. He was also the sole liaison with Australian defence officials and had forged a robust working relationship with Paxton during his time as Defence Minister.

'Well, just think about this, John. The wife of a Chinese Ambassador defects to your God-fearing country, armed with a heap of useful material for you to sift through. I would have thought that was a prize worth having,' Paxton answered.

'That's what I've always liked about you. You're a hopeless liberal, but you do have an eye for the main game. There'll be lots of red tape. Your government won't take kindly to the removal of a Chinese diplomat against the wishes of Beijing.'

Paxton smiled. 'John, this is one occasion when it's better to beg forgiveness than ask permission. Can you do it?'

'Well, Bruce, my Mom used to like to quote Jesus. "Anything is possible for those who have faith." I'll have an answer by close of business.'

At 7pm, Paxton fired off a text message to Weng.

Forster St. Hire car. 6.30pm. Tomorrow.

CHAPTER SIXTY-EIGHT

Canberra

The ABC's chief of staff, Simon Johnson, was the first to see the alert drop into his inbox. He yelled over the clamour of the newsroom. 'Prime Minister. Courtyard. 1.50.'

The bureau had been busy writing obituaries for Emily Brooks, profiles of Barry Landry, cutting grabs for radio and TV stories and pumping out online copy. Editors were scouring for vision that evoked the drama of the moment.

For a few seconds everyone stopped as the significance sank in. It was 1.40pm and a prime minister under siege had called a snap press conference scheduled for ten minutes before Question Time.

The mid-afternoon sun scorched the prime ministerial courtyard and journalists crowded into a small oasis of shade. The camera crews laboured in the harsh sunlight, sweating under their heavy equipment as they prepared for Martin Toohey's arrival.

A podium, badged with a silver Australian crest, stood before two heavy timber and glass doors. Australian flags hung either side of it, each displaying a hint of the Union Jack and all of the Southern Cross.

A security guard pushed open the mighty doors and a perfectly groomed PM stepped into the glare.

'Ladies and gentlemen, thanks for coming. I know it's hot, this won't take long. I'm going to make a statement and won't be taking questions.

'Forty minutes ago a delegation of Labor MPs came to my office, led by the Foreign Minister. They had a petition bearing the names of thirty-six party members calling for a special Caucus meeting to be convened next week, for a spill of positions and a leadership ballot.

'It is my prerogative as leader to call a ballot at any time. I have decided that this matter should be resolved today. These are serious times. We face serious domestic and international challenges. The Australian people deserve stability. The ballot will be held at 7pm.'

Toohey ignored the cacophony as he left. He walked back through his office suite and was met by George Papadakis, carrying a folder of briefs.

'Shouldn't you be on the Opposition's payroll?'

It was four minutes to Question Time. Harry Dunkley had intercepted Toohey as he emerged from his office. He'd been camped outside, knowing that the PM would take that route to the chamber.

The Australian's disgraced former correspondent had been gunning for the government for months. Now he'd overreached and been benched. As far as Toohey was concerned, it was a tiny shard of light in an ocean of darkness.

'I have to speak with you PM, it's urgent.'

'Mate, I don't have time to speak to you.'

Toohey was walking fast and George Papadakis was heaving along beside him. An AFP officer was eyeing Dunkley suspiciously, ready to step in if the journalist pushed too hard.

'Martin. You need to hear this. You've been set up. It wasn't the Chinese behind those cyber-attacks, it was the Americans.'

The Prime Minister stopped and fronted Dunkley. 'Sure, mate, sounds completely logical. If I haven't made myself clear, I don't trust you or that shit sheet you used to work for. I'm not interested in anything you have to say.'

Suddenly two metres of close personal protection stood between the Prime Minister and Dunkley.

Question Time was in full fury as Dunkley pulled up a chair at a near-empty Aussies. He stirred his flat white, gazing at the televised theatrics playing out just a few hundred metres away.

A weakened Toohey was in no position to exploit the Opposition's leadership change. Every question lashed the raw wound of his collapsed China gas deal.

'My question is to the Prime Minister. Can he tell the House where he will find six billion dollars a year to fund his mental health plan now that the Chinese have abandoned his misguided attempt to underwrite it by selling off the farm?'

The troops were in full voice, urging their new leader, Bruce Landry, into the fray. Across the aisle, Labor MPs stewed in sullen silence. In a wide shot of the House they could be seen huddled in conversation, working out the numbers for the ballot that would come within hours.

Dunkley always thought Question Time's mock outrage played as a satirical take on the famous opening from *A Tale of Two Cities*. Here the government saw the nation as enjoying the best of times, while the Opposition viewed it as the worst. The truth lay somewhere in between.

For Dunkley though, these were pitiful days.

He glanced at his watch. It was nearly 3pm and the sedate Senate Question Time would be finishing soon. Dunkley contemplated how he might approach the man who had lied to him. The once trusted source who had destroyed his career.

The journalist hadn't thrown a punch in anger in years, but thought maybe that would be a good way to start. He thought better of it as he approached the Defence Minister leaving the Senate chamber.

'Why did you do it, Brendan?' Dunkley's voice was soft, cold fury.

Ryan waved away his senior adviser and turned to front Dunkley.

'Mate, I thought the golden rule in journalism was to always check a story with multiple sources. What happened?'

'Fair point. Maybe I should be punished for that. But usually the starting point isn't a Cabinet minister lying to my face. I've always trusted you, Brendan.'

'Well, more fool you. Mate, you've been playing in the big league for a long time. You should know better than most that sometimes we do things that damage people. So be it. There are more important things than your front-page splash.'

Ryan jabbed a finger close to Dunkley's chest.

'You live for the thrill of the chase, Harry, and you don't mind who you fuck over to get a story. How many people have *you* hurt? How many careers have *you* destroyed? You thought you were doing the right thing. So did I. My job's to defend the nation and I take it seriously.'

'So I was a threat and you eliminated me.'

'If you say so. But try and get this past your ego. It's not about you. It's much bigger than you. Now I'm busy, mate, and I don't have time for has-been hacks.'

CHAPTER SIXTY-NINE

Canberra

The black Citroën appeared just after 6pm.

Harry Dunkley tensed as the greyhound-sleek figure of Charles Dancer emerged, camouflaged in the mundane suit of a bureaucrat. The spook checked his letterbox for mail, then slipped inside.

Dunkley waited five minutes, trying to steady his nerves. The path to the front door was paved with brick, a meander pattern diagonally laid across the metre-wide passage. A black metal door-bell waited to be chimed. Dunkley didn't hesitate.

He stiffened as the bell clanged. A surge of adrenalin drove up his heart-rate, his right fist clenched white.

The door opened. Dunkley lunged. Dancer swayed like a boxer, let the blow pass and then pushed hard between Dunkley's shoulder blades. The journalist slammed into the cold tiles. As he rolled, a foot crashed on his chest, pinning him to the floor. A gun was trained on his face.

'I've been expecting you, Harry. And yes, it's loaded.'

Dancer sat, imperious, opposite the journalist, a fourth-generation Glock 17 on his lap.

'Didn't I say to you once before that you were out of your depth?'

Dunkley was hurting. His mouth tasted of blood, his hip and left knee ached. He wondered whether he'd broken his wrist, but wasn't about to give his adversary the pleasure of knowing.

'Charles, I've met some liars in my time but no one like you.'

'Oh? How have I deceived you, Harry? I showed you Bruce Paxton was corrupt and dangerous. You proved he was. I've shown you that China is a threat. That's beyond doubt.'

'Maybe, Charles. But you never mentioned the Alliance. Not once. It took our friend Kimberley to discover that.'

'Tell me what's wrong with a group of patriots looking at the long game? Yes, I work for them and I'm proud of it. They're the generals and I'm their footsoldier.'

'But whose side are you on? Australia's? The United States'?'

'Both. Don't kid yourself like some neophyte. We need the US, much more than it needs us. These are the most dangerous days of our lifetime. China threatens everything.'

Dunkley probed the inside of his cheek and felt a gash where his teeth had cut the soft inside flesh of his mouth.

'And you're prepared to bring down a government. A prime minister. To lie and scheme, just like your bosses have been doing, for what? Nearly fifty years.'

'No, Harry.' Dancer's voice was firm. 'I've made you an agent of truth, alerting the Australian people to the threat. This government's fate is now in their hands.'

'What about the Lusitania Plan? Lives were threatened. Is that the work of a patriot?'

'No lives were in danger. We just showed a glimpse of the future. And make no mistake, our man in the lake, Lin An, was trying to warn us about the country he was fleeing. That embassy is a wormhole. China has tapped into our Five Eyes intelligence. Their stooge Catriona Bailey opened the door. There's a war going on, Harry, and the front line is here.'

Dunkley cursed himself as the reality of how badly he'd misread Dancer sank in.

'I've been your pawn.' Dunkley's admission was barely a rasp.

'You've played your role to perfection. And what do we do with pawns? We sacrifice them for the chance of victory.'

'Who else have you sacrificed? Kimberley?'

Dancer's arrogance wavered. He lifted the Glock with his right hand, as if he needed a shield.

Dunkley took a risk. 'Charles, I thought the three of us were working as a team.'

Dancer's control was faltering.

'She should have kept her investigation to Paxton's Chinese links. That was her job. Her duty. That's what we expected her to do.'

'But she didn't. You couldn't control her. She was an individual and asked uncomfortable questions. Like who would want Paxton eliminated?'

Dancer's hand betrayed him with the slightest of trembles.

'And now I wonder who would want to eliminate *her*?' Dunkley pointed at Dancer. 'Maybe you.'

Dancer stood and began to prowl the room, shifting his gun from hand to hand, avoiding eye contact with his captive.

'We are at war, Mr Dunkley.' His voice was harsh. 'The enemy is clear. Kimberley was never satisfied with accepting things as they are. As with her body, she forced them to fit her warped ideal. Her judgement was clouded. She threatened the project.'

Dunkley pushed harder. 'She threatened you. Confronted you with what you are. And you killed her.'

Dancer stopped. His head dropped and he inspected the gun in his right hand.

'I did.' The admission came as a shock, to Dancer as much as Dunkley. The killer turned to the journalist and his eyes shone deadly with hate and fury.

'Every day I feel the guilt of that. But it was my duty. People die in wars.'

Dancer pulled back the slide on his pistol, dragging a bullet from the magazine into the handgun's chamber.

'And, Harry, never forget who got her involved. I pulled the trigger, but you loaded the gun. You didn't care that helping you compromised her. You were chasing the only thing that's ever mattered to you. A front-page story.'

Dancer aimed the Glock at Dunkley.

'Now you are a threat. And my job is eliminating threats.'

Dunkley could see the fragility behind Dancer's facade. A man who hated himself and took out his rage on real and imagined enemies. But that was precisely what made him deadly. Dancer's masters used his self-loathing as their weapon.

Dunkley did not doubt his life was in the balance. A shudder of terror swept through him and his heart pounded. But he was surprised by the strength and defiance in his voice.

'Go on, kill me too.'

The spy dropped his hands.

'I don't have to kill you. You're already dead. No one will ever believe another word that you write. And you have no pages to write for.'

The truth of Dancer's words stung.

'I don't need a paper to expose your evil. I'll publish on the web. Everything I know. Everything.'

Dancer laughed, a rich baritone of ridicule, before throwing the Glock onto the lounge.

'And then, Harry, you'll be just another nut job on the internet.'

CHAPTER SEVENTY

Canberra

'It's a lovely view, isn't it, Brendan?'

The soft croak of her voice was nearly unrecognisable.

Catriona Bailey gazed out the window of a Senate office overlooking the lake. Her body had withered. She looked brittle, her skin like crushed paper, her hands reduced to tiny movements.

A battered rag doll in a motorised wheelchair.

Yet to Brendan Ryan she loomed as a grisly succubus. In his worst nightmares, the Labor warlord never dreamed he'd be having this meeting.

So this is what it's like to bargain with Satan.

Her left hand pushed a lever and an electric motor whirred as Bailey moved to face the Defence Minister. Her body might be broken but her eyes were a blaze of steel and resolve.

These eyes that had been her resurrection.

'They tell me you find it difficult to speak for long,' Ryan ventured.

'The tracheotomy did a lot of damage. I can talk for about five minutes. Then I have to stop.'

'Then this meeting will be mercifully brief.'

'It will, because your presence here speaks volumes. Doesn't it, Brendan?'

Ryan knew they were here to barter for the last of his dignity. He only wanted one assurance.

'The final matter to resolve is the date of the election. I will support you if you call it within a month of taking over as leader.'

'What's the rush? Toohey set September 14.'

'Frankly, I want to minimise the damage that you can inflict, Catriona. On the party and the country.'

'Yet the reason you want me back is to save the ship.'

'Don't kid yourself. The ship has sunk. I just want to stuff as many survivors as I can into the life rafts.'

Bailey's eyes, a stain of dark blue, held Ryan in their vice for a brief, uncomfortable moment.

'Done.'

Ryan stood transfixed by the view. The out-of-the-way office had been chosen to avoid prying eyes.

But he could not escape the glare of his conscience.

What have I done?

'What else could I have done?' he muttered, as he put both hands on the window sill to steady himself.

Ryan was an old-school right-winger, the son of a Victorian

Catholic who'd stayed with the Australian Labor Party when the split had torn its heart out in the 1950s. His father had lost life-long friendships in the turmoil, so he hammered a set of principles into the eager boy. Old, unfashionable ideas like duty, constancy and, above all, loyalty.

'If a man isn't loyal then he isn't anything,' his father would say. 'You pick and stick son.'

Ryan had settled his loyalties long ago. To his party, his country and its allies. Once he built those battlements, he declared war on his enemies. Life was about hard choices and a man had to realise that meant he couldn't have everything.

But Bailey?

She personified everything he hated. A dictator who had hijacked and gutted his party, a vagrant Christian who shifted like a chameleon between denominations, and a multilateralist who embraced the impotence of the United Nations.

Above all, Bailey was a clear and present danger to the alliance that protected the nation's castle walls. Ryan had suspected that Bailey was the human equivalent of a computer virus: a long-dormant but deadly infection.

One that had been cultivated by the Chinese.

Ryan slumped into a lounge chair and put his head in his hands. Martin Toohey was a decent man but had been a disaster as prime minister. Ryan blamed himself for part of that failure. He had pushed Toohey into rolling Bailey, not realising that the coup would kill both leaders.

Australians had never understood Bailey's brutal dispatch and Toohey rose from the fight with blood on his hands.

His mark of Cain.

Then again, Toohey had made plenty of his own mistakes.

'I tried to warn him. Tried to save him.' Ryan shoved a small pile of coffee-table books onto the floor and stood up.

He needed a cigarette and decided to have one; an act of defiance against another modern verity he despised. He pulled a packet of Benson & Hedges 25s from his jacket pocket and looked at the miserable image on it: a man with a gaping hole in a cancer-ravaged throat.

How appropriate.

'So this is for you, Catriona.' Ryan took a lighter from his pocket, stuffed a fag in his mouth and lit it. He drew in a deep breath and blew a long and gratifying line of smoke into the room.

He looked around for something that would serve as an ashtray before shrugging his shoulders and tapping the ash onto the carpet. He rubbed it in with the toe of his shoe, leaving a little grey smudge. He admired his handiwork. A small sin compared to the mortal one he had just committed.

I have sold out to buy my party a few seats. A slim hope of redemption.

Ryan took another long drag and blew smoke towards the window. Out of sight, just off Kings Avenue to his right, he knew there was a statue of John Curtin and Ben Chifley, frozen in a moment from 1945 as they walked to the Parliament.

Curtin, the leader who had turned to America in the nation's hour of greatest need. And the US had delivered.

Now Labor was turning from America without understanding the consequences. His party needed time in the wilderness to reassess. But he didn't want to see it destroyed and, under Toohey, that was inevitable. Bailey was the only viable choice. It was a huge gamble but a quick election would minimise the risk.

Once she had minimised the losses he would bury her forever.

And all it has cost me is my soul.

Ryan threw the butt on the carpet, lifted his shoe to snuff out the ember, and stopped.

He decided to let it burn.

'I thought you'd be with me to the end, Brendan.'

Martin Toohey's voice was laced with sadness. The Defence Minister had hoped for anger. He could cope with a fight, but sorrow was more than he could bear.

He couldn't look at Toohey, who was standing behind his desk, or George Papadakis, who was slumped on a lounge in the Prime Minister's office.

Ryan looked at his feet as he spoke.

'We had to …' Ryan caught himself trying to deflect blame for his decision and started again.

'I had to do it. I had to make a choice between my friendship with you and my loyalty to the party.'

He forced himself to look at Toohey.

'Martin, we're doomed. The people have stopped listening to you. If you lead us to the election there will be a rout and it will take a generation for us to recover.'

Toohey's eyes gleamed. Like all leaders, he had a distorted image of his powers. He still believed he could turn the ship around.

'That's not true. We can claw our way back with the mental health plan. I can beat Landry.'

'Martin, even if we get elected we can't afford another huge welfare scheme. George, you know the truth. Tell him.'

Papadakis lifted his head and fixed Ryan with hate in his eyes.

'Truth. What would you know about the truth, Brendan? And don't ever mention the word "loyalty" again. You have betrayed us for someone you despise. And if she wins what do you get? What promises has Bailey made to buy you?'

'I got nothing beyond a commitment to an early election.'

Papadakis snorted.

'You know your Bible, Brendan. "What does it profit a man to gain the whole world yet lose his soul?" I thought you were with us.'

'I didn't sign up so you could empty Treasury to build a welfare state. If you keep gutting Defence, you'll find your dreams mugged by reality. We're facing war in the Pacific and slashing Defence is endangering the nation.'

Toohey strode from behind his desk, knocking his iPad to the floor.

'Don't be such a fucking drama queen. The US and China can't afford to go to war. Their economies rely on each other. Both will come to their senses.'

Ryan shook his head.

'No one ever wants to go to war. No one can afford to go to war. But nations go to war when the alternative is unacceptable. The preconditions for war now exist. America won't be pushed back across the Pacific and China won't stop pushing.'

Toohey pointed to the map of the world on his wall.

'Then we need to sit where we are on that map. In the middle. As the calm heads at the table. Not to always fall in behind the United States. Those clowns started this fight, Brendan.'

Ryan waved at the briefs piled on Toohey's disorderly desk.

'What about the attacks on us? If a Chinese destroyer opened fire on an Australian ship, it would be an act of war. Yet Beijing has hit our airspace, banks and phones. Prime Minister, that is unacceptable.'

Toohey moved closer to Ryan. They were separated by a coffee table.

'You know as well as I do that verifying that kind of attack is dicey. I'm not starting a fight without being certain who broke the windows.

'And is it any wonder that the Chinese see us as puppets of Uncle Sam? The Yanks keep dragging us into their fights. Maybe we need to reposition ourselves for the twenty-first century. To build a more nuanced set of alliances.'

Toohey's words confirmed Ryan's worst fears.

'Really? The next warning shot might be through your brain. Hitting air-traffic control was an act of war. And when did you decide to unwind the ANZUS treaty? When did that become Australia's foreign policy?'

'I do believe I am Prime Minister.'

Ryan checked his watch.

'Martin, I'll be supporting Catriona Bailey and I'll advise others to do the same. You will lose the ballot. I'm sorry about that. But the longer we've spoken this evening the more I'm convinced that it's the right decision. You're forgetting that your first duty is to defend the nation.'

Toohey put up his hand as Ryan turned to leave.

'One last thing. Something's been bothering me. I ran into Harry Dunkley and he had the most amazing conspiracy theory – that the US was behind those cyber-attacks, not China.'

The Defence Minister weighed his answer.

'Dunkley has been discredited. And, as I recall, you've never been a fan. It does sound like a wild theory. But some claim that Churchill dragged the US into World War I by allowing the *Lusitania* to be sunk. A thousand people drowned, but maybe millions were saved. If he did, was that a good or a bad thing? The war ended. We won.'

CHAPTER SEVENTY-ONE

Canberra

It had been a gift from her mother in celebration of her eighteenth birthday, her passage to womanhood. She'd packed the pink brush when she'd left China; a link to a family and life left behind. Now it would go with her into exile.

Weng Meihui glanced around her room as she counted down the minutes.

What can you pack in one small bag when you are leaving your old life forever?

She brushed away a tear, trying to subdue a feeling of dread as she contemplated this flight from a life of certainty into the unknown.

Weng was from a Tibetan family who had embraced China. She recalled her handlers' taunts when she trained to become a Mata Hari. Perfectly suited because 'betrayal runs in the blood of your family'.

But wasn't she the one who'd been betrayed? By a state that didn't hesitate to kill when your usefulness was spent. Her life was at risk if she stayed. She had to flee.

It was 6.22pm. Eight minutes until the hire car was due. She would time her departure from the building to minimise the moments she'd need to wait on the kerb.

Her cover had been carefully thought through. The Ambassador was at a parliamentary function. She was supposedly meeting the Canadian High Commissioner's wife for a drink at the Hyatt, a short stroll away. The driver had been instructed to pick her up around the corner from the Chinese embassy, in Forster Crescent, opposite the rear entrance to the British High Commission. Bruce Paxton would be waiting at the airport.

It was time. She gathered her handbag and walked from the embassy. She nodded to the guard on the gate before turning onto the path that ran along the front of the complex.

Across the road three Falun Gong protesters still camped under their banners. She turned into the crescent. The car was there, silver and official, sporting the familiar 'HC' plates. She walked quickly to its rear door, her gaze lowered. She stepped in, collapsing into a comfortable leather seat.

Her heart surged with relief. She nodded for the driver to proceed.

The car pulled out from the kerb and indicated a left-hand turn. Weng knew the route well. They would pass in front of the Chinese embassy before turning left at the roundabout. In ten minutes, she would be pulling up at the airport.

She turned away from the embassy as they passed it on the left, nervously opening her bag to see that her brush was there.

Something was wrong.

'No. No. Turn left.' She waved in protest to the driver.

He said nothing as the limousine doors locked and the car glided up the dirt driveway to the new embassy building.

When he spoke, the voice was pure ice; his jet-black eyes cruel in the rear-vision mirror.

'Ms Weng, where *did* you think you were going?'

'Mr Paxton, your flight is ready to board.'

Bruce Paxton offered a thin smile as the Qantas attendant handed him two boarding passes. It was 7.41pm and the final short-haul flight from Canberra to Sydney was about to depart.

He'd arrived at the Chairman's Lounge an hour earlier, ignoring the high-octane buzz of those Coalition MPs who'd managed to escape Parliament and were heading home. The lounge was unusually empty because Labor's leadership showdown was still playing out.

That mattered nothing. His entire focus was on willing Weng Meihui to stroll into the lounge.

He had expected her forty-five minutes ago, positioning himself so he could nab her the moment she walked in. That was the plan. Hiding in plain sight and then a short walk to the gateway.

His phone calls had been unanswered and his fear began to rise with each empty minute.

Is she safe? Hurt? Has she changed her mind?

He was frantic. He left the lounge and looked down the escalators, hoping to see her rushing towards him.

A booming voice echoed through the cavernous space.

'This is a final boarding call for QF1494 …'

CHAPTER SEVENTY-TWO

Canberra

A dozen bottles stood discarded beside a bin quickly filling with the shredded remnants of three tumultuous years in power. In a plastic tub, Coronas and Coopers lay covered with ice, while slices of pizza and garlic bread competed for the attention of tired staff. A stereo pumped out dance tunes, rhythms from a more predictable age. On a handsome timber table, still cluttered with Question Time briefs and messages of condolence, three bottles of Clonakilla Shiraz Viognier had been shared around.

George Papadakis was opening a fourth when he felt Martin Toohey's hand on his shoulder.

'Have we declared this plonk?'

'Pardon, mate?'

'The Clonakilla. It's pricey stuff. Have we declared it?'

Papadakis blinked. Hard. His mind was blunted by several hours of solid boozing.

'Let me get this straight, Martin. You've just been dumped as prime minister. America and China are on the verge of war. Australia risks being sandwiched in the middle. And you're worried about getting done for not declaring … one … two … let's say four hundred dollars of booze …'

'Yes.'

'Martin, that'd be like getting a parking ticket an hour after being murdered. Try and get a little perspective.'

'Perspective? Like being done over by your comrades for a woman who's certifiable and … oh, for fuck's sake, George, she can have it. I'm going back to Geelong to bleed for a while. Pour me a red.'

Papadakis wasn't listening. He was bellowing out a tune, a song turned up loud, one that evoked memories of long nights in university bars, chasing skirt, solving economics tute questions, making plans. For a better life.

He loved 10cc, their quirky tales of conquest. This tune was a favourite, a melange of cricket and dark deeds in the Caribbean.

Toohey disentangled himself from several sympathisers, rejoining his chief of staff.

'All these years and I had no idea. You've got a good voice, George.'

'Well, we invented singing, Martin; the Greeks, that is.'

'What? Singing and democracy. Jesus, it must have been a busy time in ancient Athens.'

They embraced, loyal mates who'd bled for Labor, for each other. A long genuine hug. Toohey broke it, pointing at the stereo.

'I know when it all went wrong, George.'

'With what?'

'With everything.'

'You mean when you decided to roll Bailey?'

'No. Much earlier.'

'What, that day in 2006 when you backed her for leader?'

'Mate, not everything's my fault. No, I mean the day everything went completely pear-shaped. It was 1995.'

'You mean '96 – when Howard turfed out Keating.'

'No.'

Papadakis scoured his brain for anything marking 1995 as a particularly bad year for the ALP. He raised his hands in mock defeat.

Toohey licked his lips.

'To be precise, it was the twenty-eighth of March, 1995. When Queensland beat South Australia and won the Sheffield Shield ... for the first time.'

'Oh no, Martin, not one of your mad sporting theories.'

'Hear me out, mate.' Toohey was animated. 'Queensland had never won the Shield. For sixty-eight years there were three certainties: death, taxes and Queensland losing the cricket. Then came '95 and bang! It all changes. The natural order of things is overturned. We get eleven years of Howard and the next Labor PM is barking mad. Those banana benders screwed it for everyone.'

Toohey clinked glasses with a bemused Papadakis.

'Martin, that might be the silliest thing you've ever said.'

'No mate, the silliest thing I've said was, "George, how about you leave Treasury and be my chief of staff." And you bought that one.'

The two men laughed, loud belly laughs. Papadakis, for the first time in months, felt liberated.

'Martin, you promised me it wouldn't be dull, and it hasn't been. We did good things; you are a good man. And besides, we Greeks love a bit of masochism.' He wiped away a tear. Of laughter or sadness, he couldn't tell. 'So what will you do now?'

'Sulk for a while, then stand down from Corio, go look for a real job. You?'

'Try and find a job where I can't be sacked by the new Labor prime minister.'

'Sorry, mate.'

'Don't fret the small stuff, Martin. Remember?'

Toohey looked around the room, this epicentre of power, his for three years. Gone in a heartbeat. He contemplated the glass of expensive wine cupped in his hand.

'George, what did you make of Dunkley's comments, his theory that it was America behind the cyber-attacks?'

Papadakis poured another generous portion of fine Canberra red. Then he turned the volume to 11 as the Beach Boys pumped out a classic carnival melody.

God only knows …

CHAPTER SEVENTY-THREE

Canberra

The autumn cool had arrived at last. A light mist curled from the sky, barely skimming the ground baked flint-hard by an unholy summer. Across the lake, a swirl of lights – green, orange and purple – sparkled from the walls of the National Museum.

Night had descended on Nara Park, transforming a row of trees into ghostly silhouettes.

A few days earlier, Bruce Paxton had perched on this same timber bench, comforting Weng Meihui as she poured out her fears. Now they were all too real, a waking nightmare.

For the first time in a long while, he was frightened.

A dozen desperate phone calls had gone unanswered. Mei had failed to make the rendezvous at the airport, vanished without a trace. The hire car company said the booking had been cancelled with a phone call thirty minutes before the scheduled pick-up. By a male.

Paxton had asked his driver to cruise slowly past the Chinese embassy, hoping to pick up some clue. Nothing. Even the Falun Gong had packed up.

He lifted his gaze to a glade of crepe myrtles, elms, pines. The embassy and its sister compound were just a few hundred metres away, taunting him through the thick foliage.

A possum scurried across the stone path. He barely noticed it. Instead he raised his tired body from the bench, and wandered towards the lake.

Think, mate, think.

Mei had been tense but excited at the prospect of defecting, of leaving her double life behind. They'd sketched out plans – their plans – for the future. But had he misread her? Had he, the great political schemer, been had?

Or had she simply backed away at the last moment, afraid of turning against a homeland that would pursue her to the grave, no matter where she went?

Was he a fool for thinking she would discard the security of her past for an uncertain future?

Yet she had seemed so certain as she'd nestled into his embrace in this park, trembling as she told of the deaths of her three compatriots.

Her fear was real. He was convinced of it. And he was certain that, if she had willingly changed her mind, she would have sent him a message. He knew enough of her to be sure that she would not want to torture him like this.

Then what?

Had the Americans betrayed him, tipped off the Chinese, or maybe his own government, unwilling to deal with the diplomatic stink?

He reached the water's edge, shuffling along beside a stone wall that flanked water black as an oil slick. The night held a dangerous edge and Paxton, alone and friendless, held dark thoughts.

The most likely explanation was that Mei had been discovered, intercepted.

Perhaps killed.

Was she lying somewhere below this black surface?

He shuddered and pulled his jacket tight. He turned and walked towards his ComCar. Bill, his driver, was waiting, racking up the charges, reliable as the morning sun.

Paxton was resolved. If Mei was alive, he would find her. If not he would expose those who had harmed her. Nothing else mattered. He loved her, he realised, always had.

He quickened his pace, needing the security of plush leather, the reassuring idle of the Falcon's V6. Parliament House was just a few minutes away. He would take stock in the familiar surrounds of his office.

Then he would do what he did best. Exact revenge.

CHAPTER SEVENTY-FOUR

Taiwan Strait

The glow on the horizon shimmered across the ocean as Frank Vinson surveyed USS *George Washington*'s flight deck from vulture's row. The weather forecast promised a perfect day for flying, a breeze from the south, clear skies and a maximum of 69 degrees.

A roar of warplanes tore the air, peaking as jet engines and steam-driven catapult combined to hurl them skywards from zero to 165 miles an hour in two seconds. From five decks up, Vinson watched the flight-deck crews performing their dangerous dance of launching and landing aircraft.

A Hornet thundered from the carrier, trailing a ribbon of vapour. It banked as it climbed to take its place in the strike group's defensive bubble that stretched from the seabed to the heavens.

Two-hundred nautical miles out from the carrier, a Super Fudd, the propeller-driven Grumman E-2C Hawkeye, monitored the group's battle space. From 30,000 feet its long-range airborne early-warning system kept watch for air and surface threats over 120,000 square miles.

Under water, ahead of the strike group, two USN attack submarines analysed the huge volume of underwater noise their sensors recorded, searching for surface and sub-surface threats. In the relatively shallow, noisy waters, hostile subs would be hard to find. Two cruisers and two destroyers formed the inner perimeter of the picket fence.

It was a formidable armada but the 110-mile wide Taiwan Strait robbed Vinson's group of some of its defences. As large as it was, on the open ocean the strike group could disappear, moving from one point to another in a circle measuring 700 square miles in thirty minutes. But here there was nowhere to hide as it passed along the front fence of a nation that had developed 'area denial weapons' like the DF-21D anti-ship ballistic missile.

The carrier was sailing into danger.

Vinson could see the Pengjia Islet lighthouse blinking to port, just 33 nautical miles off Taiwan's northernmost tip. The fleet would sail south-west then turn towards the Taiwanese side of the cross-strait median, the imaginary line that delineated the territory controlled by Taipei and Beijing.

Two Westinghouse A4W nuclear reactors were driving the ship at a clip below 20 knots. At that speed it would take just over ten hours to pass through the Black Ditch.

The Admiral contemplated breakfast but was in no mood for eating.

He caught the tang of spray on the breeze from the China Sea, a postcard of tranquillity, and wondered how long these waters would stay calm. Not since Bill Clinton had ordered the *Nimitz* and *Independence* to sail into the Strait in March 1996 – in response to Chinese missile testing – had the threat of conflict been so real.

'Admiral, I'm going to get some coffee, can I get you one?' Lieutenant Jane Marsh was half-shouting to be heard above the jet engines.

'No thanks, Jane. I'm heading back to the flag bridge in a minute or two. Just wanted to survey this pretty morning out in the open.'

'Yes sir, it's quite a picture.'

'It is that.'

The admiral gripped the railing as his gaze turned towards the Chinese mainland, somewhere over the western horizon. He could trace his naval heritage back to before World War I, to a great uncle who'd escaped the tedium of the family's hardware business for a life chasing dreams.

Vinson had never questioned America's role in defending democracy, not even when the fiction of George W Bush's weapons of mass destruction turned public opinion against the US.

But this? Something nagged inside. His knuckles were white, and a small feeling of nausea welled in his stomach. He needed caffeine after all.

He turned one last time to the ocean. An albatross passed close flying north, a flash of white against a golden dawn. The admiral's spirit lifted. An omen, he hoped, that everything would be all right.

Hong Kong

'Sir, we will be ready to sail at 0700.'

'Thank you, sailor.'

Yu Heng mentally ticked off the orders he had been given over the preceding few days and contemplated a quick shower. It had been an arduous night, and there were long, difficult hours ahead.

Through the window, first light began to brighten the Ngong Shuen Chau Naval Base, and preparations aboard were almost complete. China's first aircraft carrier, the *Liaoning*, was ready for its mission.

But the rear admiral knew she was not ready for a fight.

He looked along the carrier's flight deck with its distinctive ski-slope bow. The *Liaoning* had been transformed from a rusted former Soviet hulk bought in 1998 under the pretext of it becoming a floating casino.

Deception had always been one of China's weapons.

The first carrier China had bought was Australia's HMAS *Melbourne*. She'd been acquired in 1985, and before being torn apart for scrap was studied by naval engineers. Two more Soviet-era ships had followed before enough was learned to refit the *Liaoning*.

At the same time, elite sailors were trained for the day the People's Republic launched its own carrier.

Yu had been moulded to lead them. Born into a military family, he had enlisted in 1990 and served with the East Sea fleet. His passion for the sea was so great he'd refused to marry until he became captain of a ship. His first command was a frigate, then a guided missile destroyer, before he was sent to the British Joint Services Command and Staff College.

His crew on the *Liaoning* had been drawn from the best of the People's Liberation Army Navy.

But like their ship they were not ready. Three months of trials in the South China Sea had shown just how much they, and the Chinese navy, still had to learn.

An aircraft carrier is useless without aircraft.

The Shenyang J-15 had been purpose-built for this ship. Known as the 'Flying Shark', the fighter jet was a clone of Russia's Sukhoi Su-33. China's media proudly reported its top speed of Mach 2.4 and range of 3200 kilometres. But at this stage of China's carrier aviation development the aircraft were for show.

More like a flopping fish.

Exhaustive trials had shown the J-15, like most carrier-borne aircraft, could not take off or land if fully fuelled and armed. But this jet's performance was much worse than anyone had expected. So they had a choice: a modest weapons load with almost no fuel; or a full load of fuel with almost no weapons. The compromise struck gave the combat aircraft an effective range of 120 kilometres.

In reality, the *Liaoning* was as yet only a training ship, not a fearsome fighting machine, and half the size of the *George Washington*.

Yu had showered and changed into a crisp white uniform when the call came through at 0625.

'Admiral Leng Sha for you, sir.'

'Thank you. I'll take it in my cabin.'

Born in 1945, Leng was Commander-in-Chief of the PLA Navy and had overseen its rise into a modern fighting force. He'd hand-picked Yu, his protégé, to command the *Liaoning*. He was a gifted student who would now carry the hopes of the navy and the nation on this dangerous assignment.

'Admiral, we will sail as commanded in thirty-five minutes.'

'Good. Then everything is ready.'

'Sir, you understand the limitations of our weapon systems. We can launch planes but they are only capable of training sorties. They are not combat ready.'

'Yes Heng. But your mission is not to engage the adversary. *Liaoning* is our flagship. You are to be seen to stare down the American strike group and make it retreat. Your systems won't be needed if it comes to a fight. Our mainland forces and our submarines can defeat the Americans. And they know it.'

'As you taught me, sir. The assassin's mace. A smaller force can wound a larger enemy if it is more nimble: with its weapons or its wit.'

'And the world will be watching. The most important weapon on this mission is the television crew. Is it on board?'

'It is, Admiral.'

'Make sure they get pictures of the planes taking off and landing.'

'Yes sir.'

'Good. Heng, America's retreat across the Pacific begins today.'

Taiwan Strait

Frank Vinson had changed into khakis. The only sign of his rank was a single silver star on his collar.

The flag bridge was a scene of ordered apprehension as senior staff monitored intelligence and kept watch over a carrier battle group that stretched across more than a hundred miles of sky and sea.

From the first deck of the ship's island, Vinson commanded the nerve centre of the fleet.

Jane Marsh, a naval intelligence officer, traced several lines of intel on her monitor, reading it twice before reporting to Vinson. 'Sir, the *Liaoning* has put to sea and is heading north. Into the Taiwan Strait. If it maintains its course, we will see her in less than five hours.'

The room fell silent around Vinson as his senior staff weighed the significance of the news.

'That ship is hardly fit to sail.' Marsh was incredulous. 'All our intelligence shows it is nowhere near ready to fight.'

The news confirmed Vinson's worst fears. His force was being drawn into a historic and extremely dangerous confrontation.

'That ship doesn't have to be able to fight. We're off mainland China. There is more than enough muscle to starboard and under us to overwhelm this strike group.'

'So why put the *Liaoning* to sea?'

The admiral turned to the sloping glass of the flag bridge, staring to the horizon.

'It's their flagship. It's the David and Goliath image they want. China is making a statement that it is now powerful enough to stare down the world's only superpower. If we sail on we had better be ready to fight. That could end in war. If we retreat the US will be humiliated.'

'So what will we do?' Marsh spoke for the group.

Vinson looked down at a screen that showed their position in the strait and weighed his options.

'I intend to complete my mission. But no one said how fast we have to travel. Alert the group, we're going to slow this operation right down. I hope the *Liaoning* commander has the sense to do the same thing. Get me PACOM. The President has to decide how he wants this to end.'

CHAPTER SEVENTY-FIVE

Canberra

The Cardinals had been sent out early. Catriona Bailey's damaged vocal cords restricted her public appearances, so the new prime minister's chorus of allies – all promised plum ministerial jobs – was out in force.

As one they trumpeted regime change and the promise of a turnaround in Labor's fortunes. The 'Bailey bounce' was already resonating with the television breakfast programs that had seized on suspect polling showing Bailey led the featureless Landry 55 to 15 per cent as preferred prime minister. The rest still liked Elizabeth Scott.

For the last twenty-four hours, the press gallery had been grinding out an endless supply of copy to feed voracious media platforms.

The federation had never witnessed such political carnage: a prime minister and Opposition leader both fed to the sharks within hours of each other.

But the drama in Canberra was dwarfed by the first flashes of a showdown in the Taiwan Strait. The world's superpower was on a collision course with the rising titan of China.

Amid this maelstrom of news, Bruce Paxton decided he would hold a press conference.

Just a few journalists gathered in the Senate courtyard, more out of duty than interest. Several defence correspondents tagged along to see if they could snag a decent quote on China to pad out their copy.

'Ladies and gentlemen, thanks for coming. As a former Defence Minister, I know better than most that defending this country is the primary job of any government. I have grave fears about Catriona Bailey's capacity to do that job.

'It was Ms Bailey who green-lighted the new Chinese embassy down by the lake. I now have information that shows that building is a direct threat to national security.

'A month ago a Chinese national died as he tried to defect. Two other men have been murdered as part of a cover-up.'

Paxton's face was glistening red.

'I also hold grave fears for the Chinese Ambassador's wife. She was planning to defect last night and she never made it.'

The *West Australian*'s defence writer, Nick Butterly, broke the stunned silence.

'How do you know the Ambassador's wife was planning to defect?'

'Because, Nick, she was meant to be meeting me as part of that process.'

'How do you know her?'

Paxton stalled. His mouth was parched. He fiddled with his tie.

'We are … friends. A relationship was forged many years ago. We have warm feelings for each other.'

'Hang on, Mr Paxton, were these "warm" feelings going on when you were Defence Minister?' Butterly probed.

'Yes. But we shared no more than a genuine friendship.'

Nic Stuart from the *Canberra Times* had never trusted Paxton.

'Sorry, what evidence do you have that two men have been murdered?' he asked.

'Ms Weng told me. And I believe her.'

Stuart was sceptical. 'That's it? How can you back up your claim that Bailey has any link to this?'

'Well, Nic, for that you will have to wait. I will be making a full statement to the Parliament in the next session.'

Butterly stepped in. 'Mr Paxton, you can't drop a bombshell like this without offering a shred of evidence. If you have anything hard, you should declare it now.'

The MP made moves to abruptly end the press conference. 'That's it for now. I'll have more to say in the next few weeks. But I do call on the police and Foreign Affairs to investigate the murders at the embassy. And I plead with them to find Weng Meihui.'

As Paxton set off he was pursued by the pack, nearly tripping up a TV cameraman who was giving chase. He ignored the flurry of questions.

But as he slipped into the supposed safety of the parliamentary building, news.com's Lanai Scarr stepped in close. 'Mr Paxton, were you having an affair with the Chinese ambassador's wife?'

CHAPTER SEVENTY-SIX

Washington

'Mr President, two minutes to broadcast.'

Earle Jackson scanned the hard copy a final time. He'd already run through the autocue twice.

The US President was preparing to address the nation and every syllable had to be perfect. It was 8pm, primetime on America's east coast. A woman dabbed powder on his face, eliminating a trace of sweat.

'Water, sir?'

'Please.'

His throat was dry. The reality of the fire that he'd fanned was dawning on him. But he could see no way out without a massive loss of face. He had to stare down the Chinese.

'My fellow Americans, as I speak to you tonight the USS *George Washington* is on a peaceful mission in international waters in the Taiwan Strait.

'For nearly seventy years our nation has stood guard over peace in the Pacific, allowing all to prosper.

'America is the brightest beacon for freedom and opportunity in the world and no one will keep that light from shining.

'The Chinese Government is moving to prevent our peaceful mission by effectively blockading the strait, a crucial trade route.

'Make no mistake. If the *George Washington* is forced to turn back, then it will mark a new and dangerous chapter in world affairs. As your President, I will not allow that to happen.

'This is not the first aggressive act by the Chinese. Since the end of last year it has been increasingly pushing the boundaries of its power. Peaceful nations like Japan and South Korea are in dispute with Beijing in the East China Sea. China claims Taiwan. And to its south, China demands waters owned by the Philippines, Malaysia, Indonesia and Vietnam.

'These are not the acts of a nation that claims its rise to power does not threaten global peace. If the twentieth century teaches us anything, it is that those who stand silent when the first signs of aggression appear are condemned by history.'

The word PAUSE loomed on the autocue and Jackson took a breath before emphasising the next sentence

'The United States will not stand silent.

'I call on President Meng to revoke China's ill-considered air-defence zone over the Senkaku Islands and to withdraw the fishermen who are occupying the main islands with his blessing.

'I call on him to talk to his neighbours, not bully them.

'And I call on him to let the *George Washington* sail unimpeded, as a sign that China genuinely believes in the right of civilised nations to freely navigate the world's waters.

'Good night. God bless you and God bless America.'

Beijing

The wash of applause from three thousand carefully chosen citizens rippled through the Great Hall of the People as Meng Tao strode onto its stage.

In just four hours the Communist Party had hastily gathered this crowd as a backdrop to the President's speech. It was another sign of the party's control over the people.

Behind a lectern decorated with a garland of flowers and bearing China's distinctive red-and-gold seal, Meng adjusted his glasses, coughed once, and spoke.

'Ladies and gentlemen, friends and comrades, these are dark and dangerous hours.

'The United States has sent a nuclear warship into waters just one hundred kilometres off the Chinese mainland.

'I ask the world to consider how President Jackson would react if he was in my position.

'But we do not have to guess. We know.

'In 1963 when the Soviet Union moved to station weapons on Cuba, one hundred and forty kilometres from America, President Kennedy said this:

The 1930s taught us a clear lesson: aggressive conduct, if allowed to go unchecked and unchallenged, ultimately leads to war. This nation is opposed to war. We are also true to our word. Our unswerving objective, therefore, must be to prevent the use of these missiles against this or any other country, and to secure their withdrawal or elimination.

Our policy has been one of patience and restraint.

'Wise words from a wise president. I agree with every one of them. We are not the aggressors here. But we will not be bullied anymore.

'As a sign of goodwill I have ordered the *Liaoning* to hold its position in the south of the Taiwan Strait. It will not advance but it will not allow the American carrier to pass.

'America now has time to consider the wisdom of its actions.

'I call on President Jackson to order the USS *George Washington* to turn around and to go back the way it came.

'Today, like President Kennedy, I am drawing a line in the water.'

CHAPTER SEVENTY-SEVEN

Canberra

Two Australian flags stood regally either side of a long low desk. A row of cameras crowded a small riser. Photographers jostled for a prime position. Journalists packed into every chair and advisers lined the Blue Room, just thirty paces from the Prime Minister's office and the exclusive preserve of the government.

It was 3.15pm. Catriona Bailey, fresh from a visit to the Governor-General, had scheduled her first press conference as the nation's leader.

This was a make-or-break moment.

The PM had to prove that Labor was no longer a rabble but was back in business.

She had to contend with the threat of a war in the Pacific.

Above all, she had to convince a sceptical media pack that she was physically and mentally up to the job.

Flanked by Defence chief, Jack Webster, Bailey scanned the packed room, her wheelchair positioned dead centre.

'Ladies and gentlemen, it's good to be back. Last night I told my colleagues that Labor could win the next election. I firmly believe, that with the right leadership, we can.

'These are dangerous times. They demand firm resolve, a steady hand and deep experience. I am the woman for this hour.'

'Any questions?'

Bailey was assailed by two-dozen voices. She dismissed them all with a single word: 'Michelle.'

The press gallery doyenne opened with a question that every one of her colleagues wanted answered.

'Prime Minister, a week ago you lay stricken in hospital. For the past eighteen months you have been kept alive by machines. Are you up to it?'

'Michelle, I had a condition that kills most people. Almost no one recovers. I did. Am I tough? You work it out.'

Bailey's minders had briefed journalists that the press conference would be limited to twenty minutes. All desperate for a question, they yelled and gesticulated, hoping to steamroll the other voices into silence. Bailey ignored them, and simply worked her way through a list of names.

'Mark Simkin.'

'PM, President Jackson has called on America's allies to stand by its side during its standoff with China. What role will Australia play?'

Bailey was resolute.

'War is not inevitable. Neither nation seeks war, so I believe it can be avoided. Australia does have a role to play as a creative middle power. This is what leadership is about.

'Because of my efforts we now have a seat at the UN Security Council. I have rung Ban Ki-moon and proposed a crisis meeting. He agrees. I will be flying to New York tomorrow to chair it myself.

'I have also called President Meng. He has warmly welcomed my intervention and invited me to Beijing for talks. Australia has a unique relationship with both the United States and China.

'I am determined to be an instrument for peace.'

For the first time, Bailey nodded in the direction of the mute and grim-faced Chief of the Defence Force.

'I have instructed Jack to revoke the order for a squadron of Super Hornets to be stationed in Guam. We treasure our historic alliance with the United States, but I feel that such a move at this time would be seen by the Chinese as provocative. And I'm sure President Jackson will understand.'

David Speers from Sky News called to Webster. 'CDF, do you agree with this decision?'

Webster shifted in his seat, a click of his tongue betraying a dry mouth.

'My job is to follow the orders of the government of the day. The Prime Minister has said the planes will not be deployed. That instruction will be followed.'

As the press conference was drawing to a close, one issue remained untouched. Karen Middleton from SBS went for the jugular.

'Ms Bailey, Bruce Paxton has made some extraordinary claims. That the Chinese Ambassador's wife was about to defect and has gone missing. That two Chinese nationals have been murdered. And that you, as prime minister, risked national security by allowing the new embassy to be built with only Chinese labour.'

Bailey's disdain bled through every word of her reply.

'I literally do not have the breath to waste on this garbage from a disgraced former member of the Labor Party. Every word is a lie. And I note he offered not a shred of evidence to support it.

'One. The Australian Government was never approached to offer asylum to any Chinese national. Two. The Chinese embassy has issued a statement saying the Ambassador's wife has returned to Beijing to visit family. Three. They completely deny these absurd claims of murder. And, Karen, neither the Federal Police nor Foreign Affairs say they have any concerns. Four. I did give the go-ahead for an embassy extension that had been on the books for years. And Australia has reciprocal rights in Beijing. Last, there was and is no threat to our security from the new Chinese embassy. Is there, CDF?'

Webster leaned into the microphone. 'As you know we do not discuss matters of national security. But I can confirm that Mr Paxton's claims are utterly without foundation.'

'And with that, folks, we have some serious work to do.' Bailey closed down the press conference and turned her chair to the door, gliding out to the bellows of scribes and the machine-gun rattle of cameras.

✱

'How the fuck did this happen?'

Every word was marinated with Jack Webster's anger. The CDF had just been reduced to a prop in a prime ministerial pantomime. But what really stung was the realisation that the fortress had been stormed. The enemy was in the castle.

Webster's office, on the fourth floor of Defence HQ, commanded one of Canberra's best panoramas, looking across the lake to the Parliament and the Brindabellas beyond.

He had ordered two of the nation's most powerful bureaucrats to join him: the Secretary of Foreign Affairs and the Director-General of ASIO.

And one other. Matthew Whelan, the Director of the Defence Signals Directorate. The 44-year-old public servant had enjoyed an unblemished career. Now he carried an indelible stain.

The Star Chamber was in session.

Whelan had spent a month trying to track down the source of the worst security breach in Australia's history. He had barely slept in the last forty-eight hours. Finally, they had identified the trail. The news was horrifying, and he feared the messenger was about to be executed.

But the awful truth could not be avoided.

'The DSD systems have been compromised. All of them.'

Webster picked at the braid on his shoulder. 'You said that. What I want to know is how the fuck it happened?'

'The adversary has managed to inject a virus into our system. We're still analysing it. But it's the most sophisticated zero-day program we've ever seen.'

DFAT's David Joyce spoke for all of the inquisitors.

'It's very important that you explain every detail of this. Clearly. What is a zero-day program?'

'It exploits existing weakness in a system. Lies dormant until it is commanded to move. The moment it starts operating is zero day. In the very best of these programs the victim never knows there has been a security breach. And, as I said, this is the best we've ever seen.'

'How does it work?'

Whelan glanced at his notes. 'It's similar to, but much better than, the US National Security Agency's Quantum program. The NSA weapon is hardware. This one is software. Once downloaded, it hijacks the host hardware and uses covert radio waves to set up a highway of information outwards. More disturbingly it sets up a pathway inwards. One that can be used for a cyber-attack. It's a work of genius. The only limitation is that the adversary needs to have a base station within ten kilometres to pick up the radio signal. But the receiver could be the size of a briefcase.'

'Or as large as a new Chinese embassy.' Joyce was shaking his head.

Webster asked, 'Why wouldn't they use the old one?'

ASIO's Richard Dalton interjected. 'Because it's hopelessly compromised, Jack, and the Chinese know it. I was part of the construction team in the '90s.'

'But Mr Whelan …' Joyce was irritated by being pushed, even briefly, off track. 'The question remains: How did the most secure building in Australia come to be infiltrated? Many of your systems are off the grid, not connected to the internet.'

'That's true. The adversary needed to jump the gap to our off-line computers. The only way to do that was to get someone inside to plant it.'

Webster jumped in. 'And who the fuck was that?'

Whelan's voice was a rasp. 'Well … we have a theory. Which I have to say is … unbelievable. But it's the only theory we have.'

'What is it?' Webster demanded.

'The only possible breach we can see dates back to September 2008. But as I say … it's just inconceivable.'

'Just spit it out!' The CDF's impatience rang in his voice.

'Well …' Whelan was fidgeting with the pile of notes on his lap. 'It was at the height of the financial meltdown. The Prime Minister was visiting DSD for the first time. She was asked to turn in her phone at security and kicked up an enormous stink. Said she was expecting a call from the US Treasury Secretary. Insisted on keeping her phone. I was called in. And … and I relented.'

'I know you don't need me to point this out, Mr Whelan.' Webster's voice was low and menacing. 'That unconscionable breach of security is a sackable offence.'

'Yes, sir.'

'What kind of phone was it?' Dalton asked.

'It was an iPhone, early model, and I hadn't seen that many of them.'

'So a sophisticated device capable of delivering a virus through a USB port,' Dalton said.

'Yes, sir.'

'But there are no USB ports inside DSD, are there?'

'Sir, there is one. In my office. We keep it for operational reasons. But it's in the most secure part of the most secure building in Australia.'

'Where was the meeting with the Prime Minister held?'

Whelan's head dropped. 'In that room.'

'And what happened?' Joyce's face betrayed the fury that was rising with every word of this briefing.

'Ten minutes into the meeting the call from the US came and Bailey insisted everyone else leave the room.'

'Including you?'

'Yes, sir.'

'How long was she alone in that room?'

'Twenty minutes. Half an hour. Long enough.'

'Did you notice anything unusual when you were allowed back in the office?' Dalton asked.

'Yes, sir.'

'What?'

'Bailey had plugged her iPhone charger cable into my computer USB port. Claimed she was running low on battery. I protested and demanded that she immediately remove it. She reminded me, again, that she was the prime minister. But she complied. After she left we ran thorough system checks. Nothing. I repeat, nothing unusual showed up.'

'Until now,' Webster said.

'Yes, sir. We believe the adversary left the virus dormant for years. Which is, in itself, remarkable. Our best guess is they activated the zero day program about three months ago.'

'The Chinese are very patient people. What have they got?'

Whelan's voice fell to a whisper. 'Everything.'

'How can we sanitise the system?' Dalton leaned forward with such urgency that Whelan flinched, as if expecting a blow.

'We'll have to shut everything down.' Whelan's shirt was damp with sweat. 'I mean everything. Every single computer in DSD, Defence, Foreign Affairs and the intelligence community is now potentially infected. Every terminal, every server. We'll have to clean them all.'

Webster, usually so clear-headed in a crisis, was visibly shaken.

He walked to his window and looked across the lake to Parliament. He wondered, briefly, if it was his duty to speak out.

Should he, the most respected military figure in Australia, warn the people that their leader was a threat to national security? An agent of China.

If he spoke she would be finished. Forever.

But so would he, as leader of a Defence establishment that could not defend itself.

And what would the Americans do?

Webster shifted his gaze to the left. There, at the heart of the Russell Defence complex, an eagle astride a globe soared 79 metres into the sky on an aluminium pillar. The Australian community had raised one hundred thousand pounds to have the American memorial built in 1954. The plaque at its base gave thanks for 'the vital help given by the United States of America during the war in the Pacific 1941–1945'. There was no more potent symbol of how deep the alliance was embedded in Australia's Defence establishment.

Now another Pacific war loomed and Australia would stand idle while the US took up the fight. Worse, his nation had blown a hole below the US waterline before the battle even began.

He turned back to the room.

'No one knows about this. Ever.'

CHAPTER SEVENTY-EIGHT

Canberra

Scoured and sanitised, the prime ministerial office retained a slight smell of industrial-grade antiseptic. In less than twenty-four hours every vestige of Martin Toohey's leadership had been scrubbed. For good.

Brendan Ryan had been waiting for an hour. It was the second time the Defence Minister had been summoned that day by Catriona Bailey, who had immediately reverted to type.

She had convened a National Security Council meeting for 9am and kept the entire defence and intelligence establishment in limbo for three hours. When she finally arrived Bailey had launched into a dissertation about US–China relations before demanding a pile of briefs that Ryan knew she would never read.

His rage was rising with every minute and Bailey's staff had stopped giving him updates about the progress of a video call with the Japanese Prime Minister.

It was 6.48pm and Ryan was tired and starving. An electric hum finally signalled the arrival of Bailey and the three staffers who trailed in her wake. Her chair glided past Ryan as he sat on the couch. She said nothing but slid into place behind her desk, forcing the minister to rise and move to a nearby chair.

'James, I need something to eat and a cup of tea. Now. And where is that brief on Taiwan's defence capability?'

One adviser hustled off as Bailey barked at another.

'When can I expect the call from Park Geun-hye?'

'Prime Minister, we haven't yet been able to get a time confirmed with the South Koreans. Their President is in a meeting with her own national security committee.'

'I didn't ask for your excuses. Just get me a time.'

Bailey finally turned to Ryan. Her gaunt face was layered with makeup to lift the cadaver pallor of her skin. She stretched a thin smile.

'Brendan. You won't mind if I have a notetaker stay. My … condition … means I need an extra pair of hands.'

'Sure.' Ryan nodded. 'But before we go any further, I was surprised you didn't flag an election date at your press conference. As we agreed.'

'In case you hadn't noticed, the US and China are one mistake from war. Ban Ki-moon has personally asked me to mediate. I am well placed to do that. Do you really think, in these circumstances, that the Australian people want an election?'

Bailey spat out the words.

'Our best hope of victory is to demonstrate that I am the only person capable of leading the nation through this crisis.'

Ryan wasn't surprised by Bailey's signature self-obsession.

'Don't kid yourself. Our best hope is that the bounce from your return lasts long enough for us to scramble a half-decent loss,' he shot back. 'Every day we wait we'll sink further in the polls. This is about the party, not you. And we had a deal.'

Bailey fixed Ryan with a don't-fuck-with-me glare.

'All bets are off.' The PM nodded to the notetaker. 'Put that brief where I can see it.'

She scanned a page and turned back to the minister. 'Brendan, I am reshuffling and offering you Human Services.'

'In the outer Ministry?'

'Correct.'

'So you're turfing me from Cabinet?'

'Correct, again.'

'You've betrayed me.'

'Well Brendan, now you know exactly what it feels like.'

Power, a surge of power, unfiltered. Blood coursed through her veins as she pressed her hands firmly on the arms of her wheelchair.

Slowly, painfully, she laboured and pushed until her body began to rise. Her legs, weak from months of stillness, moved. They joined the agonising task of trying to lift her body from the chair.

She stood, alone and unassisted, her staff banished from the office.

It was a triumph of the will. Her will to power. Power over herself. Power over others.

Her legs trembled under her weight. But they held. She focused her formidable will on moving just one foot. Her right. It slid forward.

Then, the left. Her hands pressed on the desk to hold some of her weight. Her left foot moved and she took a small step forward.

She reached the end of the desk and lifted her hands from it. She shook but did not fall.

Catriona Bailey locked her eyes on the map she'd installed on the wall, the sole relic in this office from her first dynasty. She stepped towards it.

Five triumphant paces. Each surer than the last.

She stood before the map of the world.

Australia was now hers again. She loved its shape. The way it sat at the centre of the world.

She looked up at China, the nation that had beguiled her since she was a child. From the moment she saw the intricate genius of her mother's Ming vase. She'd spent a lifetime unravelling the mysteries of the Middle Kingdom.

Across the Pacific to the United States, the twentieth-century superpower. Unwilling to share the earth with its latest and most potent rival.

Soon she would travel to New York to chair a meeting of the United Nations Security Council. To mediate as the two angry giants threatened to shatter a fragile peace.

She had been born for this, had given her life for this. Everything she'd achieved had been to prepare for this hour.

She was the bridge between East and West. Cometh the hour, cometh the woman.

She began to fashion her opening address in her mind.

'Ladies and gentlemen, the world stands at a crossroads. It can once again choose the path of war and destruction. Or it can choose the path of peace. The lives of your children and grandchildren depend on the decisions we make here today. With my guidance ...'

'Prime Minister, Prime Minister, are you all right?' The concerned tones of her chief of staff rang out, tearing at her, breaking her thoughts.

Bailey looked up, shaken awake, momentarily disoriented. She was still seated at her desk. Still locked in her wheelchair. Frozen by her illness.

'Of course I am. But could you bring me my medication?'

CHAPTER SEVENTY-NINE

Canberra

Canberra's brutal summer had finally broken. The first strains of autumn had dragged grey skies and more bearable temperatures to the capital.

Harry Dunkley idled his LandCruiser down a narrow dirt track to a place that he'd last visited twenty months ago on an arctic morning.

The same green picnic table marked the end of the dirt road. He jumped out of the four-wheel drive, his feet crunching over a thick carpet of eucalypt bark and leaves as he ambled towards the table. An empty packet of Winfield Blue and a discarded insulin vial littered the ground beneath it, a sign that people did sometimes visit this lonely clip of land. But mostly Yarramundi Reach stood empty.

Blackberry bushes ran thick along the water's edge, their thorny branches blocking access to the lake. A steady background hum of traffic from Parkes Way mingled with the rustle of trees and the cry of magpies and currawongs.

It was late morning on a Sunday and Dunkley had nowhere else to be.

He had decided to revisit the exact place where his misadventure had begun, that day when a black-and-white photograph forever changed his life.

From his car, the mobile rang. He ignored it.

Bugger it. It can't be a friend, I don't have any left.

It had been three days since Charles Dancer had trained a gun on him while revealing himself as Kimberley's murderer. The memory of it still shook him, as did his impotence to expose the killer and his masters.

He'd lost Celia Mathieson. He'd returned her calls only to find she was just checking to see how he was. As a friend.

He'd lost his job. No, it was more than a job. A calling. A crusade to hold those in power to account. Who would touch up the untouchable now?

And the one politician he had trusted without question had betrayed him.

He shivered, chastising himself for wearing shorts and a T-shirt. A south-east breeze had picked up off the lake, chilly by comparison with the recent stretch of hot summer days. Soon winter would grip Canberra, a depressing prospect.

He had devoted himself to this city for most of his adult life. He loved it, the endless intrigue, the heady layers of drama and soap.

Now, he'd been nearly destroyed by it. He realised with a jolt that he barely knew how the game was played.

Why hadn't he, the great investigative reporter, seen the clues that in hindsight seemed so clear?

You dill.

He had to consider what to do next. The lifetime reporter had fielded a couple of calls from suitors offering big bucks if he would sell his soul to work in public relations. He was appalled at the idea of becoming a spin doctor, angry with himself for even contemplating it. But he had to eat.

That one black-and-white pic had given him – what? One scalp. One cracking yarn. But at what cost?

His mobile rang again. He wandered back to the car and stretched his arm through the window. He checked the caller ID. It was the one person he was happy to speak to.

'Mate, I thought you'd be at church?'

He collapsed on the lounge, the emotion and pain of four brutal days washing over him.

'Harry, you look like shit. Scotch?'

'Yes, mate. A double.'

The Bailie Nicol Jarvie had an immediate effect, a warm medicinal balm that washed over the back of his throat.

'Jesus, Harry, sip it. That's my last bottle.'

'Sorry, Trev, been a tough time since we last spoke. Seems like weeks but it's, what, four days?'

'Wednesday night. So yeah, Harry, four days. And I've been busy too. Why don't you bring your drink over here?'

Harris motioned to the pair of iMac's. Dunkley settled into a chair as the analyst booted the machines into action.

'I've managed to decrypt the last of the files on Ben's Cloud, and mate, these are the most extraordinary of all.'

Dunkley was intrigued by Harris's enthusiasm, but a large part of him was over the thrill of the chase.

'Just to get the timing clear at the start. The email you never received from Ben, the "shades of '75" note, was sent on Monday August 15, 2011. He dies three days later, on 18 August. Three days is a long time and Ben wasn't idle. As I've told you, Harry, he stole a ton of information from DSD. But that wasn't all he did.'

Harris clicked on a folder. It sprang open and there were dozens of files inside.

'DSD's key role is to gather foreign signals intelligence. Its motto is "Reveal their secrets; protect our own". It taps into and listens to calls from across the Asia-Pacific. It's rarely allowed to tap domestic phones. But no one is better equipped.'

Harris paused and swivelled his chair towards the reporter.

'Harry, Ben trained the intelligence guns on their masters. He tapped the phones of everyone on the Alliance list. *Everyone.*'

Dunkley took a long swig of his whisky before tilting the glass upwards in mock salute. 'Well, that's my girl.'

'No question about that, Harry. But they were onto him. While Ben was raiding the DSD safe, they were gathering intel on him … and on you.'

Dunkley's face hardened.

'What do you mean, Trev?'

Harris looked down at the keyboard on his desk and brushed some dust from its edge. He was troubled.

'On 16 June, 2011, DSD got an order to open two domestic case files.'

He glanced up at Dunkley.

'One on you.'

Harris broke his gaze and stared into the glare of his computer screen. His words were laboured.

'And one on Ben. It tapped everything: your phones, computers, bank accounts. You name it.'

Dunkley waved at the screen with his right hand, still gripping the empty tumbler.

'Did she find that? Is that on her Cloud?'

'No, Harry.'

'So how do you know about all this, Trev?'

Harris sighed. 'Because I authorised it.'

A wave of nausea swept over Dunkley.

'You ... what?'

The analyst's eyes glistened. His voice turned inwards. He seemed intent on reassuring himself as much as Dunkley.

'I was operating under strict orders. From on high. They claimed that Ben was leaking top-secret stuff to you.'

Harris swivelled his chair to face Dunkley, begging understanding.

'How was I to know how this would end? I have lain awake for hours at night wondering whether I should have done something different. Whether I was responsible for Ben's death.'

'How?'

Harris pushed his chair back from the desk and stood up. He walked several paces before turning back to the journalist.

'Because on the night Ben died, a call came through to DSD asking for an exact location on him. We were tracking his movements using the signal from his mobile phone.'

'Christ, Trevor.'

'Yes ... now you understand why I left DSD.'

He paused.

'And why I'm helping you. Even though I'm breaking the law.'

Dunkley spent a long time in silence, studying the rim of his tumbler. The guilt the journalist felt over Kimberley's death was still a raw wound. He'd sought redemption by pursuing the truth and had been abandoned by everyone. So the admission by Harris had a perverse effect: Dunkley had found a traveller bearing the same burden.

'Well Trev, there's plenty of blame to go around. The only way we can make it up to Kimberley is to finish the job she started. What's in those files?'

Harris's face lightened. He nodded, moved back to his keyboard and clicked on a Waveform icon.

'Tapes, Harry. Hours of them. This one is from 17 August, 2011.'

The familiar voice of Australia's Defence Force Chief sprang out of a pair of Harman Kardon speakers.

'Brent, good news,' Jack Webster said. 'There'll be a story in *The Australian* soon, one that will blow Paxton out of the water. The Defence Minister is dead.'

For once Harry Dunkley was early. It was nearly 5pm and he ordered a beer while his eyes adjusted to the dim lighting of the Kingston Hotel.

The main bar was near empty, a handful of Sunday afternoon drinkers watching a one-dayer on wall-mounted TV screens.

From the in-house stereo, Elvis Costello was blasting out 'Oliver's Army' in 4/4, the British songster wailing about being anywhere else but here.

Here's to that, Elvis.

He wasn't a regular but Dunkley had spent enough hours sinking his wages into pool-and-gin nights to know the Kingo's back story.

The hotel had been built more than seventy years ago, and in 1963, it famously hosted a meeting of the thirty-six members of the ALP's federal conference. Labor's parliamentary leaders, Arthur Calwell and Gough Whitlam, were photographed cooling their heels in the street, waiting to be told what the party's election platform would be.

The trope of the 'faceless men' was carved into the political lexicon right here.

Nursing his schooner, Dunkley moved away from the bar. He'd been told to look for a particular poster. It was in the furthest corner, a quiet nook only occasionally disturbed by a bubble of electronic music from one of ten poker machines.

The wood-framed print carried the image of a Chinese beauty sitting on a chair. She had an open face and beguiling smile. The strap of a blue evening gown fell off her right shoulder. Her left hand was pulling back her hair. And foregrounded in the alluring scene were three packs of Golf cigarettes.

'Beautiful, isn't she?' Bruce Paxton stood captivated by the poster, cradling a long cool glass of amber. 'Ever since I came to Canberra this has been my local. I always sit right here.'

'G'day, Bruce. It's pretty old. Bit like this place I suppose.'

'Yep. The owner, Steve, tells me he picked it up in Beijing years ago for a song. Along with all the others.'

Paxton's gesture swept the room and Dunkley, for the first time, noticed the common theme of the artwork.

The MP sat down heavily on a stool. His shirt, a size too small, had one too many buttons undone. His athleticism had faded, but he was still imposing. His right hand carried a hardness that showed a history of manual labour.

And his gloved prosthetic left hand was a symbol of his wild union past.

The MP put his elbows on the table with his beer between them as he slapped his right fist into the palm of his left.

'Before we start I need to get something off my chest.'

'You called the meeting, Bruce. Go for it.'

'I always had time for you in the past, but that story you wrote about me and that Chinese money was a stitch-up. I broke no laws and you destroyed me.'

Dunkley met Paxton's stare. 'Bullshit, Bruce. The article was accurate and fair. You knew you were doing the wrong thing, otherwise you wouldn't have hidden tens of thousands of dollars from the Electoral Commission. Your bad luck was that I tracked down your sidekick Doug Turner and he decided to rat on you.'

Paxton's drawl edged up a notch. 'I was set up, Harry. You know that.'

'Well, that part is true.' Dunkley drank a generous pull of beer. 'And if it makes you happy, I was set up too. By the same people. So there you go. As you'd know, Bruce, it's a big wheel that doesn't go round twice. And I've sunk lower than you.'

'You have, mate. Welcome.' Paxton smiled and the men clinked their glasses.

'So why did you call me here, Bruce – to revel in my misery?'

Paxton shook his head.

'Actually, I thought that if there was one bloke who might understand my plight it would be you. I might be on the canvas but I've never ducked a fight. Neither have you. And clearly, Harry, you buy some outrageous stories.'

They laughed, revelling in each other's misfortune.

'Well, I've heard your story, Bruce, and it's pretty out there.' Dunkley turned sombre. 'Have you heard from the Ambassador's wife?'

'No.' Paxton glanced at the poster between them. 'And if she could get in touch she would. Even if it was just to let me know she was okay.'

Harry lowered his voice. 'She was special to you …'

'She was, mate.'

'I'm sorry.'

There was an awkward silence, broken by the ring of a jackpot and the clatter of a small wave of coins spilling into a metal tray.

'Do you have any evidence of these other murders?' Dunkley was happy to move from difficult emotional terrain to the more familiar ground of facts and questions.

'Only what Mei told me. But I'm sure she was telling the truth. She was terrified.'

'Yeah, that fits with one thing I know. The Japanese are convinced there's a killer on that compound. I have photos of him. Looks like a nasty piece of work.'

Dunkley traced the rim of his glass.

'Were you in Cabinet when Bailey gave China the go-ahead to build that compound?'

'No mate, outer Ministry. But I do know that the brass were still whinging about it when I became Defence Minister. Maybe I should have listened to them. I'm changing my views about the threat China poses.'

'Yeah, well I've completely changed my view about your fucking defence chiefs. But do you think that Bailey is a threat?'

'Look. I went to China in the '80s and Bailey was based at the embassy for six months. They tried to recruit me. And. They. Failed.' Paxton tapped his prosthetic hand three times. 'But if they tried with me they would have tried with her.'

Dunkley drained the last of his beer. 'Have you ever heard of a group of bureaucrats called the Alliance?'

'The Alliance? Sounds like a fucking insurance company. But no, Harry.'

'Well, they were the ones who wanted to kill you off, and to scuttle the gas deal with China. And Bruce, they won.'

'I had no doubt that the brass wanted me gone when I cut their cash. I didn't think there was a vast conspiracy, though.'

'Well, now it's my turn to tell an outrageous story. I think a bunch of mandarins has been interfering repeatedly to shunt the government into the arms of Uncle Sam.

'And this interference went so far as launching a series of cyber-attacks on Australia and making it look as though the Chinese were behind it. They even gave it a 007 code name: the Lusitania Plan.'

Paxton put his glass down.

'Fuck! Back up, Harry. I know about the Lusitania Plan. It's an Australian training project, based out of HMAS *Harman*, a few miles down the road. We wanted to develop the same kind of unit as Cyber Command in the United States. The Lusitania Plan was our test-bed. I ticked it off as Defence Minister. It's the sort of thing we should be putting our money into. It's twenty-first-century warfare, not the big ticket bullshit the brass is addicted to.'

The revelation floored Dunkley.

'Jesus, Bruce, I thought the US was behind this. A nudge to push us back into their tent. But this … these attacks … you say we had the capability to launch them from Canberra …'

'Well, it was the kind of capability we were developing.'

'If it originated here, it would be treason.'

'No, Harry. If they a shot down a prime minister, it would be a coup.'

The two men fell silent as they pondered the unimaginable. Around them, the hotel bar drifted through the mundane rituals of a Sunday afternoon.

'So what do we know, Bruce? The Chinese are dangerous. The Yanks can't be trusted. And there are traitors in our ranks.'

'Harry, you know what they say: politics is the womb of war. In this world you need allies. Turns out the enemy of my enemy is my only friend. Perhaps we need to forge an alliance of our own.'

Dunkley scratched at his ribcage. 'We ain't holding many aces, Bruce. Neither of us has much credibility.'

'True that, Harry. But I do have parliamentary privilege and I plan to use it. So, what have you got?'

'Well, Bruce. Turns out that I've got tapes. And they tell quite a tale.'

A broad smile split the MP's face as he downed his last mouthful of beer. He placed the empty glass on the table, diverting his gaze to the Chinese beauty before fixing his one-time tormentor with firm resolve.

'Well then, Harry. Here's to the future. Let's publish. And be damned.'

ACKNOWLEDGEMENTS

Dozens of people volunteered help and advice in the many months that it took to research and write *The Mandarin Code*. Some wish that assistance to pass unacknowledged. Those who have kindly allowed us to name them here did so on the strict understanding that we would make it clear that they do not endorse any of the book's contents.

So, thank you to:

Dr Hugh White, Professor of Strategic Studies, School of International, Political and Strategic Studies, College of Asia and the Pacific, Australian National University, for his wisdom, guidance and his book *The China Choice: Why America Should Share Power (Black Inc, 2013)*. You should buy it.

Dr Carl Ungerer, friend, former diplomat, intelligence analyst and adviser to Labor's foreign minister Bob Carr; currently an adjunct lecturer at Bond University.

Alastair MacGibbon, former Australian Federal Police agent, now director of the Centre for Internet Safety at the University of Canberra. Alastair was extraordinarily patient and generous, spending hours demystifying cyber-security and internet hacking.

The chapters on the USS *George Washington* could not have been written without the expert guidance of Admiral (Ret) Ronald

J. (Zap) Zlatoper, a former Commander in Chief of the United States Pacific Fleet. Rear Admiral (Ret) Brian Adams, AO, a former deputy chief of the Royal Australian Navy made many astute corrections to the early draft. Kind advice also came from Admiral (Ret) Chris Barrie AC, a former Chief of the Australian Defence Force, and Rear Admiral (Ret) James Goldrick AO who, among many things in his thirty-eight years in the RAN, commanded the Australian Defence Force Academy.

A serving US Air Force pilot provided expert guidance to help us write the chapter on flying the B52 out of Guam to the Senkaku Islands. Our American friend selflessly gave several hours of his time in long Skype calls detailing flight procedures for the iconic airframe.

Patrick Siu was generous in helping the authors understand the beauty of Chinese calligraphy. He is a wonderful artist.

We would like to particularly thank Amanda O'Connell, our wonderful editor, whose patience and professionalism have made *The Mandarin Code* a much better read.

The writing of *The Mandarin Code* was guided by a number of books. These include:

The Dismissal: Australia's most sensational power struggle: the dramatic fall of Gough Whitlam (Angus & Robertson, 1983) by Paul Kelly. Thanks to Paul, too, for kindly allowing us to reproduce a small part of his landmark tome.

Cyber War: The Next Threat to National Security and What to Do About It (Ecco Press, 2012) by Richard A. Clarke with Robert K. Knake.

The Party: The Secret World of China's Communist Rulers (HarperCollins, 2012) by Richard McGregor.

Party Time: Who Runs China and How (Black Inc, 2013) by Rowan Callick.

This book already had a fictional head of the US National Security Agency in it (and was all but complete) before the *Australian Financial Review*'s contributing editor Christopher Joye published his excellent interview with the retired NSA and Cyber Command head, General Keith Alexander, on May 8, 2014. But it proved, again, that some facts are stranger than fiction and we borrowed liberally from it.

Finally, we want to thank all those politicians, staffers, senior bureaucrats, members of the defence force and intelligence agencies, both here and in the United States, who enthusiastically offered ideas, stories and advice. Alas, many of you have begged to remain anonymous. But you know who you are.

More importantly, we know who you are.

A STICKY SCANDAL. A POLITICAL JAM

THE MARMALADE FILES

AN EXPLOSIVE NOVEL OF LIES, LUST AND POLITICAL BASTARDRY

STEVE LEWIS & CHRIS UHLMANN

An imaginative romp through the dark underbelly of politics by two veteran Canberra insiders.

When seasoned newshound Harry Dunkley is slipped a compromising photograph one frosty Canberra dawn he knows he's onto something big. In pursuit of the scoop, Dunkley must negotiate the deadly corridors of power where the minority Toohey Government hangs by a thread - its stricken Foreign Minister on life support, her heart maintained by a single thought. Revenge.

Rabid Rottweilers prowl in the guise of Opposition senators, union thugs wage class warfare, TV anchors simper and fawn ... and loyalty and decency have long since given way to compromise and treachery.

From the teahouses of Beijing to the beaches of Bali, from the marbled halls of Washington to the basements of the bureaucracy, Dunkley's quest takes him ever closer to the truth - and ever deeper into a lethal political game.

Award-winning journalists Steve Lewis and Chris Uhlmann combine forces in this arresting novel that proves fiction is stranger than fact.